I0757411

GET THE FIRST BOOK IN THIS SERIES FOR FREE!

Sign up for the no-spam newsletter and get BREACH.

**Details can be found at the end of
DOORS OF DESTINY.**

Copyright © 2018 Bronwyn Leroux
All the characters in this book are fictitious, and any resemblance to actual persons
living or dead is purely coincidental.
All rights reserved. No part of this publication may be reproduced, stored in a retrieval
system, distributed, or transmitted in any form or by any means, including
photocopying, recording, or other electronic or mechanical methods, without the prior
written permission of the author, except in the case of brief quotations embodied in
critical reviews and certain other noncommercial uses permitted by copyright law. For
permission requests, contact the author at info@bronwynleroux.com
https://bronwynleroux.com/

Cover design by Lena Yang Designs

ISBN: 978-1-953107-06-0

DOORS OF DESTINY

BRONWYN LEROUX

CHAPTER ONE

"What does she have that I don't?"

Tarise's plea ripped into him. Jaden tried to ignore the unshed tears glistening in her eyes, wishing for the earth to swallow him whole. Hadn't Tarise, just yesterday, said it was alright? Now here she was in his home, demanding explanations and being all emotional before he'd even had breakfast. Why were women so complicated?

Had it really only been yesterday that they were up in the mountains having fun together as a group? It seemed like a lifetime ago. Especially considering that this was when he first figured out Tarise had feelings for him. He still hadn't wrapped his mind around that one.

Her confrontation of the situation, such as it was when they parted yesterday, was so unexpected that he had floundered in the shock of the revelation. But she *had* said it was okay. Although, if he was being honest with himself, he knew that wasn't true. He had seen how she stomped away from him. And he could still feel her eyes accusing him as she glared at him right before climbing into their family's terra-porter. *Ugh, what can I say? There really is nothing that will help Tarise get over the fact that I chose Kayla instead of her.*

Getting no response from Jaden, Tarise sneered, "Is she prettier than me?"

Oh, there's no way out of that one, Jaden thought, subconsciously backing away from Tarise. Whatever answer he gave, it would be wrong. Tarise was pretty enough. She just wasn't Kayla.

As if realizing she had given him an impossible question—or one she didn't want an answer to—Tarise hissed, "Smarter than me?"

"No." Thankfully, that answer required no thought. Everyone knew Tarise was a genius. Jaden was glad she hadn't thought to ask the question more specifically, as was her wont. Kayla might not be the genius Tarise was, but she was a different kind of smart; the kind Tarise would never be.

"Then what is it? Why did you choose her?"

Jaden sighed. Nothing he could say would satisfy her. It wasn't something he could explain anyway. It was something she had to experience, and . . .

"Answer me!" Tarise demanded, her shrill tone making Jaden want to slap his hands over his ears.

"I can't. I mean, it's not that she has something, and you don't. I didn't plan for things to happen between us. They just did."

"How is that even possible? You've only known her a few days while you've known me almost your entire life!"

"Perhaps that's why," Jaden murmured.

"And what's that supposed to mean?"

Jaden flinched. Maybe those hadn't been the most prudent words. "It is possible that because I'm so used to having you around, it was difficult for me to realize how you felt?"

"And that's supposed to make me feel better?" Tarise whirled, snatched her pack off the sofa, and stormed out of the room.

Jaden sagged. *Well, that wasn't any fun. Can't Tarise just accept that Kayla and I are together without making me feel terrible about it?*

"Glad that wasn't me, bro," Atu whistled, sauntering into the room.

Jaden sent him a baleful stare. "How much did you hear?"

"Enough."

"And you didn't think to walk in sooner and save me?"

"No way! My mom always said never get between a girl and what she wants."

Jaden expelled an exasperated sigh. "Isn't that the truth?" He dropped down on the couch next to Atu. "Tarise sure was mad."

Atu rubbed his chin. "Well, look at it from her point of view. She doesn't know that you and Kayla have actually spent months together. Remember that time freeze thing that happens when we're with the gliders?"

"Ah, yes, her comment about me only knowing Kayla for a few days. Having been my friend for so long, I suppose it's understandable her questioning Kayla and I getting so close."

"Uh-huh." Atu nodded, looking satisfied.

"That still doesn't help me," Jaden commented, amused when Atu's smirk fell away.

"What do you mean?"

"Well, how do I explain gliders and Gaptors to Tarise when she can't see them, let alone the ludicrous idea of time freezes? She'd think I was making things up to excuse my actions, and that would only make things worse."

"Yeah, valid point."

"Any more sage advice?"

"Nope, you're on your own, bro." Atu raised both hands, resigned.

"Some friend you are." Jaden laughed and gave him a friendly shove on the shoulder.

Atu picked up one of the gaming controllers they had left on the table the previous evening. "How about a game to release some of that tension?"

"You couldn't have spoken sweeter words." Jaden snatched the other controller.

The pair scurried down to the basement gaming room. It had turned out remarkably well if Jaden did say so himself. The setup was still in its infancy, with none of his planned enhancements. However, it was functional. He and Atu had worked on it together since their return, and it had only taken a few days to get things set up the way Jaden had envisioned . . . only a few weeks ago?

This time freeze effect was making it difficult to keep things straight. In "real" world time, it truly had only been a couple of weeks since he showed Kayla the basement and shared his ideas with her. In reality, he, Kayla, and Atu had spent months together training with Sven and traveling to find and recover the items Zareh had sent them for. No wonder Tarise was upset. His mind drifted back to their conversation. The same question he had asked before returned to plague him. *Why can't Tarise just be happy for me?*

"Earth to Jaden," Atu prompted.

"Sorry, I spaced for a moment," Jaden mumbled. "What did you say?"

"I asked which game you wanted to play."

"You choose."

Atu obliged, all the while sliding appraising glances Jaden's way. Aware of the scrutiny, Jaden bristled. He wasn't the problem. Tarise was. And her little tirade had gotten under his skin. He needed to snap out of this funk.

As if reading Jaden's mind, Atu elbowed him. "Bet I can rack up a hundred points before you do!'

The taunt had the desired effect. Jaden's attention snapped to the virtual environment surrounding him, and he grinned. "I doubt it. Game on!"

Setting their interactive consoles and donning their lenses, they began their battle.

Jaden immersed himself in the intricacies of the skirmish, bouncing around the virtual movement quarter. Deftly feinting and slashing with his sword, he worked up a sweat as he felled one foe after another. The tension eased from his shoulders. Doing something he excelled at was exhilarating. At least here he didn't have to worry about girls, wretched things that they were.

But that was a generalization. Kayla wasn't wretched. She was incredible. Just thinking about her made him smile. He could spend hours with her and not feel one ounce of frustration. Well, unless she got stubborn about things. Or unless she was putting herself in unnecessary danger, as she seemed compelled to do. What was it about girls that got him so wound up?

Jaden sliced another beast as it rounded on him, gratified when his sword hit home and it died. A quick glance at the scoreboard showed he was losing. Unacceptable! Letting his mind slide fully away from the problem of Tarise, he succumbed to the game. Slaying one beast at a time was the only way to win.

Jaden and Atu were so engrossed in their combat that neither heard Markov greeting them. Only when the round ended and they lifted their lenses for a breather did they notice him sitting on one of the chairs along the wall. He had made himself at home and was sipping a soda, idly watching them.

"Hey, dude, sorry, I didn't hear you come in." Jaden bounded over and exchanged his usual complicated handshake with Markov.

Atu hovered in the background, waving when Markov nodded a greeting his way.

"You two been playing all morning?" Markov asked, like he just wanted to make conversation.

Jaden wasn't fooled. He knew Markov wanted answers, but Jaden wasn't about to make it easy for him. He decided to play along. "No, only for an hour or so. Want to join us?"

Markov grinned. "Do dogs have ears?"

Jaden smiled, handing Markov a console and pair of lenses. He should've guessed Markov wouldn't pass up the opportunity to beat him. Well, Markov was about to be disappointed.

After programming his console, Markov donned his lenses. "Ready?"

"Yes," Jaden and Atu responded.

The game began again. This time, Jaden didn't need any lead time to hone his focus. When the battle ended, he didn't bother checking the scoreboard. It was sad, really. Maybe they should call Kayla so he could have some real competition.

Markov dropped his lenses on the table, disgusted. "How do you always manage to pull that off?"

"At least you beat one person," Atu grumbled. "I can't seem to win with this guy."

"Join the crowd. There should be a way to give him a handicap."

"Ah, don't kid yourself," Jaden retorted. "If you won and I had a handicap, you wouldn't feel like it was justified."

"True."

"Let's have lunch," Jaden suggested. "I'm famished."

"When was that anything new?" Atu remarked.

Markov laughed. "You're getting to know him pretty well, aren't you?"

And there it was, the lead-in to the questions. "Pizza?"

His friends agreed enthusiastically, and Jaden preceded Markov and Atu up the stairs to the kitchen. In the pantry, he set the dough prepper, considering what to tell Markov. Markov had known him long enough to give him the benefit of the doubt, but that didn't mean he would believe Jaden. Heck, Jaden had lived the nightmare, and he still found it difficult to believe there were monsters out there: monsters that only seekers could see, monsters who were out to destroy this world and everyone in it.

The dough prepper beeped, and Jaden startled. He still hadn't come up with a plausible explanation. Markov wasn't one to give up. If he caught even a whiff of subterfuge, he would go at the problem all out, something that would probably entail Markov getting all or part of the rest of their group involved. Jaden preferred to avoid that. Sighing, he accepted he would have to tell Markov the truth and hope Markov would be satisfied with that. *Slim chance!* But it was the only option. And it meant one less person he would have to lie to.

Taking the dough bases with him, Jaden reentered the kitchen and dumped them on the pizza stones. Atu and Markov had already set out toppings, so the three of them dressed the dough as they discussed their game. Jaden was surprised that Markov waited through the baking time and until they had finished eating before raising the question he had come to ask.

Leaning back in his chair, Markov glanced first at Jaden, then Atu, and then folded his arms. "So are you two going to tell me what's really going on?"

Jaden almost laughed at Atu's shocked expression. He looked like a rabbit facing down a speeding truck. Instead, Jaden berated himself. Atu didn't know Markov as well as he did, and that question *had* come out of the blue. He should've warned Atu last night, so they could've come up with a plan. Too late to do anything now.

"I don't think you'd believe us if we told you," Jaden said.

"Try me." That steely resolve Jaden knew all too well glinted in Markov's eyes.

Jaden glanced at Atu for permission. Atu shrugged and gestured to Jaden that he had the floor. But when Jaden opened his mouth, he heard it: the sound he hadn't expected again so soon. At least, not here.

In one fluid motion, Jaden leaped to his feet, ripping his DD from its sheath. Pressing the DD's hilt, the curved blade of light sizzled to life. He had only a moment to notice Markov's frozen face before vaulting over the kitchen counter toward the stairwell. He almost collided with Atu, who beat him to the narrow stairway. Jaden chased him up to the roof.

The pair of them burst through the door to the landing site and stopped dead. Where were their gliders? Why weren't they here? Had their link failed? But no, Markov's frozen features could only be because he was stuck in time, meaning the gliders were close.

Hearing a familiar raucous cry below, Jaden sprinted to the edge of the landing site. Han and Aren were tearing what was left of the Gaptor with their talons. The Gaptor's inherent evil still oozed from its hideous, armored body, despite it being dead. Jaden grimaced as Han ripped the tail off. A garish version of a scorpion stinger, it landed with a hefty thump. Han didn't even wait for it to settle before sinking his teeth into the unnaturally long, scaly neck. With a twist, that also went flying. How had he done so without getting sliced by the monster's scimitar of a beak?

Aren was just as bloodthirsty, tucking into the Gaptor's wings and shredding the scraggly fingers that constituted each wing. Just as well the blades that lurked beneath the surface of the wingtips didn't release upon death, or Aren would be in worse shape than the Gaptor.

Relieved that neither glider appeared harmed, Jaden grinned. Although the eight-foot-tall gliders were smaller than the Gaptors, they were acting like the bats they resembled, darting around a fruit tree rather than a corpse. "You two having fun down there?"

Han squinted up and gave Jaden a toothy grin. "Feeling left out?"

"You bet! Was this the only Gaptor?"

"Yes." Han frowned. "It is quite unusual for a Gaptor to turn up alone."

Jaden froze. "Kayla," he breathed.

"She's alright," Han assured him. "Taz is with her, and there are no Gaptors near her home."

"How do you know? Are you sure?"

"She and Taz only left a moment ago, once they figured out you were alright and that there weren't any more Gaptors that needed execution."

"Oh." Jaden was simultaneously comforted and disappointed. *She's okay. But she was here and then she left without even coming in to say hello?*

Han snorted. "Don't make a face like a pig. She noticed your friend was here and didn't want to intrude."

"Oh," Jaden repeated. Then recovering, he added, "Well, tell her to come in next time, no matter who's here."

Han chortled, the generous sound rumbling and reverberating around the building. "I'll tell her. But don't think she'll do that just because you told her to."

Jaden rolled his eyes. "She may surprise you."

That only made Han laugh even more, and this time, Aren and Atu joined him. Jaden glared at Atu.

"What?" Atu sputtered. "You know it's true."

Reluctantly, Jaden allowed a smile to touch his face. Yeah, it was true. Kayla would do what she thought was right, one of the reasons he loved her. Studying the bloody mess that constituted the remnants of the Gaptor, Jaden hollered, "What are you boys going to do with that?"

By way of answer, Han launched himself into the air, followed by Aren. The pair circled once before turning back and diving down on the dead Gaptor. In unison, they stretched out their talons and grabbed polar ends of the corpse. Easily hefting the bulky Gaptor, they spiraled upward until they were clear of the buildings.

"You may want to take that thing far from here. Even if people can't see it, they'll surely smell it after a few days," Jaden called.

"Orders, orders, and more orders," Han grumbled good-naturedly. "Whatever happened to some gratitude that we took care of the beastie for you?"

Jaden laughed. "Of course, where are my manners? Thank you, gliders. Where would Atu and I be without you?"

Out of the corner of his eye, Jaden caught the smirk on Atu's face. Jaden and Atu sniggered as Han's griping floated back down to them. "Mercifully, he's too far away for us to hear what he's saying," Atu commented.

The pair of them lingered on the rooftop, watching until well after the gliders had passed from sight with their grisly cargo.

"Jaden?"

The voice behind them made Jaden spin around. Markov dawdled there, looking uncertain. *That's a first*, Jaden reckoned.

"How were you two able to get up here without me seeing?" Markov asked. "And what in mercy's name, are those gadgets in your hands?"

Jaden glanced down, noticing his still blazing DD. He had forgotten it was there. Yes, it probably did look like something from a science fiction movie, with its long, curving blade of light, sizzling and spitting with current. Thumbing the catch, he studied Markov as the blade slid back into its hilt, reducing it to nothing more than an innocuous carving knife. His friend was staring at him with a mixture of awe and curiosity. As he sheathed his DD under his shirt, Jaden sighed. It was time Markov knew the truth.

"I did say you wouldn't believe us," Jaden began, leading his friends down the stairs as he launched into an explanation of all that had happened since that fateful annual hike up in the Shadow Mountains.

CHAPTER TWO

Markov blinked. To his credit, his mouth didn't hang open. But Jaden knew his friend was overwhelmed. What else could he be?

"I'd think you were yanking my chain if I hadn't seen you pull that strange weapon," Markov finally muttered. "Or if you hadn't just vanished the way you did. Seriously, do you know how unnerving it was for you guys to be there one moment and gone the next?"

"Sorry, that's an unfortunate side effect of the gliders being near," Jaden said. "It was unavoidable considering the circumstances."

"Circumstances being that one of those enemy creatures was here?"

"Yes." After a pause, Jaden ventured, "You believe us then?"

"Dude, I know you, and despite that wild imagination of yours, even you couldn't come up with a story like that. Besides, you said both your folks and Kayla's have heard this story and that they've even seen the…gliders?"

Markov said the word tentatively, as if tasting the sound of it on his tongue. Jaden couldn't blame him. He had just spent most of the afternoon blowing Markov's mind with a tale so farfetched Jaden would've thought it a fairy tale himself if he didn't have the artifacts to prove it. "They have. And if our gliders return any time soon, I'll let you wear the relic stone so you can see them for yourself."

"Tell me why it is again that no one else can see these gliders and Gaptors?" Markov asked for the third time that afternoon.

Catching Jaden's exasperated expression, Atu fielded the question. "We don't know. As we said before, it's one of those things we can't explain. Although they were visible to everyone a very long time ago, that's no longer the case."

"And your family is descended from those who could see the Gaptors when they first came to our world?" Markov gave a hollow laugh. "I can't believe I just said that! *Our* world."

Jaden grinned. "Feeling like *your* world is falling apart?" That netted a smile from Markov, strained as it was. "Don't stress, dude. It takes a while to sink in."

"Tell me about it."

Jaden watched Markov, debating whether he had done the right thing. But it would've come to this eventually. Markov wouldn't have stopped until he had answers. Jaden had bypassed the circuitous path of Markov's investigation, guaranteeing the rest of their close-knit group stayed free of this mess. For now, anyway. Besides, Jaden was tired of lying. If people were stubborn enough to press him for answers, he was going to reply, whether they liked it or not.

Abruptly, Markov stood. "I need some exercise. Some time to think this through."

"Of course. Do you want to play a few more rounds?"

"Thanks, but I need a heap more cardio than that!"

Jaden chuckled. Markov would run the compound ragged working through this info dump. He and Atu followed Markov upstairs to where Markov's 'pod floated on one of the pads.

"Jaden." Markov gave him one of their complicated handshakes. Atu got the more traditional handshake. "Get Jaden to teach you the right way to greet us. Seems you're one of the crew now. Only right you should know."

Atu's wide smile broadcast his pleasure. "I will."

"See that you do. I'm glad Jaden's at least got you and Kayla watching his back."

Atu shrugged. "It's what we do. If we've learned nothing else, it's clear we need each other. We succeed together or not at all."

"On that delightfully sobering thought, I'll take my leave." Grimacing as he slipped into his 'pod, he revved the engines and sped away.

"Think he'll be okay?" Atu asked.

"Markov's resilient," Jaden observed. "It may take some time, but I know we'll be able to count on him once he's come to terms with the whole thing."

"Good to know. Now, about that handshake?"

"Yeah, let's go inside and grab a snack. Then I'll teach you."

"A snack? Isn't it almost dinner time?"

"Isn't it always time for food?"

Atu sniggered. About to head back inside, they stopped when they heard a familiar rustling. Turning, they found Han and Aren balancing on the rooftop.

"Back so soon?" Jaden teased.

"Taz wanted us to give you a message," Han responded.

"Of course she did. What does her highness want now?"

The odd expression that flitted across Han's face piqued Jaden's interest. Had Jaden offended his glider? No, that wasn't it. Before he could work it out, Han spoke. "She said to tell you that you had your day with your friends as requested. Training resumes tomorrow. And it will continue until we know what the next step is."

Jaden groaned. He knew what that meant. Hours and hours of routines. No food. And lots of exercise. Not that he didn't like exercise. It was just that Taz could . . . take things too far.

"The downtime had to end eventually," Atu sighed.

"She could've given us another week," Jaden grumbled.

"Not with what happened today," Han pointed out. "Do you know how unusual it is for a lone Gaptor to attack?"

"You know for sure that that's what it was doing—or intending to do?" Jaden asked.

Han huffed as he rustled his wings. "What else does a Gaptor do?"

"What else indeed." Jaden drew in a resigned breath. "I'm sorry if I offended you. I'm just disappointed that our vacation is over, but Taz is right. We do need to get back to things. The sooner we get on with it, the sooner it'll all be over."

Han's shoulders relaxed. "I'm glad you understand. We'll see you tomorrow." With that, he and Aren departed.

Jaden glanced at Atu. He was staring after Aren, a distant look in his eyes. "What's up?"

Atu faced him. "I hope we find my parents on this next leg of the journey."

Instantly, Jaden felt awful. Their time off had to have been difficult for Atu, forced to bide his time. "I'm sorry. We should've started back sooner."

"No," Atu said, shaking his head. "I needed the rest. After my parents disappeared, I just kept going and didn't stop. I didn't realize how desperately I needed the downtime."

Jaden considered Atu's words. "Yes, I suppose just like it was time to rest earlier, now it's time to pick up the reins again. Don't tell Taz I agreed with her, though." Jaden was gratified when a smile tugged at Atu's lips. "Shall we get that snack now?" Atu's smile morphed into a chuckle.

Jaden laughed too as they headed down to the kitchen. A flutter of excitement rippled through him. Kayla was coming for dinner, and he couldn't wait. It seemed an eternity since he'd seen her, but it had only been yesterday. Yes, getting back to training would be good. He could see Kayla all day, every day. It would be preferable if this was possible without the associated risks, but he supposed that was too much to ask. *Yes, what I said earlier. The sooner we get back to things, the sooner this will end.*

The afternoon dragged. Even his mother's scrumptious cookies didn't distract him. Jaden taught Atu the intricacies of the group's handshakes. Then they drifted back to the basement for another game, more as a means of passing time than anything else. Now they had decided to get back to their mission, they were both itching to leave. *But where are we going?* They had all agreed not to open the cube with the map until they were ready to get back on task. *Well, we'll find out soon.*

An hour before the Melmiques arrived, Atu and Jaden quit their game so they could shower and help his mother with dinner. They were putting the finishing touches on the meal when Jaden heard the pads elevating. He dropped what he was doing and bounded up to the rooftop, bursting through the door just in time to see Kayla stepping down from their 'pod. Rushing toward her, he swept her up in a fierce hug.

"Well, hello to you too," Kayla said, giggling.

Leaning in close so only she could hear, Jaden said, "If we were alone, I'd do more than hug you."

This only made Kayla laugh more as she extricated herself from his arms. Jaden was still smiling as he greeted her parents and helped them with the dishes they were unloading. Their arms full, Jaden and Kayla dashed ahead into the kitchen while her parents followed at a more sedate pace. After setting their burdens on the countertop, it was the parents' turn to hug one another, their greetings almost as exuberant as that of the teens.

Kayla skipped over to Atu and hugged him. As he returned the hug, Atu grinned at the proprietary look in Jaden's eyes. "Easy, bro, I'm just saying hello."

Jaden grimaced. "I know that." He didn't add that he'd prefer it if he could have Kayla all to himself.

Kayla turned her head and gave him one of her glorious smiles, as if she knew what he was thinking. Then, returning her attention to Atu, she said, "How are you holding up?"

Jaden shook his head. How could she remember to ask the important questions? He was glad she did though. At least one of them had a heart.

"Better now that I know we'll be getting back to things," Atu answered.

All sound died. The teens' eyes shot to the adults, who were staring at them, the same emotion painted on each of their faces. Dread.

Jaden crossed to his mother and pulled her into his arms. "It'll be okay." He could feel her trembling under him. When she smiled, it didn't reach her eyes.

"I know. You have each other—and your gliders," Clara tried to convince herself.

Over his mother's shoulder, Jaden saw Kayla move to her own mother, now in her father's embrace. Rubbing her mother's back, Kayla said, "We'll be alright."

Sadie gave Kayla a tremulous smile. "Yes, I'm sure you will be."

From what Kayla had told him, Mrs. Melmique's optimism was quite the sacrifice. Typically, she would question any assertion made without supporting evidence. According to Kayla, that was what made her such a great lawyer.

Jaden's gaze swiveled to Atu. He stood alone, watching them. He must have been wishing he could have his own parents here right now. Taking a page from Kayla's book, Jaden stretched out a hand and squeezed Atu's shoulder, pleased when Atu dredged up a smile.

The movement had Clara turning her head. Giving Jaden a tight squeeze to end the hug, she crossed to Atu and pulled him close. Jaden grinned when he saw Atu relax in her arms. *Yes, that's what he needs. Some love too.*

When Atu drew back, his eyes glistened with unshed tears. "Thank you," Atu murmured.

"Any time," Clara whispered, giving his hand a squeeze before facing the others. "Who's up for some food?"

That broke the tension. The teens picked up the hors d'oeuvres and wandered onto the deck, where they spread themselves on lounge chairs next to the moms. The dads made themselves at home next to the barbecue, grilling the meat. Conversation was a little stilted at first, all of them studiously avoiding the subject uppermost on their minds. But by the time the meat was ready, they were conversing freely.

Jaden tucked in. Glancing up, he saw Atu grinning. "What?"

"Didn't you eat an hour ago?"

"Look who's talking." Jaden gestured at Atu's plate, which was nearly as full as his own.

Kayla rolled her eyes. "Yes, we all know you boys love your food."

That produced smiles from all the adults.

A question occurred to Clara. "What do you do for food while you're…traveling?"

Motion ceased. Jaden glared at his mother. Why had she brought up the mission again?

Clara sent him a withering look. "Not talking about it isn't going to make it go away."

"Your mother's right," Ty commented, leaning back in his chair. "It would give us some peace to know." He looked inquiringly at Sadie and Vicken, who nodded agreement.

"Yes," Vicken said, "it would be reassuring to know you have a plan when you're on your travels."

Jaden stared at his plate. He couldn't tell them they never had a plan, that things just happened. That would totally freak them out.

As usual, Kayla came up with the ready answer, brilliant in its evasiveness. "We typically take food with us. But if we run out, we can catch, prepare, and cook our own food, thanks to Atu's training. He's quite the accomplished hunter."

Diverted by this unexpected turn in the conversation, the parents bombarded Atu with questions. Jaden smirked when Atu shot Kayla a subtle, accusing glance. Despite this, he deftly moved the conversation toward hunting. The parents were fascinated by the snippets he supplied, from the various ways one could set snares to which snare or trap worked best for which animal. By the time Atu reached the plants that could be used for seasoning, the adults were well and truly engaged in what he had to say.

Jaden observed Atu leading the parents away from that dangerous question, the one they really didn't want an answer to. Which made him wonder—what *was* their plan?

His gazed flicked toward Kayla, and he found her studying him. He smiled, and when she smiled back, he forgot the question. Her smile was incredible and lit her whole face. It truly was like the sunrise.

"Jaden?"

Yanked back to reality, he realized his mother had asked a question. "Sorry, I missed that. Can you repeat the question?"

Clara giggled.

Oh no, Jaden groaned inwardly. He could see it on her face. She was going to tease him about being too preoccupied with Kayla to be paying attention to anything else. *Please, don't!* he mentally pleaded. His mother's coy smile told him she knew exactly what he was thinking.

Clara repeated her question. "I asked if you had had enough food?"

Jaden released the breath he didn't know he'd been holding. His mother's eyes sparkled mischievously. "Yes, thanks, Mom."

Clara laughed, understanding that his thanks were meant in more ways than one. "Then could I ask you kids to clear the table and fetch the dessert and some plates? Oh, and will you put the kettle on for some tea too?"

Jaden smiled. "Sure, no problem."

CHAPTER THREE

As soon as they reached the kitchen, Kayla whispered, "That was close."

Jaden dumped his pile of plates on the counter. "Yeah, but thanks to your quick thinking, we didn't have to admit to not having a plan."

"Time to make one then?" Kayla asked.

"Yes, it's beyond time. Shall we find out where we're going?"

"Absolutely!"

"Agreed!" Atu exclaimed simultaneously. "Where's the map?"

"In my room," Jaden replied. "But let's wait until after dessert before we open it."

Kayla quirked her eyebrows at him, and he subtly gestured outside. Following his signal, she noticed the adults looking back toward the three of them in the kitchen. Their parents were sitting on the very edges of their seats. "That isn't a good sign."

"No, it's not," Atu murmured. "They look like they're about to jump up and come and carry us off."

"Preferably somewhere where they can keep us safe and away from all of this," Jaden added.

"But they can't. Much as they want to, there's nothing they can do to help. What a terrible predicament for a parent," Kayla sympathized.

Jaden scrubbed a hand over his face. Then he sighed. "Let's put on our happy faces, then, and at least try and make the evening fun and memorable for them."

Kayla nodded agreement, as did Atu. Collecting the dessert, plates, and spoons, the trio headed back outside.

For Kayla, every step happened in slow motion. It took an eternity to reach the parents. But it was just as well. She needed the time to adjust her thinking. When her last step placed her next to the table, Kayla had found the right balance. "You're all looking way too serious. I think it's time for some entertainment. Jaden, why don't we teach them one of Ruby's games?"

Jaden smiled. "I'll get the cards."

Kayla studied the parents as Jaden disappeared inside the house. For a moment, she didn't think the heavy atmosphere that blanketed them was going to lift. Then Sadie took the plates and handed them to Clara, who divvied up the dessert. The normalcy of the tasks eased the transition, and by the time Jaden returned, their strained expressions had relaxed somewhat. Their anxiety dissipated a little further as Jaden and Kayla explained the rules while they ate their dessert and completely vanished when they all threw themselves into the game. Things became rowdy as play progressed. Only when Sadie yawned loudly did anyone think to check the time.

"Good gracious!" Clara exclaimed. "It's almost midnight."

"You're joking," Vicken blurted, checking his own PAL. "No, you're not! Sadie, we need to get going. I have an early morning meeting."

Sadie smiled as she shrugged her agreement. "Clara, thank you. It's been a lovely evening. Would you like any help clearing things before we leave?"

Kayla flicked a glance at Jaden and saw the same panic on his face. They couldn't be going. Not yet. She hadn't had enough time with Jaden. And they hadn't opened the cube yet. They needed to know where they were headed. "Mom, Dad, why don't you go on home and send the 'pod back for me? I'll help the Jamesons clear up."

Her father sent her a grateful smile, and her mother nodded vaguely.

"Yes, dear, that's a good idea," her mother murmured.

She must be really tired. It was the only time her mother ever called her "dear." Worried, she steered her parents towards the stairs leading up to the landing site.

"Wait, I need to get my dishes," Sadie protested half-heartedly.

"I'll bring them," Kayla said. "You need to get home so you can sleep."

Her mother's wan smile highlighted the fatigue lining her face. Kayla couldn't fathom why she was so tired. She hadn't had any contracts recently that required her to leave home. Or any pressing deadlines. Was her mother was lying awake at night worrying about her? About what Kayla had to do? Deciding she needed to talk to her dad, Kayla herded her parents to where their 'pod waited. Satisfied when they hugged her goodbye without further delay, Kayla watched as they boarded and departed. When she turned to go back downstairs, Kayla found Jaden waiting for her at the entrance to the house.

"Are you okay?" Jaden asked.

"No, not really," Kayla admitted. "I think my mom's not sleeping because she's so worried about us. That's disturbing considering she's only just recovered from that nasty virus she had. I don't want her getting sick again."

Jaden crossed to her with a few quick strides, and his arms encircled her. Kayla burrowed into his shoulder, feeling Jaden's warmth through his shirt, inhaling the scent that was uniquely his. She was so thankful he was here. What would she do without him? His comfort was a balm. It gave her the strength she needed. She drew back a little and studied his handsome face. Those amazing blue eyes blazed with concern.

"I'll be alright," Kayla reassured him, lifting a hand to his face and cupping his cheek. He smiled then. That gorgeous smile. And she melted.

Bending his head, he kissed her lightly.

"No, that won't do. Kiss me properly."

Jaden smiled and did as she asked. She lost herself in their kiss. Too soon, it was over.

"Did you have to stop?"

Jaden grinned. "Unfortunately, yes. If we don't get back downstairs, my mom and dad are likely to send out a search party considering their mental state."

Kayla sighed. "Don't you wish we could just wipe their worry away?"

"That would be nice." Then after a moment, he added, "Do you regret telling them?"

Kayla cocked her head as she considered his question. "No. It's better that they know, even if it does worry them. I think it would've been way more disconcerting if we kept lying to them. We wouldn't have fooled them for long. Then they would've been conjuring up all sorts of horrid ideas to give themselves some explanation why their usually truthful children were now consistently deceitful."

"Too true." Wrapping his fingers around hers, Jaden led her downstairs. They found Atu alone in the kitchen.

"Where did my folks go?" Jaden asked.

"I sent them to bed." Atu put another plate in the dishwasher. "It gives them rest and allows us to be alone to open that map."

"Good man." Jaden beamed. "Alrighty then, let's clear this mess so we can get to that map."

It didn't take long, so they were soon up in Jaden's room. Atu took the chair, and Kayla flopped onto Jaden's bed as he retrieved the cube from his backpack.

"Shall we see where we're going?" Jaden teased.

"Open it already," Kayla chided as she giggled, rubbing absently at her birthmark.

Jaden grinned, then closed his eyes and curled his fingers around the cube. He waited a second before working the miniature panels on the sides. Somehow, he just knew what he had to do. *How did that work?* One side of the cube popped off. *Huh, that was new.* She waited for the lines of light. They didn't materialize. Glancing at Atu, Kayla saw the question on his face.

Jaden, it seemed, was just as confused. He looked down at the cube, frowning as he peered inside. Then Kayla and Atu gaped as he carefully removed a circular disc tucked inside.

Bouncing off the bed, Kayla leaned in next to Jaden and examined it. It was some sort of frosted glass sprinkled with tiny pinprick holes that were irregularly spaced. Jaden flipped the disc over, but it remained a circular disc.

"What's happening? Where's the map?" Kayla demanded.

"I think that disc *is* the map," Atu breathed.

"It can't be. Where are our magic lines of light and the moving 'x'?" Jaden refuted.

Speculatively, Kayla took the disc from Jaden and turned it over in her hands. She hissed as her finger caught on a rough edge. The bright drop of blood had her clamping a tissue over the cut. Deciding to clean it later, she studied the disc, finding a tiny chip near the edge. As she handed the disc to Atu, she warned him about it. Then Kayla examined the cube, giving it a thorough inspection. "I think Atu's right. The disc is the only thing with markings on it. It must be the map."

Jaden took the disc back from Atu and stared at it dismally. "How can this be the map? It's a piece of glass with holes in it."

"I wasn't with you the last time you guys opened the map," Atu ventured. "Can you tell me what happened?"

Jaden huffed. "How's that relevant?"

"Humor me."

"Well, I was on my own," Jaden began. "I found the disc accidentally, if that's even possible with all the other things that are so 'coincidental' with this quest."

Jaden paused, his expression sour, but neither Kayla nor Atu said anything. They waited for him to continue.

Sighing, Jaden did. "The disc was attached to the side of a toy chest that's been in our family for generations. And get this, the chest had the same markings as the key my grandmother gave me."

"Okay, so the same markings were on the key and the chest," Atu repeated. "Then what?"

"I used the key on the chest, and the disc fell off." From his curt answer, Kayla could tell Jaden was already tired of this. Honestly, she was just as mystified as Jaden.

"Now we're getting somewhere," Atu grinned.

"What do you mean?" Kayla asked.

"We're finally at the same point back then as we are now. You had the wooden disc then, and you have a glass disc now. We can figure out what we do next."

"I don't think so," Jaden pouted. "All I had to do then was open the disc, and the map floated out. This time, the cube needed opening. But instead of contour lines, we got this glass disc."

"You're still not getting it," Atu insisted.

"You're saying that the glass disc 'falling' out of the cube confirms it's the map, the same way that the lines 'fell' out of the wooden disc?" Kayla responded.

"Exactly." Atu beamed. "Last time you had to open something to get the map. This time you did the same. The difference is that last time the lines were the map. This time, it's the disc."

"Yes, I get all that," Jaden snapped. "What you're not getting is how does that help us?"

Atu looked pained. "Well, I'm not done yet. Give me a chance."

"Could we speed it up then?" When Kayla sent him a reproachful look, Jaden added, "Please?"

"Sure. What happened after you opened the disc and the lighted map came out?"

Jaden looked like he was about to blow a fuse. Kayla jumped in. "Jaden called me and invited me over to show me the map."

"Then what?" Atu pressed, his tone sharp. "Did you know they were contour lines right away?"

"Well, no," Kayla confessed. "We had to look it up. I remembered that the lines were a special kind of map, but I couldn't recall the details. An internet search revealed they were contour lines and explained what they were. With that knowledge, we then tried to fit those lines to an existing part of earth using a terrain overlay search."

"And?"

"It did the same thing that any of the other artifacts on this quest does," Jaden growled. "Gave us no result!"

"But that's not the end of it," Atu prompted, "or we wouldn't be here. Tell me what you did next."

"Nothing." Jaden scratched his chin. "We were stumped at that point. Or we were, until Kayla remembered that the lines floating around us . . ."

"Were also on a page in the book!" Kayla finished with Jaden.

They grinned at one another and then glanced at Atu. He was leaning back, a smug smile on his face.

"Alright," Jaden said, "you can say it. You told us so."

Atu raised his hands, palms up and facing them. "I'm not saying anything."

"You don't have to," Kayla chuckled. She turned to Jaden. "Where's the book?"

Jaden scrambled back to his closet, opened his backpack, and reverently withdrew the book Awena gave them. Hurrying back, he set the book on his bed between them.

The three of them surrounded the book as they slowly turned the pages, scrupulously examining the background of each page for any sign of a pattern that matched the holes on the disc. They reached the page where their last clue had been, with the splotch that read *Soquazba* when magnified, and explained it to Atu. He nodded thoughtfully but said nothing, and they continued thumbing their way forward.

"There it is," Atu whispered, vindicated.

The three of them stared at the page. The unmistakable splotch toward the bottom right corner marked it as the correct page even if the pattern on the background didn't.

Without waiting, Jaden leaped up and ran downstairs. He reappeared two minutes later, the ultra-magnifier in his hand.

"Maybe we should just keep that with us from now on," Kayla suggested.

"We will," Jaden agreed, setting the tool over the splotch.

The splotch became letters. *Happy Days.*

"Well, that's super helpful," Jaden muttered.

"Does that mean anything to you?" Kayla asked Atu.

"No. You?"

"Nope," Kayla replied, shaking her head. Turning to Jaden, she found he was no longer on the bed next to them. He was already in front of his holoscreen, entering the phrase into his proprietary search engines with that antiquated keyboard of his. Reams of information began scrolling along the multiple screens Jaden had set up on one wall.

"Would you look at that?" Jaden brooded. "Last time we only had one result. This time, the end of the world could come before we figure out which one of these entries is the right one."

Atu glanced at Kayla. "Do you have any ideas?"

Kayla shook her head. "No again. And unless we can find some way to narrow that list, Jaden's right. We don't know where we're going."

CHAPTER FOUR

For Kayla, training the next day was as expected: endless routines with little respite. It wouldn't have been any easier if her finger hadn't been aching all day. For a surprisingly minuscule cut, an infection was brewing. But they trained so intensively, she forgot to ask Atu for one of his magical potions.

Courtesy of Jaden's insight, they added more plays to incorporate Aren and Atu as a new unit and adjusted existing plays to make them more effective with three pairs of fighters instead of two. They even worked on transferring voyagers between gliders should one of their gliders become incapacitated. Then they practiced what they had learned. And practiced. And practiced, until Kayla's head was spinning. By the time Taz grudgingly called it a day, Kayla was beyond exhausted.

Everyone was quiet as they headed home, weariness weighing on them. When Taz quivered unexpectedly, Kayla went on alert. Studying the immediate area, she found no threats. Could Taz simply be tired too?

Apparently so, because their gliders dropped them at Jaden's home, agreed on a time to meet the following day, and departed without further ado. Kayla watched as they vanished in an instant, then flinched as the sun burst out in blinding, golden glory, the morning rays hot and bright.

"This time thing is killing me," Kayla moaned. "I can't believe we still have to endure a whole day before we can sleep!"

"Belay that," Atu scoffed. "I'm sleeping now. I couldn't keep my eyes open for another minute even if I tried."

"Belay that?" Jaden chuckled. "What are you? A pirate?"

"Don't laugh. My brain stopped functioning two hours ago."

Kayla nodded. "I'm with you. I plan on getting some sleep before my folks get home."

Jaden glanced at her. "How are you getting home? Want me to take you?"

Giggling, Kayla said, "Yes, please. I wasn't going to say anything, but I think Taz is as tired as I am. At least, she felt a little weak on the way home. And did you notice how she didn't complain when we said a mid-morning start? I was expecting her to veto that for sure. And if that wasn't enough to convince me, her leaving me stranded here is."

Jaden and Atu laughed, and soon the three of them had tears streaming down their faces.

"Well," Jaden eventually choked, "we'd better not say anything to her about it tomorrow. Maybe if we let things slide, she'll go easy on us."

That absurd idea had them all rolling again. Finally, rubbing the tears from their cheeks, they sighed and looked at one another.

"Ever notice how much funnier things are when you're tired?" Kayla commented. The boys nodded, looking as drained as Kayla felt.

Resolutely, Atu said, "Alright, I'm off to sleep! See you two later."

Kayla hugged him before he turned and entered the house, then smiled when Jaden took her hand. "What?"

"It's time to get you home."

Leaning into him, Kayla savored his support as Jaden guided her into the 'pod and then climbed in after her. After setting her coordinates as the destination, he wrapped his hand around hers again. The familiar comfort that action brought left Kayla wanting more. She scooted closer and snuggled up to him, dropping her head onto

Jaden's shoulder as the 'pod lifted. It was so comfortable there. And he was so warm. She closed her eyes, letting the silence, the measure of their exhaustion, wash over her.

* * *

Jaden must've dozed off because a strident beeping had his eyes flying open. When he realized it only signaled their arrival, he relaxed. That had been careless. Even tired as he was, he should've been more vigilant. A Gaptor could've attacked. He glanced down at Kayla. She hadn't stirred.

Smiling, Jaden carefully moved around her and maneuvered himself out of his seat. Then he lifted her into his arms. Groggily, she peered at him through bleary eyes. "Go back to sleep," Jaden whispered.

Her lips softened in a smile, and she burrowed into his shoulder again. Jaden marveled at how someone so small could pack such a punch when she was awake. It was just as well she had an "off" switch. What would the world do if she only had an "on" button?

When he reached her room, he peeked inside. Everything was perfectly in place, like she never used it. He shook his head. It must be a girl thing. Pulling her comforter out of the way with one hand, he settled her on her bed and then tucked the cover around her. Reconsidering, he lifted the cover again and removed her shoes. She wouldn't be too happy to wake up and find she still had them on. After placing her shoes next to her bed (he'd never have done that in his own room), he leaned down and kissed her silky head. "Sleep tight." A small smile that curved her lips was his only answer.

Jaden crept out of the room and hurried back to the 'pod. He was wasted. Flipping the switches that would take him home, he slumped in his chair, making an effort to stay awake this time. An effort it was, but he did it, thankful he didn't encounter any Gaptors along the way. Sliding out of the 'pod, he stumbled down to his room and crashed onto his bed, face down. His last thought as sleep claimed him was that he still had his shoes on.

"Jaden Jameson!'

Jaden snapped awake, feeling like he'd been run over by a truck. His mother stood in his doorway, her hands on her hips. "What?"

"How many times have I told you to take your shoes off before getting onto your bed?"

Jaden grimaced. He had thought about that, truly. It had just been beyond him to reach down and take them off before he crashed. *What's the time?* Twisting his head, he ogled his PAL. Suddenly, he was wide awake. "It's five o' clock!"

His mother frowned. "What time did you think it was? Have you been asleep all day?"

"Um . . ." It was too early for her to be asking questions like that. No, it was too late. *Ugh, why can't I get a coherent thought in my head?*

"Jaden, are you alright?"

The sudden concern in her voice roused him more than the time had. "Of course. I must've just dozed off. Sorry about not taking my shoes off." Jaden offered his mother a sheepish grin.

That did it. She smiled. "I suppose you can't be expected to take them off if you didn't plan on going to sleep. What did you boys do today? Atu's asleep too."

Uh-oh. They would have to set an alarm in the future. It wouldn't take a rocket scientist to figure out all their sleeping must be due to something besides being teenage boys. "He's still sleeping? I'd better go wake him. Kayla will be here soon."

His mother squealed. "I forgot! She's coming over this evening, and I don't have dinner going yet."

To Jaden's relief, she bustled out of the room, muttering something about food. He raked a hand through his hair. He hadn't had nearly enough rest. On the bright side, he only had to be awake for a few hours before he could crash again.

Groaning, he dragged himself from his bed and made for the guest room. Atu was more than asleep. He could've been mistaken for dead. Jaden shook Atu's shoulder. Atu rolled and came up with fists flying. Jaden took a hasty step backward. "Easy, bro. It's just me."

Atu flopped back down. "You scared me."

"You don't say."

Atu yawned. "What time is it?"

"Nearly five." Jaden was amused when Atu's eyes widened with shock. *Yeah, that must be exactly what I looked like a few minutes ago.*

"Are your folks home yet?' Atu blurted with sudden consternation.

"My mom is. She just woke me up."

"Oh no, she found us asleep?"

From that comment, Jaden knew Atu understood. "She did. She'll be asking you what we did today that we're both so tired."

"What are we going to tell her?"

"That we spent the day up in the mountains, getting some exercise."

"You don't want to tell her about the training?"

"No, she'll only worry." Jaden sighed. "Look, I know it's not the best option, but I would prefer to keep her concern on the lower end of the scale."

"I get it."

"Thanks, I appreciate that. I don't normally ask people to lie."

Atu put a hand on Jaden's shoulder. "Bro, you don't have to explain. Come on, let's go help your mom with dinner. Isn't Kayla coming over?"

Jaden grinned. He couldn't help himself. "She is. Unless she oversleeps like we did."

That made Atu laugh. When they entered the kitchen, they found Clara bouncing between the pantry and the main room as she gathered ingredients.

"What can we help with?" Jaden asked.

His mother stared at them for a moment as if they were from Mars. Then blinking, she said, "Sorry, my mind was a million miles away. What did you say?"

"We asked what we could do to help."

His mother smiled. "Oh, that's nice of you boys. If you don't mind . . ." She rattled off a list.

Thirty minutes later, the food was almost ready, and Jaden heard the whine of an approaching 'pod. He leapfrogged the stairs, catching the interaction between Atu and his mother as he did.

"There he goes again," Atu hummed, and Mrs. Jameson laughed.

"I guess he's recovered from the busy day you boys had," Clara commented.

Jaden hesitated on the stairs, just out of sight, waiting for the inevitable question about what they had done that had made them so tired. But it never came. His mother prattled on about her day. *Huh, that was strange.* Disturbed, Jaden resumed his dash up the stairs.

His worry dissolved the moment Kayla stepped from her 'pod. She looked amazing in a lime green dress that played up the color of her eyes. Her hair was swept up into that messy knot again, showcasing pretty, dangly earrings.

"Nice earrings." Jaden moved toward her and pulled her into his arms. "Did you make them?"

Kayla beamed. That smile made his day. It was refreshing to see her looking so carefree. And not so tired anymore. Despite the day's grueling activities, the dark smudges under her eyes were gone.

"I did make them," Kayla admitted shyly.

"Girl, you've got talent. Anyone ever told you that?"

Kayla giggled. "As a matter of fact . . ." She pressed a soft kiss on his lips before pulling out of the hug and taking his hand, talking a mile a minute about her online business as Jaden led her downstairs.

They entered the kitchen, still talking up a storm. But Jaden didn't miss the glance his mother swept from him, to Kayla to Atu, or the way her shoulders drooped in resignation.

"Hello, Mrs. Jameson," Kayla said.

His mother returned the greeting, her despondency fleeing as she hugged Kayla. "It's lovely to see you."

"Thank you, you too."

The whine of another 'pod pricked Clara's ears. "That must be Ty. I'll be back in a moment."

She left the room, and Kayla studied Jaden. "What's wrong?"

Jaden frowned. He would have to do better at keeping his emotions off his face. If Kayla had picked up on his concern, his mother surely had too. "Atu and I were still asleep when my mom got home today. I think she knows we did something we aren't telling her about."

Kayla put a hand on his arm. "You think she suspects we're training?"

"I don't know what she suspects. That's the problem."

"If she suspects something, wouldn't it be better to tell her?" Seeing Jaden's pending refusal, she quickly added, "I know you don't want to worry her. But sometimes it's worse not knowing something than knowing the truth."

Jaden was silent as he considered. "You may be right. I need time to think."

That was the end of the conversation as they heard Clara and Ty descending the stairs. A moment later, they were exchanging greetings and pleasantries before taking their seats at the table. They chatted through their meal, conversation flowing randomly from one subject to the next.

Jaden noticed his dad didn't ask how the teens had occupied themselves that day. Since his mother usually went up to greet his father when he arrived home, he hadn't paid it much attention. But what if she had done that today specifically so she could tell his father not to ask the teens what they had been up to? Maybe Jaden was being paranoid. But as the evening progressed, Jaden became more convinced.

Jaden picked at his meal, strung out like a steel wire stretched to breaking point. He was going to have to tell his parents, but he would need to check with Kayla first. After all, if he told his parents, hers would find out too, and she might not want them knowing for the same reason. *Ugh, this is just getting messy. The truth is so much simpler.*

When Kayla reached out a hand under the table and squeezed his knee, Jaden almost jumped at the unexpected contact. His eyes snapped to hers, and he saw the unspoken question in those sage green eyes. Hoping it conveyed that he'd tell her later, he shook his head ever so slightly. She must've understood, because she gave her own slight nod and removed her hand. Jaden wished she had left it there.

When the meal ended, Jaden said, "We'll clear the table and put the kettle on."

"Thanks, son," Ty said, standing and stretching. "I could use some down time." Ty looked at his wife. "Care to watch a movie with me?"

Clara smiled and rose, following him into the living room. Soon the vid was loud enough to prevent Jaden's parents from hearing anything else. Still, Jaden wasn't certain they wouldn't sneak into the kitchen just to catch what the teens were talking about. He needed to put some distance between them and his friends.

"You guys want s'mores?" Jaden offered.

"What's that?" Kayla asked.

"Those," Atu corrected with a grin. "You've never had s'mores?"

"Can't say that I have."

"You're in for a treat, then." Jaden smiled. "Atu, why don't you and Kayla get the fire going, and I'll get the ingredients?"

Kayla looked from the one boy to the other. "Oh, so it's a secret?"

Jaden laughed. "I think you'll figure it out."

"Some sort of dessert?"

"Yes," Atu answered as he steered her outside. "Let's get that fire going."

When Jaden joined them on the deck a few minutes later, the fire was blazing, and Atu and Kayla had pulled up chairs. Jaden grinned when he noticed Kayla inspecting the ingredients as he set them on the side table between them.

"Hmm, marshmallow, chocolate, and graham crackers. I could go with plain chocolate." Kayla broke a piece off and popped it into her mouth.

"Wait until you try the whole lot together," Atu said. "You might change your mind."

Kayla chuckled. "We'll see."

Jaden was quiet as he handed each of them a long, metal fork and passed the marshmallows around.

"So, are you going to tell us what you've decided?" Kayla asked, not looking at Jaden as she attached a marshmallow to her fork.

Jaden shot her a look. She lifted her head and gazed back, her eyes unwavering. "What gave me away?"

"Well, let's see. You were edgy all evening. You didn't eat with your usual appetite. And then towards the end of dinner, you got peace. And now you're quiet. Like you've reached some sort of conclusion. So out with it."

"I was thinking about what you said—that perhaps telling my parents that we're training again would be easier than letting them make up all sorts of horror stories about what we're keeping from them."

"And?" Kayla pressed.

"I think we should tell them."

"But?"

"If I tell my folks about us getting back to training, then it follows your parents are bound to find out too. Is that okay with you?"

CHAPTER FIVE

Kayla didn't even consider the question. "About that—I've also been thinking. Before I answer your question, I have one of my own."

Atu spoke before Jaden could. "Shoot."

"How does all this work for our gliders?"

They looked at her, confused.

"Can you be more specific?" Atu asked.

Kayla swished a hand through the air in front of her face, as if wiping a slate clean. "Sorry. What I meant is how does time work for them?" Blank stares. She tried again. "We had a whole day with our gliders, came home, and because the time freeze lifted, we had a whole day to sleep. Now we have an entire night for sleeping again—although how we'll do that I don't know. That being besides the point, do you think our gliders have this much time to recover as well?"

"Huh," Atu grunted. "I didn't think of that."

"Why is that even relevant?" Jaden asked.

Kayla sighed. "If we're supposed to be doing training, then shouldn't we be working at it like we did at Sven's? Without these extended breaks? And I say that because I'm assuming that the gliders get as much time off as we do."

"Can you get to the point?"

Kayla glared at him. "If you give me a moment, I will. Don't be so impatient."

Jaden folded his arms and sat back in his chair, lips pressed together.

Kayla groaned inwardly. *Ugh, he can be so petulant sometimes!* But he did look cute sitting there with that scowl on his face. Although to tell a guy he looked cute . . . she almost giggled. Jaden must've picked up on her humor, because his scowl deepened. *Okay, enough.* Kayla curbed her inner laughter. "We should simply stay with our gliders while we're training. That way, we'll get used to taking shorter breaks, and so will they. And it means we won't be coming home exhausted every evening, then trying to hide that from our parents."

"You're thinking this approach will negate the need to say anything to either set of parents," Atu mused.

"No, I think she's trying to get Taz to kill us with her training." Jaden's tone was mocking.

Kayla caught the twinkle in Jaden's eyes and smiled, relieved he seemed to be regaining his sense of humor. "Honestly, I'd love it if we didn't have to do the training at all. But that won't help us in the long run, now will it?"

"Regrettably not."

They sat in silence, the boys digesting Kayla's proposal. The fire crackled, reminding Kayla about her marshmallow. She yanked the charred remains from the flames. "Now what do I do with this?"

The boys snatched up their own forks, but the marshmallows were beyond redemption. The three of them replaced the marshmallows, nursing them over the flames this time. When they were all gooey, the boys showed Kayla how to assemble the s'more. She took a bite.

"Well?" Atu asked.

"Yup, pretty good," Kayla murmured. "I still prefer plain chocolate."

"What? You're not serious."

Kayla grinned. "If I was, would I have another?"

Atu eyed her, unsure whether she was teasing. When she squished another marshmallow onto her fork, he grinned and indicated that she should pass the bag. With his own marshmallow toasting over the fire, Atu leaned back in his chair. "Jaden, any inspiration about how to decode our map?"

Shaking his head, Jaden reached into his pocket and produced the cube. Reflexively, he flipped the wooden bars until the one side popped off. He freed the opaque disc and stared at it sullenly. "It's as much a mystery as ever. But at least the sharp edge on that chip has worn down, so it won't cut anymore."

Kayla rubbed her arm. She wished it would stop itching. Strange. She hadn't heard the annoying buzz of a mosquito. Maybe she should ask Jaden for some bug spray.

Kayla caught Atu staring at Jaden intently as Jaden twirled the disc in his long fingers. Her own gaze went to the disc. Kayla had to admit that the fire sparking through the pinprick holes was mesmerizing. For some reason, the tiny flashes of light sneaking through reminded Kayla of a shooting star. She almost jumped when Atu abruptly sat bolt upright.

"May I see the disc?" Atu asked, his voice tight.

Jaden handed it over. Atu peered at the fire through the disc. Kayla tried to figure out what Atu was doing when he flipped the disc and repeated his actions. Jaden seemed just as perplexed as she was.

"I know what this is!" Atu crowed.

"What?" Jaden and Kayla cried in unison.

"A star map!"

Jaden blinked. "A what?"

"A star map, you know, a map of the stars as they appear in the sky at a certain place at a specific time."

"Yeah, and that helps us how?"

"If we have the date and time the map was created, we can use those to work out the exact location on earth where this precise stellar arrangement could be seen," Atu explained.

"Um, still not getting how this helps us. We don't know when the map was created."

Atu deflated. Kayla leaned over and touched his arm. "Well, at least we know what kind of map it is now."

Atu smiled as if aware she was trying to make up for Jaden's lack of enthusiasm. "Thanks, but Jaden's right. Without a date and time, we can't identify the place."

"Here we go again," Jaden grumbled. "Another thing with other things that we need to find to get the answer to the first thing! And I know there were a lot of 'things' in that last sentence. Oh yes, I must be trying to make a point!"

Kayla rolled her eyes. Hadn't she *just* been thinking Jaden had regained his equilibrium? "Well, I'm sure that like before, we'll get the answers to those 'things' when we need them."

Her tart tone had Jaden grinning. "Look who's getting some faith!"

"Isn't that what the first clue was all about?" Kayla shot back.

Atu chuckled. That stopped them. They glared at him for a moment, but then laughed too. Smelling burnt sugar, Kayla jerked her fork out of the flames for a second time, laughing even more. When the boys realized they had forgotten theirs too, the three of them laughed until tears rolled from their eyes, tugging the blackened, smoking pieces off their forks.

"I'd say these are inedible," Kayla giggled.

"Yeah, just a tad overdone," Atu agreed.

"It's nice to hear you all having so much fun." Clara's soft voice startled them. They turned and found her and Ty standing in the doorway to the house, smiles on their faces.

"We're doing a fine job of burning things," Jaden confessed.

"Looks like you might need to brush up on some of those cooking skills Atu supposedly taught you," Ty remarked.

Jaden smiled. "Yes, it seems we should. Want to join us and test your own skills?"

Ty laughed. "Thanks, son, but no. That late night and the early start this morning has done us in. We just came to say goodnight."

"Oh, will we keep you awake if we stay out here?" Kayla asked, not wanting to overstay her welcome.

"Not at all," Clara reassured her. "You stay here as long as you want."

"Just try to not burn the house down," Ty teased as they said their farewells and retreated into their home.

Jaden waited until they were gone before he asked, "Do you think they're safe here?"

"Care to explain?" Kayla probed.

"Why do you think that lone Gaptor came to our house?"

That was a sobering thought. At the time, Kayla had been so thankful no Gaptor appeared at her home that she hadn't considered why the beast targeted Jaden's. Then she remembered Clara's dreams. "You think that Gaptor was sent here to spy?"

Atu's head bobbed as he looked from Kayla to Jaden and back again. "Why would a Gaptor need to spy on your folks?"

Jaden scrubbed his face, then dropped his hands to his knees, leaning forward and looking worn-out. "Because my mom had this dream—" He gave Atu the facts in bullet-point format.

Kayla realized Jaden was too fatigued to explain in more detail. The thought of his parents being kidnapped because of him was nagging at him, wearing him down. She stretched out her hand and clasped Jaden's. He smiled absently as he continued recounting his mother's dream. His tepid response had Kayla wondering whether her gesture had given him any comfort at all. That wasn't good. If this small amount of contact couldn't break through that wall of worry, it must be insurmountable.

She would have to discuss this with Jaden. There were clearly issues he wasn't addressing, and Kayla couldn't have him distracted while they were on their next journey. It was far too dangerous—for Jaden and for the rest of them. Kayla couldn't lose him. And on a practical level, Jaden was the only one who knew how to open the maps. Kayla's worry would've spiraled some more, except that Jaden gave her a genuine, heartfelt smile just then, like her hand on his had registered. But that didn't negate the need for Kayla to have that talk with him. Jaden had to deal with this, one way or another. Realizing Jaden had stopped talking, she focused on Atu, puzzled by his response.

Atu's face was ashen. "Maybe that's what it was doing."

"Pardon?" Jaden asked.

"Spying," Atu spat. "I'm pretty sure we had a Gaptor near our house before my parents disappeared. I didn't see it, but I got the same feeling back then as I do now every time a Gaptor is near." Atu paused. "Do you think my parents were taken for the same reason?"

Kayla's eyes swung to Jaden. He looked like he'd been kicked.

"That's more than possible," Jaden admitted.

"Which means my parents could be in danger too," Kayla concluded.

Glumly, they stared at the flames licking the edges of their marsh-mallows. *That's how I feel. Like that marshmallow. Slowly getting roasted until I'm all burned up.* She wallowed in self-pity for a split second, then shook herself. What was she thinking? Was she going to allow this monster to get to her? To win?

Kayla squared her shoulders. "I don't believe for a second we're going to lose. And we have to play to win. If we think our parents are in danger, we should call Pallaton. Maybe the Legion can camp out here and keep an eye on our families while we're away."

Jaden's face brightened. "That's an excellent suggestion. And it also makes me far more comfortable with staying up in the mountains while we train."

Kayla smiled. She should've known his reluctance would've run deeper than just being wiped out. Those he loved meant everything to him. And he would do what he had to in order to protect them. "We're agreed then? No telling the parents because if we stay away while training, the time freeze will keep them ignorant? And we get Pallaton here to keep an eye on our families while we're away?"

The boys nodded their agreement.

"Perfect. Now let's see if we can get some of these things cooked without burning them."

CHAPTER SIX

Jaden stirred his coffee absently, staring into space. Training had made it an exhausting week. Taz had been merciless. Their first day was rough, since, just as Kayla had predicted, none of the teens had slept well the night before. Taz's own tiredness was a small mercy. Not that she would've admitted it. But after Kayla pointed out the anomalies in her behavior the previous day, Jaden had paid more attention and found Kayla was right. Taz was slower than usual, hadn't been so quick to get them back to training after lunch, and had definitely dragged by early afternoon. Of course, Taz had made the excuse that the teens were tired, and that was why they cut the day short. Jaden suspected Taz would revoke her offer if he even hinted that she was equally tired, so he'd kept his mouth shut. That had been the only day with some respite. A day was all Taz needed to regain her strength, and it was all business after that.

Groaning, Jaden took a sip of coffee. *Ah, heaven in a mug.*

"You look like you needed that," Atu piped up next to him.

Jaden almost fell off his chair. "Do you always have to sneak up on people?"

Atu grinned. "I wasn't even trying. You were so absorbed I think a herd of elephants could've trampled through here and you wouldn't have noticed. What's on your mind?"

"That I'm glad we're home. It was a tough week."

"Yeah," Atu agreed. "I think Taz was a drill sergeant in another life."

Jaden smiled. "Isn't that the truth! Want some coffee?"

"I'll help myself, thanks." Atu strolled to the counter and picked up the coffee pot. 'Did you already have breakfast?"

"Not yet. I'm getting my caffeine fix before I attempt anything else."

Atu chuckled. "I'll let you wallow in your coffee then."

The two of them sat in companionable silence as they drank. Jaden's thoughts drifted to the map. Why hadn't they deciphered it yet? Time was wasting away, and they were no closer to their next destination. Would Zareh make an appearance to give them some help? Jaden dismissed the idea. Zareh wouldn't intervene without dire need.

Jaden tugged the cube from his pocket and flipped the bars, opening it and removing the disc. It glowed softly, backlit by the sunlight streaming through the kitchen window. Such a small thing, and yet it held the key to saving the world. *Or at least one of the keys.* Jaden sighed as he mindlessly rocked the disc back and forth along the counter between his fingertips.

Atu's morose expression mirrored Jaden's feelings. Sighing again, Jaden took another sip of coffee.

His mother marched into the kitchen, finding both boys staring into space and not saying a word. "You boys look like you didn't have enough sleep."

"I didn't," Jaden admitted, surreptitiously curling the disc into his fingers and hiding it.

"Maybe your body's finally realizing it's on holiday, and now it wants to catch up on all the sleep it lost while you were studying."

Jaden assessed his mother. She knew he'd already had few months to recover, albeit while time in her world had been frozen. Her haggard expression was all the explanation he needed. "You don't look much better yourself."

"I didn't sleep well last night," his mother confessed.

"Can we do anything for you so you can catch a nap?"

"You could do the grocery check and authorize the order," Clara replied hopefully. "The laundry needs to be loaded, and the kitchen needs cleaning."

Jaden laughed. "Alright, you can stop there. You'll come up with a lot more if I give you the chance."

Clara giggled. "Too true. Would you be able to do those for me at least?"

"Sure."

"Thank you. In that case, I'll make you some breakfast before I head back to bed. A few more dishes won't be a problem, will they?"

"Not at all." Jaden grinned. "Especially if it means a cooked breakfast."

"You!" Clara chuckled, swatting him with the dishtowel she was holding.

Laughing, Jaden ducked, throwing his hand up to grab the dishtowel. But he'd forgotten he was holding the disc. It rolled free and skimmed merrily along the countertop until it slowed, curled in a circle, and dropped to a stop right in front of his mother.

Clara's laughter died, and her face drained of color. Slowly, she took the disc off the counter. "Jaden, where did you get this?"

Her reaction was enough for Jaden to know she was familiar with it. And not in a positive way. "You know what it is?"

"I have no idea what it is, but I've seen it before. Where did you get it?"

There was no way around it. If Jaden was going to get answers from her, he had to give her some of his own. "We got it on our last journey."

"Oh, I suppose that makes sense," Clara croaked.

"Mom, where have you seen it before?"

She ignored his question and asked another. "What's it for?"

Jaden glanced at Atu, who nodded his head. "It's the map for the next part of our journey."

His mother collapsed into the chair she had been standing next to.

Suddenly, she looked very old. Alarm bells went off in Jaden's head. "Mom, you're worrying me. What's going on?"

This time she put a finger up in the air, acknowledging she had heard his question but indicating she needed a moment to compose herself. When she spoke, it wasn't to give an answer. "Would you please get me a glass of water?"

Jaden obliged, bringing the filled glass back and putting it into her trembling hands. Then he placed his hands on her shoulders, standing next to her. Tension rippled through her as she tried to order her emotions. After a few moments, she placed a hand over one of his.

Turning, Clara offered Jaden a shaky smile. "Thank you. I think I'll be okay now."

Jaden nodded but said nothing. He wasn't so sure.

Clara gulped down the water. Then she pulled Jaden in front of her so she could see him and Atu at the same time. "Remember the dreams I told you about?"

Jaden's heart sank. Her reactions made perfect sense now. "You saw this disc in your dreams?"

"Only in one of them."

"Not all three?"

"No, just the second one." His mother shuddered. "It was so out of place and in my face. I couldn't ignore that it hadn't been in the first dream, and it was obvious when it wasn't in the last."

Jaden glanced at Atu, noting how quiet his friend was. Atu gave a slight shake of his head, indicating they shouldn't interrupt. Jaden would have to thank him later for giving Clara the space she needed. He returned his attention back to his mother. She sat perfectly still, her hands in front of her clutching the disc.

His mother sucked in a deep breath. "Remember the visions I got of what our future could look like?" Jaden nodded, and she continued. "Well, this time, when I found myself on the street with all the chaos around me, an image of this disc appeared in front of me, like an opaque wall blocking my way, filling the sky from top to bottom."

"No wonder you didn't forget it," Jaden breathed.

"I could hardly ignore it! The disc in my dream had the same coloring, appearing as a thick curtain of mist. There were holes all over the curtain in the same pattern as this disc." She fingered the disc pensively for a moment. "Although there, in the dream, of course, the holes showed black through the white. Here I can see sunlight through the holes. A much brighter perspective."

Jaden squeezed her shoulders. "Yes, light is preferable to darkness."

Her answering smile didn't reach her eyes. Jaden debated whether to ask her more questions or give her a breather. But they needed to figure out where they were going. And she seemed to have regained her composure. "Mom, did anything in that particular dream give you an idea of the time and place you found yourself in?"

Clara frowned. "No, it was just the disc, taking up all the space in front of me. Except for the holes."

"Could you see any details, any little thing through those holes?"

"No, I'm sorry. The holes were pure black. Black like I hope never to see again, but plain black nonetheless. No relief or breaks in the color at all."

Black like a Gaptor's face. I'm more familiar with that black than I'd like to be. Their current situation was almost as dark. They were still no closer to an answer. Jaden slumped onto his chair.

"I take it that wasn't the answer you were looking for?" his mother said.

"We were hoping for something that might give us a time and place for when the map was created."

Clara fingered her cheek thoughtfully. "This might not be relevant." She shook her head. "Only it's so odd, it's probably exactly the sort of information you need."

Atu finally spoke. The hint of hope had him running out of patience. "Yes?"

"Well, the second time I had the dream, the time when this disc appeared, we weren't at home," Clara revealed.

That doesn't make sense. "Correct me if I'm wrong, but don't you have the dreams when you've come into contact with the medallion? Surely you didn't take the medallion with you?"

"That's just it! I didn't take it. We were away on vacation, and there's no way I would've taken the medallion with me, given all your grandmother's hype about not losing it."

"So you didn't touch the medallion that day?"

"No," Clara rushed on. "I did."

"But if—"

"I don't know how it got there, but it was just there. You had scraped your knee, and I was cleaning it in the bathroom of the cottage we had rented, when suddenly there was this green glow on the bathroom counter."

"A green glow?" Jaden choked.

"Yes, like the glow you get from a light stick."

"And then?" Atu asked.

"Naturally, I investigated. It was coming from my toiletry bag, so I pulled things out."

"And you found the medallion," Jaden concluded.

"Yes! If I had known that's what it was, I wouldn't have put my hand in there. But I did. And when I pulled the medallion out, I could hardly believe my eyes. My first thought was that your father had packed it, but when I asked him about it later that evening, he denied it. So I went to fetch the medallion to prove to him that it was there . . ."

"And then you couldn't find it," Jaden finished.

Clara looked put out. "How did you know?"

"Something Zareh told us about the medallions. But I'm still not sure how this helps us with a time and place."

"That evening was the night you had your . . . dream?" Atu ventured.

"It was." Clara nodded.

"Bro, I think we have our time and place then." Atu grinned.

"Oh, I get it!" Clara bounced on her chair. "The time was when we were there, and the place was where we were staying!"

"You said it.!"

"Hmm, I don't know," Jaden murmured. "There's so much that was left to chance. What if my mom hadn't seen the disc? Or she hadn't remembered that it was in the dream? Or . . ."

"Which is exactly why I think it *is* the time and place we're looking for," Atu broke in. "Think about it. Has any of this been clear for any of us to see? At any point in our journey?"

Jaden had to admit it wasn't. The answers were always there, but hidden just beneath the surface, waiting for them to scratch the right piece of dirt away. "I guess not. Since we have nothing to lose, we should go there and see if we can find a solution to our problem."

CHAPTER SEVEN

They had to go back several years and wade through three years of records before Jaden's mother found the right file. Jaden had been nine on that vacation. He let her "ooh" and "aah" over the photo folders for a while before reminding her they needed a name and location. Reluctantly, Clara closed the folders and opened another file with the corresponding receipts. She flicked the information over to both the holoscreen and Jaden's PAL.

Jaden scanned the receipt, then did a double take when he saw the resort's name. *Happy Days Campground and Cabins.* How could a book written so many centuries ago contain the same name? He shook his head. Solving that puzzle was a formula for insanity.

Skimming the rest of the receipt, he found the location: Lake Pleasant. *Yes, it had been.* Although he'd bitten back impatience as his mother flipped through the photos, they reminded him of how much he'd enjoyed that particular vacation. He hoped it still lived up to its name and would provide them with answers. Stepping from the room, he pressed his CC and ordered the call to Kayla.

"Hi," Kayla answered, gracing him with one of her incredible smiles.

"Hello." Jaden grinned. He couldn't help himself.

"What's up?" Kayla asked when Jaden said nothing.

"Oh, right." Jaden remembered he had called to give her information and not stare at her. "We might have a destination."

"Really? Where? And how did you find it?"

"It's a story, but we can fill you in while we travel." Being with her again, all day, every day would be heavenly. Jaden was suddenly aware of Kayla's accusing gaze. "What?"

"In case you hadn't noticed, I'm a girl."

Well, duh. What was she going on about?

Kayla rolled her eyes. "Girls need a little more information when they travel. Like where they're going so they can pack the right clothes?"

Oh. Jaden grinned. "I thought you didn't fuss about things like that. Besides, our smart suits will keep us comfortable, no matter what the temperature."

Kayla's eyes flashed. "You don't think there may be times I'd like to get out of that suit?"

Jaden was tempted to say, *I'd prefer if you stayed in it.* But now was not the time to tease. "We're heading south east, down towards the coast."

"Thanks. I'll be ready in an hour or so. I'd like to take one last shower before we leave."

Jaden grinned. "A fine idea. Atu and I will be there in ninety minutes. That is, unless the gliders pick up on the fact that we need them. Then we'll see you when they collect us."

"Sounds like a plan." Kayla signed off.

Jaden stared at the screen. Just like that, she was gone. It was a rude reminder of how temporary life could be. Wandering back to the family room, he found his mother poring over the photos again. He plopped next to her on the sofa, wanting to take some time and enjoy her company. When Clara reached out her hand and took his, he knew she felt the same way.

"You're leaving soon?" Although Clara tried, she was unable to hide her sadness or apprehension.

"Yes. The sooner we get this done, the sooner we can get back to our everyday lives."

Clara sighed. "I suppose. Is it selfish of me to say that I wish it wasn't you or Kayla or Atu who had to do this?"

Jaden folded her hand into his. "Not at all. It tells me you love me. And that's what makes doing all this worthwhile."

Clara's lip trembled, and a tear slid down her cheek. Jaden pulled her closer, so she was against his side. There was no need for words. He let her cry, holding her and rubbing her arm soothingly.

When the tempest had passed, Clara squeezed his hand before rising. "Enough melancholy. I'll make some sandwiches to get you through at least the first part of your trip."

"Thanks, Mom. That would be fantastic."

Sending him one last watery smile, Clara headed for the kitchen. Jaden watched her leave. How was he going to keep his parents safe? Sure, Pallaton and the Legion would be here to keep watch, like when Jaden, Kayla, and Atu had done their training this past week. But what happened if the Legion was overwhelmed? The last group of Gaptors had been substantial, and Jaden doubted the Usurper had stopped sending them through. How large would the next group be?

How many Gaptors were there on the gliders' world? Jaden would have to ask Han. And could Zareh send more gliders to match the increased number of Gaptors?

But he was getting sidetracked. There had to be a way to find his parents if the unthinkable happened and they were taken. When he first heard about the arcachoa and its ability to send him back in time, Jaden thought he might be able to use it to help him track his parents. But that wasn't possible. The arcachoa would only take him back in time if that specific place had an artifact. And his parents weren't artifacts.

But what if his parents had an artifact with them when they were taken? Surely he could use that? What artifact could he give them? Not the relic stone. They needed that for killing Gaptors. Then he remembered his grandmother's key. It had unlocked the disc from his family's toy chest to give them the first map, so hadn't it served its purpose? But was it an artifact? How had Han—or was it Taz—phrased it? An artifact was an object that was present in both their worlds. Surely the key was an artifact because Zareh had to have crafted it in his world. Then again, Zareh could've had both the key and chest made here.

Jaden's mind went around and around. Then he remembered the strange markings on the key and chest. He raced upstairs and retrieved Awena's book. Plopping onto his bed, he paged through the book, taking his time. On the fifth page, he found them. Faint, but definitely there in the background. The same markings that were on the key and toy chest. The key had to be an artifact.

He tucked the book back in his closet, then rummaged in his backpack until he found the key and strode downstairs.

His mother looked up when he entered the kitchen. "I'm not finished yet —"

"I want you to keep this with you," Jaden interrupted, handing her the key.

Curious, she took it. "A key?"

"Yes. I want to know I can find you."

"How will this help you find us?" Clara examined the key.

"The key's an artifact, something that comes from the gliders' world, but which is here in our world now. It can lead me to you."

"I still don't understand how it works. Does it send out some sort of tracking signal?" Then, perplexed, she changed her line of questioning. "Why would you need to find us? We're not going anywhere, or at least, not that I know of."

Jaden hadn't wanted to explain, but she just wasn't getting it. "In case your dream comes true. In case they come for you and Dad."

"Oh." His mother's reply was weak, understanding crushing the breath from her.

"It's just a precaution," Jaden reassured her. "Maybe the dream is only that, something meant to give us warning, not something that will actually happen."

Clara sighed. "Jaden, if the dream does come true, you know you can't come looking for us. That's why I told you what could happen—so you would know it's a trap."

Struggling to suppress the anger that bubbled up, Jaden managed a measured reply. "And because you told me it's a trap, I'll know to be careful. Mom, I'm not letting him have you or Dad!"

Clara hesitated. "Thank you. I'll keep it with me."

Jaden smiled, relieved. "I know it will probably be a pain to carry around, so maybe you could put it on a necklace? You know, the same way Kayla keeps her medallion with her?"

"Yes, that's an excellent idea. I'll go find one now to put it on, shall I?"

Jaden waved her on her way, noticing the beginnings of a smile quirk up the corners of her lips.

"Alright, I'm going already." Clara hustled out the kitchen.

His burden lifted, Jaden was suddenly starving. He picked up one of the half-made sandwiches on the counter, finished making it, and then took an enormous bite.

"I hope that wasn't one of the sandwiches I was making for your trip."

Jaden gave his mother a sheepish grin. "It was."

She giggled, the musical sound tinkling in the air. Jaden grinned. She was almost back to normal. "How about I make another two sandwiches for those I'm going to eat now and then help you finish the ones you've already started?"

"Deal," Clara approved.

"What are we doing?" Atu asked, joining them.

"Making lunch and some food to take on our journey," Jaden answered.

"We're leaving?"

Jaden grimaced "Sorry, I told Kayla and then meant to tell you, but I got sidetracked. Would you be ready to leave in about thirty minutes?"

"Sure." Atu nodded, grabbing a sandwich.

It was actually forty-five minutes later when Jaden left his room, wearing his smart suit and with his backpack slung over his shoulder.

Would their gliders be waiting on the roof? Stopping outside Atu's room, he asked, "You ready?"

"Yes, good to go." Atu slung his own pack over his shoulder and followed Jaden to the stairs.

When they exited onto the roof, Jaden was astonished to find his father waiting with his mother.

"Your mother called and told me that you were leaving on the next part of your journey," Ty explained. "I wanted to be here to say goodbye."

Jaden pulled his father into a hug. "Thanks, Dad. That means a lot."

His dad held onto him for a while, not letting go. Jaden didn't begrudge him the farewell. For all they knew, this really was a final goodbye, and it couldn't be rushed. When his father released him, Jaden allowed his mother the same rights. Over her shoulder, he saw his dad pull a shocked Atu into a hug. He caught his dad's eye and smiled.

"You boys take care of each other. And Kayla," his dad ordered, his voice gruff.

"We will," Atu promised.

Jaden stepped back from his mother and looked toward the 'pod. They would have to take it after all.

"Dawdlers!" Kayla called.

Jaden whirled. Kayla and the three gliders hovered off to the side. "Nice to know our gliders can still sense when we need them."

"Of course we know," Taz huffed.

Grinning at her indignation, Jaden caught his parents' startled glances in his peripheral vision. "Our gliders are here, along with Kayla." Then, after a moment's thought, he removed his relic stone and handed it to his mother. "Why don't you say hello?"

His mother grinned like she'd just won the lottery. Sliding the ring onto her finger, she began conversing with the gliders. Jaden's father stepped closer, and Clara filled him in on the parts of the conversation he couldn't hear. As he observed, Jaden realized something. Two things, in fact. First, there was a slight time delay between when the gliders arrived and when the time freeze kicked in. Second, perhaps more importantly, while his mom wore the ring, the time freeze didn't affect his father. Did the relic stone nullify the time freeze effect?

His attention returned to his parents, a mixture of joy and grief washing over him. They looked so delighted to be talking with the gliders. Ultimately though, they would have to allow the teens to leave.

As if sensing Jaden's thoughts, Taz cleared her throat. "Lovely as it has been to see and talk to you, we must be getting on."

Clara bit her lip as she removed the ring and returned it to Jaden. "Here you go, love."

Jaden eyed her as he placed the ring back on his own finger. "We're going to be okay."

"Yes, you are," his mother said vehemently. "And so are we."

Jaden quirked an eyebrow, and Clara lifted the necklace that had been hiding under her shirt. Attached to it was the key. Jaden smiled.

Atu glanced at Jaden. "Now?"

Jaden nodded. They had agreed they would wait until they were actually leaving before summoning Pallaton for the second time.

Atu blew on the reed. Then he nodded to Clara and Ty. "See you soon." With that, he leaped toward Aren, and they arced away, making space for Han to drop down for Jaden.

"I love you both. We'll be back before you know it," Jaden said, before making his own leap.

His mother's comment to his father drifted up. "I don't know that I'll ever get used to that."

"Me either," his dad agreed. "I wonder if it will make a difference this time, knowing they're gone."

"It won't. If we wait here a few moments, they'll suddenly reappear like they did last time—even though they were gone for all those months."

Jaden never heard his father's reply because Han lifted beyond hearing at that point. Sighing, Jaden faced forward, hoping his parents wouldn't have to wait long.

CHAPTER EIGHT

Kayla, Jaden, Atu, and their gliders circled the area, waiting for Pallaton and the Legion.

"Healer, you called?"

Kayla relaxed. Pallaton's voice was a welcome sound. Jaden was also more at ease. The lines that constantly creased his brow during their week of training had vanished.

On their third day away, when it was just the two of them huddled close to the fire, she had cornered him about it, and Jaden confessed his fears that his parents—or hers—would still get taken despite Pallaton and the Legion's protection. His concern for her family's welfare had warmed her heart, and she snuggled into his shoulder, snaking her arms around his waist. Savoring the hard lines of his body pressed against hers, she had melted into him when he kissed her and scattered her thoughts. That was the end of the conversation, but the lines had persisted. What had changed between then and now to give him such peace?

Jaden addressed Pallaton. "Thank you for coming. I apologize for calling you back again so soon."

As they talked, Kayla noticed they weren't the only ones exchanging greetings. The legion's chirps and twitters mixed with those of their own gliders. Would what she saw last time the groups met reoccur? On cue, gliders circled closer to Taz, then dropped beneath her. Definitely bowing, or giving her some sort of obeisance. Kayla swiveled on Taz's back and watched the members of the Legion approach Han. They drifted closer, floating next to him and peeling off, but they certainly didn't drop away under him as they did for Taz.

"Taz, are they bowing to you?"

Slight as the movement was, Kayla felt Taz jerk in surprise. "What makes you say that?"

"That's what it looks like. And you didn't answer my question."

Taz tensed under her. "Now is neither the time nor place for that conversation."

"It seems that's the standard reply whenever you don't want to give an answer."

"There's a good reason this time, believe me!" Her terse reply warned Kayla that she was serious. Kayla glanced around, wondering who or what was making Taz skittish. She didn't see anything unusual. Then again, just because Kayla didn't see anything didn't mean there wasn't anything to worry about.

"All right," Kayla conceded, keeping her voice low. "But I expect an answer sooner rather than later."

Taz relaxed under her. Was Taz aware of another danger she hadn't told the voyagers about? Only time would tell. Taz wouldn't divulge something she wasn't ready to share.

As they left, half the Legion detached themselves from Jaden's home and headed towards her own, comforting Kayla. Not having to worry about her parents' safety meant one less thing to distract her. Kayla eased into the rhythm that was flight. A while later, she glanced at Jaden on her right and noticed his grin. "What?"

"Want to race?"

Kayla giggled. "What's the point when we know who's going to win?"

Jaden laughed. "Too scared to try then?"

Kayla lifted her chin at Atu, flying on her left. "What's your take on this?"

Atu shook his head, raising his hands in the air. "I'm not getting involved. You two sort it out. Aren and I are just here to enjoy the scenery."

Kayla looked down. It *was* breathtaking. The air was clear, and she could see for miles. Glittering lakes shimmered with the promise of cool water. Fields dressed in emerald, gold, and rust, waved as they passed. Small clumps of trees in all shapes and sizes invited them to take respite under their shadowed forms. The combined effect was picturesque enough for a postcard. "Maybe I'll side with Atu on this," Kayla told Jaden.

Jaden visibly slumped on Han. "You guys are no fun."

But he was taking in the scenery too. They flew on, enjoying the changing view. Soon, the landscape took on the red hues and barren characteristics of the semi-desert they had crossed over once before, although not in the same place. Kayla could feel Taz's impatience rising. "Hey boys, let's do that race."

As if Taz had been waiting just to hear those words, she put on a burst of speed, and Kayla felt the familiar crawl of her face mask over her skin. The goggles snapped into place, and the aerolator followed as Taz accelerated further. Kayla laughed with sheer delight. This was flying!

Jaden and Han streaked past, and she stopped laughing. "They're not beating us," Kayla told Taz.

Taz chuckled, increasing her speed to match Han's even though she wouldn't be able to maintain it for long.

Reading her mind, Taz murmured, "Set a finish line."

Kayla yelled to Jaden. "The finish is that strip of sand on the horizon." In a quieter voice, she said to Taz, "Close enough?"

Taz only nodded as she pushed her limits. They shot ahead of Jaden and Han.

"Catch them," Kayla heard Jaden yelling to Han.

"I can't," Han bit out. "She's always been faster over shorter distances. And smarter too, it seems, since she set the goalpost within reach."

Jaden's chuckle floated across the distance as he said, "I believe it was Kayla who called the finish line."

"And who do you think told her to do that?" Han growled.

Jaden roared with laughter, and Kayla turned then to see him rub Han along his neck. But Jaden kept his voice low this time, and whatever he said to Han was for them alone.

Looking past them, she was shocked to see Aren and Atu keeping pace. Aren looked like he was out for a Sunday afternoon stroll. "Aren looks too relaxed by far. Is he faster than you?"

"He's chosen not to reveal that," Taz said. "Although why he would hide his abilities is beyond me."

Kayla studied Aren, confirming that he did seem to be taking his time. Or maybe that was just how he looked when he flew. All relaxed. Sighing, she decided she wouldn't know the answer until Aren had a reason to show his true potential.

A second later, Taz shot over the finish line ahead of Han and angled her wings to glide for a while.

"Nice work," Kayla congratulated, massaging the silky ridge of fur along Taz's neck.

Taz purred. "Be careful when you do that, or I might forget to keep us in the air."

Kayla giggled. "You enjoying the massage?"

"What do you think?"

"Yup, silly question. I never say no to a back rub."

The boys caught up and took their places to her left and right as before.

"Nice win." Jaden grinned.

Hmm, that grin is way too smug. He's up to something. "Thanks. Are you going to tell me what's going on in that head of yours?" His stunned expression was priceless. Kayla laughed. "What, do you think I don't know when you've got something up your sleeve?"

Jaden opened his mouth, but no words came out.

"I think it's about time for food," Atu commented, inserting himself into the conversation.

Jaden snatched at the straw. "Definitely."

Kayla chuckled. "Don't think you're getting out of it that easily. We're not landing until you tell me what you were thinking."

This time, Jaden had a ready reply. "Ironically, I was thinking we only lost because we needed some sustenance."

Kayla wasn't sure she believed him. Although she *was* starved. Something about being out in the fresh air and flying with Taz boosted her hunger. "Alright, I'll let that pass. Taz, let's find somewhere where we can have lunch."

In a few minutes they were on the ground and tucking into the sandwiches Mrs. Jameson prepared. Kayla wasn't sure if Mrs. Jameson was simply an excellent cook or if it was because she was so hungry that the food tasted heavenly. When Kayla finished eating, she flopped onto her back. Taz noticed and ordered them back into the air. Kayla groaned. "Isn't there some sort of rule about not flying too soon after you've eaten—you know, like the one about swimming?"

Taz sniffed. "Perhaps you should've eaten less. Han, Aren, and I are leaving. You can either come with us or stay here. If you elect to come, we'll be back for you in five minutes."

Taz leaped into the air. With apologetic shrugs, Han and Aren followed.

Kayla scrambled to put things back into the respective packs. "I can't believe she just did that."

"Well, she did," Jaden said, his hands working just as quickly.

Kayla huffed. "I guess she was tired of arguing. It'll serve her right if one of us barfs while we're up there this afternoon."

They were all still grinning when their gliders picked them up. However, the afternoon passed without any gastronomical eruptions. If they'd had to do any rolls or routines, Kayla's grim wish might've come true. In truth, the afternoon was so dull she might've even fallen asleep if the terrain under them hadn't begun changing again as they set a more easterly path.

Washed-out reds and dreary grays transformed into more vibrant colors as trees and grassy hills filled the canvas beneath them once more. Kayla revived and began enjoying the day again. It wasn't long after that when she noticed Jaden squirming. "What's up?"

"I'm not sure."

Kayla watched as he turned this way and then that, looking down at the ground and then off to the side. He kept twisting on Han's back, as though trying to pinpoint something. "Jaden?"

He ignored her, still turning on Han's back. Suddenly, he said, "We need to land. Over there!"

The gliders eyed him suspiciously.

"Why?" Taz demanded.

"I don't know. I just have this feeling that's where we're supposed to be. Please!"

Kayla recognized Jaden's agitation for what it was. "One of those 'feeling' feelings?"

Grimly, he nodded.

Kayla was instantly alert. "Taz, I think—"

"We should do as he says," Taz finished. Kayla's eyes widened in surprise. "Yes, this isn't the first time he's had those when we've been around."

Kayla smiled. *No, it isn't.*

Taking their cue from Taz, Han and Aren tilted their wings, chasing after Taz as she aimed for a sizable wooded area. "Be on your guard," Taz commanded.

Cautiously, they circled the area Jaden specified. After two complete circuits without Gaptors rising to attack them, Taz determined they would need to land to get a grip on things.

"But I don't like it," Taz stated. "It smells like a trap. Once we're on the ground, it'll be more difficult to fight enemies lurking there."

"If there are any Gaptors down there, they would be at the greater disadvantage," Jaden pointed out.

"True," Taz allowed. "That doesn't mean we should be any less vigilant. Jaden, can you point out a more precise area we should be focused on?"

Jaden indicated a spot near the western edge. "There."

"Alright, this is what we'll do," Taz said.

Kayla listened as Taz outlined her plan, impressed. Taz hadn't had long to come up with that. When had her glider become such an excellent strategist? Then again, Taz had been the one with a plethora of exceptional ideas when they were caught in the desert with all those newly arrived Gaptors.

The plan agreed upon, Taz circled one last time before ducking toward the tree line. Kayla's arm abruptly itched in earnest. *Not now!* Much as she wanted to scratch, she needed freedom of movement to disembark at Taz's stipulated time. Her arm only itched all the more, so much that she nearly missed her drop point. Taz had to hiss to remind her to jump.

Narrowly missing a raised tree root, Kayla landed hard. Dropping into a roll soothed her screaming knees and ankles. She didn't stop until she came up near a tree trunk. Then she scuttled behind it, settling into a crouch and surveying the area. Her hand went to her birthmark, and she scratched at last, fighting the urge to close her eyes in relief.

Listening to the muffled thuds as Jaden and Atu landed, Kayla kept her eyes peeled for any sign of danger. The black depths of the trees held no movement. Kayla relaxed as she felt Jaden creep up behind her and put a hand on her arm. His touch was exactly what she needed.

"You okay?" Jaden asked. "You had a pretty rough landing."

Kayla smiled at him over her shoulder. "Yup, I was a little distracted."

"By this?" Jaden asked, gently touching her arm where she was still scratching.

Snatching her hand away from the offending spot, Kayla nodded irritably. "Yes."

"You still owe me an explanation."

Kayla sighed inwardly. Sometimes, she wished Jaden wasn't so attuned to her and her needs. Telling him about the birthmark would only make him worry more. But not answering his question would make him more adamant. "I do, but later. We have more pressing issues to deal with." Turning, she peered into the darkness. "I can't see a thing. Are you sure this is the right place?"

Jaden shuddered. "Yeah, it's the right place."

Without a word, the three of them drew their DDs. The brilliant slivers of light that extended when they released the safety catches seemed unnaturally bright in the shadows.

"Please, there's no need for those." The voice emanated from the murky area directly in front of them. "I promise, I'm not here to harm you. In fact, I think you're looking for me. I'm coming out. Please, don't use those weapons."

CHAPTER NINE

A lean girl of middling height stepped from behind a tree, hands raised in surrender. Kayla couldn't help but notice her enviable locks of lustrous, dark brown hair. The stranger moved with the grace of a gazelle—and was about as quiet too. *Someone who's accustomed to moving in these woods.* Slowly, as though the stranger didn't want to scare them into doing something they would regret, the girl approached until she stood only a few feet away.

"My name's Iriyessa, but you can call me Iri," she offered.

"What makes you think we were looking for you?" Jaden challenged, not giving his name.

"Because I have one of those too." Iri nodded toward Kayla's medallion, dangling on its chain on the outside of her smart suit. "And because I can see things other people can't, like those giant bats that brought you here."

The tumblers fell into place. "You're a seeker?" Kayla asked.

"If that's what you're called, then yes, I suppose I am."

Atu held out his hand. "May we see your medallion, please?"

Iri nodded, then cautiously lowered one hand, indicating via a tiny wrist motion that she wanted to remove something from inside her outer shirt. After receiving approval from Jaden, she continued the measured movement to extract her medallion.

Where had she hidden it? While the girl's unbuttoned outer shirt had about as many pockets as her cargo pants, the shirt under it had no hiding spaces at all. In fact, it hugged the girl's figure like a second skin, showing off her toned body to perfection. She must have hidden it in her bra. Kayla slid her gaze toward Jaden and smiled when she caught him staring. At that moment, Jaden turned his eyes toward Kayla. He shrugged and grinned sheepishly. *Well, if a girl's going to hide things there, she should expect people to look*, Kayla thought wryly.

Atu, on the other hand, seemed quite unaffected. Taking a bold step towards the girl, he inspected her medallion. "Yeah, it's real. I'll let Taz and the others know we're not in any danger."

Kayla nodded. "Thanks. We wouldn't want to get the sharp side of her tongue again."

Atu pulled a face, showing how disagreeable the idea was, before disappearing into the trees.

Iri watched him leave, her curiosity plain. Then she used her raised hands to point at their DDs. "Will you put those things away now?"

"Oh, sorry." Kayla flipped the safety so that the sizzling blade retreated and stretched out a hand. "I'm Kayla."

Iri shook her hand and smiled. "It's really nice to meet you."

Kayla's gaze sharpened. Something in the girl's tone made her wonder how long it had been since Iri had spent time with anyone. "Do you have any friends skulking about?"

The girl shook her head. The movement sent a wavy strand over her face, which she tucked behind her ear. "No, it's just me."

"You're out here in the middle of nowhere—on your own?" Jaden blurted.

Kayla noticed the girl's immediate withdrawal. "Jaden," Kayla gave him a meaningful glare, "don't be rude." She turned to Iri. "Ignore him. Sometimes he speaks before he thinks."

Jaden shrugged. "I'm sorry. I didn't mean to offend you. In case you hadn't gathered, I'm Jaden."

Iri gave a tentative smile as she shook his offered hand. "How did you find me?"

Jaden scratched his head. "It's difficult to explain. Let's go with I had a feeling we had to be here."

When Iri nodded like Jaden's explanation was the most natural thing in the world, Kayla's suspicions were heightened. How was it that this solitary girl had no qualms about them meeting her the way they had? In fact, the more Kayla studied her, the more perplexed she became. The girl was nervous around people. But she had a confidence that was contradictory. Atu's return only added to Kayla's confusion. As soon as he arrived, Atu wandered over to Iri to introduce himself, but she took a quick step away, lifting a hand to her nose.

"I'm sorry, but would you mind putting that pricklepine root in this bag?" She handed Atu a thick, plastic bag with an airtight seal.

Atu's face went from suspicious to crestfallen to bewildered in as many heartbeats. "Sure," Atu mumbled, taking the bag and reaching into his pouch. When Iri took another step backward, he mimicked her action as he pulled something green from the pouch and sealed it in the bag.

As soon as the seal closed, the girl removed her hand from her nose. Approaching him, she extended her hand. "Sorry about that. My nose is sensitive to some things. I'm Iri."

"Atu." He shook her hand, his incredulity evident. "I've never met anyone who could smell that well."

Iri smiled. "Like I said, a sensitive nose."

Kayla couldn't shake the feeling that there was more to that statement. However, she couldn't consider it further because she heard Taz calling. "Are we ever going to meet this new voyager?"

The imperious, demanding tone was so like Taz that Kayla giggled. At Iri's raised eyebrow, Kayla said, "That's my glider, Taz."

"That's what those giant bats are called? Gliders?"

Kayla nodded. "Want to meet them?"

"Do you even have to ask?" Iri grinned.

Kayla masked her surprise as she turned to leave. She had half expected Iri wouldn't want to go near the gliders, given her skittish-ness around people. Yet again, though, Iri reacted in contrary fashion. She certainly wasn't predictable. When they stepped from the cover of the trees, they found Taz, Han, and Aren hopping around anxiously.

"You took your time," Taz commented, shooting Kayla an acerbic look.

Kayla had to stop herself from rolling her eyes. Taz was only worried about her, which made Kayla feel cared for. Smiling a little at the thought of what Taz would say if Kayla brought that up, Kayla made the introductions.

Iri almost ran to meet the gliders. "You're so big!"

Han's rumbling chuckle washed over the group. "And you're so small."

That had them all laughing.

Kayla watched, astounded, as Iri touched each glider in turn, emit-ting excited squeaks. She showed no hint of fear, nor was there any of the reverence Atu and Sven displayed when first meeting the gliders. Iri behaved as though being confronted by these majestic creatures was an everyday occurrence. When Iri faced them again, a clear ques-tion burning in her eyes, Kayla was beyond being surprised.

"Yes, you can fly with them. You might want to ask them first, though," Kayla suggested.

Iri didn't hesitate. "May I please fly with one of you?"

Shockingly, Aren dipped his head in assent. Kayla had expected Taz to take the lead, control freak that she was. Kayla watched, flab-bergasted, as Aren knelt to let the excited girl claw her way onto his back. Iri didn't need to be told to get up to Aren's neck or to hang onto the thick ridge of fur there—or to use her legs to grip the bat. It seemed to come naturally.

Iri grinned down at Kayla. "Don't look so surprised. This isn't all that different to riding a horse."

Kayla clamped her mouth shut. Had her skepticism been that obvi-ous? "Oh well, good for you that you've ridden horses," she mumbled. How would Taz react to being compared to a horse? But she didn't seem to mind.

Iri didn't hear Kayla's reply as she urged Aren to fly. Aren obliged, and Iri let out a wild, joyful shriek. The shrieks continued as Aren soared higher.

"I hope Aren's ears survive," Atu said, watching his glider curve away from them.

Jaden smiled, placing a hand on Atu's shoulder. "I'm sure he'll be fine."

"He'd better be," Atu muttered.

"Aren will tell her to tone it down if she gets out of hand," Taz assured him. "She seems . . . interesting."

Kayla's attention was seized for the third (or was it the fourth?) time that day. Taz's tone held undercurrents of uncertainty. "What do you mean?"

"There's something about her—something I just can't put a name to, but it's there. Like a memory you can't quite put a claw on."

Thoughtfully, Kayla nodded. "You picked up on that too then." Kayla turned to Jaden. "Your spidey-sense tingling?"

Jaden laughed. "No, but it doesn't work that way."

Kayla tried not to be distracted by his disarming smile. "How *does* it work, then? You sensed that she was down here, but you're not sensing something off with her?"

"That's about the gist of it."

"But these feelings of yours, they act like warnings, don't they?"

"Yes, but—"

Kayla kept talking. "Why then would they warn you about the presence of another seeker? Surely she's the other one Zareh told us to find? Which means she shouldn't be a danger to us, right?" Jaden said nothing, and Kayla forged ahead. "But if you had that feeling about her presence, doesn't it follow that she must be a danger?"

When Jaden still didn't answer, Kayla looked at him and noticed his mild irritation. "Are you going to let me speak now?"

Kayla half-smiled and took his hand, capturing it between both of hers. "Sorry, I just don't understand."

Jaden nodded, accepting her apology. Kayla saw him look down at their clasped hands and then back at her. His eyes were so blue, his face so earnest, Kayla couldn't stop herself from reaching out a hand and placing it on Jaden's cheek. He leaned into her touch, then raised his eyebrows questioningly. "I truly am sorry for cutting you off. I really do want to understand."

"That's okay. It's difficult for me too. These feelings I get—most of the time, they warn me about danger. Occasionally though, they are simply warnings that I need to be aware of something. So whether for danger or an alert, there's no way to tell."

"Well, that's frustrating," Kayla grumbled.

"You have no idea. The worst part is that I only really get to find out which of the two it was when the danger confronts me directly. And then it's usually too late to stop whatever it is from happening."

Kayla made up her mind. "In that case, we'll just have to be sure to keep tabs on Iri. We wouldn't want her betraying us unexpectedly."

"I don't think that's likely." Atu's entry back into the conversation was understated as usual, but the certainty in his voice made Kayla frown.

"And why is that?"

Atu tilted his head sideways as he considered. "Whatever's going on with her, I don't think it's that she's a traitor."

"Well, I'm glad you're so sure, but at least allow me my suspicions."

Atu nodded but said nothing more on the subject. Instead, he looked up at the sky. "They've been gone a while."

Kayla giggled. "I'm sure she'll bring Aren back in one piece."

Atu gave her a baleful stare. "It's not your glider she's taken."

"True. Shall we go find them?"

Atu brightened. "Yes, let's."

In seconds, they were in the air, Atu and Jaden on Han while Kayla flew solo with Taz.

"How will we find them?" Kayla asked when they had gained some altitude.

"We'll use our link," Taz replied.

"Wait, it works with Iri already?" Kayla felt unreasonably jealous. How could Taz already link with her?

Taz sent her an affectionate smile, as if pleased Kayla didn't want to share her. "No, but we share a link with Aren."

"Oh. Let's get there then."

Taz increased her speed, and a thought struck Kayla. While she had felt sympathy for Atu, it hadn't been empathy until now. She would have to apologize for teasing him.

Finding Iri and Aren didn't take long. Atu sighed in relief when he found Iri was no longer shrieking, which made Kayla smile. Would Atu insist Iri ride with Kayla and Taz so that he could have Aren all to himself again?

As it turned out, Atu had a more generous spirit. After confirming that Aren was coping, he seemed content to let Iri maintain her solo position. But another issue soon presented itself.

"We're too slow for a fight," Taz confided to Kayla.

"I was wondering about that. Iri needs a suit and an aerolator, doesn't she?"

"She does. And she needs her own glider too."

"We should've thought about the suit when we left Sven's. We knew we had to find another seeker."

"While it's regrettable that we didn't think of that at the time, there's nothing we can do about it now. We will simply have to make a plan to get her a suit as soon as possible."

"Should Atu summon Pallaton?"

Taz paused. "I'm not sure that's the best idea. Pallaton may think we're in trouble and bring the whole Legion. Then who would be left to protect your parents?"

Fondly, Kayla rubbed Taz's neck. "Thank you," she whispered.

"You're welcome," Taz purred. "But we will need to solve these issues. The sooner we do, the sooner we can begin training her."

Kayla laughed. With Taz, it was all business. Well, most of it was. "Yes, ma'am."

Taz ignored her and sent them into a roll. "Speaking of which, it's about time for some practice."

The afternoon sped by. Iri was a quick study and learned the routines annoyingly fast. Kayla found herself questioning Iri again, but she shook her head. If she distrusted Iri, she would only cause division. She had to give Iri a chance to prove herself and only change her mind if Iri gave Kayla a reason to doubt her. Besides, if Iri had been living on her own for so long, she must've learned some skills. The routines were no doubt just an extension of that. Kayla relaxed, relieved to have temporarily resolved her misgivings where Iri was concerned.

The sun was slipping down to the horizon and its associated dangers when they touched down for the night in a clearing that bordered a stream. Kayla was grateful that Taz opted to comply with her request to find a spot where they could at least clean up. As she leaped off Taz, Kayla dreamed of showering. She moved aside so Han could drop the boys, then the three of them watched as Aren dipped and landed. Kayla smiled as Iri half-fell, half-stumbled off Aren.

"Here, let me help." Kayla moved forward and grabbed Iri's arm as she helped her to her feet.

"Whew, that was exhausting," Iri admitted. "I like to think I'm in pretty good shape, but I didn't think it would be that tiring. You all make it look so easy!"

Kayla grinned. "Believe me, we felt the same way after our first day of flying. You'll adjust—and quickly if Taz has anything to do with it," she whispered conspiratorially.

Iri laughed. "I'll bet." Then she placed a hand on Kayla's arm. "Thank you."

"For what?' Kayla asked, surprised.

"For making me feel at home and part of this group."

"Sure," Kayla stammered, feeling guilty.

Iri studied her. "You know, for a while there back in the woods, I didn't think you were going to let me in."

Kayla struggled to hide her shock. How did Iri know? Kayla had spent her entire life hiding her feelings from others—and all the moving they had done over the years had only allowed her to perfect that art. Was this girl just that good at reading people? If so, she was a lot better than Kayla. And Kayla would have to be on her guard if she didn't want Iri guessing anything Kayla didn't want her to know.

CHAPTER TEN

Instead of the day or two it would've taken with a smart suit and aerolator for Iri, it took a week to reach Lake Pleasant. For the first two days, Jaden chomped at the bit, trying to get the gliders to squeeze more distance into each day. By the third day, he'd accepted they weren't going to get there any sooner, so he chose to enjoy each day for what it was: time to spend with his friends. More specifically, Kayla. Having her near him every moment of every day was beyond wonderful. Unfortunately, they had no opportunities to spend time alone. Nonetheless, Jaden didn't complain. Being near Kayla was better than not having her close at all.

Nearing the lake, Jaden realized the scenery looked way too familiar. Then the reason hit him. They weren't just getting to the lake today. They were getting to the lake at almost exactly the same time of year he and his parents had visited all those years ago. He punched commands into his PAL to verify the date of their last stay. Almost to the day. There was no such thing as coincidence anymore, only design. Jaden shivered. *But whose?*

"Where would you like us to land?" Han's question garnered his attention.

"My mom said we were on the eastern side of the lake, in one of the cabins along the shore."

"Anywhere along the eastern shore then?"

"Yes, as long as it's near the cabins."

As Han took the lead, Jaden overheard Kayla questioning Taz. "Will you leave once you've dropped us off?"

Taz shook her head. "No. This area is probably on the Usurper's radar, which means the likelihood of Gaptors is high. Besides, if we stay, you'll have the liberty of exploring free of the people vacationing here now."

"Ah, yes, the time freeze. That will certainly work to our advantage."

"I'm glad you approve."

Jaden wasn't the only only who detected the disappointment in Taz's tone.

Ruffling the fur along Taz's neck, Kayla said, "And knowing you're near will reassure me."

Taz's teeth gleamed as she smiled. Yes, Taz wanted to know she was as important to Kayla as Kayla was to her. Jaden took consolation in knowing Taz wasn't going to let anything happen to Kayla any more than he would. Or, at least, Taz would help Jaden keep Kayla as safe as they could in the circumstances they found themselves in. So much was beyond their control. Jaden sighed, accepting he couldn't change it.

Their gliders dipped low, discharging their voyagers before looping back to land next to them. The group surveyed their surroundings.

"I doubt any Gaptors are hiding in those narrow spaces between the buildings and trees," Kayla remarked.

"And we can't go there either," Taz lamented. "Han, Aren and I will get back in the air. Up there, it'll be easier to see danger coming and keep an eye on you as you traverse those narrow trails between cabins."

Kayla nodded. "Be safe."

"You too. We'll be close." With that, the three gliders took to the skies once more.

"Shall we?" Jaden asked.

"Yes, let's," Kayla agreed. "What cabin number are we looking for?"

Jaden pulled up the receipt on his PAL. "232."

The four teens crossed the field to the playground and set off along the main path to the cabins. Smaller trails branched off at regular intervals, some leading to cabins and others going deeper into the forest. The first cabin closest to the path was on their right, numbered 205. The next one on their left was 275. A little further along, an offshoot of a side trail led to another cabin on the left, 268.

"This numbering is all messed up," Jaden muttered. "Shouldn't these things be sequential?"

"I think I know how they did it," Kayla offered. "Let's see what this next one on the right is."

"206," Atu announced.

"I think I understand," Kayla said. "They numbered all the cabins on our right first. Somewhere up ahead, these cabins come to an end, and then the numbering picks up at the cabins on the left. I think the missing numbers indicate that there are cabins deeper in the woods off these side trails."

"We'll keep going straight then," Jaden declared. "The cabin should be on our right since those are the ones next to the water."

In fact, cabin 232 was the very last cabin in the row before the numbering flipped to the cabins on the left. "I should've guessed my folks would've picked a cabin where we didn't have neighbors on one side!"

They entered the cabin cautiously. Even though they had spent months with their gliders, this was the first time they were actually entering a place where strangers existed with the time freeze in effect. Would the people still be there, but just frozen in place?

To their relief, they found the cabin empty, although there were signs of habitation: discarded garments on the floor in the bedroom, toiletries in the bathroom, and dishes in the sink.

"Eerie, isn't it?' Kayla murmured. "To know that someone's here but not actually see them."

"Totally creepy." Iri shivered.

"Not really," Jaden said. "It's just like walking into someone's house when they're not there."

"Yeah, but usually you only do that when you know the people," Atu countered. "Here, I feel like an intruder. And I'm left wondering when the homeowners will appear to defend their property."

Jaden remembered something Han had told him. "The homeowners aren't going to appear. Han said the time freeze creates a bubble around us. When the gliders are near, we're safe inside that bubble. Everything outside freezes."

"Okay, stop, you're making it worse," Iri complained.

"How?" Jaden looked incredulous.

"The way you described that makes me feel like a goldfish in a bowl. Like the world out there is gawking at me and I'm oblivious."

Kayla grimaced. "Okay, that does sound unappealing."

"No one's outside the bubble looking in on us. They can't see us any more than we can see them," Jaden argued.

Atu chimed in. "Maybe try thinking of it like a parallel universe. We're in the same place as everyone else, just in a different universe— one that parallels this world in every way, except we're the only people in it."

Iri raised a hand. "Enough! Can we stop talking about being trapped?"

"Anyone ready for food?" Kayla asked.

The abrupt change in subject made Jaden wonder what Kayla was up to. Then he noticed Iri's face. She was totally frazzled. "Always. Let's use the picnic table outside. The gliders will be happier if they can see we're okay." *And Iri won't feel like she's trapped.*

Kayla took his hand as they headed outdoors. Jaden smiled, understanding she was grateful he'd picked up on her goal. He squeezed her hand, and that lovely smile appeared. How he adored making her smile!

Delving around in their packs, they removed the last of their food.

They would stock up at the lake's store before they left. Jaden smiled when he caught sight of Han leading the others. He waved, and Han dipped his wings in acknowledgement. Then the gliders turned and cruised toward the other side of the lake.

"I wonder where they're going," Iri said.

"Probably to get their own meal," Jaden replied. "There are plenty of berry bushes along that side of the shore."

"You remember that?" Kayla blinked in surprise.

"Without looking at the photos of this vacation with my mom before we left, I wouldn't have. But they helped me remember plenty."

Kayla's answering smile made Jaden wonder what she was thinking. He quirked an eyebrow at her, but she only shook her head. She wasn't willing to share in a group setting. Nodding acceptance, he continued watching her, hoping for some clue. A smile still played around the corners of her mouth. It was fascinating. Her whole face had softened, her green eyes going dreamy and faraway. He ached to be close to her. He had to find a way to carve out some alone time for them—he needed to hold her, feel her next to him, and oh yes, he wanted to kiss her again. Desperately.

Kayla glanced his way, her eyes catching his and sticking. As he stared into those soft green pools, an electric current rippled through him. It had been far too long since they were alone.

Jaden dropped his gaze, breaking the spell just in time to catch Atu's question. "What are our plans now?"

Jaden sighed. *Why do they all look to me for guidance? We're all in this together, aren't we?* Then he scrubbed a hand over his face. They were only asking him because he'd been here before, and the map was somehow linked to this place. "Atu, you know more about star maps than I do, but I'd guess we have to compare the disc to the stars here to make sure we're in the right place?"

"You'd guess right. We might just have to wait all night because the stars move across the sky, so the pattern may only be fully revealed later rather than earlier."

"We have to stay up all night?" Kayla groaned.

"Not necessarily." Atu chuckled. "I did say 'might' in that last sentence. For all I know, they could appear as soon as it gets dark."

"In that case," Jaden said, "I suggest we get some sleep this afternoon. It could be a long night, even if the pattern appears right away."

Sated by their meal, the idea was appealing enough that no one complained.

"Where are we going to sleep?" Iri asked, looking worried.

"In the cabin," Jaden answered without thinking. "There are plenty of beds there."

Kayla was watching Iri. "I don't think she wants to sleep where people might suddenly appear."

"Oh, that again." Jaden waved dismissively. "The gliders said they would stick around, and they aren't ones to change their minds."

"Not without good reason," Kayla murmured so that only Jaden heard.

Jaden had to give her that. "Alright, we can take shifts keeping watch if you want. I think it's a waste of time, but if it helps Iri sleep, we'll do that."

Iri nodded vigorously. "Thanks, that would help tremendously."

Jaden set up the shifts, and Iri offered to go first. "I won't complain." Jaden grinned. "A sleep right now sounds perfect."

"Baby," Kayla teased.

Jaden laughed. He and Kayla were covering the last two shifts, so they would have a nice long stretch of sleep before they had to wake up. "Call me what you want, I don't care. I'm grateful for the sleep. See you all later."

* * *

The boys disappeared inside the cabin. Kayla lingered with Iri to make sure she would be okay.

"I'd rather be awake than sleeping," Iri admitted. "In fact, I don't know that I'll even be able to sleep once my shift's over."

"The thought of people suddenly appearing here is that unsettling?"

"Yes."

Kayla waited to see if she would share more, but Iri remained silent. After a while, Kayla said her farewells and made for the cabin. Without a doubt, Iri was hiding something. But Kayla would have to wait until she was ready to spill. Whatever it was, it didn't seem to be something that would undermine the trust Kayla had in her, and that was reassuring.

Kayla smiled when she noticed that Jaden and Atu had left the main room for her. She snuggled under the covers, only then getting an inkling of what Iri had been referring to. There were other people actually living here, even if they weren't here at this exact moment. But they were going to sleep in this bed again as soon as the voyagers and their gliders were gone. Sniffing her clothes, she smelled the smoke from their fire of the previous evening.

Crawling from the bed, Kayla yanked her sleeping shell from her pack and dumped it over the sheets. At least it would provide some barrier to the smell. With that thought, she crashed.

She awoke to Jaden's soft touch what seemed like only moments later. Groggily, she looked at him. "What's up?"

"Time for your shift." A smile creased his handsome face. "Or what's left of it."

Kayla squinted at her PAL. "Jaden, you should've woken me earlier. You let me sleep though almost half my shift."

"It's alright. I got in a decent sleep before my shift started, enough that I didn't feel like going back to sleep when my shift ended. I thought I'd let you sleep a little longer. But maybe I should've left you sleeping."

Kayla smiled. "No, I'm glad you woke me. That is, if you aren't going back to sleep?"

"I'm not. Why?"

"Because," Kayla said, extricating herself from her sleeping shell and sliding toward him, "it means we can finally have some time together."

Jaden grinned. "To be totally honest, that was part of the reason I didn't let you sleep your whole shift."

Kayla giggled and threw a pillow at him. "You crafty weasel!"

"Weasel! Couldn't you have thought of a better adjective?"

Kayla laughed. "What would you prefer for me to have said?"

Jaden shook his head. "That's not for me to decide. You come up with something, then let me know."

"Alright." Kayla eyed him. Then she rose onto her knees on the edge of the bed next to where he was standing. Stretching her arms, she could only just reach around his neck. He was so tall! But she didn't let that stop her. Gently, she tugged on his neck, pleased when he bent his face closer to hers. She smiled and gave him a soft kiss, then pulled her mouth away to gaze into his eyes.

Without a word, he reached down and lifted her into his arms. Kayla squeaked in surprise.

"Shh, you'll wake the others," Jaden warned.

She giggled, then turned her head into his shoulder to muffle the sound. She felt like a naughty schoolgirl, sneaking away to get up to mischief.

Jaden grinned and carried her outside to a secluded spot behind some trees that sheltered the patio. It was invisible to those who might look out of the cabin's windows, but any threat to the cabin could be seen from here. She surveyed the sky as Jaden set her down. "Wow, look at that sunset."

"What's in front of me is far more beautiful."

Turning from the golden sky, Kayla gazed into Jaden's eyes. What she saw there made her heart skip. Then he tilted his head and kissed her.

Not nearly enough time alone together, Kayla thought, as she heard Atu and Iri emerging from the cabin some time later. She and Jaden had moved to a couch on the patio, and Kayla was leaning back against Jaden's chest, his arms around her. Kayla grinned when Iri's steps faltered as she spied them. Iri glanced back at Atu, but he continued forward, unafraid to interrupt. Taking her cue from Atu, Iri resumed walking.

"Pleasant sleep?" Jaden asked.

"Not really," Atu answered, still cheerful somehow.

Iri still eyed them warily. "Surprisingly, I did sleep, and for the whole time."

Kayla was suddenly uncomfortable. When Jaden tensed behind her, she looked up, expecting danger. Finding the sky empty, she turned her head and raised an eyebrow at Jaden.

"I'm getting that feeling again," Jaden muttered.

Kayla inhaled sharply. "About Iri?"

Jaden nodded. "It's time we figured out what's going on."

CHAPTER ELEVEN

Iri remained where she was, a few feet away from Jaden and Kayla, studying them. When she first met them, the bright blues swirling around them told her of the bond they shared. The depth of the colors showed the true extent of their feelings for one another. Right now, faded oranges swirled like mists overlaying the blues. What were they anxious about? When Jaden subtly shifted Kayla so that she was somehow behind him, Iri recognized the action—an attempt to keep Kayla out of harm's way.

Fearless, Iri looked up. She was curious to see these Gaptors the others had told her so much about. But the sky was clear. Confused, she glanced at Jaden again. He had moved to stand in front of Kayla, and Atu had crossed to stand next to Jaden. The two of them presented a wall in front of Kayla. Then she understood. "You think *I'm* the danger?"

"Why is it," Jaden said, "that I keep getting this feeling about you? What is it that you aren't telling us?"

Iri froze. He couldn't know. Could he? Her face flushed as fear gripped her. How did he know? Her muscles tensed as she prepared to flee.

"Tell them," a quiet voice behind her said.

Iri whirled, ready to fight. Taz perched on the roof of the cabin, gazing down at her. Taz knew? She was trapped. Sweat ran down Iri's back. She had to get away. They would be just like all the others.

"Tell us what?" Kayla stepped out from behind Jaden and Atu.

Taz rolled her massive shoulders. "It's not my secret to tell."

Iri stared at the three people facing her. She couldn't tell them. Not them. They had been so accepting. Well, Kayla had shown some reservations, but she got past those.

Kayla glanced from her glider to Iri, then back at her glider. "Taz, this thing Iri has to tell us, is it something that will put us in danger?"

"Do you think I would've allowed her to travel this far with us if I thought she would harm you?"

Tense, Iri watched Kayla. The orange mists melted to a golden yellow. Iri released the breath she had been holding, but she still backed up when Kayla took a step toward her.

Kayla raised her hand in a pacifying gesture. "Iri, it's alright. You can tell us. Whatever it is, we won't judge you."

Iri didn't dare believe Kayla. Others had told her that, and they hadn't been true to their word. Iri couldn't face this group's fear or ridicule or unbelief or any of the dozen other negative responses she had received when she had lowered her defenses and shared her secret.

Kayla took another cautious step toward her. "Iri?"

"How do I know you won't act like all the others?" Iri blurted.

Jaden's cautioning hand went to Kayla's shoulder as Kayla made to take another step forward, but Kayla glanced back at Jaden and gave him a soothing smile. "I've got this."

What does that mean? Iri wondered. *That Kayla will make me leave if I don't tell them?*

Jaden let his hand drop, and Kayla shuffled closer, stopping when Iri made to bolt. "I can't promise we won't act like the others you mentioned. All I can say is that we *will* try and understand."

Motionless, Iri analyzed the colors surrounding Kayla. The yellows were now interlaced with white. Kayla was at peace. Iri sucked in a deep breath. *Yes, I can smell it now, the pure, sweet scent of truth.* But a tiny piece inside her was still set on self-preservation. "How are you at believing things that seem impossible?"

Kayla smiled. "That's an easy question. How do you think we've made it this far?" Iri nodded, and Kayla continued. "You haven't had a chance to see this for yourself yet, but Atu can do some pretty unbelievable things when it comes to healing. And Jaden gets these 'feelings' that he can't explain, but they're early warnings that he needs to pay attention."

Iri understood now. "That's how he knew I was hiding something?"

"Yes. Whatever it is that you're afraid to tell us, it can't be more unbelievable."

Iri shrugged. "I guess." She would have to tell them eventually—and it'd be better to tell them sooner so the rejection could happen before she made any deep, lasting connections. In a rush, she confessed, "I can see and smell people's emotions. Other things too sometimes, but mostly to do with people."

Iri wasn't sure what she expected them to do. Run for the hills. Laugh. Stare at her like she was a mental case. But they did none of those things. In fact, they waited quietly, expecting her to say more. "That's it!" She threw her hands up. "There isn't anything else. Say something!"

Atu was the first to speak. "That's quite a talent."

The quiet acceptance in his voice brought unexpected tears to Iri's eyes. Never, never, had she ever had anyone say that to her.

"Wow—that's quite something!" Jaden whistled. Iri could smell a hint of envy coming from him.

"So that's how you could read me so easily." Kayla chuckled. "I thought I was losing my touch."

That did it. Iri began sobbing. When Kayla's arms closed around her, it didn't help, just turned the faucet all the way open. Iri had spent so many long, lonely, painful years on her own, rejected time and time again. And here, out of the blue, were three people who accepted her as she was. It was too much.

It was a long time before she stopped crying. When she did, Iri looked up, expecting pitying eyes. But Jaden and Atu were tending the fire in the pit next to the patio. Their white halos indicated their peace. Judging by the mouthwatering aroma, dinner would soon be ready. When Jaden and Atu noticed she had lifted her head, neither stared nor avoided her gaze. They simply nodded and carried on with their business.

Iri sucked in a wobbly breath. She couldn't remember anyone ever doing that, just letting her be, without pressure to conform. Iri snuck a peek at Kayla.

Kayla smiled. "Feeling better?"

"Yes, thanks." Iri drew back from Kayla with a watery smile. "Thanks for not . . ." She floundered. "Well, you know." Iri waved her arm in the air in a helpless gesture.

Kayla nodded. "Sure. I understand how much that means more than you realize." When Iri gave her a quizzical glance, Kayla explained that she had had to deal with countless rejections because of all their moves.

"Oh, Kayla, I'm sorry." Iri put her hand on Kayla's arm. She read the hurt Kayla still felt, though Kayla had buried it deep.

"I didn't tell you so that you would feel sorry for me. I just wanted you to know I understood."

Iri smiled. "Thanks for sharing that with me. It means a lot."

"Shall we join the boys? That dinner smells wonderful."

Iri laughed. "And I thought the boys were the ones always thinking about food."

Kayla giggled. "Well, I at least have the excuse that it is dinner time —those boys will eat any time you let them."

Atu and Jaden were just taking the meat off the fire when they joined them. Iri didn't miss the way Jaden smiled at Kayla. When she smiled back, the simple act lighting her whole face, Jaden looked like he had momentarily lost track of what he'd been about to say. But from the colors around him, he was grateful Kayla had taken care of her.

"Is that plate for me?" Kayla put an arm around Jaden's waist and winked.

Jaden looked down at the plate he still held. "Sure, you can have this one." Selecting another plate, he handed it to Iri. "And you can have this one."

"Tuck in," Atu encouraged when the girls took their plates and waited for the boys to get theirs. "We didn't cook this food so that it could get cold."

Kayla snorted. "I bet you didn't."

As they ate, the darkness around them deepened, and the first stars popped up.

"I think we should get the disc," Atu said, pointing at the sky.

Iri glanced up. Overhead, the sky was sprinkled with sparkly silver lights, as though someone carelessly tossed glitter over a dark, velvet blanket. It was breathtaking.

"Wow, you don't see stars like that in the compound," Kayla whispered.

Jaden reached for Kayla's hand, the blue hue around him becoming more vibrant. "Spectacular, isn't it?"

Shifting her attention, Iri relaxed, watching the panoramic view expand.

"Ugh, I'm getting a crick in my neck," Kayla said. "Let's get our sleeping shells and spread them on the grass. It'll be way easier to watch the sky that way."

"And far more comfortable," Iri agreed.

"While we're doing that, we may as well pack up," Jaden said.

"Why? We don't even know if we'll find anything," Kayla countered.

"But if we do, we may have to leave in a hurry. Remember finding the second relic stone?"

Iri wondered what had happened. The oranges around Kayla were muted, but unmistakable. Noticing her confusion, Kayla explained. "We didn't expect to find the second relic stone. Suffice to say it resulted in a hasty exit with a Gaptor in pursuit. Jaden's right. We should be ready for anything when we find the map."

Jaden did a double take. "Say what? Can you please repeat that?"

Kayla slapped him playfully on the arm. "I'm not the only one who's ever right!'

"Yeah, that's true." Jaden grinned, snapping his fingers. "I forgot, Taz is also in that elite group!"

Kayla only laughed. "Tease all you want. Let's clear dinner and make sure we haven't left anything in the cabin. That would be disturbing for the people who are living here when time returns to normal."

Iri groaned. 'Did you have to mention that?"

"I thought you'd be glad to be getting out of here."

"I am. The sooner the better."

They made short work of packing up. Thirty minutes later, they were sprawled on their sleeping shells, their heads resting on their packs and the last bag of cookies on the ground between them.

Jaden handed the disc to Atu. "Here, I think you'll be better at finding what we're looking for than I will."

"I'll do my best." Wasting no time, Atu held the disc up to the sky.

"Find anything?" Iri grinned at the eagerness in Jaden's voice.

"No, but that patch of stars at the very edge of the horizon looks promising." Atu handed the disc back.

Iri wondered about Atu. Of the three, his color palette changed the least. Based on the dominant whites surrounding him, he had no issues with life, except for the purple tinge that was always there, underlying the white. She wanted to ask what sorrow troubled him, but she didn't feel like she knew him well enough. And it was a big part of him right now. She didn't want to jeopardize the group's unconditional acceptance.

Jaden took the disc and compared it to the cluster of stars Atu indicated. "Yeah, those do look like part of the pattern. When do you think the rest of it will be visible?"

"A few hours at least," Atu replied. "I suggest we check every hour or so, long enough that we don't drive ourselves nuts and short enough that we don't miss anything."

Jaden set the alarm on his PAL, and the four of them relaxed on their sleeping shells. Iri was delighted when Jaden began filling her in on their stories. This was their first chance to catch her up when any or all of them weren't too exhausted to do anything except sleep. And catch her up they did, each sketching various parts of the story between their regular checks of the stars. When she heard about Atu's missing parents, she understood the purple hues and was thankful she hadn't had to ask.

It was well past midnight before they had her up to date. "It sounds like you've had more than a few adventures without me. Zareh is interesting, but it seems you don't know a lot about him?"

"That would be because that's what he intends," Jaden bridled. "Believe me, you'll understand if you ever get to meet him."

Iri chuckled. "If you say so. I wonder why we didn't meet before you retrieved that last artifact? Seems you could've done with help fighting off those Gaptors before the Legion arrived."

"A question we'll never know the answer to," Atu put in. "I do believe that there is a reason for everything, though. If you were meant to be with us before now, I'm sure that would've happened."

"Atu's right," Jaden agreed. "The gliders mentioned that same thing once before. Or was it Zareh? Either way, it seems there is a design to all of this. And that means that you must be necessary now, or you would still be wandering the woods."

"Thanks," Iri said dryly, "that really makes me feel wanted."

"Sorry, that's not what I meant. I only . . ."

Iri grinned and put a hand in the air. "It's okay. I'm just teasing."

Jaden relaxed. "I'm glad we found you. It means we're making progress."

Kayla rolled her eyes.

"What?' Jaden asked, dumbfounded.

"What he means," Kayla explained, eyeing Jaden as she did, "is that he's glad you're with us."

Iri smiled. If Kayla hadn't corrected Jaden, she wouldn't have noticed that his revision hadn't been any better than his first faux pas. That was a revelation. She must be more comfortable with these people than she'd realized.

"Yes, what Kayla said," Jaden admitted, looking sheepish.

After that, he didn't say more. Was he was worried he would upset her to the point of making her cry again? The colors around Kayla shifted as she sensed Jaden's discomfort. Kayla wriggled closer to Jaden, resting her head on his stomach, and Iri smelled the calming effect Kayla had on him. Jaden began running his fingers through Kayla's tresses, and his remaining tension eased. Having someone that you could rely on so much must be wonderful. Iri never had anyone she could do that with—until now. Here were three people she could share her burdens with. And that was a gift to be treasured indeed.

CHAPTER TWELVE

With Jaden's hands running through her hair, Kayla closed her eyes and indulged in the exquisite pleasure.

"I think we're getting close." Atu's unexpected statement got everyone's attention.

Kayla sighed as she sat up, regretting the loss of contact with Jaden. Turning, she found Atu holding the disc up against the starry sky.

"May I see?" Jaden asked, impatient as always.

Atu grinned and handed the disc over—to Kayla. She took it with an impish grin.

Jaden shook his head. "Yeah, go ahead and laugh. Have fun while you can."

"Is that an invitation?" Kayla asked gleefully.

"No," Jaden grumbled, not bothering to look at her.

Kayla grinned as she studied the stars. Her perusal complete, she smiled sweetly at Jaden before handing the disc to Iri. Iri began her own comparison of the tiny holes in the disc to the twinkling canvas overhead. Kayla stifled her burgeoning laughter as Jaden fidgeted. When Iri lowered the disc, Kayla nudged her, and Iri obligingly raised the disc once more. But when Kayla made to nudge Iri again, Jaden caught her.

"Okay, hand it over," Jaden ordered, holding out his hand. The girls giggled as Iri complied. Resigned, Jaden sighed and raised the disc for his own inspection. "You're right. It should be soon."

"An hour or two at most," Atu guessed. "Since I fell short on sleep this afternoon, is it okay with all of you if I nap?"

"And if I join him?" Jaden quickly added.

From the bags under his eyes, Kayla knew his extended shift from the afternoon was catching up with him. She almost regretted teasing him. Almost. He hadn't bitten her head off despite being tired, so he was making progress with that temper of his. And she couldn't refuse his request. Not after the cherished time they spent alone this afternoon. And not after he allowed her to sleep longer than she should've. "Yup, cool with me." Iri nodded her consent, and the boys snuggled into their shells.

When Iri pulled a book from her pack, Kayla blinked. If Iri lived at the back edge of beyond, where did the book come from?

"Don't be so shocked." Iri grinned. "Just because I prefer living by myself doesn't mean I avoid civilization altogether."

Kayla grimaced. "I can see how this reading emotions thing is going to get us all in trouble."

Iri laughed. "You don't know the half of it yet." She paused. "So you and Jaden are…close?"

"We are."

"Isn't that complicated? I mean, with the mission and all?"

"It could be, if we let it. Or you could see it like we do—because of the mission, we've realized that time is fleeting and life is short. You have to make the most of things while you can because you don't know how long you have."

"That's a rather morbid outlook!"

"Perhaps, but a realistic one considering the circumstances we find ourselves in."

"I guess." Iri waited a few moments. Then she blabbed the question that was clearly bothering her. "I assume you've thought through all the consequences?"

Kayla studied Iri. "Why don't you just spit it out?"

Iri reddened. "Well, what if something happens to one of you?"

Kayla sighed. There it was. The question that plagued her from the time she first allowed herself to accept what she felt for Jaden. "I could say that we'll be strong enough to put our personal feelings aside until the mission is over, but I won't know if that's really true until the time comes."

Looking guilty, Iri put a hand on Kayla's arm. "I hope it doesn't come to that."

"You and me both," Kayla murmured. "You have anyone special in your life?"

"No. I don't get to meet any cute boys living like a recluse."

They lapsed into silence. Kayla was sure she dozed, because when Jaden's PAL beeped, indicating two hours had passed, she felt like it had only been moments since she and Iri had been talking. Stretching, she looked around and found Iri watching her. The boys were still trying to rouse themselves. "Did I nod off?"

"You did." Iri grinned.

"Sorry," Kayla mumbled. "You should've woken me. Some companion I am falling asleep on you."

"No problem. I enjoyed having time to myself. You all talk too much."

Kayla laughed. "I bet it seems that way when you're used to having peace and quiet. Let's wake those boys."

The boys had been waiting for those words. They popped their heads out of their sleeping shells.

"No need for anything drastic," Jaden blurted, spotting Kayla as she moved toward him. "I'm awake."

"Ah, and I thought I'd get to mess with you." Kayla grinned.

Laughing, Jaden inched out of his shell. "Maybe we can tag team Atu," he threatened, noting Atu hadn't moved since poking his head from the shell.

Hurriedly, Atu sat up, pushing his shell down to his waist and reaching up to rub his eyes. "Leave a guy to wake up in peace, would you?" His grumpy tone had the others chuckling.

"Someone didn't get his beauty sleep," Jaden teased.

"Yeah, and someone had too much," Atu retorted, shoving out of his shell.

Jaden opened his mouth to say something else, but Kayla placed a warning hand on his arm. "Give him a moment," Kayla said in an undertone.

Leaning close to her, Jaden whispered, "Yeah, he's not exactly Mr. Nice Guy when he wakes up. The last time I woke him, he came up with fists flying."

Kayla giggled as she took Jaden's face between her hands and planted a quick kiss on his mouth. "I'm glad he didn't make contact."

Jaden chuckled. "No chance." He took her hands in his own and kissed the palm of each before releasing her and turning to dig in his pack for the wooden cube.

Kayla laughed when he found the cube and made a show of holding it up like he'd found treasure. "Idiot!" That produced a smile, and she took a moment to take a mental photo. If anything, that smile made him more appealing than any man had a right to be.

She watched, fascinated like always as his long fingers spun the sides of the cube until the disc fell free. Then he stood there with the disc in hand, waiting for Atu to finish wrestling his shell into his pack. Jaden's patience impressed her. When Atu eventually stood, flushed with annoyance, Jaden offered him the disc. "Care to do the honors?"

Atu glared at Jaden, still trying to find his sense of humor. It was a full minute before Atu huffed and took the disc. "Sure, why not?"

"Good man," Jaden said, clapping Atu's back.

Atu managed a shrug, but his grouchiness lingered. He took a moment to rub his eyes again before lifting the disc to the heavens. "Yes, perfect timing. It's all . . ."

Yelping, Atu leaped back. Bright light streamed through the holes in the disc from somewhere unseen, angling away from his face and toward a point behind him. His sudden movement shifted the disc, and the light disappeared as abruptly as it had materialized.

"Dude," Jaden breathed, "what did you do?"

"Nothing! I just held the disc up to the sky."

"Please, Atu, do that again," Iri urged, so softly that the others strained to catch her words.

"Why?" Jaden caught sight of Kayla's frown and said in a more amenable tone, "Did you notice something?"

"I think so. I'm sure the beams were converging on something on the ground."

Jaden rounded on Atu. "Well, what are you waiting for?"

Grumbling, Atu apprehensively lined the holes in the disc up with their matching stars. When light flared through the holes again, Kayla chuckled. Atu got more of a scare the second time—probably because he'd been expecting it. She smiled apologetically when Atu honed his glare on her.

"Where's the light coming from?" Intrigued, Jaden peered behind the upheld disc.

Kayla focused on the light, then squealed. "Who cares! Look where it's pointing!" As one, the others followed her gaze.

"My backpack?" Jaden ventured.

Kayla bounded over and upended it.

"Hey," Jaden whined, "that took a long time to pack."

Any further complaints died as the beams of light realigned themselves. When they settled, something on the ground began glowing—the book Awena gave them. In one leap, Jaden was beside Kayla, flopping down and opening the book. Instantly, the light went from white to golden as the rays were absorbed. The light faded, and darkness returned.

"Okay, what just happened?" Kayla asked.

Jaded scratched his head. "I think the book sucked the light in."

Iri and Atu joined Kayla, and the three of them peeked over Jaden's shoulder as he flipped through the pages. When the glowing page appeared, the four of them gasped as one. Giving their eyes a moment to adjust, they took a second look. The page as a whole wasn't glowing. Rather, certain letters on the page burned brightly.

"B-u-r-i-e-d-f-o-r-," Jaden spelled out.

"The Buried Forest? Oh man!" Atu whistled, his eyes widening as he took a step back.

"What's that? Or where's that?" Kayla demanded.

On top of her words came Jaden's. "You know this place?"

"I do." Atu nodded. "But only by legend. I don't think anyone has spoken of it for centuries."

"And why's that?" Iri probed. At Kayla's inquiring glance, she raised a hand in the air before she explained. "Atu smells . . . cautious, and the orange hues around him denote uncertainty."

"Let's just say it's not a place you want to visit." Atu grimaced. "And it has that name for a reason."

"It's buried?" Jaden blinked.

"It is."

"How do the trees grow then?" Iri asked.

"Only one of the mysteries of that forest."

Kayla studied Atu. "I'm sensing there's a lot about the forest you *aren't* saying?"

"Yes, not the least of which is that I don't know exactly where it is." Atu spat the words.

"But I thought you said you knew the place." When Atu's glare resurfaced, Jaden backed down. "Sorry, dude. Why don't you tell us what you do know?"

"Everything I've been told about that place boils down to the same thing: don't go near, stay away, don't look for it, if you accidentally find it, run. Clear enough?"

"Crystal," Jaden acknowledged. "Unfortunately, we still have to go there. Do you have any idea why it's so dangerous?"

Atu shook his head. "No. When it did come up in stories, which was rarely, it was glossed over. And it never came up in casual conversation."

"So, it's a place that we know little to nothing about, other than that it's dangerous—and Atu only has a vague idea of where it is. Fantastic!" Jaden clenched his fists. "This is Zareh again! Next time I see that critter, I'll hang him by his cute little ears until he gives us all the answers."

Kayla sighed. She would have to stop Jaden before his rampage got out of hand. Leaning closer, she kissed him on the cheek. He blinked, pausing mid-tirade and focusing questioning eyes on her. She knew the moment it clicked. "Oh, you want me to stop?"

Kayla smiled. "Can you think of a more effective way to tell you that?"

He returned the smile, the anger draining from him. "No."

* * *

Jaden took Kayla's hand, gazing at her. He would never understand how Kayla always seemed to know the right thing to do when it came to him, but he was glad she did. His smile widened before he noticed how the others were all looking at him. Had he made that much of a fool of himself? But no, it was something else. They were waiting for him to give them direction. He sighed. Of course they were. "Let's saddle up, then," Jaden said, reluctantly releasing Kayla's hand.

As if on cue, the gliders appeared.

"We saw the light," Han called. "Everything alright down there?"

"It is," Jaden replied, stepping away from the others to converse with Han. "Perfect timing on your part. It's time to go." Jaden thought he heard Taz muttering. Probably something about it being time they left. He smiled. She was so predictable.

Han circled lower. "Shall we pick you up where we dropped you yesterday?"

Jaden considered, then shook his head. "We need supplies. There's a twenty-four-hour store just on the other side of the cabins, up there, past that ridge. Can you and the other gliders pass from range in about ten minutes or so? That should give us enough time to get there. Then we need about fifteen minutes to stock up, after which we can meet you in the berthing area south of the store. It's empty most of the time, so it shouldn't be a problem with the vanishing act we do. Does that work?"

"It does, but we'll give you thirty minutes in the store. You know what women are like when they shop. You'll probably take longer than you think."

Jaden chuckled. "You're undoubtedly right. See you in about forty minutes, then?"

Han agreed and then flew back up to the others to relay the plan.

Kayla wandered up to Jaden. "What was that about?"

"Where and when the gliders will fetch us." Beckoning for Iri and Atu to join them, Jaden explained what had been agreed. "Let's get going."

The others waited while Jaden piled his scattered belongings into his pack. "You should be helping with this," Jaden grumbled at Kayla.

"You're doing just fine without me." Kayla smirked, watching him with folded arms.

Jaden laughed. Seeing her in such high spirits was wonderful. He slid the last of his things into his bulging pack and stood. "Shall we?"

Their stop at the store was efficient. As they waited for their gliders, they agreed Iri would fly with Atu. Minutes later, they were all airborne.

"Where to?" Taz's tone as imperious as ever.

"Back the way we came." Atu sounded glum, but he'd evidently resigned himself to the fact that he was going to the one place his family had repeatedly told him to avoid.

"I thought you didn't know where the Buried Forest was?" Jaden asked.

"I don't. I only have a general idea. This starts us in the right direction. How we find the forest after that, I have no clue."

Jaden nodded. That gave him an idea, but he would wait until lunch to discuss it with the others. Trying to talk to each other while flying was challenging at best.

Hours later, when his stomach rumbled, Jaden said to Han, "I think it's time for lunch."

Nodding, Han drifted closer to Aren and then Taz, passing along the message. As soon as they had settled on the ground and unpacked their lunch, Jaden made his proposal.

CHAPTER THIRTEEN

"How far north are we going?" Jaden began.

Atu finished chewing before answering. "Pretty far."

"Anywhere close to Sven's?"

"Not quite, but close enough that we could get there with another day or two of traveling. Why?"

"You're thinking of getting Iri a smart suit?" Kayla guessed.

"Yes, but not only that." Jaden smiled. Kayla was quick on her feet. Would she figure out the rest? The frown creasing her face and her delayed response told him she hadn't thought it through to the end. He waited.

"Could you just tell us already?' Atu complained. "Watching the two of you having this silent debate is tedious."

Jaden frowned. Atu wasn't usually testy, but ever since he'd heard where they were going, he'd been on edge. If Atu was worried, this place had to be all it was cracked up to be.

"Well?" Atu hissed.

The grumpy demand reminded Jaden he hadn't replied, and Iri and Kayla were looking at him as though they'd like the answer too. "I thought we'd ask about comms for the smart suits."

"That was it!" Kayla snapped her fingers. "I'm glad you remembered."

"I just wish there was a way to get hold of Sven in advance." Jaden sighed. "It would be nice if he could have something ready and waiting for us when we arrived. Last time, we spent way too long there."

"We did, but we learned so much," Kayla said. "And it was tough to leave."

Jaden, Kayla, and Atu smiled at one another as fond memories resurfaced.

"Perhaps we could split up?" Iri suggested.

Jaden immediately shook his head. "No, we can't be separated when we reach our next destination. Even if it isn't as ominous as Atu's made it out to be, we all need to be there. I can feel that."

"Is that one of those *feelings* of yours?" Kayla asked, more attuned to Jaden than the others.

"It is. I'm not sure why, but we need to stay together." He caught Iri studying him. Her gaze made him feel like an insect under a microscope. "What?"

"I've seen those colors on you before. I wasn't sure what they meant. Now I do."

"That I'm sensing something?" Jaden asked, incredulous.

Iri nodded, but hesitantly. Had she been nervous about how they'd react to this confession?

"Anything else?" Jaden asked, hoping she would share.

Iri waited a moment before answering. "Yes, I can smell your ability too."

"That's amazing!" Atu's enthusiastic endorsement made Iri smile, but she still glanced furtively at him and Kayla, as though expecting revulsion. When she didn't find any, the hunted look left her eyes. But Jaden sensed she was still holding back, as though she didn't want to get too attached.

Iri nodded at Atu. "Thank you. I have to say, I can't remember anyone ever being excited about what I can do."

Atu shrugged. "I guess they're the ones who've been missing out, then."

Jaden glimpsed hope fluttering its battered wings ever so briefly in Iri's eyes. Then the emotion was gone. "Thank you again," Iri said.

Wondering what Kayla was making of this, Jaden glanced her way in time to glimpse the speculative gaze she leveled at Iri. *What has her attention this time?* When Kayla swung her gaze toward him, he raised an eyebrow. Inclining her head to one side, she shook it slightly.

The line of Kayla's neck and throat was far more interesting to Jaden than her reply; he wanted to run his finger along that appealing curve. It reminded him of the graceful lines of the gliders when they were in flight. *The gliders!*

"Oh yes," Jaden spewed, "I meant to say we should take a detour via our homes if we're going back the same way. We can connect with Pallaton and hook Iri up with a ride of her own."

Kayla regarded him. "Someone's been doing some thinking this morning."

"Someone has to—and not just daydream while they're flying!"

Kayla laughed. "Point taken."

"I get my own glider?" Iri squealed.

Jaden grinned. "You do."

Over lunch, they agreed to detour via Daxsos to get Iri's glider and then go to Sven's before searching for their destination. Hopefully, this route would give them more time to figure out exactly where they were headed. Their gliders returned, and Kayla waved them down.

Clearly, they hadn't planned on landing, as evidenced by Taz's annoyed glare. Despite this, the gliders dropped to the ground, perching on the stubby grasses of the prairie.

"What?" Taz demanded.

Kayla looked to Jaden, expecting him to lay out their plans. He waved a hand at her.

"We think it would be best if we return home first, then . . ." Kayla began.

Taz interrupted. "We need to reach the next destination. That is our priority."

"No," Jaden corrected, stepping in, "we need to work as a team. And to do that, Iri needs a suit and a glider. Both will make her a more effective team member."

Taz cocked her head. "Getting Iri her own glider will increase our chances of survival. And adding the suit means we won't be hindered by these prehistoric speeds."

"Now you're getting the picture."

"Your home it is, then," Taz accepted.

As Jaden connected with Han, he wondered whether Taz agreed so quickly because she really did see the value of their plan, or because she just needed them to be on their way again. She had been increasingly restless. What wasn't she saying?

He had to wait three days for his answer. Even then, it was indirect: their gliders began commenting on the fact that they hadn't encountered any Gaptors. Repeatedly. They belabored the point all day, then that evening, they disappeared for their meal as usual after depositing their voyagers. However, unlike previous evenings, they returned earlier than was their norm, assuming protective positions around their voyagers who were enjoying the cozy campfire.

As Taz settled next to Kayla, she worried. "It's most unusual for Gaptors to stay away, especially when they have prey."

"It's as though you want them to attack us!" Kayla exclaimed, sitting up from her spot resting against Jaden's chest.

"No," Taz snapped, "it's because there's something wrong with this picture."

She'd said something like this before, only Jaden hadn't understood what she was hinting at. Now, it hit him like a cement truck. Trying to calm himself, he said, "What exactly are you saying Taz?"

He must've let something slip in his tone, because Kayla's head swiveled toward him, her eyes wide and alarmed. Jaden wanted to reassure her, but if he was right, he didn't think he could. He took her hand in his, but he couldn't relax. And sensing his tension, he felt Kayla's hand tighten around his own in response.

Chittering, Taz moved her head from side to side. "I don't know. Something's not right, but I can't say what."

Jaden took a deep, steadying breath. It wouldn't do to get angry with Taz. She was already upset. "Let's start with what you do know. You said they don't usually stay away when they have prey, right?"

"Yes, yes, they live to attack. But we've been traveling for almost two weeks, and we haven't seen a single Gaptor. We should've encountered at least one by now."

"You're sure they can find us?" Jaden asked. "They have a way of tracking us?"

"Your medallions," Taz hissed.

"Ah, yes."

Distressed, Taz rolled her shoulders. "I'm sorry, I shouldn't be so short with you. What I should've explained, is that yes, while the Gaptors can find you, it will sometimes take them a while to do so. But this . . ." Helplessly, she waved a wing in the air. "It's too long."

"Let's list the possible reasons then," Jaden said. "The first and most obvious explanation is that more Gaptors may not have come through yet. That lone Gaptor that appeared at my home could've been one that somehow escaped our last battle."

No one knew how much Jaden wished that were true. If it was, the Gaptor hadn't been spying like they surmised. It had merely been trying to find someone with a medallion. And logically it had come to his house, since there was a stronger . . . signal, or whatever it was that attracted them because Atu was there too. *Two medallions have to make for a stronger signal than one, right?* Deep down, though, Jaden knew he was lying to himself.

"Yes, that's a distinct possibility," Taz twittered.

Her fervor for the idea was too pronounced for Jaden's peace of mind. Looking around, he asked, "Any other ideas?"

"I know this is unlikely," Kayla offered, "but is it possible Zareh's found a way to turn off whatever it is that's attracting the Gaptors to the medallions?"

Atu shook his head. "Why would he suddenly do that? Besides, cantankerous as he is, wouldn't he have found a way to tell us that he was planning to do that? Or that he had accomplished it?"

The others nodded.

"There is another reason," Iri ventured.

Jaden sighed. "What?"

Her expression made him wonder whether Iri had used her gifts to know he already had an answer. Her next sentence proved him right. "When I'm hunting, there are only two reasons I stop. The first is that I've killed my prey. The second is that—"

"Something better came along," Atu finished for her.

"Precisely. What I can't fathom is what could be more interesting for them to hunt than us."

There. She said it. Jaden's eyes flicked to Kayla. Her face drained of color.

"Our parents!" Kayla cried, leaping to her feet.

Bounding up after her, Jaden caught her in his arms. Kayla struggled, trying to free herself, but then she slumped against him. "They'll be alright. Pallaton's there," Jaden whispered.

Kayla burrowed into his shoulder, hiding her face. Tension radiated off her in waves. After a moment, she pulled herself together. Looking up, she smiled weakly, still clinging to him like her legs wouldn't support her. Jaden cradled her closer as he returned her smile, although he wasn't sure his attempt was much better than hers. Even though Pallaton was there, there was no guarantee that her parents—or his—were safe.

"Wait!" Iri yelped. "Your parents have medallions too?"

Jaden was grateful when Atu pulled Iri aside, giving him more time to comfort Kayla. Although, he had to admit, she was just as much of a comfort to him. In short, concise sentences, Atu explained what had happened before they left Daxsos. It was something they hadn't thought to tell Iri when they shared their adventures.

"Now it makes sense," Iri said when Atu finished.

"What does?"

"That Jaden was worried about what I was going to say. It was as though he knew what the problem was before I spoke it."

"You saw that?" Atu asked, eyes round.

"Yes, but I wasn't sure why."

"This gift of yours—it's truly incredible," Atu stated, not for the first time.

Iri blushed. "It's not that great. It can tell me some things, but sometimes, it's more confusing than if I hadn't been able to see or smell those emotions in the first place."

Iri's gift is certainly unique. But how is it going to help us? Jaden tossed the thought away. He already had too many questions and too few answers. He noticed Iri watching them.

"Will they be alright?" Iri asked Atu.

"Yes, I think they just needed a moment. In fact, from the way Taz is dancing around over there, I wouldn't be surprised if we leave shortly."

"And travel at night?" Iri asked, shocked.

Atu laughed. "It's not so bad. Besides, the gliders do better at night than during the day. Daytime travel is more to accommodate our needs than theirs."

"That's noble."

Atu snorted. "Don't let Taz catch you saying something like that. She'll expect the rest of us to be beholden to her too."

Iri giggled. "The way you three talk about her, one would think she was royalty."

Atu chuckled. "Don't give her any ideas, would you? Let's get our things together."

Iri and Atu glided back to the fire to collect their scattered items. Jaden released Kayla from his embrace but kept his hands on her shoulders as he appraised her. She lifted her chin and smiled at him. This time, the smile was more confident. "Time to leave, I suppose?"

"If you're ready?" Jaden answered.

"I'd rather stay in your arms and not think about where we're going or why. But that won't change things, so why wait?"

Jaden gave her shoulders a gentle squeeze before pressing a kiss to her forehead. "Atta girl!"

They joined Atu and Iri, and the four of them packed up and made sure the area was clean.

"Kayla's home?" Atu asked when they finished.

"Yes." Jaden nodded.

Atu grinned. "We should tell the gliders. Taz is about to rock right off her feet, she's so antsy."

Worried as he was, Jaden couldn't help but smile. When he turned and actually looked at Taz, the smile became a quiet chuckle. "Yes, let's put her out of her misery."

They strolled to where Taz waited and only grinned more when Taz hopped to meet them halfway.

"I assume we're headed back?" Taz chirped.

"We are."

"About time." Jaden wasn't sure how she did it or if she even communicated what they were doing to the other gliders, but when she took to the air, the others followed.

"Some communication system they have going there." Iri's voice behind them made him jump.

"Snuck up on us, did you?" Atu remarked.

"I wasn't trying to. Sorry!"

"Sure you weren't! Either I'm off my game, or you're really quiet."

"Considering I hunt to keep myself fed for the most part, I'd go with the second option." A smile dimpled Iri's cheeks.

"I think I will," Atu grinned. "Are we all packed up?"

"We are," Iri confirmed as Kayla joined them.

"Let's get this show on the road, then," Jaden said, watching their gliders approach.

CHAPTER FOURTEEN

As they flew, Kayla fretted. It was taking forever to get home. What would they find when they got there? She didn't notice her own silence until it was suddenly oppressive. With that realization came the awareness of a tension between the group members that grew with every mile they covered. Kayla couldn't get a handle on the reason until she overheard Iri and Atu.

"How can our gliders keep flying with so little rest?" Iri asked.

"These speeds are nothing to them," Atu answered. "They're accustomed to flying much faster. Think of it like taking an extended walk instead of sprinting. Same principle. It doesn't require nearly as much effort, so we can go much further."

Apparently, the analogy was helpful because Iri nodded. Then Kayla noticed the slight change in her demeanor. And when Iri sent a worried glance her way, Kayla understood. Iri was afraid they would blame her if something happened to either set of parents. After all, she was the one slowing them down.

Would I stoop to that level? It wasn't Iri's fault that she didn't have a suit—or that they'd found her when they did. Kayla opened her mouth to assuage Iri's fears, but the words stuck in her throat. The revelation was disconcerting. Kayla glanced at Jaden. He was doing his own brooding, oblivious to what was happening around him, even Kayla's attention. She sighed, and the silence grew louder.

By the time they reached the outskirts of Daxsos, the tension was unbearable. It ratcheted up when they encountered gliders carting away the carcasses of Gaptors. Iri's face drained of color as she got her first look at the monsters—or what was left of them.

"They're not as invincible as they seem," Kayla muttered, unsure how she was feeling. Worried, angry, resentful. She shouldn't—couldn't—blame Iri, yet Kayla wasn't feeling particularly charitable towards her, either.

"How can things like that exist?" Iri whispered, her attention honed on the corpses. "They're more than ugly. They're somehow . . . evil."

"You can see that?"

"No. Because they're dead, there are no colors or smells to tell me more about them." Iri sent her a sidelong glance, and Kayla remembered she should be aware of her emotions when Iri was around. Iri's eyes telegraphed her doubt about whether she would still have Kayla as a friend after this.

Kayla *had* to let go of this ridiculous notion that it was Iri's fault if anything had happened to her parents—or Jaden's, so she forced the words out. "Look, you don't have to worry. It's not your fault if something's happened to . . ." Kayla swallowed. She couldn't say the words. She could barely even form the thought.

She was spared further conversation when a large glider abruptly blocked their way.

"Pallaton," Taz said.

"Tazanna," Pallaton replied, dipping his head.

"What happened?" Taz demanded.

Pallaton's reply was cut short by Kayla's own demand. "Are my parents safe?"

"They are." Kayla all but melted onto Taz's back with relief. "But I regret to inform you that we were unable to do the same for Jaden's parents."

The words hung in the air. No one spoke. No one moved. *It's as though we're in a time warp.* Then sound and emotions came crashing back down.

"They took them?" Jaden croaked.

"They did," Pallaton admitted. "We were outnumbered—and outmaneuvered. Almost unbelievable considering our enemies usually don't have a brain to spare between them. But the fact remains that we were unable to keep your parents from being taken. I am sorry."

Rigid, Kayla watched Jaden. She wished the gliders would land so she could go to him, comfort him. He looked stunned. Although, considering his mother had warned him this would happen, she couldn't fathom why. Maybe he hadn't believed it would actually happen. Or he hadn't thought it would happen so soon. Then Jaden straightened, and his eyes didn't seem so bleak anymore.

"Jaden? Do you want to go home?" she asked.

Her questions must've cut into his contemplations, because he looked at her, startled. "Sorry, what?"

"I asked if you wanted to go back to your home?" Kayla repeated.

"No, there's no point. They're gone. Nothing we can do about that now."

Kayla felt like her eyes would pop out of her head. He was holding something back. After his initial reaction, he was now too calm. He should have been ranting and raging at everyone in sight. "Jaden, is there something you want to tell us?" His guilty expression confirmed her suspicions, but that haunted look lurking in the background told her it was also something he didn't want to discuss. Not here. Not now.

Deciding to let it go, Kayla said, "Would you like to come and see my parents then?" That got his attention. He seemed to realize he had been so wrapped up in thoughts of his own parents that he hadn't spared a thought for hers.

Chagrined, Jaden said, "Yes, thanks. I'm really glad they're okay."

Kayla nodded. "Me too."

It didn't take long for the four voyagers to disembark and enter the Melmique home. But it was only when they reached the living room and found it empty that Jaden put it together.

"The time freeze. It's still in effect. We'll have to wait until the gliders are gone before we can speak to your parents."

It was a tedious wait. Jaden paced the living room floor until Kayla thought she would go insane. When she couldn't take it anymore, she pulled him down onto the couch. Then Jaden's leg bounced a mile a minute until Kayla put a hand on it. He gazed at her hand, then up at her face. Kayla watched him, her concern growing.

Evidently, Jaden couldn't face her questions right now because he sprang back up and began pacing again. This time, Kayla left him to work off the nervous energy. She felt like pacing too. It was as though they were trapped in an invisible cage.

She could see Jaden's mind working. Then some fearsome thought must've caught him mid-stride because he stumbled. Not only that, he . . . deflated. Then Jaden wilted onto the couch. Kayla leaned toward him, but something else occurred to him right then because his shoulders drooped even further.

Alarmed, Kayla placed a hand on his shoulder. "Jaden, what's wrong?"

His breathing was rapid, and sweat beaded his forehead. Was he going to throw up? Kayla lifted her hand toward his head. Jaden halfheartedly swatted her arm away. But Atu was unexpectedly next to him, looking as anxious as Kayla, and his hand reached Jaden's forehead before Jaden could counter the move.

"Bro, what's up?' Atu felt the perspiration but shook his head to tell Kayla he didn't sense a fever.

"He looks like someone who just got really bad news," Iri observed from her place across the room.

"Jaden, talk to us." Kayla didn't need Iri's abilities to tell her something was terribly wrong.

Swallowing, Jaden opened his mouth, struggling to squeeze the words out. "My parents—I can't get to them."

"We know," Kayla answered, bemused. How did this suddenly make things worse? He already knew this. Or was that what he had been hiding earlier? "Jaden, what's really going on?"

Jaden shook his head. He couldn't look at her.

Gently, Kayla touched his chin and turned his head toward her. "Speak to me."

"I thought I had a plan to save them. But it's not going to work."

"What plan?" If she heard the plan, she might be able to figure out the issue.

Swallowing, Jaden explained in halting sentences. "I gave my mother the key my gran gave us, since I'm pretty sure it's an artifact. I thought I could use it with Han's arcachoa to rescue my parents if . . . if my mom's dreams came true. But I forgot that Han told us that the arcachoa doesn't allow for any physical interaction. Therefore it's impossible to bring them back because there's no interaction across timelines." Jaden swallowed again. "If that's not enough of a blunder, I also just remembered something Taz said. That the arcachoa will only take us back in time if there's an artifact in that exact place. And right now, I have no idea where my parents are. I can't use the key to find them any more than I can lift a five-hundred pound weight!" He dropped his head into his hands, struggling for breath. "This can't be happening. I planned it so carefully."

Kayla gave him a hard stare. "So, without knowing where your parents are, the key can't be used with the arcachoa to draw you to them. And even if you knew where they were, you can't pull your parents back from there because it's crossing timelines."

Jaden nodded, looking sick. His head dropped lower, as though waiting for the recriminations he was sure would come. When none did, he looked up.

Kayla smiled. But it was the sort of smile a cat might give a mouse right before it pounced. "You thought you could do this all on your own."

"I didn't want to put anyone else at risk."

"That kinda sucks, bro," Atu said. "Aren't we a team? Shouldn't you at least have given us the option to choose for ourselves what we would like to do?"

Jaden sighed. "I guess I was too caught up in my emotions to be thinking clearly. You're right. I should've told you. I'm sorry."

After a moment, Kayla relented. A little. "Don't do it again, or we might have to lop off an arm or something."

Jaden almost smiled. But Kayla could tell he knew she was serious. "Yeah, I'll keep that in mind."

"Do that. That said, I'm sorry your plan didn't work. But perhaps if you include us next time, we can come up with a better strategy."

Jaden snorted. "Next time? I don't think this will happen twice."

"Yes, poor choice of words. What I should've said, for those so obsessive about saying exactly what we mean, is that planning together will help mitigate issues like this in the future." Her tone wasn't friendly, and from the way Jaden angled his eyes, he understood how upset she was. *Good. He might remember this lesson.*

Their silent conflict ended when Atu spoke. "Bro, you need food. You haven't eaten since breakfast, and you'll feel better with something in that hollow stomach of yours."

The mention of food had Jaden's stomach growling. "I don't really feel like eating, but I suppose my stomach can go with that."

Kayla relaxed. His agreement was a good sign. Kayla steered them toward the kitchen.

They prepared their food, ate, and then sat around sipping tea for a while. It didn't take long for that to get old. Jaden became restless again. His gaze settled on Atu. She wasn't sure what to make of his expression.

"Sorry all this is taking so long," Jaden said.

Atu started, looking surprised. "It's not your fault. The Gaptors have to be cleared away."

"No, I meant sorry it's taking so long for us to find your parents."

Understanding lit Atu's eyes. "Yeah, thanks, I appreciate that. You'll see. It gets easier to accept the waiting when you're doing something."

"I think I get that already."

Iri cleared her throat. "Maybe we should do something then?"

When Jaden didn't respond, Kayla was the one who asked, "What do you have in mind?"

"For starters, you could get me hooked up with a glider." Encouraged by their nods, she continued. "And then perhaps we can head to

Sven's so I can get a smart suit?" Jaden's dark look silenced her suggestions. Iri looked worried, as if she was afraid of pushing too far.

"Those sound like excellent ideas." Kayla smiled at Iri before casting an inquiring glance Jaden's way.

Jaden didn't miss her implied question. "We can't leave yet. There are some things here that I need to get squared away."

Kayla nodded. Yes, he would probably want to speak to her parents, and perhaps Pallaton and the other members of the Legion, to find out exactly what had happened before he went anywhere.

Noticing the silent exchange between Jaden and Kayla, Atu made his own proposal. "How about if Iri and I go to Sven's then, while you and Kayla take care of that?"

Kayla waited for Jaden to object, but he said nothing. Kayla would have to step in. When she looked at Iri, Kayla almost giggled. Iri stared at Atu, wide-eyed, like she couldn't quite believe he was willing to go with her. Interesting! How had Atu been able to surprise Iri? Kayla would have to ask him. She would love to have a way to keep from being such an open book where Iri was concerned.

Iri finally stuttered, "Thanks, I'd like that."

Atu nodded, like it had all been settled. "Alright! Kayla, okay with you if Iri and I take some supplies to keep us going until we get there?"

Dazed by how quickly this decision had been reached, Kayla nodded. "Sure." Then she came to her senses. "Here, let me show you where you can find everything."

CHAPTER FIFTEEN

Kayla watched Iri hop from foot to foot on the rooftop landing deck. Her excitement was contagious. At least it gave Kayla something to think of besides Jaden. He had insisted up until now that they should all stay together, but he wasn't stopping Iri and Atu from leaving. Had he meant to say nothing, or was he too absorbed in his thoughts to register what was happening? That was disconcerting. Kayla would need to find a way to help get him over this hurdle. Although she had no idea how she would do that.

Shoving those thoughts aside, Kayla focused on the issue at hand. Was it the right decision for Iri and Atu to leave? If not, it was up to her to stop them. She glanced at the sky, wondering what was taking Pallaton so long.

Right on cue, Pallaton appeared, followed by some of the Legion. He must wonder why they had called him again so soon, or he was expecting trouble. Either way, he had come prepared. "You called?" Pallaton asked.

"I did, Ancient One. Thank you for your prompt response," Atu replied.

"I take it there is no danger?"

"Yes, no threats. We called to ask if you might assign a glider to Iri?"

"Of course." Pallaton grinned. Studying the gliders he had brought with him, he signaled a lithe glider near the front. "Satinka."

Eagerly, she came forward. "Yes, Ancient One?"

"I would like to pair you with our newest seeker. Do you accept?"

"With great pleasure." Satinka faced Iri. "I'm Satinka, and it will be my honor to serve on this quest with you."

From the way Iri grinned, Kayla didn't need Iri's gifts to know Iri planned to "help" Satinka lose some of that formality. "I'm excited and pleased to meet you too. My name is Iriyessa, but call me Iri."

Satinka inclined her head. "Thank you, Iri. Are we planning on flying together soon?"

"Right now, in fact." Then she reconsidered. "That is, if you're okay with that?"

Light, chiming laughter pealed from Satinka. "I am. Shall I land so you can alight?"

"Well, I prefer aerial connections—how about you?"

"That would be my preference too," Satinka smiled.

In seconds, Iri and Atu were gone, and Kayla hadn't stopped them. Dazed, she stared at the empty sky. Well, for better or worse, the decision was out of her hands now. Kayla trudged back downstairs. Jaden was still on the couch where she had left him. He hadn't even said goodbye. Irrationally, Kayla was irritated. "You know, you can't sit there and mope forever."

Jaden's eyes blazed. "And I suppose if the situation were reversed, you would be all A-Okay and ready to go?

The anguish in his voice made Kayla back down. It was still all too raw. He wasn't in a place yet where she could goad him into action. Kneeling on the floor in front of the couch, Kayla reached to take his hands into her own. When he pulled back, she gently but firmly extended her reach until she grasped his hands. Gazing into his dark blue eyes, stormy now with emotions he couldn't or wouldn't express, she said, "I'm sorry. I can't imagine what you're going through."

The dam burst. The self-control he had been holding onto so tightly evaporated, and tears streamed down Jaden's face. Wordlessly, Kayla climbed onto the couch next to him and pulled him into her arms. She held him there as he gave in to his sorrow, wishing there was more she could do but thankful he was finally expressing some emotion. The cold, automaton that had been Jaden for the last few hours had been alien to her, and she hadn't known how to deal with him. This Jaden, full of emotion, was the one she understood, the one she could help.

When the storm passed, Jaden leaned out of Kayla's arms to take her in his own. He pulled her toward him in a fierce embrace. His voice was husky. "Thanks, I needed that."

Kayla nodded slightly, not wanting to move. She was at home here, tucked against his chest where she could hear his heart beating. Here, she felt alive. And she could feel the life in him too.

The door to the landing pad banged open, and Kayla shot upright. "Someone's here."

Jaden crossed to the stairs ahead of her, peeking up the hallway. It was a shock when Kayla's parents appeared.

Kayla streaked past Jaden and up the stairs, pulling her stunned parents into hugs. "You're back."

Worried, Sadie studied Kayla. "We didn't go anywhere. It was only a few moments ago that we said goodbye. Did you not go?"

It fell into place for Kayla then. Of course! They must've been on the roof all this time, except the voyagers couldn't see them with the time freeze in effect. The gliders must've finally moved out of range. She took a moment to consider her reply. "We did. Remember, I told you that it would seem like time hadn't passed for you at all."

Sadie's eyes widened. "You're done then? You've finished whatever it was you were trying to do?" Then, a split second later, "How long were you gone?"

Kayla realized they were all still standing on the stairs. "Let's go down to the living room, and I'll answer your questions there."

When her mother fixed Kayla with a penetrating stare, Kayla

understood something in her tone had sent alarm bells ringing in her mother's head. She jumped when she saw Jaden at the bottom of the stairs. "Oh, hello!"

"Hello, Mrs. Melmique," Jaden replied, giving her a hug and then greeting and shaking Mr. Melmique's hand. Kayla herded her parents into the living room.

Sadie glanced around. "Where's Atu?" Her face paled. "Is he alright? Please, tell me something didn't happen to him!"

Kayla took her mother's hands in her own and led her to the couch. "He's fine, Mom. Don't panic. I'll tell you everything just as soon as I get you and Dad some tea."

"Kayla, I don't want tea. I want you to tell me what happened. Now."

Sighing, Kayla took a seat opposite them. She was immensely grateful when Jaden came and stood behind her, placing a supportive hand on her shoulder. She took a deep breath. He was with her. She could do this. As succinctly as possible, Kayla updated her parents on all that had transpired since their departure, ending with Iri and Atu leaving for Sven's and omitting anything about Jaden's parents.

Vicken broke the sudden silence that filled the room when Kayla finished. "You found the last seeker then?"

"We did."

Her father had chosen to act in character and would ask his questions later. Her eyes went to her mother. And when Sadie frowned, Kayla knew her mother had also ferreted out the issue. "I don't understand. Why did you come back home then? You have the last seeker, and you know where you're supposed to go. Why the detour?"

It was the question Kayla had dreaded. She knew how close her mother and Mrs. Jameson had become. In a way, their friendship reminded her of what she had shared with Grailynn. Something so special was rarely found: that deep connection, knowing and understanding what the other person thought or felt before they even said it. And now Kayla would have to tell her mother that her best friend was missing.

* * *

Jaden watched as Kayla explained what had happened to his parents. He could see her distress at having to share the awful news. What would he have said if her parents were taken instead? He was thankful that wasn't the case. All the same, he wished he never found the medallion. Then his parents would still be here.

If only he knew how to find them. Would Markov have any ideas? He had always been good at strategizing, maybe because of all those years playing on the gridpost team. Whatever the reason, Jaden could rely on him to work out a plan. A chilling thought occurred to him. Markov knew the truth. Was Jaden also putting him in danger because of it?

No, he couldn't spiral into blaming himself. Markov had asked; Markov had wanted to know. And Markov was quite capable of looking after himself. What of Jaden's other friends? Would they also become targets whether they knew the truth or not? What if they were taken? Would Jaden save them too?

No, saving the world was more important. Only that wasn't true. If any of his friends were taken, Jaden would try and save them as well.

He circled back to his original question: would Markov have any ideas? Then Jaden almost laughed out loud. Of course Markov couldn't help. He couldn't even see the Gaptors or gliders!

How will all this play out? He couldn't keep chasing his tail to try and keep people safe. If he allowed himself to travel down that road he would become paralyzed by fear, unable to do what was required. And that in itself would be failure. The only solution was to complete this mission.

"Jaden?" Kayla asked.

Jaden started. "Pardon? I'm sorry I didn't catch that."

"My parents wanted to know if you'd like to stay for dinner."

"Thanks, I appreciate the offer, but I have to get home and see if I can find any clues there." Catching Kayla's worried frown, Jaden shrugged. "I know it's unlikely that I'll find anything, but I have to look."

Jaden wondered about the glance that passed between Kayla's parents. Maybe he was imagining things, but it seemed like Mr. Melmique wanted to say something. Jaden gave it a moment, but Kayla spoke first. "May I fly you home then?"

"Please—unless the gliders are waiting when we get to the roof." Jaden turned to the Melmiques. "Thanks again for the offer of dinner. I'm sorry I can't accept. Stay safe."

They only nodded, still too staggered by the news of his parents' capture to say more. Jaden and Kayla made their way to the roof. When they found the gliders absent, Kayla fired up the 'pod and had Jaden home in minutes. Although he would've relished more time with Kayla, he didn't linger on his goodbyes, settling for a fierce hug and a short kiss before ordering her back home. "Ping me when you get there."

"Are you sure you wouldn't like me to come inside with you?"

"No, thanks. I'd like to do this alone. Get home to your parents. They need you. And let me know when you get home."

"I'll do that." Kayla settled back into the 'pod and took off.

Jaden stared after her, wondering whether he should've spent more time with her. Then he shook his head. What was wrong with him? Why was he being so indecisive? Maybe because there was nothing he could do. Why had he told the other voyagers he needed to stay? What could he possibly find? A piece of his parents? Heaven forbid! Or a clue to where they were taken? *Yeah, that's likely.* A clue *why* they were taken? No, Jaden knew why they had been taken.

Jaden most likely wouldn't find any clues, but that didn't mean he wasn't going to look.

Marshaling his thoughts, Jaden took his time getting downstairs. He searched the rooftop landing site first. Nothing was out of place. Had his parents still been up here when they were taken? Or had the time freeze effect been broken, and were they already back inside the house? How could the Gaptors have reached them there? Jaden would need to interview Pallaton.

Then Jaden remembered something else. The day Markov came to ask his questions, Markov "lost" them when they ran upstairs and the time freeze went into effect. But when the gliders passed from range, Markov had not been waiting in the kitchen where they left him. Instead, he joined them on the roof. Jaden allowed that to sink in for a moment. Did this corroborate his earlier observation that there were "windows" within a time freeze allowing for a pause between leaving and arriving?

Jaden opened the maintenance room door and went downstairs. No sign of windows or doors scratched up by talons. No sign of any disturbance in the house. No sign of his parents. Slumping onto the couch, Jaden realized he wouldn't learn how or when his parents had been taken and that he would drive himself crazy if he kept trying to figure it out. Dropping his head back, he closed his eyes. Then he lurched back up. The book might have a clue. Jaden dashed to his backpack and retrieved Awena's precious book, trying to control his impatience as he inspected each page thoroughly before turning to the next one. But there were no clues there either.

Why had he stayed? There were no clues, no indicators of where his parents had been taken. Or even that they had been taken. Could the Usurper have planned it so Jaden would think nothing was wrong? But no, there were all those dead Gaptors. *Something* had happened. Then again, did the Usurper know that his parents' capture hadn't been flawless? In fact, did the Usurper know Jaden knew that his parents had been taken and by whom?

Another thought struck Jaden. He leaped to his feet. Dashing from room to room, he searched for it. He looked on the kitchen table. He read the comm unit on the refrigerator. He checked his bedside table. And his PAL. He looked anywhere someone might have left it, where it would be in plain sight, where it would be clearly visible. But he found no ransom note.

How would the Usurper contact him? *Would* he contact Jaden, or did he have some other devious plan to draw Jaden to him so that Jaden wouldn't suspect he was being lured into a trap? Either way, what was Jaden going to do when Slurpy did? There was only one thing for it. They had to get back to the mission and complete it before the Usurper could message him.

But to complete the mission, he would need the team. What had he done? How had he permitted Atu and Iri to leave? Or was that another of the Usurper's ploys? To get Jaden so upset that he allowed the team to split up? Suddenly, Jaden had a very bad feeling. Iri and Atu might be in real danger. Jaden had to get Kayla. They had to leave.

CHAPTER SIXTEEN

Covertly, Iri watched Atu as they flew. The colors and hues floating around him rarely changed, and his scent remained odorless. She had seldom met someone with such an even temperament. Was he deliberately keeping it that way? Or maybe it was just who he was. Satinka veered right, and Iri grabbed at her neck fur. She had to pay more attention to her flying and less to the strange boy flying alongside her.

They flew in silence. It was strange to not have Taz barking orders. Aren and Satinka seemed content to just get where they were going without practicing any of the endless routines Taz always insisted on.

But that didn't sit well with Iri. Sure, flying was fun with the breeze whipping in your face, but it was dull. "Shouldn't we be practicing our routines?"

Atu looked at her as though she had lost her marbles. "Now why would you want to do that?"

"Aren't you bored just sitting here?"

"No, there's plenty to see if you just watch what's happening underneath you. And it's peaceful. It allows me time to think."

Iri wasn't getting anywhere with Atu. He was in his zone and quite happy to stay there. Appealing to Satinka, she said, "Don't you think training is important?"

"Of course. We trained with Pallaton every day."

"So, shouldn't we be doing that now?" Iri was irritated that Satinka wasn't picking up on the hint. When she sent Iri a curious glance, Iri realized Satinka had no clue what she was talking about. Satinka hadn't been around when Taz had made them practice all those routines. "Taz made us learn and practice routines each day when we flew. I think it would be worthwhile to keep those up. Besides, you need to learn what I have so that if we meet a Gaptor, you'll know the plays."

"Tazanna ordered us to get you to the Armorer without delay." Aren's explanation was unexpected. Atu's glider had appeared to be in the zone just like his voyager.

"Oh." Iri was momentarily speechless. "Taz said to not even practice on the way?"

"Practicing takes time. Flying in a straight line is faster than doing rolls and loops. And for some of us who repeatedly fall off," Aren intimated, "that would delay us even more. So no, we don't practice. We get you to the Armorer with no delays."

Iri slumped. How was she going to survive the tedium? "Atu, tell me about this Armorer."

Atu blinked, as though annoyed his meditations had been disrupted. But Iri didn't notice any of the colors she would've associated with the emotion. How was he doing that? She had never met anyone who could mask their emotions. "He's been a friend of my family's for a long time."

His placid tone made Iri reconsider. Maybe he wasn't annoyed. That would explain the lack of a color change. Satisfied, Iri listened as Atu elaborated.

When evening came, Iri groaned as she slid off Satinka. Incredibly, she was more exhausted than when Taz made them do all those strenuous exercises. *Must be the boredom factor.* Dinner was quickly dispensed with, and Iri slipped into her shell, grateful for sleep.

The air was noticeably cooler the next day. When Iri began shivering, Atu surprised her by calling for the break. Once on the ground, he pulled a jar from his ever-present pouch. Handing it to her, he said, "It will ward off the cold. Use it like a lotion on any exposed skin."

Dubiously, Iri took the jar but the fragrant lavender that escaped when she popped the lid set her at ease. Although she wasn't so sure about the goo a minute later when her skin began tingling and then burning.

"The effect will wear off," Atu said when she squirmed. His calm tone was unnerving, just like the colors around him that still hadn't changed.

The sameness was beginning to bother Iri. She would have to press him into some strong emotion to see if anything changed. If it didn't . . . well, at least she could confirm he had some way of tricking her senses.

Realizing that the unwelcome effect of the lotion had worn off, and she wasn't feeling the cold anymore, she relaxed. At least Atu didn't seem bent on harming her. Passing the jar back, Iri said, "Thanks."

Atu merely nodded, put the jar away, and then pulled out his lunch. Iri didn't know what to make of him. He had seemed so affable when they had first met. But his feelings towards her seemed to have cooled—or was that just her imagination? She couldn't think of a reason for the abrupt change in his behavior. With her senses potentially blind when it came to him, she would have to feel her way through things like a normal person.

The silence they had shared for most of the trip continued through to early the next afternoon when they arrived at the pass to Sven's home. By then, Iri wasn't feeling particularly benevolent toward Atu.

"We need to land and walk from here," Atu said.

"Why? There's nothing around for miles," Iri snapped.

"That's what we thought last time, and we were wrong." Atu's answer was calm as always.

As they landed, all Iri could think was that she wanted to wring Atu's neck. Couldn't he show a little emotion? About to prod him so see if she could rile him up, she paused when a shout echoed down the pass.

"Friends, you have returned!" Rushing towards them was a bear of a man, a grin plastered on his broad face.

The pink hues flaring around Atu were a balm to Iri's frayed nerves. At last! Some emotion! Atu rushed into the man's arms, embracing him. "Armorer! It is wonderful to see you again."

"And you." The man's Gotskienian accent was unmistakable. His eyes went to Iri and their gliders. "And who do you have with you this time?"

Atu was quick to make the introductions.

"Two new gliders and a new seeker. You've been busy while you were away," Sven said. "But come, let us return to my home so we may catch up where it's warm and comfortable, no?"

They weren't kidding about all Sven's traps, Iri thought some time later as she settled in his home with a cup of tea.

"Now, you will tell me more?" Sven asked, sitting down with his own drink.

Atu smiled and obliged. Iri watched Atu as he talked, disappointed that the colors around him had resumed their usual hues. But there had been that spike. Her senses weren't totally blind. She would just have to adjust to this level of emotion.

When Atu finished, Sven leaned back in his chair, smiling. "So, you are triumphant then!"

"Partly. We only have one of the three artifacts," Atu replied.

"Why have you returned?"

"We were wondering whether you had another smart suit and aerolator for Iri."

"And?" Sven prompted.

"Whether you could install some communication system in the suits so we can talk to one another more easily when flying?"

Sven slapped a meaty hand to his head. "Of course. That's something I should've thought of."

"And, if it's not too much trouble," Atu continued, "perhaps we could work on a way we can communicate with you without compromising safety? It would've been helpful if we could've communicated our needs to you before we arrived so that you had time to prepare."

Sven looked thoughtful for a moment. "That last request is more problematic." He noticed Atu's resigned expression. "But it is not insurmountable. Come, we eat and sleep, and then tomorrow we solve these problems, no?"

Grinning, Atu nodded, and Iri followed them into the kitchen.

"So Iri, you will tell me your story?" Sven asked as he began preparing dinner.

Iri hesitated. She was going to share her abilities with *another* person? Well, Sven was part of the team. And he would find out eventually. Taking a deep breath, Iri told him the fraction of her story that she had shared with the others. Afterwards, Iri dared to gauge Sven's reaction. She still felt shocked when Sven just nodded. How was she lucky enough to have found so many people in such a short time who accepted her just as she was?

The next morning, Iri woke refreshed and ready for the new day. Wandering into the kitchen, she was surprised to find she was the only one there. It was still early, but Atu had proven that he was an early riser. Sven didn't strike her as being one to tarry in the mornings either. After grabbing a yogurt out of the fridge, Iri strolled to the front door.

The snow outside sparkled in the early morning sunshine. The pristine white of the snow offset the dark greens of the fir and pine trees perfectly, and the air was redolent with their sharp scent. The quiet was almost eerie. But it was so peaceful. Then she heard muted banging. Following the sound, Iri found another building off to the side of the main house. It had a door but no handle to open it with. Eyeing the intercom next to the door, she pressed the button. Instead of an answering voice, the door clicked open.

Stepping inside, an array of machinery, pieces of tech, chemicals, lab equipment, and a wall of holoscreens confronted Iri. She was still trying to make sense of the confusing jumble when she heard Sven call to her. "You are up early, no? Were you uncomfortable? Too cold?"

"No, I slept well, thank you. I'm just an early riser. What is all this stuff?"

"Oh, this and that." Sven waved. "All things I need for tinkering in my workshop."

Iri nodded. "This is where the magic happens, then. What are you working on?"

"A communications system for your smart suits." Sven grinned, wiping his hands on a nearby towel. "Would you like to help me test it?"

Iri's eyes widened. "It's ready?"

"Of course. Is simple task. Here, your suit." Sven handed her a suit identical to those worn by the other voyagers.

"Thank you." Iri grinned, taking the suit and retreating into the bathroom Sven had indicated. When she reemerged a few minutes later, Sven handed her a rubber hood and the silver tube the others called an aerolator.

"Here, let me show you how to attach them." Sven leaned over and helped her. When the hood and aerolator were connected, Sven grinned. "Now where is your glider?"

Iri shrugged. "I have no idea. They seem to come and go at will."

Sven emitted a chuckle that sounded more like the distant rumble of an avalanche. "You haven't learnt yet that they will appear when you need them?"

Iri reddened. "I . . ."

Sven immediately stopped laughing. "I'm sorry. I did not mean to embarrass you. You will learn like the others, no?"

"I guess," Iri sighed.

"Come, we go outside," Sven suggested. "We see if your glider is there, no?"

It turned out he was right. Not only was Satinka waiting for her, but Aren floated nearby too. Why was he there? Did they always just fly in pairs?

"Good morning." Atu exited the house. "What are we up to?"

Atu's appearance answered Iri's question. "Sven wanted to test the comm system in the suits."

Atu gaped. "You're finished already?"

"It wasn't that difficult." Sven shrugged. "Will you join us?"

When Atu nodded, Sven herded them back to the workshop and showed Atu how to install the tiny wires and intercoms of the new tech. "I wish Jaden was here," Atu grumbled, "This is more in his wheelhouse."

"You will remember." Sven gave him an encouraging pat. "Is not that—"

"Difficult," Iri and Atu finished for him.

Chortling, Sven removed the system he had just installed and made Atu run through the installation on his own. Iri watched as his nimble fingers manipulated the tiny components. In seconds, he had the system installed to Sven's satisfaction.

"Is good now. You put hood on, and you and Iri go fly. We shall see how effective the system is."

Atu grinned, reattaching his hood. "Shall we?"

His smile distracted Iri. Had he always been so attractive, and she just hadn't noticed? Or was his disarming authenticity making her take a second look?

Atu quirked an eyebrow. Iri blushed. Had she been staring?

"Yes, let's go try these puppies," Iri blurted.

Turning, she loped outside, relieved to find Satinka had already taken to the air. When Satinka spotted her, she turned and came in for the aerial connection. Only when they were airborne did Iri register she hadn't asked Sven how to use the comm system. Was there a button?

"Hello?" Iri tested.

"Yeah, I can hear you loud and clear," Atu answered.

"As can I," Sven affirmed.

Iri glanced around, trying to find Atu and Aren. They were nowhere in sight. "Atu, where are you?"

"Aren and I flew in the opposite direction. We thought we'd test the range on this comm unit."

That sounded like something Jaden would've done. Iri wondered whether Atu had done this on his own at Sven's behest. "Okay, so how far away are you?"

"He is almost to the perimeter of my property." Sven sounded delighted. "Atu, you should turn back now. My defense system does not extend much further."

"Alright, I'll . . ."

Atu's sentence cut off.

"Atu?" Iri asked. "You still there?" Silence. Iri tried again. "Atu, speak to me. Sven, did he pass from range?"

Sven grunted. "No, it should be working. I need to check something." Sven's breathing changed. He was running somewhere. But where? Then she heard cursing. Well, it sounded like it, anyway. With Sven reverting to his native tongue, it was impossible to tell. But when his frantic English returned, she knew she'd been correct. "Iri, you need to go after Atu. My perimeter defenses have been triggered."

"What does that mean?" Iri asked, even as Satinka changed direction. *Huh, Satinka must have really good hearing. I didn't even have to tell her what Sven said.*

"We have company. And I think it's the kind we don't want."

"You mean Gaptors?" Iri's pulse spiked.

"Yes, I mean Gaptors," Sven barked. "Now get to that mountain pass that got you to my home!"

"Alright, no need to yell. Satinka and I are on our way."

"Can I fly faster now that you have the suit the other voyagers have?" The urgency in Satinka's voice alarmed Iri.

She had almost forgotten about the suit. Hesitantly, Iri said, "I think so."

Satinka's sudden burst of speed had Iri grabbing for a handhold, then sucking in a sharp breath when her smart suit yanked her upright again. When the hood crawled over her face, Iri shivered. Did it feel this creepy for the others as well? The hood snapped into place, and Iri blinked, adjusting to the goggles that now protected her eyes from the wind. She blinked several times as her eyes focused. She knew they had to be going really fast when the aerolator covered her mouth, allowing her more oxygen. Somehow, the speed didn't seem real. Wanting to test the suit, she moved her shoulders slightly, almost giggling when the suit moved her back to a more aerodynamic position. *Oh yeah, this is going to be fun!*

Her glee was cut short when she saw Aren and Atu ahead of them. Atu was slumped over Aren's back. "Atu? Atu! Speak to me!"

Atu didn't move, and Iri's concern shot off the chart. Frantically, she scanned for Gaptors.

"What's happening?" Sven's worried voice reminded Iri someone else could help.

"I don't know. Atu looks like he's hurt. He's not answering on his comm. Give me a second and Satinka and I will be close enough to ask Aren what happened." Iri hadn't finished her sentence when Satinka drew level with Aren.

"I couldn't dodge fast enough," Aren moaned. "The Gaptor's talon clipped Atu and he fell off. I caught him, but he's bleeding."

Iri winced at the wide gash slicing across Atu's forehead, angling from his right eyebrow across into his hairline. "We need to get him back to Sven's. Where's the Gaptor?"

Aren nodded behind him. The monster was enormous. And ugly. And lying in the snow as if thrown there by some unseen force. Its limbs were at odd angles, and the wings were a mess, twisted all over the place. It didn't move.

"Sven, how can I tell if this Gaptor's dead?" Iri worried that if she didn't confirm it, the Gaptor would magically revive and resume its attack.

"No need to worry about him," Sven informed her curtly. "He won't be a problem. How is Atu?"

"Good to know I don't need to worry. Yeah, Atu has a pretty bad cut on his head, but I think he'll be okay." Out of the corner of her eye, Iri saw Aren relax. She should've reassured the glider earlier. "We're on our way back. See you soon."

CHAPTER SEVENTEEN

Kayla sighed. Jaden hadn't said more than two sentences since they'd left. Worried, she scratched at her birthmark. The action drew Jaden's attention. "You still haven't explained that to me."

Finally! Something Jaden was interested in. "There really isn't that much to tell," Kayla began. Then, noticing the way Jaden hunched into himself, she sighed again. She would have to give him something. "Remember how I told you that my mom insisted that I learn that ancient language?" Jaden nodded. "Well, I fought her on the issue until I visited my grandmother and saw the books I would use to learn the language. The cover of each book had a strange symbol on it."

Jaden perked up. "The medallion?"

"No, but good guess. You want another?"

"It has something to do with this quest we're on?"

Kayla giggled. "Well duh! And you can't be that vague. Try again."

Jaden smiled. "Alright, give me a clue."

Kayla drank in the smile that had been absent for far too long. It drew some of the tension from his face and lit his eyes with mischief. Positively wicked! Her own face creased into a smile. "What were you just asking about?"

"Your birthmark." A heartbeat later, Jaden added, "That's what the symbol on the books was?"

"Yup. When I saw that, I was understandably more open to the idea of learning the language. I'm not sure if my mother or grandmother knew why I had changed my mind, but I think they thought they wouldn't ask in case I reneged."

Jaden grinned. "Good thing you didn't. We would have been well and truly sunk trying to find that first artifact if you hadn't been able to interpret the language."

A burden Kayla hadn't known she was carrying fell away. Seeing Jaden smiling again made her realize just how much she had missed his smile. And now that it had reappeared, she was petrified of chasing it away. What could she talk about that would keep it on his handsome face? Avoiding further talk about the birthmark was a start. She couldn't tell him the mark had meaning or what that meaning was. But what could she say? "Is there perhaps another way we can use the key you gave your parents?"

Jaden's startled expression warned her she had changed topics too quickly. Kayla held her breath. Would he analyze her answer and then quiz her further on her birthmark?

Jaden frowned. "Do you want to explain that?"

Swallowing her sigh of relief, Kayla realized Jaden nor pressing her about the birthmark meant he was more distracted than she'd thought. But she wasn't going to complain. "Well, you said that you had planned to use the key to find them. Just because you don't know where they are now doesn't mean you don't know where they were before they were taken."

The spark of interest in Jaden's eyes was encouraging. "You're saying I should go back to the time I gave my mom the key?"

"Yup. That's the one place you know you can find them." Even as she said the words, she saw Jaden's dismay. "What's wrong?"

"How is that going to help? It won't stop them from being taken." Jaden paused. When he continued, the words spilled out. "And my mom already knows there's a chance they'll be kidnapped. I won't be telling her anything she doesn't already know. The key was supposed to help me rescue them from wherever they were taken to. Going back in time isn't going to change what's already happened."

"Can't you tell her that you now know when they'll be taken and that she needs to leave you a clue—or clues—that you can follow?" Kayla spoke in desperation, hoping to reverse the pessimism that was taking hold again.

Her suggestion had the opposite effect. Jaden shrunk even further into himself. "Therein lies another problem. We can't communicate across timelines."

"I don't remember you saying that," Kayla began.

"I told you there was no interaction across timelines."

Kayla understood now. "And that includes communication."

"Yes."

Kayla was fresh out of ideas. And even if she could come up with one, she doubted she could drag Jaden from the mire a second time. The flash to her left surprised her. Taz dropped twenty feet in a split second and Kayla sucked in air. What was . . .? A bright light to her right. Jaden's DD.

An attack! Kayla whipped out her own DD. *Where's the Gaptor?*

"Five!" Jaden yelled.

Without thought, Kayla and Taz rolled into the play. Kayla's head tipped up as she watched Jaden and Han streak away to the left. She still couldn't find their attacker. Or attackers. "Did you see the Gaptor?" Kayla asked Taz.

"Barely," Taz muttered. "It appeared out of nowhere again."

"You never did explain how they do that!"

"I'm just as much in the dark as you. I think the comment one of you made about them appearing like that because they were coming through the breach is the most likely explanation."

"But how would they know where to come through? Surely the Usurper hasn't devised a way to open the gate at exact locations on our world?"

"Who knows what he's been able to come up with during the time he's been in hiding. A more disturbing question is how he's able to pinpoint our location. We know his minions can track your medallions here in this world. But how is he able to do that from our world? It is information we need to pass on to Zareh."

"You have a way to communicate with him?" Kayla squeaked.

"Yes, indirectly. There is a place we can leave him coded messages."

"And you're only just thinking to tell me this now?" Kayla was miffed that Taz hadn't trusted them with this information before.

Taz hesitated. "I apologize. It hadn't occurred to me that you might like to know."

Kayla was stunned. An apology from Taz. That was—

Bam! The Gaptor struck with enough force to throw Kayla off. She flailed; then her smart suit kicked in, and she regained control of her limbs. Tumbling into the forward-facing position that would make it easier for Taz to pick her up, Kayla turned her head, alert for approaching Gaptors. There he was. Coming straight for her and raising his antennae again. Silly beast.

The current that zinged through her body was as unexpected as it was unpleasant. Kayla jerked, her body reacting to the current. It felt like ice cold gel flowing over her, numbing every spot it touched. Within nanoseconds, she was totally encased. She couldn't feel a thing. She had no control over any part of her body. *What's happening to me?*

When Taz crashed into her, Kayla was aware of the motion only because of the sound. It was sickening. Had Taz been injured, too? There was no time to find out. Kayla bounced off Taz into open air again. Even her smart suit seemed to have lost the ability to help her. Kayla struggled to see how far from the ground she was, but the tiny muscles around her eyes refused to work. As she tumbled over to face the ground, Taz bashed into her a second time. That impact was going to hurt when feeling returned.

Kayla wanted to scream with frustration when she slid off Taz yet again. But why wasn't she scared? It was as though her mind had been numbed with the rest of her body. Like this was happening to someone else and she was just a spectator. Hopefully she wouldn't feel the panic—or pain—when she smooshed herself all over the ground.

Kayla didn't feel Jaden's arms slipping around her. She was only aware it was happening because his arms passed across her limited vision for a second. Then she heard his voice, close to her ears. Was he pressing his head against hers?

"Got you!"

How is that going to help? Kayla wondered. *Neither of us is on a glider, so we'll both die now instead of just me.*

Han loomed under them. Kayla heard the crunch as they landed. Hopefully that wasn't Jaden taking the punishment. Han cursed, so no, Jaden hadn't. Jaden was trying to tuck her between his arms; her head lolled as he moved her. Her frozen eyes caught his worried frown, then open sky, then his chest. And her vision remained fixed there, so he must've maneuvered her into a position he was satisfied with. If only she could demand a position where she could see what was happening. But her voice didn't work any more than the rest of her body did.

She'd have to settle for using her ears. Straining to hear past the roar of the wind, she caught nothing for what seemed like an eternity. Abruptly, the wind calmed from a roar to a whisper. Kayla wanted to move more than anything, but she was still paralyzed. Then her eyes caught the sky. Jaden was moving her again. *Are we being attacked?*

"It's alright. Calm down," Jaden reassured her.

Kayla could see his hand moving past her eyes. Was he holding her face or moving her hair from it? *Ugh, this is so infuriating!*

"We're on the ground. I'm going to set you down so we can figure out what's wrong."

On the ground? How did Han land with two of us? Oh no, are Han and Taz alright?

Jaden must've sensed her agitation. "Han and Taz are fine. And the Gaptors are dead." Again, she must've communicated something non-verbally, because he added, "There were only two."

The sky changed back to his chest for a moment. Then she caught sight of his face, and he bent over her. The blue sky returned. Kayla wanted Jaden to stay where she could see him. Instead, Han and Taz's familiar faces appeared in the space. Han was worried. Taz was . . . perplexed.

"I don't understand what's wrong with her," Taz said.

"Here, let's put this back on," Jaden said.

The sky moved. Something shiny passed in front of her eyes. The sky settled back where it had been. Why didn't they talk to her?

Jaden obviously understood her unspoken plea. "You lost your medallion when the Gaptor knocked you off Taz. I just put it back on."

And that's helpful to know because? Why are they all looking at me like that?

"It's not helping," Han rumbled.

Jaden's face appeared in her line of vision. "Kayla, can you hear me?"

What does he expect me to do? Suddenly start talking again?

"Can you blink?" Jaden asked.

Some of Kayla's agitation left. He was answering all the questions she would've asked. He understood her. The knowledge settled her.

"Kayla?"

Oh yes, I'm supposed to try blinking. Kayla concentrated. Was she blinking?

Jaden sighed and disappeared from sight again. "I believe she can hear us. But it's like the rest of her is paralyzed."

Duh! Can you just figure out why already?

"Let's think this through. Taz, you said when the Gaptor attacked, he seemed to deliberately go for Kayla's medallion?"

When did Taz tell him that? Is that what happened?

"Yes. The Gaptor was so focused on Kayla's medallion, he left himself open to attack. When he extended his talon to rip the medallion off, it was easy to sink my teeth into his neck."

Jaden nodded. "He died for the medallion. Do you think the Gaptors were trying to take possession of it, like the original Gaptor used to?"

"I don't think so. When the medallion fell free, the other Gaptor didn't chase after it. Instead, he approached Kayla slowly."

"So why would they try and get the medallion, but then leave it to drop as soon as it fell off?" Jaden wondered.

Kayla remembered that Gaptor approaching. Then she remembered *how* he had approached. With his antennae raised. Was that relevant?

"Why did the Gaptor leave Kayla unharmed?" Han muttered.

"Pardon?" Jaden's sharp tone would've made Kayla smile. He was getting all protective over her.

Han rushed to reassure Jaden. "Not that I'm complaining. I meant that it had to take considerable skill for him to place his talon to get the medallion off without even breaking her skin. And he was willing to sacrifice himself in the process."

"Most abnormal," Taz said. "You're right, Han. He made a concerted effort to leave Kayla unharmed. Why?"

"Taz, you said the Gaptor approached Kayla slowly. Were his antennae raised?" Jaden asked.

Now we're getting somewhere. Our minds are definitely in sync.

"Yes, but I don't see how that's relevant. They always do that before they attack."

"And the first time they did that, in our first battle with them, I remember how confused they were," Jaden said. "Like they were expecting something to happen, and it didn't. I think the reason they left Kayla unharmed was to test a theory."

Spit it out already, Jaden!

"And that was?" Taz snapped.

"Whether they could use their EMP on her." When Taz looked skeptical, Jaden explained. "I'm pretty sure that when they raise their antennae, they're using that EMP weapon of theirs. But you and Han must be impervious to its effect, or you would've known that that was what they were doing and warned us about it. I'm guessing that when Zareh made the medallions, he put something in them that would also nullify the effects."

"That's plausible," Taz admitted. "How does that help Kayla, though?"

Atta girl! Kayla cheered silently.

Jaden floated into Kayla's line of vision again as he scrubbed a hand over his face. He looked utterly defeated. Kayla wanted to reach up and . . . *Jaden, please, come up with a solution already!* As the plea crossed her mind, Kayla saw Jaden stiffen. *What now?*

"If the relic stones can destroy the Gaptors, do you think they can remove the Gaptor's EMP effect?" But Jaden wasn't waiting for an answer. Kayla saw him lift her left hand in the air above her. Then her right hand. "Where is Kayla's relic stone?"

"She normally keeps it in her bag when she isn't wearing it," Taz replied.

Kayla heard her backpack being upended while Jaden muttered about her keeping her best weapon packed away. Then Jaden appeared over her, deliberately putting her hand right in front of her face as he slid the ring on.

The ice that encased her receded the same way it encroached. The first thing she felt was the throbbing pain in her cheekbone, where she had smashed into Taz when Taz tried to pick her up. The pain went from throbbing to flaring. Sensation ebbed back into the rest of her limbs.

Jaden hovered over her, eyeing her like a hawk. She smiled. His answering smile was like a slice of heaven touching her soul. Lifting her arms, she pulled his head down towards hers and kissed him thoroughly. Kayla didn't care if the gliders were watching. Jaden did, though, because he drew back, looking sheepish as he glanced their way.

"Thank you for solving that," Kayla said. "You have no idea how aggravating it was to not be able to do anything."

Jaden grinned. "Of course."

Kayla studied their gliders, who were still watching her anxiously. "I'm alright. Thank you for all you did to save me too. Without you, I would've just been a red splotch on the ground."

Taz visibly relaxed. Han flashed that toothy smile that had scared her so much when they first met. Kayla felt renewed. It was good to be back in the game. "We have a leg up on those monsters again." Kayla grinned.

"How so?" Jaden asked.

"They think they know that if we don't have medallions, they can use their EMPs on us. What they don't know is that the relic stones negate that. So even if they come after our medallions, they still don't have a way of winning!"

The effect of her words on Jaden was not what she had expected. He went very still. An expression flitted across his face so fast Kayla almost didn't catch it. It was gone before she could interpret it, replaced by a grin and a chuckle. "Yes, we do have a leg up on them."

But Kayla wondered if they were still on the same page. In fact, Kayla was sure Jaden was in a different book. What was he plotting now?

CHAPTER EIGHTEEN

Jaden kept a close eye on Kayla as they resumed their journey. Although she appeared totally recovered, a fact he was grateful for, he was worried about latent effects. Hours later Kayla still showed no indication of being otherwise affected, and Jaden relaxed, reviewing the morning's events.

Their brief interaction with the two attacking Gaptors hadn't been like a normal fight. Was that more or less troubling? Only two Gaptors had come after them to test the Usurper's theory, and that was also disturbing. Surely the Usurper would've sent more Gaptors if he really wanted an answer? And why did they only attack Kayla? Had her medallion been visible, making her the target? As always, there were more questions than answers. But he could get an answer to one question now.

"Han, how many Gaptors are there in your world?"

Han shrugged. "It's difficult to say."

"Tell me in general terms then. Are there more Gaptors than gliders? And approximately how many more or less?"

"It's not like that. When we encounter Gaptors, we eradicate them. They are aberrations that shouldn't be allowed to exist. Because they are hunted, Gaptors hide and avoid inhabited areas. This is why it is difficult."

"You're saying, then, that it's possible there could be five or ten or fifty times the number of Gaptors than gliders, and you wouldn't know?"

"It's possible," Han admitted. "Our world is extensive, and there are many places the Usurper could hide a force that size without it being noticed."

"Don't you think you should find out, then, if such a force exists? I mean, if that many could be hidden, what are our chances if they come here?"

"Zareh is close to a solution for that," Taz chimed in.

Jaden hadn't noticed the girls had drifted closer. "A solution to what? Finding out the size of the force there or stopping that force from coming here?"

"I believe he's found a way to track the Gaptors. Right before we left our world, Zareh told us he had discovered that the Gaptors emit a unique frequency from their bodies. Zareh's technicians are designing a machine that can ferret that frequency out. When that machine becomes operational, he will have a means of finding the Gaptor nests and destroying them."

"Do you know if the machine is operational yet or whether the nests have been destroyed?" Jaden quizzed.

Taz shook her head. "Unfortunately not."

"Then we're back to where we started," Jaden muttered. "Up a creek without a paddle."

Kayla broke in. "Do you think Atu, Iri, and their gliders are okay?"

The abrupt change in subject reminded Jaden of their current mission. Or rather, their most pressing one. While their end goal remained elusive, this was something tangible they could act on right now. "I'm thinking that if the Usurper only sent two gliders after us, maybe he only sent two after Iri and Atu as well, which bodes well for their chances."

"I hope so," Kayla worried. "Taz, how much longer until the pass?"

"We're almost there."

In less than ten minutes they crossed into the valley that would lead them to the pass, allowing access to Sven's home. As they drew near the entry point, Jaden said, "Let's land and enter on foot."

The gliders did as he suggested, and the four of them began the long walk up the pass. It wasn't long before they found the dead Gaptor.

"Oh no!" Kayla cried, running forward. "You were right. The Gaptors came after them too."

Jaden's mouth set in a grim line. "This is what I was afraid of if we split up. Come on, let's hurry. We need to find Iri and Atu."

"How much further before we can fly again?" Han puffed.

He and Taz were stoic about having to hop up the pass, but Jaden knew it was tiring. "Sorry, friend, but I have no idea how far Sven's gun can send that weird ray that affected you last time. Do you think you can last a little longer?"

"There is no need for that," a familiar voice boomed from a nearby boulder.

Jaden almost jumped out of his skin. Han actually fell sideways, which made Jaden want to laugh, but that would embarrass his glider. Stifling the grin that threatened to break free at any moment, he crossed to the boulder and inspected it. A speaker had been concealed in a sheltered crevice. "It's good to hear your voice, Sven."

"And yours, my friend. But this is not the best place for us to catch up, no? You and your gliders will fly to my home, as quickly as possible." Jaden didn't like the sound of that last sentence. Sven had sounded tense, as though there was a reason they should hurry.

"Sven, are Iri and Atu with you?"

"They are. But come. You get here, and then you can see them for yourselves, no?"

Jaden flicked his gaze toward Kayla. Her frown confirmed she had picked up on the unspoken message. "Han, buddy, let's do what the man said."

Han and Taz were only too eager to oblige, but not so elated that they didn't pick up on Jaden and Kayla's tension. "Are you going to tell me what's wrong?" Han asked Jaden as soon as they were airborne.

"I would if I could. I only know there's something Sven isn't telling us. So let's get there so we can find out what it is."

Soon, their gliders were dropping them in the open area they had used for testing the relic stones. Jaden and Kayla sprinted for the house. By the time they got there, their gliders were tucking their wings behind them on the side of the house where they had access to the interior. Together, the four of them entered Sven's home.

The first thing Jaden noticed was the blood. It was on the floor. It was on the couch. It was on the rags that had been tossed aside in the kitchen. Jaden glanced at Sven, standing in the middle of the living room floor. "Sven, you'd better tell me right now where Iri and Atu are or . . ."

"Still as hot-headed as ever," Iri murmured from somewhere near the couch.

Kayla beat Jaden there. The sight that met them was not entirely unanticipated after all the blood, but it was a lot better than they imagined. Atu sat propped up on the couch, a bandage around his head and a glass of something nasty in his hand.

"That looks disgusting," Kayla commented.

Atu grinned. "It is. But it will heal my injury faster than anything else. It's nice to see you too."

Kayla laughed. "And I suppose that was meant to shame me into saying hello and all the pleasantries that go along with it?"

Atu chuckled. "It was."

Kayla leaned down and gingerly hugged Atu. "It's wonderful to see you. And you too, Iri." Kayla turned to her for a hug with more substance to it. Iri grinned self-consciously, and Kayla crossed to Sven, hugging him as well.

Jaden watched Kayla move effortlessly between the members of the team, passing along light and hope. He was proud that he wasn't jealous when she hugged the male members of their group. Then he realized it was more because of who she was than any emotion he was capable of controlling. Yes, she was certainly special.

Motivated to act in a similar fashion, Jaden stepped closer and touched Atu's shoulder. "It's a relief to see that you fared better than that Gaptor."

"Yes, that is a rather nice bonus," Atu grinned. "Did you pass him on your way in?"

As if their conversation had reminded Sven of something, he rushed from the room, returning a few minutes later with a bunch of electronics piled high on a cart.

"What's this?" Jaden asked, wandering over so he could inspect the items.

Kayla grinned. "Can't keep you away from tech, can we?"

Jaden laughed. "I wasn't the one who asked to see it. Sven rolled this right in front of me like a dessert cart in a restaurant. Can you blame me for wanting to taste?"

"I suppose not." Kayla giggled.

While Sven set up the equipment around them, the four teens exchanged news.

"Wait, you were attacked too?" Atu asked, trying to sit up straighter. "Were either of you injured?"

Jaden assured Atu that he and Kayla were both okay, then went on to give more details about the attack, the assumptions they had made, and the conclusions they had reached.

"Those rings of yours gain value each time I see you," Sven commented, sitting back and wiping a meaty hand over his forehead. "Let me show you my latest application of their power."

Jaden felt his fingers curl around his ring. Sven didn't want to use it again, did he?

As though sensing Jaden's possessiveness, Sven beamed. "No, you do not have to share your ring with me. I have used the same power I created for your DDs and converted it. See for yourselves!"

Throwing up an enormous holoscreen along the far wall, Sven indicated they should watch. At first, all they saw was a snowy landscape. Then the downed Gaptor came into view.

"You've not only set up a communication system for entry into that pass, you've installed cameras too?" Jaden whistled.

"Yes, but that's not what I want to show you." Sven sounded impatient. "Watch!"

As the teens did, a bright, white beam sliced across the screen. It hit the Gaptor, an explosion of black smoke puffing up. When the cloud cleared, there was no sign of the Gaptor.

Jaden took a moment to process what he'd seen. "You made a cannon to fire the beam?"

Sven clapped his hands in delight. "I did!"

Jaden chuckled. "Sven, you're the most remarkable man I think I've ever met!"

Sven beamed. When the rest of them added their praises, his face turned pink with pleasure. "Just something I had to try with all you nonsenses leaving me on my own. I had to find something to keep me occupied."

Kayla giggled. "Sven, with your mind, I don't think you'll ever run out of things to keep you occupied."

Sven rubbed a finger along his jaw. "Yes, I think you are right. Now if I can turn this into a missile, we'll be golden."

Jaden nodded. "If anyone can do that, it's you. But before we get sidetracked, have Iri and Atu had a chance to tell you why we came?"

"Iri already has her suit, hood, and aerolator, and we were in the process of testing the comm system when they were attacked."

"Just as well we had the system, or things might not have gone so well," Iri commented.

Talk shifted to more general matters after that, then toward thoughts of food as the dinner hour approached. The teens helped Iri find her way around the kitchen, and they prepared dinner as they updated Sven on their adventures.

"Now, if we'd had a way to communicate with you after we left, you would've known all this already," Jaden hinted. "It would also have allowed us to let you know that we were returning and given you advance warning of what our needs were."

Sven chuckled. "Yes, I believe that isn't the first time you've mentioned that, no? But setting up a system where we can communicate so that the signal won't be intercepted by either the people who are looking for me, or by this Usurper, assuming he is capable of such technology, is the difficult part. I will think on it some more. If there is a way it can be done, I will do it. You are correct that we should be able to communicate with each other while we are apart. That way, I can keep you informed of any new weapons I develop that would be useful on this quest."

"Now *that* would be handy," Jaden agreed.

Atu yawned. "It's bedtime for me. Sleep is nature's best way of curing what ails us. Can someone help me to my room?"

Sven rose. "Of course! Then I will prepare another room for the girls."

"Sven, there are enough bunk beds in there for all of us to sleep on two per night if we wanted. We'll make do, thank you," Kayla assured him, placing a hand on his arm and giving him a warm smile.

"We shall retire then and catch up some more tomorrow?"

"Yes," Jaden answered for all of them. "We could all use the rest."

It didn't take long for the teens to settle into their old routine. They showed Iri where everything was as they went along, sharing some of the funny things that happened the last time. While they didn't rush, they didn't take their time either. They were eager to get some sleep.

When Jaden woke the next morning, he felt more refreshed than he had in days. He wasn't sure whether it was the mountain air or the exercise or them actually doing something that lifted his spirits, but he was thankful for it. Kayla might stop looking at him with her worried face now. Jaden glanced at his PAL, surprised to find it was mid-morning. Well, at least they hadn't woken up to explosions as had happened on their last trip here. *Small mercies.*

Noticing the others were still asleep, he dressed and slipped out of the room, heading for the kitchen. He wasn't surprised to find it empty. Sven was probably in his workshop, designing some new marvel. Jaden helped himself to breakfast, almost dropping the bowl when he turned to find Iri right behind him. "Way to sneak up on a guy!"

Iri grinned. "You were being so noisy, it was impossible not to."

Jaden grunted. "Cereal's in this cupboard. Yogurt, milk, and eggs are in the fridge. Bread is in the bin over there on the counter. Knock yourself out."

Jaden felt Iri watching him as he padded toward the table and took a seat. He took a mouthful of cereal. "Quit staring at me." He slurped back the milk that threatened to run out of his mouth. "What do you want?"

"It's nice to know you have such perfect table manners." Iri put a bowl of cereal together for herself and took a seat opposite him.

"And you didn't answer my question."

Iri didn't immediately respond. Jaden watched as she moved the cereal around in her bowl, not really eating it. How long would he have to wait before she told him what was on her mind?

"I know we should be getting on with our next mission, but do you think we could perhaps stay here? I mean, for even a day or two? We don't have to stay very long."

Jaden leaned back and eyed her, waiting. She was ogling him in that strange way she had. What was she seeing and smelling on him with those senses of hers?

It must've been positive, because she resumed speaking. And this time, the words tumbled out of her. "Satinka and I haven't really had much time to get used to flying together—only the short time it took to get here. And then she and Aren said that Taz had told them that we shouldn't take any time doing routines. We did that, but when Atu was attacked and Satinka and I went to find him, all I could think was that I didn't have a weapon, that I didn't remember the plays, and that Satinka wouldn't know any of the things I could or couldn't do. I didn't know if I was even going to be able to help Atu when we reached him."

The torrent stopped so suddenly, Jaden blinked. He was about to speak when Iri added, "And I don't like not knowing what to do or feeling helpless."

Jaden gave it a beat. "I think that a day or two here getting you and Satinka caught up would be an excellent use of our time." Iri's shoulders relaxed. "Besides, we don't even know where we're going yet.

And Sven will no doubt want to teach you how to use a DD before he lets you loose with it." A hint of a smile tugged at the corners of Iri's mouth. "And what's with this Satinka business? Give her a nickname already!"

Iri giggled. Jaden leaned back, pleased he had been able to pull her from whatever uncertain place she had been in. "Alright." She thought for a moment. "How about Tinks?"

Jaden guffawed. "Oh yeah, that'll be perfect."

Iri chuckled. "Yeah, she's so formal. I can't wait to see her face when we tell her."

"Whose face and tell her what?" Kayla asked.

Jaden turned, still grinning. His breath caught. She always looked so angelic in the morning. Her hair was all over the place as usual, not yet tidied into the ponytails she preferred while they were flying, and her eyes were still half closed with sleep. Despite this, they itched with curiosity. Did Kayla think Iri and Jaden had been discussing her?

"Satinka's face when we tell her that her nickname is Tinks," Jaden supplied hurriedly. When Kayla's face morphed into a wicked smile, Jaden took a mental picture. This was how he wanted to remember her. Always.

"I don't know if that's going to fly." Kayla giggled. "But I'd like to be there when you tell her."

CHAPTER NINETEEN

Kayla gaped when Atu entered the kitchen. His head bore no sign of injury.

"Dude, you're all better!" Jaden exclaimed when he saw Atu.

"You didn't think I would be?"

"I told Kayla this a while back, but I'll say it again since it's still true. The only thing I can expect on this mission is the unexpected."

Still not believing her eyes, Kayla closed in on Atu and took his head in her hands. After a thorough inspection of the area, she declared, "Incredible! You really have to tell me some day how you get things to heal so fast."

Atu only laughed. "So what's for breakfast?"

"Whatever you dig out of the cupboard," Iri informed him.

Muttering, Atu made for the refrigerator.

"What's that?" Kayla asked.

"I said, considering we all survived attacks yesterday and that this is the first day we're all back together again, we should at least share a decent breakfast."

With that, he slapped cheese, milk, peppers, onions, and bacon on the table. When Kayla saw the eggs in his hands, she dashed over and rescued the carton before he could slam it down as well. "Atu, what's wrong?"

He stood still for a second before crumpling into a chair. Then he stared blankly for a long time. "I could've died yesterday. And I wouldn't have rescued my folks yet."

Kayla sat next to Atu. Pulling his hands into her own she held them until he looked at her. "But you didn't die. And you have us to help you find your parents." Although Atu nodded, he didn't speak. Kayla wasn't sure this was helping. Atu needed something to *do*. Knowing someone was on your side was all well and good, but sitting around just made you feel helpless. Kayla glanced at Jaden, relieved when he understood the plea in her eyes.

"You just going to leave all these ingredients sitting there? How about you and I make that breakfast you mentioned?" Jaden goaded.

Atu studied Jaden. For a moment, Kayla didn't think he would accept. Then he sighed heavily. "Yeah, alright."

Iri picked up on Atu's emotions and Kayla's intentions with those senses of hers. She leaned back in her chair and deliberately pushed her bowl of cereal aside. "I could get used to this."

Kayla grinned and winked at Jaden. "Yes, boys, let's see what you can cook up!"

Jaden gave her one of his glorious grins. His mouth quirked so perfectly at the corners that Kayla was tempted to kiss him, then and there. But she resisted the urge. It'd undo all the work she, Iri, and Jaden had begun.

When Jaden continued staring back, Kayla realized he was stuck in his own thoughts about her. Or she hoped so. Despite the happy bubble that surged inside her, Jaden needed to get back on task. When Atu poked his head in the refrigerator, Kayla gave Jaden a quick shooing motion and furious stare. He blinked and began discussing breakfast options with Atu.

Slowly, they drew Atu into the conversation. By the time the boys served breakfast, Atu's depression had retreated, and he was somewhat back to normal. Although, since he was so quiet by nature, it was difficult to tell where his head was at. As she studied Atu, Kayla concluded this was a contented quiet, so she relaxed. When Atu turned away for another plate of food, Kayla smiled at Jaden and Iri and mouthed, "Thanks."

"So, what are our plans?" Atu took his seat and tucked into his food.

Kayla almost choked. *Atu* was the one to raise the subject? Swallowing, she recovered from her bout of coughing. "I think Jaden and Iri have that covered."

When Jaden said nothing, Kayla gave him a pointed look. "Uh, Iri and I were discussing that earlier. She mentioned that she'd like some time to get used to her smart suit. She also wants to learn how to use her DD and practice with it. Then we need to get Tinks caught up on our plays—" Jaden broke off when Atu began laughing.

"Tinks?" Atu sputtered. "That's what you're going to call her?"

"What's wrong with it?" Iri challenged.

"Oh, it's perfect. I just want to see her face when you tell her." Atu chortled.

"You and everyone else." Iri grinned. "We'll do that as soon as we see them today."

"Let's just make sure we've had some time to let our food settle before we summon them," Jaden begged. "I'd hate to spoil a good meal by going flying right afterwards."

The others agreed, and they finished breakfast, their levity restored. Afterwards, they went in search of Sven. They decided they would start their day teaching Iri how to use her DD. Then they would run her through the training programs Sven had made them do so she could get accustomed to her smart suit and acquire some self-defense skills. After that, they would take stock and make further plans accordingly.

As it happened, they spent the whole day on the ground because their gliders didn't reappear. Not that any of them were too concerned. It gave the voyagers time to bond without their gliders. Sven even spent time with them—first instructing Iri on the safe use of her DD, then later when he donned his own smart suit and showed the teens the mat in hand-to-hand combat. The teens were still commenting on Sven's ability (and surprising agility) when they ended their day, tired but happy. Entering the house, they discovered Sven had another surprise for them in the form of a traditional Gotskienian dinner, all ready and waiting to be eaten.

"Sven, you magician! How is it we got so lucky with you?" Jaden clapped the big man on the back.

Sven's booming laughter rumbled around them. "I think it's the other way around. But we won't argue, no? We eat?"

"Absolutely," Atu affirmed with enough enthusiasm to make everyone laugh.

The evening was just as pleasant as the day. Kayla wasn't the only one reluctant to leave the table.

"I wish we didn't have to be responsible and get some sleep." Kayla groaned. "But if we don't, what's the bet Taz will be here at the crack of dawn to whip us through our training regimen?"

"A bet not even worth taking," Jaden answered. "Sven, thank you for a wonderful day and that delicious meal." The other teens added their thanks before they succumbed to bedtime routines.

Kayla slept soundly and opened her eyes the next morning, refreshed. But when she saw Jaden pacing their room, antsy and irritable, she knew today wouldn't be so easy. A fact that was confirmed when she discovered that their gliders were already outside waiting for them before they'd even had breakfast.

"What was that you were saying last night about Taz being here to whip us into shape today?" Jaden grumbled.

Kayla only nodded. Jaden's early morning pacing had her worried. Iri, on the other hand, looked like she would ricochet out of her chair before she'd even finished the breakfast they were scarfing down.

"Why are you so excited?" Kayla asked.

"We get to see how Tinks reacts to her nickname," Iri bubbled.

That brought a round of smiles. *At least we have something to look forward to.*

Predictably, when Iri bounded out of the house and greeted her with, "Heya, Tinks! What's up?" Satinka's face was priceless.

Tinks finally found her voice after her expression had gone from confused to taken aback to carefully studied. "If by Tinks you're referring to me, then I am well. May I ask why you are using that name?"

Taz spoiled their fun then. "Because that's what they do—take a perfectly good name and shorten it to something they think is endearing. Don't let it bother you. It means they like you. Now, shall we get to practicing? Satinka has a lot of catching up to do."

And that was the end of it. A merciless training session followed. Kayla struggled to keep her mind on what they were doing. She kept worrying about Jaden, who seemed even more distracted than she was. What was going on in that head of his?

* * *

Jaden's mind kept circling back to Kayla's encounter with the Gaptors. Something was niggling at the back of his mind, something to do with the relic stones and their ability to nullify the numbing effects of the Gaptor's EMP. The numbing effects. Yes, that was it!

When his mother relayed her dream, she mentioned that when she woke up, she felt numb. She couldn't move or speak. But she could smell his father. And hear him. That sounded a lot like what Kayla had experienced. Could that be what happened to his parents? That this was how they were subdued?

Excitement tingled in his veins. He was onto something. Han flipped, and Jaden fell off. He hadn't been paying nearly enough attention to what Han was doing or Taz's instructions. Jaden relaxed, allowing his smart suit to turn him into the required pickup position. Han floated up under him, and they connected. Without a word, Jaden scooted back to his usual position.

"What was that?" Han asked.

"I fell off." Jaden wasn't in the mood for a lecture. He was trying desperately to hang onto the idea taking shape.

"I know that," Han snapped. "Why?"

Jaden held back the sigh. "Because I wasn't paying attention."

"And what happens when you do that?" Taz asked sternly, coming in fast and positioning herself to get up in his face.

"I put myself and everyone else at risk," Jaden replied by rote. He reined in his irritation. It would only result in a longer lecture.

But surprisingly, Taz didn't pursue the error. "I'm sure I don't need to expand on the gravity of your lapse in judgement?" When Jaden gave a shocked nod, she said, "Excellent, because we still have a lot of work to do. Get your head in the game, and we can all end the day early."

End the day early? Really? Jaden doubted that would happen. Taz was *such* a perfectionist. But he would do as she asked, although not before committing his thoughts to something more permanent than memory. "Can you give me a moment to make some notes and then you'll have my undivided attention?"

Taz wasn't the only one to give him a curious glance. Kayla's sage green eyes lingered speculatively. Could she guess what he was thinking? No, that wasn't possible. But Kayla always knew when he was up to something, so without question, he would have some explaining to do when they landed. Taz shrugged, then gave a quick nod of assent before moving toward Tinks.

Jaden dictated his thoughts into a note on his PAL, aware Han could hear every word. At least the others couldn't hear thanks to the mute button Sven had built into the comm system.

When he finished, Han looked back at him, his eyes grave. "Is this something you're really considering?"

"Yes, but please don't tell the others. I need to work out the details before I share the idea with them."

"As long as you do share it with them before you take action, I'll keep your secret."

"Thanks, Han." Jaden smiled, giving his glider a vigorous rub around his shoulders.

"And if I didn't know any better, I'd think you were trying to bribe me with that neck rub," Han grunted.

Jaden laughed. "No, I'm just showing some gratitude. But we'd better get back to following her highness's orders or we'll be back in the dog box."

Jaden wasn't sure, because Han turned his head, but had that question surprised Han? As Taz began yelling orders, the question was swept away, and Jaden threw himself into their training.

The comm system was marvelous. It would be useful when the smoke from destroyed Gaptors filled the air, like when they were attacked near the temple. Jaden's delight only increased when he discovered they could range further apart, allowing more maneuvers. They trained Iri and Tinks on the basics, then began working on enhancements.

Jaden was just getting to grips with the new scenarios when Taz called it a day. "Don't look so startled," Taz told him when she and Kayla zipped past. "I did say we would end early if you applied yourselves. And you did."

Jaden could only shake his head and watch as Taz and Kayla took the lead. They were home in minutes, and the teens gratefully leaped off when their gliders swooped down near Sven's home.

"Well, the day went better than I thought it was going to," Jaden commented.

"Yes, finishing early is always a bonus." The way Kayla grinned made Jaden wonder what she was up to. "Now that the gliders aren't with us anymore, are you going to tell us what had you so distracted this morning? And about those notes you made on your PAL?"

Oh yes, he had forgotten. "Why don't we get dinner on the table, and I'll tell you while we eat?"

"I can live with that."

CHAPTER TWENTY

An hour later, dinner was ready, but Sven hadn't joined them yet. Accustomed to his unusual work habits, the teens didn't wait. They took their places at the table, tucked into their food, and listened as Jaden outlined his idea. "I'm going to go back in time and see if there's another way I can help my parents."

Kayla's face scrunched up. "Not this again! I thought we'd decided that wasn't possible. And even if it is, you can't pull them through from the parallel universe or wherever it is you go when you use the arcachoa. I also distinctly remember you saying you can't communicate with them across timelines either!"

Jaden held up a hand to stop her tirade. She glared, and he sighed. "Didn't I promise that if I was going to make plans that I would discuss them with all of you first?" Kayla raised her eyebrows. "So this is me keeping that promise. Just because I'm floating an idea doesn't mean I'll actually do it."

That calmed Kayla. She gave him a tight smile, leaning back in her chair and folding her arms. "Okay, so let's hear what this plan is, then."

Yup, she's definitely already biased against it. Aloud, he said, "So you know how the relic stones counter the numbing effects of the Gaptor's EMP?" Nods all around. "When my mom told Kayla and I about her dream, she said the first thing she remembered after waking up was that she was numb. She couldn't move or speak, but she could hear and smell. Sound familiar, Kayla?"

Kayla blinked. "That sounds exactly how I felt after the Gaptor zapped me. You think that's what happened to your folks?"

"I do. And I think if I can get the relic stone to them before they're taken, they'll be able to counter those numbing effects."

"How will that help?" Iri asked.

"If they aren't numb, perhaps they'll be able to escape." Jaden anxiously twisted his relic stone around on his finger as he waited for their response.

"The first problem is that we don't know where they are—you said so yourself," Iri pointed out.

"True, I don't know where they are now," Jaden agreed. "But I do know where they were when I gave my mom the key."

"And you think because of that, you can use the arcachoa to take you back there, then give them your ring?" Kayla reasoned.

"Yes."

"Bro, you're forgetting you can't cross timelines," Atu reminded Jaden.

"No, I haven't forgotten. But there's something we haven't considered. What if artifacts can cross timelines?"

No one said a word.

"You're going to risk using the arcachoa based on a hunch that you might be able to pass the relic stone across timelines?" Kayla finally rasped.

"I think it's worth a shot." Jaden looked at Atu. "What would you be willing to risk if it was your parents?"

Atu didn't even have to think about it. "I'd do the same thing."

Kayla still seemed unhappy. "Have you discussed this with Han?"

"Yes, he heard me making the notes on my PAL. And before you get all upset with him, he only agreed to say nothing if I promised to share my plans with you."

"That's not an answer." Kayla huffed. "Let me be more specific—what does Han think of this idea?"

Jaden wanted to shake her. Why wouldn't she just agree with him? She knew how much his family meant to him.

As if she had read his mind, Kayla said, "I'm not saying you can't do this. I just want to be sure we've evaluated all the implications before we make a mistake we can't correct. What if you destroy your relic stone trying to do this? Or if doing this gets you trapped in that other world like Taz said happens sometimes?"

That made Jaden pause. They were valid points. "You're right. And to answer your question, Han was dubious about the plan."

"Well, doesn't that tell you that perhaps it's not such a great idea?" Kayla snapped. "We should get the gliders to weigh in on this before we make any decision. And I think we should get Sven's input too."

"I agree with Kayla," Iri piped up.

Jaden shot her a look. *Is she using those senses of hers again? Does she know I'm thinking of simply going ahead anyway?*

Kayla tried again. "Jaden, I know how much your family means to you. I think we all just want to be sure that there are no downsides like there were last time."

Yes, he had made mistakes when he gave his mom the key because he hadn't bounced his ideas off the rest of the team. But Jaden was sure this plan would work. Would he have an ally in Atu? "What do you think, dude?"

"We've only scratched the surface, and Kayla has already raised two very real risks. What others haven't we thought of yet? And could they be even more dangerous? I think the gliders can provide information that will help us reach a more informed conclusion," Atu suggested carefully. "Shall I go see if they're outside?"

Jaden slumped in his chair. They were all going to veto the idea before it was off the ground. Then he leaped up. "No, I'll go."

Before anyone could object, Jaden was halfway to the door. If he gave them enough time, they would come up with more reasons why he shouldn't, but he just had a *feeling* that this had to be done. He was so engrossed in his own thoughts, he nearly ran right into Han. "Oh, you're here." How was he going to get Han to agree without getting the others involved? "Are the other gliders with you?"

Han studied him before answering. "No, I told them I would investigate why we felt we were needed and summon them if necessary. But I am sensing you're happier now that you know it's only me. Why?"

Jaden wished he'd had more time to come up with a plan. But he had to get out of here before the others realized what he was doing, and Han coming alone seemed like a sign. "What I am planning is better if it's only you and I."

"I presume this has something to do with that recording you made this morning?" Jaden nodded. "You told the others, but they don't agree with you?"

Jaden winced. That made him sound like a spoiled kid throwing his toys out of the cot because he didn't get his own way. "They don't understand. I know this is what we have to do. But they're all sitting there and debating it like we have all the time in the world to reach a decision."

Han's gaze sharpened. "When you say you know we have to do this, how do you know that?"

"I just have a feeling it's the right thing to do." Jaden shrugged. "I don't have any hard facts or evidence . . ."

"Just one of those feelings of yours," Han concluded.

Jaden nodded, then sighed. "Do you think this is a terrible idea?"

"That question can't be answered without a full assessment of the plan. What I can say is that I think it's foolish to take action without considering the consequences."

"But we don't know what the consequences *are*. All we can do is guess. Look, can we discuss this in the air? I don't want the others walking out here and finding us."

"I suppose there's no harm in that. I'll be back."

Han took to the air, and Jaden forcibly relaxed his aching jaw. He hadn't realized how tense he had been. A second later, Han dropped down, and Jaden aerial-connected. Seconds after that, they were high above the house. It was cold, and Jaden was glad he hadn't removed his smart suit before dinner.

"Alright, explain yourself more fully," Han said.

"As I was saying, we can only guess at the consequences. You and Taz don't really know any more about using the arcachoa than we do. That means whatever course we take will be risky. Shouldn't we just take the chance and trust this feeling I have? I mean, there should be a reason why I sense things, and if this mission isn't a good reason, then what is?"

"Stop, you're making my head hurt with all that circular logic," Han moaned. After a moment's silence, he added, "You're obviously set on this. Much as I'm sure I'm going to regret it, I'll go along with your plan."

Jaden almost stopped breathing. Had Han just agreed? "Wait, you'll let me try giving the relic stone to my mom?"

Han's shoulders rolled under Jaden as he sighed. "Yes. When are we planning to do this?"

"How about now?"

"What? You have no supplies with you. And it's two days back to your parents' home. Because that's where we'll need to be for this to work."

"I have my smart suit, my DD, and my relic stone. What else do I need?"

"Food and water." Han smirked. "With food being your priority, of course!"

"I can order a cash pickup with my PAL. Can we go already? Don't tell me you're getting cold feet!"

"No, I'm just wondering about giving up the relic stone when it's such a powerful weapon."

Jaden sighed. "Yes, I thought about that. But we don't know of any other artifact that cancels the numbing effects of the EMP, so what choice do I have?"

"Fair enough. Have you contemplated the fact that there may be repercussions for passing the relic stone across timelines?"

Jaden groaned. "Not you too! I was getting enough of the third degree inside."

"No need to get upset. I don't know what topics you and the other seekers covered. I only want to be certain you've factored in the possibility of . . . other things happening that we might not expect or want."

"I'm sorry. You're right. And yes, the others were already more than eager to tell me there could be unpalatable side effects. But I haven't changed my mind. Are you still with me?"

Han chuckled and wheeled away from the house. "Young one, you will be the death of me."

"Ah, don't say that." Jaden grimaced, leaning forward and rubbing the back of Han's ears. "We'll be fine!"

"You'll be the one explaining all this to Tazanna when we succeed, then." Han grinned.

"Oh, that's what you meant." Jaden laughed. "Yeah, she's going to be a spitfire when she figures out what we did."

The journey home didn't take as long. They didn't encounter any Gaptors along the way, so that helped, as did the fact that Han was trying to get them there before the others caught up. By the time they reached Jaden's home, they were exhausted. However, they ignored the desperate need for sleep. If the plan didn't work, they could sleep until the others arrived.

Floating above his home, Jaden removed his medallion from his wrist pouch. "Ready?"

Han nodded, and Jaden placed the medallion in Han's arcachoa, the medallion-shaped indentation just below the ridge of Han's neck. This time, Jaden was more prepared for the harrowing trip. When he and Han popped out the other side of the time tunnel, he was relieved to see his mother through the kitchen window.

"Try not to interact with yourself in this timeline," Han cautioned as Jaden prepared to dismount.

"Yeah, time travel 101," Jaden replied, making Han frown. "Never mind. I just meant yes, I'll do that."

Jaden leaped off Han, landing on the roof. He took a moment to prepare himself before he opened the door. When he glanced back to give Han a thumbs up, he couldn't help but notice how worried his glider was. "I'll be alright. I won't take chances. I'll get in, try to give my mom the ring, and get back out."

Han growled. "See that you do. I'll be waiting."

With a final salute, Jaden opened the door and entered. It was more than strange to be in his home in this alternate timeline. The hairs on the back of his neck rose as he closed in on the kitchen. Was that a warning? *Too late now*. He reached for his mother.

Jaden wasn't prepared when his hand passed right through her. *What did I expect?* Taking a breath, he pulled the ring off his finger and held it against the area his mother occupied. He almost had a heart attack when his mother jumped.

"Where did you appear from?" Clara asked. "I thought you were upstairs packing!" She trailed off, and abruptly, fear marked her features.

Jaden almost didn't work it out. Why was she afraid? He scanned the kitchen, expecting to find danger, but saw nothing. His eyes drifted back to his mother. The way she retreated, then peered all around her gave him the clue he needed. The relic stone was no longer touching her. Had he just disappeared when that happened? Stepping toward her, he gingerly placed the relic stone in the area she occupied again. This time, he did his best not to jump away even though she let out a small shriek.

"How do you keep doing that?" his mother demanded. "Stop it! It's creepy."

Jaden grinned. It was so good to see her again. Then his smile faded. "Mom, I am upstairs packing." His mother's confusion was understandable. "The 'me' standing in front of you right now is from the future." He gave her a moment to process that, then moved on. "I'm sorry if all this sounds unbelievable, but can you trust that what I'm saying is true?"

His mother nodded. "Why are you here?"

Jaden sighed. "Mom, there's no easy way to say this. Your dream, the one you had about —"

"Yes, I know the one you mean. Get on with it." A grim expression settled on her face.

"It came true."

Clara stumbled toward a chair. The sudden movement made her

lose contact with the relic stone again. Her eyes searched the room frantically as Jaden hastened after her and put the ring in place again. "Mom, you need to stay connected to the relic stone, or I'll keep disappearing."

"Oh, so that's how you keep doing that," his mother croaked.

"I'm sorry, I know this is a lot to take in, but I have to hurry. I don't know how long I can safely be here."

She waved a hand at him to continue, too overwhelmed to speak.

"This ring counters the numbing effects of the Gaptor's EMP." When his mother stared at him blankly, Jaden tried again. "You said that you were numb when you woke up after being taken. I think this ring will counter that. I've come back from the future to try give this ring to you, but usually there isn't any interaction across timelines." He was losing her again, so he waved an agitated hand in front of her. "Never mind. Can you see if you can take the ring from me? But don't let me lose contact with it."

His mother reached out and grasped the ring. "I have it."

"You can feel it?" Jaden asked, hardly daring to believe this was working.

"Yes," Clara sighed. "Now what do we do?"

Jaden suddenly realized how much of a burden he had laid on her. Keeping his hand closed over the one holding the ring, Jaden pulled her into a hug. "Mom, I'm so sorry. I know how difficult this is. But I said I would find a way to help you, and I believe this is it."

His mother stayed where she was, just enjoying the contact. Then she pulled back and gave him a watery smile. "Thank you. Now, what do I have to do with the ring? You said you didn't have much time."

Jaden sensed the need to return to Han. "Keep it with the key on that chain—and keep it hidden. Hopefully it will stop you from being numbed so that you and Dad can escape. I wish I could give you more help, but I don't know where you are, so you'll have to help yourselves until I can figure that out."

"Will do." Clara lifted a hand and placed it against his face. "Now you should go."

Jaden lifted his own hand, closing it over his mother's and giving it a squeeze. "I love you."

"I know, and your father and I love you too. Go. Be safe."

Jaden turned before she could see the tears welling in his own eyes. As soon as his hand left the ring, he felt a chill. No, more than a chill. Like something fundamental had changed in the world around him. Panicking, Jaden raced up the stairs and burst onto the roof. At least Han was still there. "We need to leave," Jaden shouted.

Han wasted no time, curling up and away before speeding back down for Jaden. Jaden was barely in place before he wrenched his medallion free of the arcachoa. The tunnel of light almost blinded him, appearing out of the blackness that surrounded them. Then he and Han were sucked through, all sounds silenced. In a rush, they were through and thrown back into their own time. But the dread hadn't dissipated. It sat in his throat, clawing at him, making him want to retch. Something had changed. But what?

CHAPTER TWENTY-ONE

"Just what did you think you were doing?" Kayla's voice cut the air, sharp with iciness. Calling her angry was an understatement.

Jaden struggled to free himself from the effects of the time tunnel. Kayla's presence was unexpected. He hadn't thought the others would catch up so quickly. Or had he and Han been gone longer than he thought? And were the others here too?

Shaking his head to clear the fog that lingered, screaming that something was wrong, he opened his eyes. Why had his eyes been closed? Did that happen last time he and Han used the arcachoa? Reality snapped back into focus. Yes, they were all here. They were safe. At least that hadn't changed. The relief coursing through him made him weak, and he tightened his grip on Han before he slipped off. Geez, he was exhausted! How long since he had slept?

"I asked you a question," Kayla hissed.

Jaden finally looked at her—really looked at her. Anger etched every line of her face from her stormy green eyes to the thin line of her lips. Under the surface though, he saw relief. The two opposing emotions warred with one another, twisting her face into a mask. He sighed. *Time to pay the piper.* "I'm sorry. You were all taking forever to reach a decision. And I just had a feeling that I was supposed to do what I did. I—"

"You had a feeling?" Kayla lashed out. "You had a feeling? Why didn't you lead with that when you were telling us your idea?"

"I didn't have a chance. Before I'd even fully shared the idea, you were all listing the things that could go wrong. Then you wanted to bring the gliders into it. There wasn't time. I couldn't wait for you to thrash out all the pros and cons. I had to go!"

"And you thought it was a good idea to join him on this foolish expedition?" Taz snapped at Han.

"It's not his fault," Jaden interjected. "I talked him into helping me."

"And I suppose you also made him fly?" Taz fumed. "You lifted those great wings of his and made them flap?"

Jaden almost laughed. The idea was ludicrous. Laughing would've been a terrible idea, though. Kayla and Taz were glaring as if they wanted to roast them like pigs on a spit.

"It's alright, Jaden," Han said. "Tazanna, I beg your forgiveness for the manner in which we left. We should've at least informed you."

Just like that, the wind went out of Taz's sails. Jaden watched as she opened and closed her mouth a few times, but no words came out. Finally, she sighed. "I suppose I cannot fault you for supporting your voyager."

"Thank you," Han murmured.

Taz's radical change in behavior was odd, but Han's was even more so. Jaden turned curious eyes on Han. Had there been a real thread of emotion there when Han addressed Taz? How much trouble would Han have been in if something happened to Jaden? Jaden felt sick. How could he not have considered what this meant for Han?

"Han, I'm sorry I put you in that situation." Jaden placed a hand on Han's massive head. "I shouldn't have asked that of you."

Han turned his head and gave Jaden his toothy smile. "I made the choice. It wasn't something you bullied me into."

"I see your relic stone is missing. Did your plan work?" Kayla's tone was still snippy.

Jaden would have to do damage-control there, and soon. Since he couldn't get close to Kayla or speak to her without the others hearing, she would have to make do with what he could offer right now. "Kayla, I'm sorry for worrying you. I should've been more patient and at least allowed you—and the others—to hear that my plan was based more on one of my 'feelings' than just a random idea. Will you forgive me?"

Kayla chewed on her cheek as she considered. "I will. But don't do that again. Why is it that I have to keep telling you not to do things?"

Her last sentence conveyed the vestiges of her irritation. Yes, he would have to do some serious groveling when they were back on solid ground. He was tempted to throw back a humorous reply, but that wouldn't fly. "I'm sorry."

Kayla rolled her eyes. "Yes, you already said that. Now tell us if your plan worked."

Han turned his head and added his request. "Yes, what happened while you were in the house?"

"You left him *alone* in the alternate timeline?" Taz exploded.

Uh-oh. We aren't out of the woods yet—not with either female.

Han took charge this time. "Tazanna, you have already made it clear that you disapprove of our actions. Can you at least hear what the boy has to say before offering up more judgements?"

Yes, there's definitely a tone there that only Taz can understand.

Taz glared at Han, then addressed Jaden. "Well?"

"I was able to not only pass the relic stone across the timeline but speak with my mother as well," Jaden elaborated. "That is, as long as we were both touching the ring."

"Your assumption was correct then," Taz commented. "Artifacts can cross timelines."

Jaden hesitated. Should he share the rest? Yes, he'd already done enough harm to the trust they shared. "Maybe not all my assumptions were correct."

Taz pounced on this. "Explain!"

"When I actually passed the relic stone over to my mother so that I could return, I got a really bad feeling," Jaden admitted.

"One of *those* feelings?" Kayla asked.

"Yeah. It felt like something had changed, but I don't know what or whether the change is beneficial. Maybe I was projecting, and I felt that way because it wasn't the best idea for me to hand over my relic stone. It's the one weapon we had in our arsenal whose powers we don't fully understand yet. Or it could be more than that. I simply don't know."

A loud beeping interrupted him. Jaden was too startled to make the connection.

"Jaden, is that your PAL?" Kayla asked, her eyebrows raised in surprise.

Jaden glanced down. "Yeah. Huh, I don't remember our PALs ever working before when we were with our gliders."

"Who is it?"

"Oh. It's Markov."

"Well, answer it!"

Jaden swiped his hand across his PAL so that the holoscreen popped up. Everyone would be able to see and hear. "Hey, dude, what's—"

Jaden was cut short as Markov interrupted. "What did you say those monsters of yours looked like?"

"You mean the Gaptors?"

"What other monsters would I be talking about?' Markov barked.

Jaden shook his head. "They . . ."

"Do they have crazy-scary beaks and weird, fingered wings and a badass stinger for a tail?"

Jaden didn't remember giving him that much detail. "How do you know that?"

"Because I'm looking at them right now. They're all around our house. And I think they're trying to get inside!"

"Wait, you can see them?"

"Dude, get your head in the game. They're here, and I need you and Atu and those weapons of yours!"

"You said 'them.' There's more than one?" Jaden persisted.

"Way more! And—whoa, what are those things? Jaden, I think they're trying to break the—"

They all heard the crash as the glass behind Markov shattered. Markov had to be diving away from the chaos because the screen rolled and lost focus as it moved.

"Markov, are you okay?" Jaden shouted.

Markov's face appeared again. "Yeah, but you'd better hurry. They broke the window, and now they're clawing at the frame. I'm heading for the basement. Get here already, would you?"

Markov cut the connection. Jaden looked up to see the others gaping back at him. What stood out the most was Kayla's pale face. "Atu, you and Iri okay with heading over to Markov's? Kayla and I will join you as soon as we've checked on her parents." Kayla's bleak smile was all the thanks he needed. "And we'll bring what part of the Legion Pallaton can spare."

"Yeah, Iri and I can take care of that," Atu agreed, although Iri looked dubious.

Right, because of his actions, she hadn't had the time she had wanted to get up to speed on things. Jaden nodded at her. "Iri, you'll be fine. Atu will help you."

"As will I," Tinks affirmed.

Taz nodded. "Yes, your glider has been a quick learner, the same as you. You and Atu are capable of the work assigned to you."

Iri grimaced. "I hope so."

"Aren, let's go," Atu said, not giving Iri any more time to think.

Aren streaked away, and Tinks followed. As Jaden watched them leave, he hoped that he hadn't been overconfident in Iri's ability. They would have to hurry so he could join them as soon as possible. "Han, let's get to Kayla's."

But Han was already en route with Kayla and Taz right behind. When they reached Kayla's home, Jaden was relieved to find no battle in progress and no incoming Gaptors. But one glance told him Pallaton had been expecting them.

"Good, you're here," Pallaton said. "My scouts report Gaptors coming through not far from here. What are your orders?"

There it is again. All of them expecting me to make the decisions. Mustering his thoughts, Jaden said, "Kayla, you and Taz should stay here with some of the Legion. If you spot any Gaptors headed this way, use your comms to let us know. I'll take the bulk of the Legion over to Markov's. If there are as many as he says, I think it'll be the fulcrum of the battle. Any objections?"

"No. Just—be safe." Kayla's face told him she wished she could've expressed herself with more than words.

Jaden could've kissed her because she didn't argue. "I'll be fine. And so will you."

At least she'll be out of the battle. It was the best he could do to keep her safe right now. Unfortunately, he wouldn't be able to protect her forever. He'd have to deal with that when the time came.

No point worrying about it now. Jaden had a battle to win. "See you and Taz later." Jaden nudged Han to take them away.

Han needed no second invitation. As they streaked towards Markov's home, Jaden turned, surprised to find the bulk of the force circling Kayla's house following them. How had Pallaton communicated the order? They would have to find out when they had more time.

Jaden's attention shifted back to the sky in front of them. Markov hadn't been kidding. Scores of Gaptors circled the area, attacking anything that moved. Frightened people huddled behind transports and under trees to escape the menacing skies. They scrambled to get inside houses whose owners were opening the doors to anyone in need.

A Gaptor dived for a man sprinting across an open area. The beast's trajectory was wrong, and Jaden knew it would miss before it did. Intrigued, he watched as another Gaptor swooped down on a teen dashing out from behind an antiquated car. *Huh, same thing.* The Gaptor missed. Was it deliberate?

Jaden spotted another Gaptor, this one headed their way. It didn't seem as self-assured as the Gaptors they encountered in their other battles. In fact, Jaden noticed a slight wobble in the Gaptor's flight. Calmly, he drew his DD and called the play. "Four."

Han waited until the monster was almost within striking distance. Then he tucked his wings and dropped the few feet needed for Jaden to reach overhead just as the Gaptor passed. Jaden sliced open its belly. Foul black blood sprayed from the wound. Adeptly, Han shifted so that they avoided most of the gore.

"That was almost too easy," Jaden muttered. Speaking louder so his comm system would register, he said, "Atu, Iri, where are you?"

"Southwest of Markov's home. Look for the giant hole in the sky," came Atu's terse reply.

Giant hole in the sky? Is everyone losing it today?

"You heard right," Atu hollered. "Could you hurry it up?"

Jaden scanned his surroundings but couldn't find a "giant hole." Han didn't bother. He sped toward an area where the sky was black with Gaptors. No wonder Jaden couldn't see anything.

"Ready for Gaptor blood?" Jaden asked.

"Always," Han grinned.

And into the fray they plunged. Jaden had no time to call plays. He could only slice through Gaptors left and right. The Legion went to work, killing Gaptors with impunity. It was almost too easy—these Gaptors were nothing compared to the ones they'd faced at the tower. But he couldn't dwell on it. Another monster was always replacing the one he'd just struck down.

Furiously, he swung his DD in arcs. When the blade didn't hit quite right, it sheared off limbs, but when it hit home, it sent Gaptors to oblivion with a flash of light, sound, and smoke. The smoke soon polluted the air, and Jaden was thankful for his aerolator. A Gaptor's neck stretched toward him, and Jaden slashed it with his DD, closing his eyes against the light as it was destroyed.

When he opened them, they were in empty sky. No more Gaptors obscured his view. But what he saw made Jaden suck in a sharp breath. Circling in front of him was a massive round opening, its rim defined by a ring of light. The only thing visible beyond the opening was inky blackness. Gaptors poured through it.

Jaden couldn't quite accept it. He was seeing the actual breach.

"Jaden!" Han's urgent voice wrenched him back.

"What?"

The question was unnecessary. The stream of Gaptors now swung toward them, like they knew Jaden was there. Of *course* they did. They could sense his medallion. For a second, Jaden wished he still had his relic stone. The Gaptors were lined up like pins in a bowling alley. The relic stones would've taken care of them perfectly. If he . . . No, it was in a better place. Besides, he would've needed Kayla here with her relic stone to pull that off.

The Gaptors closed in.

"Atu, we're at the opening. Where are you and Iri?" Jaden bellowed.

"No need to shout! Sheesh, my ears," Atu complained.

Jaden was about to repeat his question when Iri and Atu popped up on either side of him. Jaden grinned maniacally, then called the play. "Seven."

Iri, Atu, and their gliders shot off along the lines of an imaginary V while Han and Jaden stayed where they were at the V's point. Would this play work with so many Gaptors lined up in their sights? Only one way to find out.

"Now!"

They all let loose with their DDs. Gaptors crashed into one another, trying to avoid the sizzling currents. In seconds, the swathe of Gaptors was reduced to less than ten. As they finished their run and neared the breach, Han and Jaden prepared to turn. Unexpectedly, Iri and Tinks smacked into them.

Dazed, Jaden fell. His limbs whipped around as his smart suit tried to compensate. A bright light to his right. The opening! He was going to fall right into it. He was going to—

An electric surge speared his body. Not unpleasant. More like it was boosting his energy levels. No, it was power. Jaden grappled with the strange sensation. Whatever it was, it was all bottled up inside him now. He felt like a loaded spring. If he flexed his arms and threw them outward—

The light was unbearable, the sound deafening. A powerful blast knocked him sideways. Blackness consumed him.

CHAPTER TWENTY-TWO

Kayla tried again. "Jaden!" He still didn't move. "Han, what happened up there?"

Han puffed out air. "Satinka and Iri crashed into us —"

"We didn't mean to," Iri babbled. "I just couldn't remember which way we were supposed to turn at the end of that run. Tinks told me we should be going the other way, but I didn't listen. I'm so sorry!"

Kayla put a hand on Iri's arm. "It's alright. It was an honest mistake. You haven't had much time to practice the plays." Kayla returned her attention to Han. "Then what?"

Han ruffled his wings and rearranged them, tucking them tightly against his large frame. "He fell off. Right into the gate."

"When you say 'into the gate,' do you mean he fell through that hole or just touched it?"

Han thought about it. "It's impossible to say. He got near the edge, then there was that explosion, and then the gate was gone and severed Gaptors were dropping like flies."

"Do you think the Gaptors coming through the hole were sliced when the gate vanished?" Atu asked.

"Yes. But I don't think the gate vanished. I think it was slammed shut."

"Because if the gate vanished, it would've taken the Gaptors with it. But if it closed, it would be like that light around the edges cut through the Gaptors, the same as our relic stones and DDs can," Kayla mused.

"Exactly."

Kayla glanced at Jaden. His head was cushioned on her lap. She ran her hands through his long, dark blonde hair. "That still doesn't explain what happened to Jaden."

"Do you think he'll be alright?" Markov asked.

Kayla had almost forgotten he was there. What with Taz hovering over her shoulder like a mother hen and hopping from one foot to the other as she eyed Jaden, Taz had all but blocked Markov out. "I don't know. There are just so many things we don't know. Most of the time we're guessing what we have to do. Atu, are you sure none of your potions can help?"

Atu shook his head regretfully. "I've tried everything I have. And I can't think of any other remedies that would help."

Kayla felt Jaden's head move. "Jaden?"

His eyes blinked open. "Hey you!" Putting a hand to his head, Jaden groaned. "Where are we?"

Kayla threw her arms around him and bent over, kissing him, not caring that the others might be watching. He was conscious! She tried to stem the tears that suddenly spilled over. She pulled away, then stroked her hands down his cheeks and cupped his face. His handsome face. And those eyes. So blue. Awake! Alive!

Kayla smiled through her tears. "We're on Markov's roof. Our gliders are becoming experts at catching and conveying unconscious voyagers."

Jaden nodded slowly, moving his hand from his head to her face as he traced away a tear with his finger. "Hey, there's no need for tears."

Kayla gulped back the hysterical giggle, forcing a smile instead. "Says you! You gave us quite a scare. What do you remember?"

Jaden moaned as he eased up. He rubbed a hand over his face and then the back of his neck, rolling his shoulders. "Blackness."

"Jaden, come on," Kayla begged. "No teasing. Not now, please."

Jaden took her hand in his. Looking into his eyes, Kayla could see how exhausted he was. And that little furrow that appeared between his eyes when he was thinking seemed deeper than usual, like the lines were becoming permanent. This mission was aging them all.

"I'm not teasing. That really is all I can remember. One moment Han and I were getting ready for the next run, then—oh!" Jaden's head turned as he looked around for Iri. "You're alright. Is Tinks okay?"

Iri smiled. She clearly had used her senses to gauge how genuine Jaden's relief was. Kayla wasn't sure whether Jaden's pleasure that Iri was unharmed or his lack of blame about her crashing into him pleased Iri more. Either way, Iri was more reassured by Jaden's reaction than Kayla's words. And wasn't that a beautiful thing for someone so uncertain of her place with them?

"Tinks is fine. We just turned the wrong way at the end of the run. Sorry!" Iri offered.

"It happens." Jaden grinned.

Taz finally ran out of patience. "What else do you remember?"

Jaden took a moment. "That's about the last thing I do remember. Colliding with Iri and Tinks, then falling, then . . . blackness."

Taz harrumphed. "You need to do better. Did something happen before? Did you feel anything or touch anything?"

Kayla watched the furrow reappear. She turned to Taz. "Is there a reason you're asking?"

Taz gave Kayla a pointed stare. "What is it you're not considering?"

It was Kayla's turn to frown. Then it came to her. "We've been so focused on what happened to Jaden that we haven't considered what closed the gate!"

Taz gave a satisfied smile. "That's my girl!"

"Wait, you think Jaden closed the gate?" Kayla squeaked.

"It's a possibility we should explore." They both looked at Jaden.

Jaden shrugged. "I genuinely don't remember. I was falling, then nothing."

"Do you remember the explosion?" Han tried.

"Explosion? Something blew up?" Jaden rasped.

"It's the best way to describe that massive amount of light and sound that happened right before the gate disappeared."

Jaden appeared confused. "The gate? What gate?"

"You know, the huge hole in the sky that all the Gaptors were coming through," Atu coaxed. Kayla quirked an eyebrow at him. "What? Jaden's taking forever to get it together!"

Kayla eyed Atu. It wasn't at all like him to act like this. "What's eating you?"

"Nothing." Atu turned away, looking like he wanted to kick something.

"So that's what he meant," Jaden murmured.

Everyone's attention turned back to Jaden.

"That's what *who* meant?" Kayla asked. "And about what?"

Jaden's smile was crooked. Not the open, friendly, amazing smile Kayla was used to. *Was that guilt?* "Uh, there's something I probably should have told you earlier."

"Another thing?" Kayla groaned. "This is getting to be a habit with you."

Jaden hunched his shoulders. "I know, right?"

"Out with it," Taz ordered.

"Remember when we were at the tower?" They nodded. "I thought I saw the Usurper just before we left."

"He was there?" Taz exclaimed, glaring at Han.

"I didn't see him," Han contested. "Jaden said he saw him when he leaped from the tower, but I was looking at that exact spot so I wouldn't miss catching Jaden, and I certainly didn't see the Usurper!"

Jaden nodded. "Han's telling the truth. When I told him I'd seen Slurpy, and that he'd spoken to me, Han told me I was imagining things, so I dismissed it as the after-effects of using the arcachoa. But now, I'm not so sure."

"That's why you didn't tell us then?" Kayla asked. "Because you didn't think it was real?" Jaden nodded. "So what's changed?"

"When I jumped out the tower, Slurpy—"

"Please, stop calling him that." Taz shuddered.

Jaden raised an eyebrow but didn't comment as he continued. "Well, he called me 'Gatekeeper.'"

"That troubles you?" Iri asked. Kayla glanced at her, wondering what she saw or smelled on Jaden.

"Yeah," Jaden admitted. "I didn't know what he meant. But just now when Han said the opening was called a gate, and then Taz pointed out we didn't know who closed the gate—well, it's not a stretch to think perhaps he called me that because I can close the gate to the other world."

Taz bounced her head excitedly. "That's logical. It would explain why the gate closed when you came into contact with it, and why you weren't cut in half like all the others caught in the opening."

Jaden sighed. "Well, even if that's the truth of it, the problem is that I don't remember how I did it. I don't even remember touching the gate."

"Dude, you have super powers," Markov breathed, reminding them all that he was there.

Kayla studied Markov from under her lashes. Little did he know Jaden wasn't the only one with powers. Atu could heal, Iri could see and smell emotions, and Sven could create weapons no one even dreamed of. But what was her ability? Was it only to interpret languages?

"Kayla?" Jaden's voice filtered through.

"Sorry, what? I missed that last part."

"I wanted to know whether you had noticed anything strange today," Jaden repeated.

Kayla frowned. How much of the conversation had she missed? What were they on about now?

"Are you okay?" Jaden asked, putting a hand on her shoulder.

His worried face encouraged Kayla to concentrate on his questions. "Yes, I'm fine. And, yes, now that you mention it, I guess this was strange. Just before Taz and I left my home, my mom came out onto the roof and asked if Taz or I wanted something to eat."

Jaden chuckled. "She asked if you wanted something to eat?"

Kayla slapped his arm. "Yes, what's so funny about that?"

"It's just such a bizarre question. I mean, why would . . . Oh!"

"Oh? What's that 'oh' mean?" Kayla tensed.

"Such a mundane question might mean she had seen you out there for a while before she thought to come upstairs and offer food," Jaden explained.

"Huh, I hadn't thought of that. I just thought it was odd that she was up there and talking to us like we weren't invisible. Which we weren't!" Kayla shouted.

Jaden wasn't the only one who jumped.

Kayla grinned. "My mom normally needs to be wearing the relic stone to see Taz. How is it that she could see Taz without it today?"

"And how was it I could see those monsters earlier?" Markov added. "Or that those people out on the streets knew they were under attack? Or that I can see all your gliders now?"

Jaden snapped his fingers. "*That's* what changed!" He noticed their bewildered faces. "Remember how I told you I had a bad feeling when I left the alternate timeline? Well, I think that when I gave my mother the relic stone, it made Gaptors and gliders visible to *everyone* again. That also means it's possible the time freeze effect doesn't work when they're around anymore."

Stunned silence followed Jaden's revelation. Kayla shivered. Such a small thing Jaden had done. And yet it had such far-reaching ramifications. They really didn't know what they were doing. Worse, when they left on their travels now, her parents would know she was gone and for how long.

Jaden's hand slid into hers. "What's troubling you?"

"We won't be able to keep my parents oblivious to our travels now —or the perils we're facing." Jaden's hand tightened around hers. Kayla was thankful for the warmth and the comfort his touch always brought.

"I'm sorry," Jaden murmured.

Kayla nodded. It wasn't his fault, not really. He hadn't known it would happen. "Just promise me that next time you have one of your crazy ideas or those feelings of yours, you'll tell us, and we can really thrash out the options before you go haring off and doing your own thing again?"

Jaden gave a grim smile. "You've got it."

"I hate to interrupt, but what are we going to do now that we know all of this?" Markov asked.

He wasn't the only one looking to Jaden for an answer. Poor guy! Leadership wasn't getting any easier. Jaden's face showed the strain. Although, to his credit, he didn't snap at anyone. "From the Gaptors' behavior today, it wouldn't be a stretch to say war is imminent. An incident like this won't stay under the radar. And when more people start seeing Gaptors, there's going to be panic. The military will get involved, if they aren't already. I guess that's when we'll find out whether our conventional weapons will kill those monsters. With luck, they will, and we'll be able to go on with our mission without worrying about those abominable creatures anymore."

"And if they don't?" Markov asked.

Jaden looked him square in the eye. "That's the more likely scenario. And if that happens, then it'll be up to us to fight them."

"What are you saying, bro?" Markov asked.

"Exactly what you think."

"Which is what?" Atu asked, looking from one to the other. "You two may know what you're agreeing on, but the rest of us sure as little eggs do not!"

That's the second time today that he's lost it. Something was definitely going on. Was Atu wishing he could've helped his parents the same way Jaden had? Or was it something else? She would speak to him as soon as Jaden had laid out his plans.

The long stare Jaden gave Atu before answering indicated Jaden also noticed Atu's strange behavior. "We have to build an army. We have to train more people on the gliders. Pallaton's been preparing the gliders for centuries, so I don't think they'll need much training. But they will need people to fly with them. And we'll need a boatload of DDs. I hope Sven's up to the task."

"Who's Sven?" Markov asked.

"Our friend, fellow seeker, and armorer." Jaden grinned. "Do you know he invented pulse weapons?"

Markov looked incredulous. "No way!"

"Yes way! He's phenomenal! He crafted these babies for us." Jaden drew his DD from its sheath, slipped the safety off, and set the bright blade slithering free. "Sven's been working on something that'll pack a bigger punch. Let's hope he's ready for mass producing those too."

"You mean a cannon?" Markov looked way too excited. Boys and their toys.

Although Kayla had to admit she loved her own weapon. And the smart suit. She shouldn't be a hypocrite. "Alright, boys, I know the weapons are thrilling, but you're getting sidetracked. Jaden, what's the plan for now?"

"Simple. We call the rest of the group and see who's interested in joining this grassroots resistance. Then we summon Pallaton and the Legion and send them with whoever wants to fight to Sven's for training. I know Sven has more smart suits, but I don't know how many. Hopefully enough that people can train in rotations. But that's his problem to figure out—one I'm sure he'll probably excel at."

"When you say the 'rest of the group,' you mean Stovan and the crew?" Markov asked.

"I do. I know our group. I know I can trust you guys." He put a hand on Markov's shoulder. "And I'm going to ask you to lead the group that I'm sending to Sven's. What do you say?"

Markov blinked. "Dude, you know I'm clueless about any of this. I don't know that I'm the best person."

Jaden smiled. "I didn't know anything about all of this a few months back either. You're not in a unique position. The difference here is that I need someone I can trust to lead this group. And you're it."

Markov shrugged. "In that case, I accept."

"Excellent." Jaden grinned. They exchanged one of their complicated handshakes. Then Markov did the same with Atu. When had that happened?

"It's time to fill the others in," Jaden said. "I'll ping the crew. Can we meet here?"

"Sure. When?" Markov asked.

"It will have to be soon. Before news of this gets out. Maybe in an hour or so?"

"Yeah, that works. Better that we do it earlier anyway. I think Bree and Stovan are working this afternoon, and Shianna's scheduled for one of her wildlife exhibits tonight. Man, can you imagine what she's going to be like with the Gaptors and gliders?"

Jaden laughed. "That's going to be interesting. I'll have to warn the gliders beforehand. What about Tarise?"

Markov scratched his head. "Not sure. She's been a little off-grid lately."

Why had Jaden tensed when Markov answered? Had something happened with Tarise? *Ugh, why do I have so many questions today! It's aggravating!* Eager to act and not be standing around thinking of more questions, Kayla said, "Should Atu summon Pallaton?"

Jaden shook his head. "Not yet. I'd like to speak to the group first and see who's interested in going. Once we know that, we can call Pallaton. We'll have to get more voyagers too—or whatever they're called if they fly with gliders but aren't seekers. Perhaps Pallaton will have some ideas on how to recruit more people. Once Pallaton gathers that force, whether he gets them here or along the way or gets Sven's help enlisting them, he and Sven can start training them."

"What if there are more people who want to fight than there are gliders?" Iri asked.

"Zareh could perhaps send more gliders through. But there's no point in worrying about problems that haven't presented themselves yet. Let's cross one bridge at a time. The first would be letting our group know what's going on."

"Actually," Kayla said, "there's something else we should do first."

Jaden's eyebrows shot up. "What?"

Kayla turned and focused on Atu. "We need to deal with whatever's bothering Atu."

CHAPTER TWENTY-THREE

Atu squirmed. "Nothing's bothering me."

Kayla placed a hand on his arm. "That's not true. Are you worried about your parents?"

Atu scowled and moved away. "Of course I am."

"But that's not the issue, is it?" Iri pressed.

Kayla could've hugged the girl. Iri's senses corroborated that something was genuinely troubling Atu.

"What's this? Pick on Atu day?" No one said a word. They just looked at him. Atu kicked at a stone that had somehow ended up on the roof. Probably from one of the transports.

"Fine!" Atu eventually spat. "But I still think all this is a bad idea."

"What is?" Kayla prompted.

"Going to the Buried Forest."

Kayla almost smiled as she noticed Jaden trying to contain his excitement. "You've remembered how to get there?"

"Not quite." Atu sighed. When they resumed their silent vigil, he huffed out a breath. "I remembered asking my grandpa how I could avoid the Buried Forest. He told me there was no way to find it intentionally. Most people who ended up there did so by accident. Except he had heard there was one person who could find it."

"Who?" Jaden breathed.

"You, I think," Atu grunted.

"Me? I wouldn't have the first inkling of where to start," Jaden sputtered.

"Wait, you said you *think* it's Jaden," Kayla interrupted. "Why?"

"Because when I asked my grandpa, he said this person could find it because he would be able to sense it." Before they could guess, he added, "I think it has to do with those 'feelings' Jaden gets. That's how we find the Buried Forest."

"What about me?" Iri asked. "I have senses too."

Atu rubbed the back of his neck. "I guess it could be you. But my gut is telling me it's Jaden."

Markov held up a hand. "Wait, you all have super powers?"

Kayla rolled her eyes. "You seem upset that you don't."

"Darn straight! What are yours?"

"I don't seem to have any either. Well, not anything that's awesome like what the others can do." Kayla shrugged.

"How do you think it works?" Jaden asked, ignoring Kayla and Markov.

Atu shook his head. "I couldn't say. What is *your* gut telling you?"

Jaden laughed, but it was a mirthless sound. He turned away and paced toward the edge of the landing site. For a moment, Kayla feared he might just jump off the edge, but he swiveled and paced back. Anger punctuated every step. "I don't know. Why don't we just get on our gliders and fly around until I *feel* we should change direction? Then we can keep going until I get another one of those feelings, and we can change direction again. Oh, it might take a hundred years to get where we're going, but I guess that's what we have to work with."

Kayla put a hand on his arm. Just when she thought he'd managed to get his temper under control. "Jaden, don't."

Jaden glared at her, but to her surprise, instead of turning away or continuing with his tirade, he pulled her into his arms and nuzzled her hair. "What would I do without you here to help me?" Jaden whispered. He held her there for a few more minutes until his heartbeat slowed and his breathing calmed. Then he released her and stepped back.

Kayla peeked at the others. They were all watching them. Again. She sighed. Time for her to step up to the plate. "Let's get hold of the group. That's what we can do today, so that's where we start."

Within the hour, Jaden's friends surrounded them. It was lovely to be with all of them again. Bree, bless her heart (and her now purple-tipped hair), had arrived with a mountain of food, claiming she had been testing some new recipes and needed guinea pigs. Stovan looked like he had just stepped out of the gym, his clothes still stained with sweat. Shianna was clutching a file filled with photographs of wildlife. Ignoring what was going on around her, she took a seat on the couch and began making notes in the file.

As Kayla studied each face in turn, wondering how they would take the news, her eyes fell on Tarise. She was holding herself stiffly. When Jaden sat beside Kayla and took her hand, Tarise looked away. But not before Kayla saw the anger that flared in Tarise's every feature. Ziggety! Had Tarise confronted Jaden about him and Kayla? Kayla sighed. Just another thing she would have to deal with.

Jaden cleared his throat. "Thanks for coming. I'll get right to the point. Did any of you notice anything strange today?" With the exception of Markov, they all shook their heads. "Well, pretty soon you'll be seeing things you won't believe. You'll be wondering if you've lost it. Do you remember the annual spring hike we took right before finals?"

"You mean the one where you had altitude sickness?" Bree asked.

"Yes, that one." Jaden grimaced. "Only I wasn't suffering from altitude sickness. What I was seeing was real, except it was hidden from the rest of you. When you start seeing it too in the next few days, you'll believe me."

"And what's that?" Stovan asked.

"A monster so terrible you'll know that you couldn't find it in even your worst nightmare," Jaden replied.

Shianna tossed her hair over her shoulder. "Jaden, you know there aren't such things as monsters. Why don't you describe it to me, and I'll help you identify it?"

Kayla watched, incredulous, as Jaden began laughing. "How about I let you see the monster first, and you can tell me then whether monsters are real?"

Shianna frowned. "I don't think —"

"They're real. Believe me, I saw them today," Markov said.

"Where?" Shianna demanded.

"Right here. Outside my house. If you want proof, why don't you come look at this?"

The entire group rose and followed Markov. When they reached the shattered window, they seemed surprised, but they weren't unduly concerned. That was, until they saw the claw marks around the window frame.

Shianna immediately stepped closer and began inspecting the gouges. "These are impressive claws."

"They're actually talons," Jaden corrected. "And if you think those are scary, wait until you see the beak. The tail will totally blow your mind."

"These were made by a bird?" Shianna inquired.

It was Markov's turn to laugh. "Not any bird you'll ever be able to identify!"

"Okay, before we get into any arguments," Jaden said, "let me tell you the rest of the story. Shall we go back to the lounge?"

The group traipsed back and took their seats. This time, Shianna didn't pick up her photographs.

"Before I start, can I ask that no one interrupts until I'm finished?" Jaden requested. When they agreed, he began their story. An hour later, Jaden flopped back into his chair, drained.

Kayla waited for the questions. As she did, she examined the faces around them, all shocked. The bounce was definitely gone from their bungees. What would they make of all this? Would they believe Jaden? She didn't have to wait long to find out, but the question was not what she expected.

"So you and Kayla have known each other for a few months already?" Tarise challenged.

Jaden shifted uncomfortably. "Yes, and Atu has known us almost that long as well."

Kayla wondered whether the others had noticed Jaden's marked inclusion of Atu. Tarise nodded but said nothing more. *We tell her some fantastical tale, and that's all she's interested in?*

"Well, that's an incredible story," Shianna commented. "If I didn't know you so well, I'd think you were yanking my chain. But if what you say is true, I think I'd like to meet these gliders of yours."

Jaden grinned. "Just because you implied you believe me, why don't you join me on the roof? You can meet them now."

Shianna squealed and rocketed out of her chair. "Really?"

Kayla laughed with the others as they headed for the roof. Stepping onto the landing deck, Kayla smiled at Taz. Jaden had warned the gliders what to expect when it came to Shianna. "Taz, I'd like you to meet Shianna," Kayla said with a wink.

Taz huffed. "Let's get on with this then."

It took another hour for Jaden's childhood friends to fully acquaint themselves with the gliders. By that time, Kayla was tired of all the questions. She was thankful when they went back downstairs and into the kitchen. Food! She was starving. Risking a glance at Jaden, she noticed how drawn his handsome face was. He was more than tired. When was the last time he had slept?

"Bree, thanks for bringing the food," Kayla said as she helped Bree open the containers. She handed Jaden a plate. "You need to eat."

His wan smile confirmed his gratitude. Jaden piled on the food and then made way for the others. Before wandering over to join Jaden, Kayla added food to her own plate. The others were just as eager to sample Bree's creations, and they huddled around the island of food as they ate and discussed Jaden's revelations.

Kayla was thankful that Markov took the lead as they finished their meal. "Now that you all know what's going on, who wants to come with me so we can learn how to fly with these gliders?"

Markov didn't even have to plug Sven or his accomplishments before everyone agreed. Even Tarise. Shocker! But Kayla was glad they had been able to keep Sven's name out of the conversation. The fewer people who knew about him, the better. He had been so careful to escape the life he despised. It would've been wrong for them to compromise that.

Kayla turned to Jaden. "I think I'm going to head back home. I need to tell my parents what's happening. And if I know them like I think I do, they might want to join Markov."

Jaden's face was priceless. "They'd want to go flying around on gliders, fighting dark and dangerous beasts?"

Kayla giggled. "You've seen them with the gliders. They're totally besotted. Besides, there's a side to them that you don't know. My dad's . . . skills will be useful. And even though my mom's a contract lawyer now, she was a prosecutor before. She's not one to back down from a fight."

Jaden raised an eyebrow. "Exactly what does your dad do? All you've ever said is that he's a contractor."

Kayla hesitated. "Let's just say he's good at security."

"Ah. I'm guessing the kind that likes guns and knives and uses stealth?"

"Yup. You should've seen him when I showed him my DD. To say he was fascinated would've been an understatement."

"I'll bet." Jaden grinned.

Kayla grinned too, then sobered. "I've probably already said more than I should have, so can we leave it at that?"

Jaden led her away from the others and pulled her into his arms when they were alone. "Of course. I'm sorry. You're just always so secretive about his work."

"And now you know why." Kayla shrugged. "But I should go. My folks will be worried."

Jaden gave her one last squeeze before taking her hand and leading her upstairs.

Taz was waiting for them. "Time to get back?"

"Yes, please." Kayla turned to Jaden. "I'll see you soon. Please tell the others I said goodbye."

Taz streaked back, and Kayla leaped on, urging Taz to take them higher and faster. She needed time to unwind. Taz must've sensed this because they weren't headed directly back to her home. She rubbed Taz's neck.

"Want to talk about it?" Taz asked.

"I'm worried about Tarise. I think she may have thought she had a chance at more than friendship with Jaden, and then I came along and put a spanner in the works. And instead of accepting this and being happy for Jaden, she's obsessing about us."

"Since I am no expert on human emotions, I'm afraid I can't really help," Taz confessed. "However, I will say that I did find her attitude quite unacceptable."

"Oh?"

"Yes, she was quite aggressive. An atypical response like that by a human towards gliders usually warrants closer inspection."

Kayla thought for a moment. "You're saying we should keep an eye on her then?"

"That would be my recommendation."

They flew for another thirty minutes, much to Kayla's delight. By the time Taz took her home, Kayla felt more like herself. Waltzing into the kitchen, she found it empty. She followed the hall to her mother's study. "Hi, Mom."

Her mother looked up, surprised. "Back already? I thought you'd be gone longer."

Only then did Kayla notice the tight set of her mother's shoulders and her white-knuckled grip on her pen. Kayla walked around the desk and hugged her mother where she sat. For a moment, her mother's posture held. Then Kayla felt her tremble. "Oh, sweetheart, it's so good to see you," her mother whispered.

"I know, Mom, I can't imagine how difficult all this must be for you. Not knowing where we're going or when we'll be back."

"That part's okay," her mother asserted. "It's those things you have to fight that worry me more than anything else."

"What would you do if you had the chance to join the fight?" Kayla asked.

"How? We can't even see those things."

Kayla quirked an eyebrow. "So how did you see Taz this morning without the relic stone?"

"I—oh! Yes, I did, didn't I? But how is that possible?"

Kayla released her mother and sat on the edge of her desk. "This won't be easy to hear. You know how Jaden's parents were taken?" Her mother nodded. "Well, Jaden got it into his head to go and do something about it—something he didn't fully think through. Now you're going to be seeing a whole lot more of the other world than you probably would've wanted."

"What did he do?" Sadie asked.

Kayla explained only the essential details. "The point is, now that you know you'll be able to see these monsters and that there's a war on the horizon, do you think you'd want to be part of it?"

Her mother's face was grim. "If there's a chance I can help you and your friends, I'm taking it. What do we need to do?"

"Don't you want to discuss this with Dad?"

Her mother laughed. "Do you really think he'll want to skip out on this? It's right up his alley!"

Kayla had to smile. *Yes, it was.* Her hand went to her arm, and she rubbed her birthmark.

Her mother stopped laughing. "While we're on the topic of difficult questions, there's something I've been meaning to ask you."

"Shoot."

"I never pressed you about why you changed your mind about learning that language Grammy insisted on. Can you tell me why you did that?"

Kayla studied her mother. "Why is that question coming up now?"

Her mother pointed at the arm Kayla still held. "Your birthmark."

Kayla immediately felt defensive. "What about it?"

"No need to get touchy. It's just that . . . Well, right after we moved here, I was putting your laundry in your room when I saw the books Grammy gave you."

"And?"

"The emblems on the covers of those books have the same shape as your birthmark. I don't know why I never noticed it before. But that day, there it was, glaring at me like I should've paid attention." Her mother paused. "Is there something you want to tell me?"

Kayla ignored her mother's question as something that had been nagging at the back of her mind coalesced. "That's why you've been acting so strange since we got here! I thought you'd just gotten an upgrade on your mom-radar. You've suspected since then?"

"Well, since you met Jaden and you two started going off on those 'fact-finding' missions of yours. I mean, the library? You loathe printed books!"

Kayla had to smile. "Yes, I suppose that was a dead giveaway."

"So will you answer my question?" Sadie pressed.

Sighing, Kayla stood. "Yes, it's the same shape. And yes, those books have something to do with this mess we've been thrust into. The language in those books is what I had to use to decipher a code when we were in the tower. I'm expecting to have to do more translating as we travel this path. But why my birthmark is the same shape as the emblem on the books—who knows? I just used it as a sign that I should learn the language."

"That's why you changed your mind so abruptly?"

"Yes. Speaking of the books and coincidences, I have a question for you. How did Grammy get those books?"

"From what Grammy told me, she bought them off a traveling saleswoman. You had just begun to show your talent for linguistics when this lady appeared at Grammy's front door with books teaching language. Grammy couldn't resist."

Kayla wanted to reach behind her and pick off the spiders feathering up her spine. But they weren't real. "Mom, did Grammy tell you anything about the woman who sold her the books?"

Her mother frowned. "Hmm, the only thing I can remember my mother telling me is that she wore the most outrageous clothing. And she had the quaintest shoes—with real, old-fashioned buckles."

Kayla sank into the nearest chair. "Awena!"

"You know the woman?" Sadie croaked, hand to her throat.

"You could say that," Kayla murmured. "Just another one of those 'coincidences.'" She filled her mother in on their encounter at the library. Then she sighed. "But that's something else we can't do anything about. Let's focus on what we can do. How about we call Dad and see if he can come home early? The others are anxious to leave, and I told Jaden I wouldn't keep them waiting past tomorrow."

Her mother stood, nodding firmly. "Yes, let's do that."

The next few hours passed in a blur. Before Kayla succumbed to sleep, she sent Jaden a message. "Folks are in. Don't let the others leave without them."

It was late, so she was surprised that Jaden replied. "Excellent. Couldn't think of a better way to keep them safe with the Legion heading up to Sven's."

Trust Jaden to think of that. Bless him for it because the thought hadn't even crossed her mind. She had assumed Pallaton would leave some gliders behind, but that really wouldn't have been feasible. Yes, Sven's would be the best place for them to hide out while she and the other voyagers embarked on the next part of their journey. Her parents would be too preoccupied with their training to worry about her, and they wouldn't know when Kayla left or how long she'd been gone for. A truly inspired solution.

Yes, she would have to thank Jaden. Tomorrow. She allowed sleep to claim her.

CHAPTER TWENTY-FOUR

Jaden groaned. He wallowed in his bed, not wanting to get up and face the day. What he wouldn't give to hear his mother nagging him to get up. Or smell whatever delicious thing she was cooking. But the harsh reality was that his parents weren't here.

Had he been wrong to give his mother the relic stone? How long would it take for them to free themselves? Would it even be possible? Jaden felt sudden horror. Would the relic stone function in the alternate timeline? Its powers here were no guarantee there.

Too late to second guess what he'd done now. Jaden had to have faith his actions hadn't been in vain. He rolled out of bed. Time to move on.

An hour later, Jaden and Han hovered outside Kayla's home. Taz drifted next to them. Kayla made sure her parents were safely in their 'pod before aerial connecting with Taz. Then they assumed positions on either side of the 'pod, ready to escort Kayla's parents to Markov's.

After a journey without incident, Kayla's parents stepped onto Markov's rooftop landing site. Jaden grinned as they stood rooted in place, their heads turning as they surveyed the Legion. Yes, they would be fine with the strange situation they found themselves in. Jaden and Kayla dismounted, joining her parents on the roof.

"Aren't they magnificent?" Sadie breathed, reaching for her husband's hand.

Vicken's eyes glittered as he surveyed the gliders around them, and for the first time, Jaden glimpsed the man behind the mask. It was a terrifying sight. Just as well not many people saw that side of him. Vicken and Sven would get on like a rocket burning fuel.

Jaden turned as the door to the home opened and the rest of his friends joined them, including Atu and Iri, who had spent the night at Markov's in case any Gaptors reappeared. Jaden noticed his childhood friends had taken his advice and were appropriately bundled up. They also had backpacks loaded with supplies slung over their shoulders.

Vicken released his wife's hand and reached back into their 'pod, removing a few bags of his own. Sleek, black bags that bulged menacingly. Noticing Jaden's interest, Vicken grinned. "No harm in bringing a few toys along, especially if they get us there a little more safely."

"Yeah." Jaden was unsure how much he should say. Although they were still some distance from the others, he wasn't positive that they wouldn't be overheard. Even so, did that mean Jaden could discuss things? Had Kayla told her father that she'd revealed his secret, although not in so many words?

Vicken chuckled. "Yes, Kayla told me."

Jaden started. *How does he know what I was thinking?*

"When you do what I did for as long as I did it, you learn to read people really fast. And you're an open book, kid." Vicken winked.

Jaden blinked. *Alrighty then!* "So you're okay with me knowing?"

"Yeah. I'm not in that covert line of work anymore. I branched out a while back with my own security firm. Since then, I've been looking for a place to base our HQ. And I think I've found it here."

"That's why you won't be moving around anymore like you did before?" Jaden guessed.

Vicken nodded. "About time too. Not only is this location prime, but my wife and daughter are happy here. What more could a man ask for?"

"A gun and a mission?" Jaden quipped, gratified when Vicken howled with laughter.

"A man after my own heart." Vicken clapped Jaden on the back and unloaded the last of his bags. Looking at the not insubstantial pile, he said, "I thought the other gliders Kayla told me about wouldn't mind carrying the extra load. Do you think they will?"

Jaden shrugged. "Why don't you ask them?"

Jaden called Pallaton. When Pallaton drifted right up to the edge of the landing site, Jaden greeted him and then introduced Vicken Melmique. Jaden was amused when he noticed the way Mr. Melmique sized Pallaton up.

The two conversed for a few minutes before Mr. Melmique obtained the required consent. This done, he turned to the rest of Jaden's friends, still hovering near the home's exit. "You chaps going to hang out there all day, or are we going to learn how to fly with our allies?"

That got them moving. Would Markov even get a chance to lead with someone as capable as Mr. Melmique around? But they would have to work that out. He and the other voyagers had their own mountains to climb.

Stepping forward, Jaden instructed the group on how to climb onto their gliders, where to put their legs and hands, and what to expect when their gliders launched them into the air. "Don't forget to hold on tight!"

"Or you'll end up on your backs like Jaden did." Kayla grinned.

Jaden smiled, remembering the first time he and Han had flown together. "Someone please fall off so that I'm not the only one."

But none of them did. Even Bree. She did need Stovan's help getting onto her glider, but once she was on, she stuck like glue. Watching his friends climb onto the backs of the gliders that floated down to become their steeds was almost painful. Had Jaden looked that clumsy climbing onto Han the first time? Thankfully, those days were long gone.

When the Melmiques and all his friends were on their assigned gliders, the voyagers aerial connected with their own gliders and joined the group hovering overhead.

"Time for us to part ways." Jaden had given Pallaton directions and warned him of Sven's intrusion defense system. Pallaton had seemed eager to meet the man who had come up with weapons that could kill Gaptors. Pointing at Pallaton, Jaden addressed the newbies. "That's Pallaton. He's the leader of the Legion. He'll get you where you need to go. Good luck with your training. And stay alive!"

Jaden wondered whether he should've added that last part when he saw Bree's face drain of color. But no, they needed to know that this wasn't fun and games. He just hoped they would all survive the ordeal.

Kayla called one last farewell to her parents as the Legion left. "I hope they're going to be okay."

Jaden nodded. "Don't worry. Your dad's dope. They'll be just fine."

Kayla smiled. "Yes, he is really good at what he does." She nodded as if confirming something in her own mind. "Yes, they'll make it to Sven's, whatever they come across."

"I bet they will." Jaden glanced at Atu. "Okay, dude. What general direction would you say we should start out in?"

Atu shrugged. "What are those feelings of yours telling you?"

Jaden sighed. "It's not like I tell them when I want answers. They just come."

"Let's head north," Kayla suggested. "Atu did say we were headed somewhere in the general area of Sven's home, so aiming there until something changes makes sense."

Jaden sent her a grateful smile. How did she always know exactly what he needed? Thankfully, it meant one less thing he'd had to take the lead on.

They flew in silence for the next couple of hours despite being able to carry on a conversation thanks to their new comm system. Jaden wondered whether they were all keeping quiet because they thought it would help him figure things out.

Analyzing each of them in turn, he decided that wasn't the case. Atu looked like a thundercloud. Iri alternated her gaze between the voyagers. What was she seeing on them? Kayla looked like she was just enjoying the scenery. Jaden followed her lead, and soon he began to relax.

He was eyeing a ridge below them when it happened: that spine-tingling sensation telling him he needed to pay attention. He jerked upright.

Iri's voice reached him over the comm system. "Jaden, do we need to slow down?"

Ugh, Iri must've used her gift! Jaden had hoped to be able to figure this out without drawing attention to himself. That clearly wasn't going to happen. "Yeah, let's slow down."

Kayla and Taz pulled in closer, taking up a position on their immediate right. When Iri and Tinks did the same on the other side and Aren and Atu placed themselves right behind Jaden and Han, Jaden realized they were surrounding him with protection so he could concentrate on where they were going, not unexpected Gaptor attacks.

Time to figure this out, then.

Jaden focused on what he was feeling. A pull. Towards the east. Getting stronger the longer they travelled north. Geez, if he didn't get them to change course soon, it might just pull him off Han. He had never experienced such an intense feeling before.

"East!" Jaden yelled as his body curved in that direction.

Han must've felt it too because he immediately altered course. Jaden relaxed when the sensation left and his body was his own again.

"That was different?" Iri asked.

Jaden nodded. "You could see that?"

"Yes, the colors were more vibrant. And so bright it was almost painful to look at you."

"Well, I doubt I'll miss another one like that, but if I do, I'm sure you won't." Jaden grinned. He glanced at Kayla and saw the clouds in her lovely green eyes. "I'm fine. Don't worry. It was just the strangest sensation. Like I couldn't resist it even if I'd wanted to."

"I thought you were going to topple off," Han commented.

"It sure felt that way. Atu's grandfather was right, which means we'll be able to find this place after all. Who would've thought this was the way we'd find it?"

Atu scowled. "It would be better if we didn't have to find it at all."

"Dude, you've got to get over it. We don't have a choice. If we have to drag you in there resisting like a mule backing away from a snake, we will. Although I'd prefer it if we didn't have to be that drastic."

Atu grunted but said nothing. Jaden let him be. About ten minutes later another one of those quirky sensations grabbed him. "South," Jaden called, before it became as strong as the first.

Less than ten minutes later, the next direction came. Then the next in an even shorter time. The feelings came at increasingly closer intervals until Jaden wondered whether they were flying in circles.

"I feel like we're going nowhere," Taz commented, echoing Jaden's thoughts. "Let's stay in this area for a while and see what transpires."

It didn't help. The directions came one on top of the other, like microscopic adjustments were bring made. Jaden felt like he was on the inside of a blender running at high speed. Bile rose into his throat. On the last call, he barely managed to get the words out before his body twisted sideways so violently he thought he would fall off. Then the next pull came, and he did fall. The blissful sensation of only air tugging at his body was a relief. Jaden relaxed as his smart suit rotated him. Glancing down, he tensed. The ground was way closer than it should be. Han wouldn't get under him in time!

Jaden closed his eyes, bracing for impact. But it never came. He continued floating.

Jaden's eyes snapped open. What he saw was not what he'd expected. He was high above a forest, so vast it stretched into the horizon in every direction. He looked up. The sky above was distorted, as though a giant piece of rippled glass had been placed over it. His limbs jerked as Han burst through. *What?* Jaden stared as the others came through the—ceiling?—in short succession. Han wasted no time picking him up.

"What happened?" Jaden demanded.

"I thought I'd lost you," Han moaned. "You were falling and then I couldn't find you. You just disappeared!"

Jaden rubbed his neck. "Turns out I'm not that easy to lose, buddy." Han purred. "What happened after I fell?"

"You were there one moment and gone the next. It was surreal."

"Hah, payback!" Jaden chuckled. Han looked at him askew. "When Kayla and I first met you and Taz, that was how it felt when you two left us. You flew so fast that you were there one moment and—"

"Gone the next," Taz finished dryly. "Yes, we get it. Atu, is this the place?"

Atu squirmed on Aren, his face ashen. "It is."

"Now that we're here, it there anything else you remember?" Kayla asked, her tone gentle.

Atu glared at the sky overhead. "That thing we passed through to get here, it's what we're going to find all over this place. We can't trust our eyes. They will lead us astray, into danger."

"That doesn't sound ominous at all. How are we supposed to get where we're going if we can't use our eyes?"

"We use my 'eyes,'" Iri said. The others looked at her. She in turn looked at Atu. "It seems we were both right. We needed Jaden to get us here, but I'll have to get us through this place."

Atu nodded. "Perhaps that's why Jaden felt we should stay together." He gave Jaden a reluctant smile. "Okay, bro, you've convinced me. If anyone can navigate this accursed place, it's this team."

"That's the spirit," Jaden said. "Iri, what do you see? Any ideas on which way we should go?"

Iri whistled. "If only you could see what I can. There are these doors."

"Doors?" Taz objected. "I don't see any doors."

"Oh, trust me, they're there. Just waiting for us to pick one." She studied the area for a while longer, then glanced at Atu. "I know you don't like to discuss the stories you heard about this place, but can you at least tell me if the few people that made it out had anything in common to say about the forest?"

Atu fidgeted. "They all admitted that everything was very ordinary at first. They were just minding their business, walking or riding along, when they found themselves in the Forest with no idea how they got there. After that, they entered purgatory."

"Can you explain a little more?"

Atu shivered. "Not really. Their stories were all different. Walking through the forest one moment and then facing some calamity the next. What those calamities were seemed different for each person."

"When you say 'calamities,'" Jaden said, "do you mean something had happened and they had to fix it?"

"No, I mean it was life-threatening. They had to survive it to get out."

Iri hummed. "And they each only faced one calamity?"

Atu frowned. "I don't remember. In fact, I don't recall what the calamities were either. I think I was so terrified after hearing the stories that I just blocked the details out."

Jaden glanced at Iri. "What was that 'hmm' for?"

"From what I can see up here, the doors are all at the same angle, although they're different colors and at different places all over the forest. But some of them are closer to the end point than the others."

"The end point?" Jaden repeated.

Iri squinted. "Yes, the doors are on one end of the forest and there's something on the other side. I'm calling it the end point because the doors would lead there if there was a path. But I can't see what's at the end point. Every time I try and look at it, it kind of fuzzes. Like whatever is hidden there is not meant to be seen."

"Let's take a closer look, then," Taz recommended. "Which way are we headed, Iri?"

Iri pointed to her right. "That way."

"Wait!" Jaden ordered. "Before we go hurtling in that direction full tilt, we should consider Atu's first warning that we can't trust our eyes. I suggest we go slowly, so that if there are any surprises, we aren't kicked out of the game before we've even started playing."

Taz nodded her agreement. "Single file formation, then. Iri, you and Satinka take the lead. Perhaps your talents will give us an advantage."

Iri nodded, and she and Tinks took point as Taz directed. Jaden watched the rest of them form up. He and Han were at the rear. Their pace was sedentary. Jaden had almost forgotten the gliders could fly this slowly.

Still, it didn't seem long before Iri said, "It's close now. About two hundred yards ahead. I think . . . Tinks, stop!"

Her words were cut off as Tinks hit something. Jaden watched, stunned, as Tinks crumpled, then launched Iri headfirst into whatever she had smashed into. Impossibly, Iri turned so her shoulder connected with the obstacle rather than her head. Then she dropped like a stone. Jaden was about to command Han to collect Iri when Tinks shook her head to clear it, all the while sliding down an invisible wall. With supreme effort, she twisted herself backward, falling away from the obstacle upside-down. She then curled out of her inverted position and flew away from the barrier. In a flash, she was back and under Iri.

The whole incident took less than two seconds. Jaden and the others drew level with Tinks and Iri.

Tinks asked Iri, "Are you alright?"

"I think my shoulder will survive," Iri moaned. "How about you? How's your head? I'm sorry, I didn't see that wall until we were right on top of it."

"Don't fret. My head is pretty hard," Tinks assured her.

"You didn't get any of those feelings of yours?" Kayla's worried frown was more disturbing to Jaden than the collision.

"Not a one," Jaden confessed, still puzzling over Kayla's response. What was she afraid of? She knew the danger. Then he understood. The safety of the group partly depended on his feelings. If he wasn't getting any, the bar had just lifted immeasurably higher. Only Kayla would think of the others before herself. Didn't she know she was just as valuable to the team? And even more so to him? He wished he had a private channel to speak to just her, but he had to settle for speaking to her at all.

"We're going to get through this. All of us," Jaden reassured her.

Kayla attempted a smile, but it didn't reach her eyes. Jaden wished he could do more, but that was impossible without being able to hold her. He sighed. And that did it for her.

Her smile widened as she guessed what he'd been thinking. "Me too," Kayla mouthed.

Jaden chuckled. Kayla's smile was infectious.

"Although you did warn us to go slowly. That was fortuitous or that collision could've been fatal," Taz pointed out, oblivious to the silent conversation Jaden and Kayla were enjoying.

"I'd like to make sure Iri and Tinks are really okay. Can we land?" Atu asked.

"Yes, we should." Jaden was really thinking he would be able to make good on his wish. "Iri, any particular spot you can point out to us?"

Iri peered down. "The only suitable places are in front of the doors. Do you care which one we choose?"

Jaden considered. "Pick the door that's closest to that end point you mentioned."

Iri directed the gliders, and they retreated from the invisible wall, flying even slower than before. Soon, the others saw the clearing Iri was leading them to, but the door still eluded them.

At Taz's insistence, they circled the area, alert to any sign of danger. But to Jaden, nothing seemed amiss. The others concurred.

"Alright, I'll go first," Jaden said. "Once I've made sure the area's clear, I'll signal you. Make sure you come in one at a time. I don't want us clumping together in case I overlooked something. Also, if some of you are still in the air, you can see something approaching that the rest of us can't. It's a bit of a jungle down there."

The others nodded, and Jaden and Han moved away as Han prepared for the descent. Muting his comms, Jaden spoke to Han. "Be ready for anything. I don't want you flying into one of those invisible walls. And I don't want us to be caught unawares if something leaps out or attacks as we get closer to the ground."

Han nodded. "I'll drop you and then return to the air until the other voyagers are on the ground. I'll be more effective if I can attack from above. Although I'm not happy that you'll be on the ground on your own. Just don't go into the forest where I can't see you."

"I won't," Jaden said. He didn't point out that there could be other rabbit holes down there which would vanish him like the ceiling over the forest. As he prepared to dismount, he could only hope that wasn't the case.

CHAPTER TWENTY-FIVE

Iri studied the area. She didn't see any incandescent colors like those that had pulsed on the wall she and Tinks had crashed into. But did that mean there was nothing to fear?

Too late, she thought as Jaden leaped. Anxiously she watched Jaden land, roll, and come up in a crouch, his DD flaring to life. He surveyed the area, then paced the circumference, peering into the dark recesses of the trees. Eventually, his DD disappeared, and he signaled the all-clear.

They lined up: Kayla first, then Iri and Atu last. Iri scanned the surrounding forest as Kayla dismounted, but the only thing drawing her attention was the door. Kayla landed without incident, and Iri tensed as Tinks took them down.

"Is something wrong?" Tinks asked.

"Not that I can tell," Iri told her. "But last time I didn't see the wall until the last second."

"You'll let me know if anything changes?"

"I will." Iri smiled. "Just join me as quickly as you can. You sure your head's okay?"

"I do have a pretty hard head." Her confident tone reassured Iri.

Minutes later, Iri was on the ground and off to the side of the clearing, watching Aren approach. He came in fast. Now that Iri was paying attention, she noticed how graceful Atu was when he dismounted.

Atu loped over to them, his stride easy. "Let's take a look at that shoulder."

Obediently, Iri sat on the ground, then waited as Atu's gentle fingers probed the area. She winced when he hit a tender spot. Atu stopped and frowned, concentrating on the area for a while before resuming his examination. Did the purple swirls of worry around him seem darker than usual?

Probably not, because he sat back, a grim smile on his face. "You seem none the worse for wear. A little bruising and tenderness, but that will pass. It will heal faster if you apply this lotion. Kayla, can you help her with that?"

Kayla stepped forward to take the tube Atu proffered. "Shall we?" Iri followed Kayla to the edge of the clearing.

"Stay where we can see you," Jaden cautioned. He snagged a towel from his pack. "Here. It'll allow some privacy without you having to go into the forest."

Iri inspected the blue sparks flashing between Jaden and Kayla with fascination. She had never seen such a strong connection between two people before. Would it be the same for her if she ever fell in love? She almost laughed. Would she even see the colors on herself? She'd never been able to before. Did that mean she also wouldn't see them on the person she fell in love with?

She eyed Atu again as she slipped behind the towel Kayla had propped between two branches. Was this the reason Iri could only see purple around Atu? One color that dominated all else? Or was he just that good at hiding his emotions from her? She'd never met anyone with that ability before.

Iri hissed as Kayla began rubbing the cream in. Kayla paused. "You okay?"

"Yeah." Iri chuckled. "I just wasn't expecting it to tingle like the cream he uses to shield against the cold."

Kayla examined the tube. "This is definitely something different. Different container, different smell. Should I carry on or wait a bit?"

"No, carry on. It's already helping."

"I wish he'd share some of his secrets with me." Kayla sighed. "These potions are extremely effective. I wonder if it really is all in the way it's mixed together, like he says."

Iri giggled. "Probably not. Did it ever cross your mind that he has a gift, but he presents the potions as a way to explain it?"

Kayla smiled. "The thought has occurred to me several times."

Tinks landed, interrupting them. Something about it wasn't quite right. "You almost done?" Iri asked, eager to get to her glider.

"Yup, done," Kayla confirmed.

Iri tossed her shirt back up over her shoulders, thanked Kayla, and trotted over to where Atu examined Tinks. "Is she alright?"

Atu glanced her way, but continued running his hands over Tinks's head. His fingers abruptly stopped, and he pulled his hands away. They were covered with blood.

Iri sank down next to Tinks. "A pretty hard head, huh?"

Tinks gave an abashed smile. "I thought it was."

Iri rubbed Tinks along her shoulder, her eyes on Atu as he dug in his pouch and pulled out another tube of something. Gently, he dabbed the contents onto the wound. "There, that should help close the cut. Fortunately, it's not deep. Have you experienced any dizziness?"

"A little," Tinks confessed. "As I landed."

Atu nodded. "Felt sick at all?"

"No."

Atu laid his hands on her head and rubbed behind her ears. Iri smiled as Tinks's eyes closed in pleasure, and she began purring. The sound grew louder. Iri bit back a laugh. She would have to remember this trick the next time she got into trouble with one of the gliders.

When Atu removed his hands a few minutes later, Tinks opened one eye and looked at him. Atu grinned. "No, that's all you get. How's the dizziness?"

Tinks opened the other eye and moved her head. But Iri could already tell from her scent that Tinks was healed. Kayla was right. Atu really did have a gift.

"Gone. I feel wonderful." Tinks smiled. "Thank you, Healer."

Atu returned the smile. "My work here is done."

Jaden stepped forward. "Are we good to go?"

"We are."

Jaden faced Iri. "Ready to lead us through that door we can't see?"

"Of course." She took a step away, but Jaden stopped her.

"Before we open the door, any ideas about what we can expect?"

The others crowded around as Iri examined an area in front of them. "Well, this door's white. Assuming the color lines up with what I know about colors, it indicates peace, tranquility, contentment. But that's an assumption. I really can't say if it will be true."

"Is the door big enough for us to follow you?" Taz asked.

"Yes. Any more questions before I open it?" The others shook their heads.

"I'll go first. The rest of you cover me," Jaden asserted.

"Here we go then," Iri said, opening the door.

She knew the others couldn't see what she could because they all stood there staring, their expressions unchanged. "You can't see that?" Iri breathed.

"What?" Kayla demanded.

"It's like paradise in there." Iri stumbled forward. The heady scents filled her nostrils, and her head swam. She needed to get closer. The fragrance beckoned, an invitation to decadence.

Jaden threw out a hand to stop her. Iri glowered at him, but Jaden ignored her. "Me first, remember. Since we can't see what's going on in there, you need to enter last. No one else will be able to see if there's trouble. Okay?"

Iri sighed and dragged herself away from the entrance with difficulty. "Alright." The tantalizing aromas were still teasing her senses, so she stepped further back until the air was clear again.

Then they watched as Jaden marched forward. Iri wasn't sure if the others saw him cross the threshold. She suspected not as they all continued staring, their colors and scents unchanged.

She glanced back at Jaden, standing just inside the door. His mouth hung open as he surveyed the scene.

Palm trees waved lazily over an impossibly white beach, the sand so fine that it rippled as the warm breeze brushed over it. The sea, just beyond, was a dazzling aquamarine. Its waters were clear enough to see tiny fish clumping together in silvery schools, darting this way and that. Further up the beach, a thatched hut invited shade and rest. Its bleached deck was dotted by sprawling lounge chairs, their cushions plump and inviting. The clink of ice turned Iri's attention to the orange juice waiting on round wicker tables next to the loungers. Tiny beads of condensation dribbled down the crystal tumblers. Beyond the hut, the lush jungle took over again. Shrieking monkeys played in the emerald depths, their shenanigans disturbing the branches. It was like something out of a magazine.

Iri returned her attention to Jaden, walking towards the hut. Han had entered and was following Jaden. Kayla had one foot in front of her to step inside. Then the colors around Jaden blinked out. Iri blinked in turn. What had happened? Now Han's colors winked out.

As Kayla moved, Iri yanked her back. "Wait. Something's wrong." Iri watched, almost unbelieving, as Jaden sank onto the lounger and stretched out, closing his eyes. When Han loped over to the jungle to swing around the branches like a gymnast on the parallel bars, she was certain.

"Why's Jaden lying down on that fallen tree trunk?" Kayla whispered.

Iri noticed bright orange swirls of alarm slithering around Kayla like an anaconda. "You can still see him?"

"Yes, he's right there, in front of us. Stretched out on that tree like he plans on taking a nap."

Iri understood. Jaden hadn't vanished when he had walked through the door. The others still saw him in the forest. But while Iri could see the "truth" of the situation, Kayla could not. "In that place on the other side of the door, Jaden thinks he's on a tropical beach, lying on a lounger."

Kayla giggled. "Really?"

"So what does Han think he doing?" Taz sniped. "He's behaving like a toddler!"

Iri grimaced. "I think he thinks he's a monkey—or he's trying to play with the monkeys he sees there."

"Wait." Kayla turned to Iri. "You're saying there's another whole world in there that we can't see but they can?"

"Yes, but that's not the problem. Something is making them forget who they are and why they're there. I think the white door did mean tranquility, but not in a good way. It's robbing them of their identity, their thoughts. I wouldn't be surprised if they soon forgot to even eat or drink. It's a honey trap. We have to get them out!"

"What makes you so sure?" Atu asked.

"You know the colors I see around people?" When Atu nodded, she continued, "Well, there aren't any around Jaden or Han anymore. Sorry to be blunt, but that only happens when something's no longer alive."

Kayla panicked. "Jaden's dead?"

Iri put a calming hand on Kayla's arm. "No, but he's been stripped of his will to live."

Kayla shuddered. "How do we get them out without getting caught ourselves?"

"Quickly," Iri muttered. "They were in there for a few minutes before the colors disappeared. Enough time that we could conceivably dash in and drag them out, but only if we don't allow ourselves to actually look at that idyllic place. That won't be easy. Even from here, it's mesmerizing. I could stare all day and not get tired of the view."

"Alright, we'll only send one person in. And we'll tie a rope around them beforehand, so we can pull them out if necessary," Atu directed.

"We have rope?" Iri chirped.

In answer, Atu slipped a coil from his backpack. "After the tower, Jaden thought we should have some."

Iri grinned and glanced at Aren. "We'll need a glider to get Han. I doubt Kayla and Atu together would be strong enough to pull him out. Are you up for that?" Aren nodded, and Iri turned to Taz. "Will you and Tinks be able to pull Aren out if he gets lost in there?"

"Yes," Taz replied, as though this was a silly question.

Iri smiled. Taz was as imperious as ever. "Alright, we're set. Atu, you good with going in?" For a moment, Iri thought Kayla might object. But she must've realized Atu was the wiser choice because she said nothing.

As Iri finished tying the rope around Atu, she repeated her warning. "Don't look at anything except Jaden. Just focus on getting to him and getting out of there. If I'm right, the temptation to look around will be almost irresistible. Don't!"

"Okay, I get it. Can I go in now?"

"One moment." Iri pulled a clothes peg from her pack and clipped it over her nose. When Atu and Kayla raised their eyebrows, she said, "I need to block the smell that's coming from that place. Its pull is just as strong as the images. And I don't have to be inside for it to draw me in."

The orange hues around Kayla burned. Iri placed a hand on her arm. "It's okay. As long as I can't smell, I won't fall under the influence."

Kayla's smile was unsure, but Iri didn't try and convince her further. They needed to reach Han and Jaden— before it was too late. Iri led Atu to the door, and then she and Kayla took hold of the rope, feeding it through their hands as Atu lunged inside.

"I'm trusting you to tell me when to pull," Kayla said.

"Yeah, I'll let you know." Iri watched Atu like a hawk. He sprinted toward Jaden. A good sign. When he reached the lounger, Atu wrapped his arms around Jaden and threw him over his shoulder. Then he began jogging back. A few steps from the door, the colors around him began to dim. "Now, Kayla! Pull!"

The girls heaved. The sudden tug knocked Atu off his feet, and he spilled Jaden onto the ground in front of him. Jaden landed on the rope, immediately making it harder to pull.

"Tinks, help, we need to get them out of there!" Iri called.

Tinks snatched the end of the rope in her claws and took to the air. The rope jerked taut. With an almighty yank, they dragged Atu forward. Iri could see he was totally under the effect of whatever it was inside there. The colors around him had disappeared completely, and he was staring at the sky, spellbound.

"Just a little more," Iri puffed to Kayla.

"Yup, I might not be able to see that other world, but I can tell they aren't that far away, maybe a few feet. It's tempting to run over there and just haul them back."

"It is." Iri's hands strained on the rope. "But don't."

The roped jerked a second time as Aren joined in. For a moment, the load resisted. Then, with a sudden release, the boys flew backward and out the door. The rope went slack, leaving the boys in a jumbled heap.

Rushing forward, the girls separated them. The boys lay on their back, unmoving, their eyes glazed. Iri felt Kayla's frantic gaze.

"They're going to be okay, right?" Kayla demanded.

"Yes, their colors are returning. It may take a while before they're fully lucid."

In fact it took nearly five minutes. Taz, Tinks, and Aren hovered nearby. Atu was the first to snap back. He bolted upright, looking around as though he expected snakes to strike. He relaxed when he saw Jaden and then the others.

"We made it?" Atu croaked.

"With a little help," Aren answered, his own relief plain.

It took Jaden longer, and he was still out of it when he sat up. "Why are you all staring at me?" Jaden asked, yawning loudly.

"You don't remember?" Kayla asked.

"Remember what?"

The goofy grin on Jaden's face as he looked at Kayla was too much. Iri giggled. He glanced her way.

"Why are you laughing?"

Iri shook her head. "I'll explain some other time. Do you feel strong enough to pull on a rope?"

Jaden's brow furrowed. "Why would I want to do that?"

"Because Han's in trouble. He needs your help," Kayla told him.

Iri wished she had thought to say that. The colors around Jaden flared, orange flames flickering around him as he searched for Han.

Grey flecks of confusion tinged the edges when Jaden saw Han and his antics.

"What's he doing?" Jaden gaped.

"He thinks he's a monkey," Iri explained for the second time.

"He—what?" Jaden started laughing.

"I wouldn't laugh if I were you," Kayla admonished. "You don't know what you did when you were in there."

"I hope I was at least as entertaining as Han."

"Nowhere close." Kayla smiled. "But we need to get Han out. You ready to pull on that rope?"

Jaden stood. "Ready as I'll ever be. You'll have to explain later what you mean when you say we have to get him 'out.' He's just over there in the trees." Jaden began walking toward Han, shocked when more than one pair of hands wrenched him back. "What?"

"You have to stay here. Even though we can see Han, he's in a different place. A place that will claim you again if given the chance," Iri growled.

For the first time, Jaden looked shaken. "Okay. Tell me what to do. Then you really will have to explain."

Atu and the others tied the rope around Aren's massive chest. Finding a place to secure it where it wouldn't slip off was difficult, but they eventually managed it. Iri repeated her warnings to Aren and then led him to the door.

"Atu didn't have as much time as I thought. Get to Han as fast as you can and get back even faster," Iri ordered.

Aren nodded. "Can I fly once I'm through this door?"

Iri shrugged. "It's big enough. You should be able to."

Aren stepped through the door and launched himself toward Han. But Han saw him coming and, twittering, took off further into the jungle.

"He thinks this is a game." Jaden's face was pale as he watched Han skip around to avoid Aren.

"Aren! Grab him!" Atu roared.

The group watched, helpless, as Aren chased after Han. They danced among the trees, flitting like moths around a flame. Then with a sudden lunge, Aren crashed into Han, and the two bumped and rolled over the canopy as they grappled. Iri saw Aren's mouth moving, but she couldn't hear what he was saying. Then his colors dimmed.

"Oh no, Aren's starting to lose it," Iri said. Unexpectedly, the colors around Aren flickered to life again. "Wait, he's fighting it. Somehow he's resisting." Again, Aren's mouth moved. Then Iri understood. Aren was telling them he needed help. "Pull!"

With a grunt, the teens did. Hearing the command, Taz and Tinks took to the air with their end of the rope. Aren and Han came hurtling back toward the opening. Aren was still fighting off the effects of the realm, flapping his wings madly and doing what he could to aid their efforts. He had a firm grip on Han's feet with his own, so Han now hung upside down, a limp weight under Aren.

As they reached the door, the rope snapped.

Iri stared, confused. What had happened? Then she noticed the absence of colors around Aren. He lay on the ground just inside the door, dazed. Ignoring the danger, Iri ran forward and tried dragging Aren over the threshold. He was too heavy. Suddenly, Atu and Jaden were beside her, helping. Together they managed to drag Aren out. When Iri looked back, Han was crawling towards the jungle again.

A blur of black almost knocked Iri to the ground. Instinctively, she stepped aside, watching with awe as Taz bowled Han over. Then Taz twirled and latched onto Han's legs.

In a flash, it was clear to Iri. She poked her head inside the door to be sure she was heard. "You can't fly out with him. I think that's what made the rope snap."

For a heart-pounding moment. Iri didn't think Taz heard. She barreled back toward the opening. She must've been using Iri as a marker, because at the last moment, Taz dropped Han and landed on top of him. He wriggled, trying to fight her off, but she settled herself more squarely, squashing the resistance out of him.

Eyeing Iri, Taz said, "This would be the part where you all rush in and help me!"

Iri grinned. Only Taz. For the second time, Iri dashed inside, followed by Jaden and Kayla. Taz maneuvered herself so she could restrain Han while still helping the teens heave him over the doorway. The group collapsed on the other side, breathing hard.

"Could you please close that thing?" Jaden begged.

Too tired to stand, Iri kicked at the door. It closed with an audible click. *Well, audible to me anyway.*

"Ah, thank you. That feels so much better," Jaden sighed.

They rested where they were until the weariness passed, by which time Aren was back to himself. Han still suffered the effects. Atu eyed him, then reached into his pouch for the third time that day. He extracted a jar of purple liquid and held it under Han's nose. That cleared the after-effects right up.

"No comments from the peanut gallery about what went on in there," Han growled. "What was that place?"

Iri saw anger, confusion, and helplessness still clinging to him. "I'm sorry. I didn't know it was a trap until you and Jaden were already caught. While it's true the place offered peace, it wasn't the kind you would ask for. It would've dragged you down to death."

"So perhaps the door closest to the end point held the most danger, even though it seemed like the shortest route," Jaden theorized, his brain back to its usual analytical norm.

Iri shrugged. "Perhaps. The only thing that seems certain is that these doors hold traps designed to keep us from that end point. We can't fly to the end point, and the gliders can't fly out of a doorway. However we do it, we will have to choose one of the doors and then traverse its dangers, or we'll never accomplish what we came here to do."

CHAPTER TWENTY-SIX

Jaden wondered how they would choose the door. If Iri was right, all the doors held dangers. But only one door was required to lead them to their destiny. "How about we visit each door and assess its dangers —or at least try to? Iri can use her senses to assess the dangers behind each. Once we've considered what may or may not be lurking behind each door, we'll rate our options. Any complaints?"

There were none. But before they took to the air again, they ate a meal together, partly to restore their energy and partly to allow for more recovery time. Han had been in that awful place the longest, and he still seemed to be grappling with the after-effects.

When their meal was over, Jaden asked, "How are you doing, buddy?"

"Better now, but it feels like the fallout after too much marula fruit," Han admitted.

Taz gave a snort. "Then you should be right as rain after some elderberries."

Han's face brightened. "You're right. Have you seen any?"

"I have not. But I'll take a quick look around and see what I can find," Taz offered.

"You're not going alone," Kayla told her.

The annoyance that flashed over Taz's face amused Jaden. Yeah, she really didn't like being told what she could or couldn't do. Then Taz's face softened as she saw Kayla's own determination. Jaden chuckled.

"What?" Kayla asked.

"It's like you and Taz were made for each other."

"What does that mean?" Taz sniffed.

"Never mind," Kayla said. "I don't think we want to know. Shall we?"

In seconds, they were gone. Above them, the dome that formed the ceiling was visible. Jaden studied it. Would they be able to get out that way too? If they had "fallen in," would they be able to "fall out" again? He pondered their options.

Abruptly, he was aware of the time. Where were Taz and Kayla? Jaden was about to contact them when they returned. Leaping off Taz, Kayla landed gracefully, several branches clutched in her hand.

Han sniffed. "Yes!"

Jaden grinned. Kayla held the branches out for Han, and he tucked in. Stepping up behind Kayla, Jaden slid his arms around her waist. "I was just getting worried. Did you have any trouble finding the berries?"

Kayla tilted her head back against his shoulder and angled her face up at him. "No, they were just further away than we'd hoped they'd be. But I like the result of taking that extra time and making you miss me." Kayla snuggled back against his shoulder.

"You do, huh?" He dropped his nose into her hair, inhaling her sweet scent. They stayed like that until Han finished devouring the berries. Unfortunately, that didn't take long. With a sigh, Jaden released Kayla.

He studied Han. Already, the glider was more stable on his feet, and some of the spark had returned to his eyes. "How much longer should we give you before we start opening doors?"

Han flexed his wings, then rolled his shoulders. "I'm good to go."

"Excellent!"

The others had heard and were already preparing to leave. They were just as anxious as Jaden to get out of this place, so they took to the skies. Iri directed them to the next door, blue this time.

"What doe blue mean?" Jaden asked.

"It usually signifies love or true friendship."

"In that case, let's take it to mean the opposite," Jaden said.

They landed, and Iri opened the door. Jaden couldn't tell if her reaction meant what was behind the door was good or bad. "So?"

"It looks just like the rest of this place," Iri murmured. "Lots of foliage and not much else."

Jaden scanned the ground until he found what he was looking for. He handed a stone to Iri. "Here, toss it inside and tell us what happens."

Iri did as requested, then jumped back quickly, scaring the rest of them. "Uh, yeah, we're not going through that one."

"What happened?" Kayla pressed when Iri didn't explain.

"The stone was attacked by the vegetation." Iri gulped. "Those plants came alive like some alien species, all trying to get their jaws around it."

"Jaws?" Kayla giggled. "I know there's a joke in there somewhere."

"Hah, jokes aside," Jaden interrupted. "Iri, were they really trying to eat the stone?"

"Yes, like overgrown Venus fly traps. They had mouths and sharp teeth. And they were all snapping at each other like the stone was theirs. Absolutely no love or friendship evident anywhere."

"Okay, let's move on to the next door," Jaden ordered.

In minutes, they stood in front of another door, this one red.

"I'm almost afraid to open it," Iri admitted. "Red means anger, or in this case, danger."

Jaden thought a moment. "Atu, how much rope do we have?"

"Only the short piece that was left on the outside of the white door."

"That will have to do." Jaden took the rope and tied it around Iri. Then he took a firm hold, asking Atu, Han and Aren to add their strength. "Alright, Iri, if something tries to nab you, we'll get you out."

Iri didn't even open the door two inches before she slammed it shut again.

"No go?" Jaden asked.

"Not when there's lava flowing towards you!" Iri looked back at the door apprehensively. "I think we should get back in the air as soon as possible. Just in case the door can't stop it."

The rest of them hastened to follow her advice. And so it went. A black door with an inky interior that Iri couldn't see into and that no amount of light could penetrate. Well, what could you expect from the color signifying death? Then an orange door, with a world inside turned upside-down and inside-out. Iri described paths curving into the sky, animals strolling on vertical walls like gravity had been subverted, and insects with soft innards where shells should've been. Getting lost would have been too easy in a place where nothing was as it seemed. According to Iri, the place even smelled wrong, like the laws of nature had been perverted.

The pink door (signifying joy or happiness) was the last. Despite being the furthest from the end point, it held the most promise. Iri described pleasantly rolling hills, a rushing river, and orchard trees offering sustenance. A rock thrown through the door produced no reaction. They would have made a fatal mistake if a bird hadn't flown through the open door. It made it only a few feet in before dropping dead. Even Iri's sensitive nose hadn't detected the toxins emitted by the environment. Iri hastily shut the door.

"Now what?" Kayla asked, sinking onto the soft earth in front of the door.

Iri frowned. "Would you all indulge me? Could we go back to the place where we fell through?"

"Is something wrong?" Jaden's sense of foreboding flared for the first time since entering the accursed place.

"I'm not sure. I know I saw something when we came in, but I can't work it out. Going back might jog my memory."

"Since I'm getting one of those feelings of mine, I think we should do as Iri asks," Jaden said.

Kayla turned her lovely green eyes on him. "You are?"

"Yeah. I have to say, it's a little disquieting. They've been notably absent since we got here."

His words put a damper on the already silent group. *Well, that can't be helped*, Jaden thought as they flew back. If nothing else, all this flying around had shown them the only wall in the space blocked the path to the end point.

They reached their starting point, and Tinks turned so Iri could survey the area. "Red, blue, orange, green, white, black, and pink." Iri pointed at each door in turn.

"Wait, say that again," Jaden ordered.

Iri obliged. "Red, blue, orange, green—"

"We never went to a green door," Jaden interrupted.

Iri grinned. "That's what was bothering me! I must've known that I'd missed one. Actually, looking at it now, it's difficult to see against the backdrop of the trees. Probably why."

"And how's that spidey-sense of yours doing?" Kayla quizzed Jaden.

Jaden eyed her, unsure whether to be annoyed or ignore her. She knew he didn't like that term.

Something on his face must've shown, because Kayla said, "Sorry, I meant . . . Well, what do you want me to call it?"

Jaden sighed. Now was not the time to get into an argument with her. "I'll live with it. To answer your question, the green door beckons."

They landed a few minutes later. Jaden waited as Iri stepped up to the invisible door. She opened it, then stood still, staring ahead.

"What do you see?" Jaden asked, even though he sensed this was the door they had to go through, no matter what was inside.

"Just more of the forest. Like what we saw behind the blue door." Iri shivered. "I hope this one doesn't have those carnivorous plants."

"Only one way to find out." Jaden handed her a stone.

They all held their breath as Iri tossed the stone inside. This time, she didn't jump backward.

"Nothing happened," Iri stated, answering the group's unspoken question.

Jaden didn't relax. "That may be, but it just means there's probably something else in there that we aren't aware of. I still feel this is the door we should use, but be on your guard. There's no telling what's going to happen. We'll enter one at a time again. Iri, are you and Tinks okay with going last?"

Iri nodded agreement. Jaden sent Han a questioning glance before stepping forward. Han followed Jaden. They stood side-by-side just inside the door and studied the area around them. Jaden didn't feel any of the blissful effects that had washed over him when they had entered the white "room." Hopefully, nothing here would affect their minds again.

Cautiously, Han and Jaden crept forward, alert for anything untoward. But they made it a good way in, and nothing seemed amiss.

Jaden glanced back at Iri. "See anything?" Iri shook her head. "Alright, let Kayla and Taz come in."

The others entered in pairs until all eight of them stood where Jaden and Han had stopped.

"Maybe I should go first now?" Iri suggested.

"Have you had any more of your premonitions since we entered?" Kayla asked Jaden.

"No. So perhaps it's best if Iri does lead us. Her senses are more likely to pick up on any anomalies."

They rearranged themselves, and Iri started down the path that led through the trees.

The path gave Jaden pause. "Do you think we should be following the path?"

Iri paused and looked at him. "Are you getting a bad feeling about it?"

"No, not per se, but it just seems a little too convenient."

"We follow the path until we find a reason not to," Taz stated, putting an end to the debate.

Iri nodded and led them forward, her pace slow and careful. After walking for five minutes without incident, Jaden breathed a little easier. Ten minutes and he allowed a little tension to drain away. Twenty minutes and he relaxed further. At thirty minutes, he began to wonder what he'd been worried about. He was about to suggest a break for food when Iri yelped.

"Off the path!"

Iri dove left into the bushes, followed by the rest of the group. Jaden would've laughed at the gliders trying to squeeze themselves into the undergrowth if the situation hadn't been so dire.

Iri stayed where she could see the path. The way she eyed it made Jaden focus on it too. At first, he didn't see anything. Then, in the blink of an eye, the blades of grass marking the path shot up to five times their size, each blade glinting with edges so sharp that they sparked when the blades brushed against one another.

"Whoa!" Kayla breathed.

"How did you know?" Jaden asked Iri.

"I didn't—not exactly. The path just began to glow red."

"I'm glad you're with us," Atu murmured.

Iri sent him a tight smile. "Thanks. Let's hope I can stay ahead of whatever this place tries to throw at us."

They wouldn't be able to use the path again. The blades swayed, searching for the prey that had eluded them, with no indication they would retract soon. And now they'd been awakened, they would certainly react more swiftly to any disturbance.

Iri drew her DD and turned to face the underbrush. "Not sure if this is what Sven had in mind when he designed these, but let's see if they work." She chopped at the brush in front of her, clearing it away with a hiss.

"Oh, that's not good," Jaden muttered.

"What do you mean? It did an excellent job!"

"You weren't with us when Sven was designing these things. Long and short of it is that they shouldn't be able to cut through anything organic, anything real. They only work on things that are unnatural."

Iri shuddered. "Alrighty then!"

"It's not unexpected," Atu said, breaking his customary silence. "We just haven't acknowledged it yet. Think about it—a place that few people get into and even fewer get out of. Invisible doors hiding unseen snares, invisible walls blocking travel to the end point. Did we really think this place was something natural?"

His quiet summation of the facts settled the matter for their group, especially Iri.

"What are we waiting for? Let's get out of here," Iri said with renewed resolve, hacking through more vegetation.

Slowly but surely, they pressed ahead. Every tiny ribbon of forest cleared felt like a conquest. Jaden didn't allow himself to relax again. He skimmed the area around them, vigilant for any sign of danger. It wasn't only him. The gliders kept ruffling and rearranging their wings, ready to fly at a moment's notice. But Iri again sensed the danger before anyone else.

She had just lifted her arm to strike at the vegetation blocking her way when she stopped, mid-swing. "Any of you smell that?"

The gliders noses moved up and down, tasting the air.

"The sharp smell?" Han asked.

"Yes. Something's off about it," Iri muttered. "Can you tell which direction it's coming from?"

Kayla's scream of pain stopped Jaden's heart. He whirled, ready to face her attacker, but saw only her. Then Iri cursed. Jaden's gaze swung in her direction. Simultaneous cries from Atu and Han confused Jaden even more. Where was the threat?

Something stung his wrist. The pain was intense, and Jaden muttered his own curse. Glancing down, he noticed a small red spot. As he watched, it blossomed in size, the pain increasing with it.

A bright flash drew his attention. An unnatural coppery blob dripped off a leaf above Kayla's head. Jaden dived into her, knocking her out of the way. His leg wasn't so fortunate. Jaden howled as the drop ate into bare skin.

"It's coming from the leaves above us." Jaden lay there, clutching his leg, his eyes on the trees overhead.

Iri looked up. In the few short seconds since the first drop hit, the blobs had multiplied, like a swarm of ants fleeing their nest. Unbelievably, Iri closed her eyes.

"What are you doing?" Jaden yelled. "We need to get out of here."

"I know. Just be quiet for a moment, would you?" Iri snapped.

Jaden pursed his lips. Much as he wanted to say more, Iri wasn't one to waste words. The seconds felt like hours. Jaden and the others dodged the falling missiles as best they could.

Then Iri's eyes snapped open. Without hesitation, she said, "This way."

Iri set off swiftly. How was she clearing a path in time? Then Jaden noticed she wasn't. She was putting her arms in front of her, and the vegetation simply moved aside. Something she hadn't told them about? Why hadn't she just done this earlier? They moved through the forest rapidly now, putting distance between themselves and the coppery blobs of pain.

Iri didn't slow until they reached a clear stream. Setting her pack on the ground, she faced the others. "Don't touch the water. It's toxic too."

Jaden gaped. It was like she had become another person. Her eyes glowed with a faint luminescence. Nothing creepy, but more than could be explained by the light filtering through the trees. "How were you able to clear the forest like that?"

Iri shrugged. "I don't know. I've never done that before. When I closed my eyes, I scented the direction we should go. And when I opened them, I just knew to put my arms out like that."

"You mean there's hope for me getting some magical abilities too?" Kayla teased.

But something in her tone made Jaden take a second look. Was it envy? No, Kayla wasn't that petty.

Studying her, Jaden saw her uncertainty. He went to her. "What is it?" Jaden said in an undertone so that only she could hear.

Kayla folded into his arms, her mouth against his chest. When she spoke, her words were muffled. "Nothing. It's silly."

"Tell me." Jaden ran his arms up and down her back.

For a moment, Kayla was silent. Then the words rushed out. "Everyone has something useful to offer the group. You have your feelings, Atu can heal like no one's business, and Iri has her abilities. What do I have?"

Jaden understood. Kayla needed to feel like she was contributing. "Without you, do you think we would've been able to solve that riddle or get the next clue?"

Kayla lifted her head and looked into his eyes. "Okay, so I can interpret things. But that's not any magical power like the rest of you have."

"Does it need to be?" Jaden challenged.

Kayla frowned. "No, I suppose not."

Jaden smiled. "But you'd like it to be."

Finally, a smile lit her beautiful face. "Sure, who doesn't want superpowers?"

Jaden pulled her closer and kissed her. She felt heavenly in his arms. So soft, her curves pressing into him in all the right places. He wanted to lose himself in her. But that wasn't what the kiss was about, not this time. He drew back. "You do have superpowers. At least, when it comes to me."

Kayla giggled. "Yes, Jameson, keep telling yourself that."

The fire in his wrist and leg ratcheted up a level. Jaden pulled away from Kayla. "Sorry, but Atu really needs to do something about these." Jaden indicated the red patches, which were now the size of quarters and blistering.

"Tell me about it." Kayla gently prodded the skin around her own injury.

"Well, if you two are done canoodling, then I can help you." Atu's tone was mild. They turned and found him standing nearby with a tube in his hand.

"Thanks, we are. Kayla first," Jaden answered. He looked at Iri. "Any idea how much longer we'll be in here?"

"We follow this stream," Iri said. "I can smell fresh air in that direction. And based on how strong the scent is, I don't think much further."

Iri was right. As soon as Atu dealt with Jaden and Kayla's burns, they set off again. In under ten minutes, Iri said, "I can see the door. It's right ahead, over there. But there's something between us and it. I can only see red. I'm not sure what the danger is, but it's there."

Jaden thought a moment. "Going slowly only woke up whatever dangers were dormant. I say we make a run for it. Iri, can you clear the way?"

Iri nodded. "Ready when you are."

Jaden glanced at the others. "Anyone not good with this?" They all shook their heads. "Alright, Iri, lead the way."

Iri sprinted forward. Instead of backing away, the vegetation curled into her. Jaden watched, horrified, as vines stretched out of the undergrowth, wrapping their tendon-like arms around her ankles. Iri stumbled and fell forward. The vines crawled over her like snakes over a rat in a pit. If they didn't do something soon, the vines would choke her or squeeze her to death.

A black shadow swooped down, obscuring Iri for a second. Jaden was halfway toward Iri, his DD extended, when he realized what had happened. Tinks had taken hold of Iri in her talons, lifting her voyager up, away from the danger. But the vines were relentless. The more Tinks tried to lift, they tighter they held on.

With a war cry, Jaden rushed the spot and slashed at the vines. Han dove down and helped Tinks. Then Taz, Kayla, Aren and Atu were there, hovering above him as well. Psychotically, Jaden hacked at the green ropes, his blade severing whatever it touched.

But the vines held their own revenge. As they slithered back to the ground, they released small puffs of particles. *Thorns*, Jaden corrected when his arm brushed through them. They sank into his skin, burrowing in and taking a thousand tiny bites out of his skin.

Abruptly, he was in the air. Jaden glanced up. Han was lifting him. Looking down, Jaden realized Iri had been freed. Their gliders increased their height, removing their voyagers from danger.

When they were clear, Atu tossed Jaden the same tube he'd used earlier. "Use it now. Those thorns will burrow all the way through if you don't."

Slathering the lotion over the affected area, Jaden groaned with relief. Tiny specks ejected themselves from his skin. The raw skin that remained slowly covered over until his skin was back to normal.

Jaden really didn't know how Atu did it, but he was glad Atu had the gift he did.

The others were discussing strategy, but Jaden had been distracted. "What's the plan?"

"We'll fly to the exit, then drop down at the last moment so we can walk through," Han informed him.

Even as Han said it, Iri and Tinks slid down and ran forward. Iri had marked the spot. The rest of them followed her lead, and soon they all stood on the other side of the invisible door.

Iri slammed it shut. "Good riddance!"

Jaden expected to find more jungle, but this place was far from it. Jaden tensed. *What now?*

CHAPTER TWENTY-SEVEN

Kayla stared. The scrupulously manicured lawns, landscaped flowerbeds, and sculpted trees looked like something out of a fairy-tale. She glanced around, half expecting to find a palace, but she was disappointed. There were no buildings, only the lush, sweeping gardens, surrounding them on all sides as far as they could see. What was this place? More troubling, who had been maintaining it?

"Is this the end point?" Kayla asked Iri.

"I don't know. I couldn't really see what was here, just that there was an end point."

Kayla nodded, thoughtful. "Jaden, how about you? Any of those feelings of yours?"

"Nope! I wish there were, though, because this place is eerily perfect."

"You're not the only one thinking that."

Jaden nodded. "Well, we aren't going to get anywhere just standing here. Let's explore and see what we can find."

"As long as we don't go up, we're fine," Iri commented. They all looked at her. "You can't see the ceiling?"

Kayla studied the sky overhead but saw nothing. When she glanced at Jaden and Atu, she gathered she wasn't alone.

Iri grimaced. "Okay, so the ceiling up there is like that invisible wall we flew into before. It might even be part of that same wall. And I'm thinking it has the same purpose."

"You mean to stop us from flying to the end point if this isn't it?" Kayla clarified.

"Yeah. Wherever we're supposed to go, we'll have to walk."

"Fantastic." Taz's sneer indicated it was anything but.

Kayla hid a grin. She couldn't blame Taz. Who would want to walk when they could fly? "I suppose we should start walking then."

They set off in no particular direction, meandering down the gently sloping lawn towards the pond that reflected the sun like a polished mirror. Apart from the lush lily pads bobbing idly on the water, there was nothing noteworthy about it. They angled towards some sculpted trees, shaped into animals and artfully placed around a loose gravel oval with white stone benches. Although Kayla would've loved to sit and admire the trees, there was no time. They pressed on and entered a section with flowers so flamboyant, they were taller than the gliders.

If there are such things as fairies, this must be what it feels like for them. Hiding amongst all the blossoms with their heady scents was almost intoxicating. Just when Kayla began to worry that this was another trap, they exited into the sunshine again. A short way in front of them, a hedge blocked their way.

"Do you think that's meant to be a wall around the garden?" Kayla guessed.

"Let's find out," Jaden muttered.

Kayla glanced at him, noting his sour expression with amusement. Apparently the tunnel of flowers had done nothing to improve his disposition. She caught up to him and snagged his hand with her own. Startled blue eyes the color of cobalt focused on her.

"Try to relax. You know there's nothing we can do to expedite this," Kayla whispered.

Jaden smiled, albeit grimly. "How do you always know the right thing to say?"

Kayla chuckled. "I don't. I just say what I'm thinking, and it turns out to be what we both need."

Jaden squeezed her hand. This time, his smile was that gorgeous one that she loved. The one that tipped the corners all the way up and made crinkly lines around his eyes.

"Have I told you lately that I'm grateful you're here with me?" Jaden asked.

"And here I thought you wanted to keep me wrapped up in cotton wool and away from all of this." *Finally, a chuckle!*

"If only."

Hand in hand, they approached the hedge and began walking along it. They didn't have to go far before discovering its true purpose.

"A maze!" Kayla exclaimed, as a break in the hedge revealed a parallel hedge a few feet away with a sharp corner opening onto a perpendicular path. She scratched at her arm, irritated that it would choose this moment to start annoying her.

"We're in the right place, alright," Atu murmured, drawing up next to them. When everyone gazed at him, he pointed down.

On the ground, conspicuously placed at the entrance to the maze, was a concrete paver. The molded stamp on its square face was unmistakable.

"The medallion!" Kayla breathed.

"Bring back any memories?" Jaden asked.

"Yeah, the floor of the tower," Atu remarked. He glanced at the sky. "At least, there aren't any Gaptors around this time."

"Did you have to say that?" Iri moaned. "You know you've jinxed us now, right?"

Atu shook his head. "There's just no pleasing some people."

But his tone was light, and Iri smiled. Some mild entertainment was welcome right now.

Kayla turned to Jaden. "Do we go in?"

"I don't see that we have much choice." Jaden sighed. He glanced at the gliders. "What do you think?"

Taz, as usual, spoke for all of them. "We will follow where you lead."

Jaden grunted. "That's not really an answer." Despite this, he gripped Kayla's hand more firmly. "Ready?"

"Yes," Kayla answered.

Together, they stepped into the corridor of the maze. They stopped there, expecting something to happen. Nothing did. Iri and Atu joined them, followed by the gliders. Jaden and Kayla moved further down the corridor to make space for them. *That's* when things changed.

Kayla gasped as the hedge's walls reshaped themselves in front of them, forging a tunnel leading away from where they stood. The light at the start of the tunnel only allowed them to see so far. Beyond that, all that remained were the dark recesses of that closed space. She began to feel claustrophobic. This was like those black spaces in the tower.

Kayla shuddered. Jaden's grip on her hand became almost painful, but ironically, it comforted Kayla. Having him close was all the support she needed. This time, Kayla took the first step.

As they walked, Kayla was surprised and relieved when the light overhead didn't disappear. The tunnel stretched in front of them and behind, a dark void, but their area remained a bright, sunny spot. *Not sure how that's working, but at least we have that going for us.*

Although the tunnel seemed endless when it appeared, it didn't take long to reach the exit. Her gratitude at leaving the tunnel was replaced by confusion. A stone wall blocked their way. Kayla stepped closer. An *inscribed* stone wall.

"Looks like we've got a message." Kayla released Jaden's hand and dropped her pack. In seconds, she had her notepad in hand. She grinned as Iri ran her hands over the markings.

"You understand this?" Iri sounded awed.

"You can thank my Grammy for that." Kayla set to work. Copying the symbols into her notepad, Kayla began the tedious process of crossing out and rearranging them so that they formed a translation. As she studied the completed work, she frowned, her mind caught on the third sentence. Was she reading too much into it? Should she tell the others about the double meaning? Then she dismissed her concern. This mission was making her paranoid about everything.

"Finished?" Jaden asked, stepping up behind her.

Kayla smiled up at him. "Yes. Want to do the honors?"

Jaden read through the words. She knew he'd reached the last line when his face drained of color. "You're sure about this?"

"Yes. But the last riddle had something about a boy and burning, and that didn't happen. I doubt this will either."

Her words didn't reassure Jaden. He looked ill. Kayla tried again. "Jaden, first of all, it probably isn't even talking about us. Secondly, there are two girls here, so it could just as easily be Iri. Either way, stop worrying about something that may or may not happen. Fear will cripple us if nothing else does."

Jaden wasn't convinced. He stared at the paper for so long that Kayla wondered whether he was going to share it with the others. Just when she thought she needed to prod him, he shook himself and motioned the others closer. Anxiously, they crowded around Jaden.

"What does it say, bro?" Atu asked.

Kayla was surprised that he had been the one to ask. But then, he was also the most eager to leave this place.

Jaden read the words she had written:

In the mural of deceit
The elusive tiers defeat
Judge the leaves with care
Of dangers beware
Do not despair at this time
Find what leads you to sunshine
Not if you should hope
But when you should hope
Stop the steel from flying
Stop the girl from dying

Iri glanced at Kayla. "You think this girl in the riddle is one of us?"

"No," Kayla answered firmly. "The last riddle had something similar, and that never came to pass. So perhaps these last two lines are only there to scare us."

"As if all this isn't sinister enough," Atu muttered.

"Okay, ignoring the doom and gloom," Iri said, "what does it mean?"

Kayla took the notepad from Iri and flipped back a few pages to the last riddle. Running her eyes across the words, she compared the two. "Well, the first line last time had to do with where we were. Based on that, let's go with the theory that this riddle was written the same way."

"The 'mural of deceit' being the wall in front of us?" Iri asked.

"Perhaps. It could also be the garden we just passed through or the entire Buried Forest. I mean, the whole place is practically one big lie," Kayla noted.

"Go on," Jaden encouraged.

"The next three lines on the first riddle told us what we had to do: go out the tower and climb the steeple to find the hidden item."

"I'd say we've defeated the 'elusive tiers' already." Jaden frowned. "Isn't that what we did when we tried all those doors?"

"I don't think so," Kayla murmured. "Something you need to understand about this ancient language is that the way words are arranged is almost as important as the words themselves. The three lines need to be viewed together. And before you say all of them can apply to what we've already gone through, let me reiterate. The way the words have been arranged, the placement of the symbols on the wall, and how I had to get the translation imply future tense, not past tense. I'm inclined to say these lines refer to something we still need to do rather than something we've already done."

"Alright," Jaden acquiesced. "Think the 'tiers' are the layers of stones in the wall?"

Iri shrieked, startling them all. "Look, leaves!" Running along the bottom of the wall were leaves stamped into the stone. "But don't touch!"

"Why not?" Jaden asked, his eyes round.

"They smell bad."

Kayla almost wanted to laugh. How could inanimate, stamped leaves smell like anything? Hadn't Iri said she couldn't sense things that had no life? Were they in fact alive? But Iri was sniffing the air as she moved toward a small bush with long, thin leaves that had grown up right alongside the wall. Its coloring exactly matched the wall, making it blend in. If Iri hadn't pointed it out, they wouldn't have noticed it.

"These leaves, however, they smell right." Iri gently pushed them aside.

Kayla inhaled sharply. The space Iri opened revealed another medallion stamped into the wall. This time, the medallion wasn't oversized. In fact, it was the exact size of their medallions. Absently, she rubbed her arm, wishing she hadn't indulged the itch the first time. The prickliness was just getting worse.

Jaden crouched next to Iri, examining the engraved image before removing his medallion from his wrist pouch. He glanced at the others. "Zareh did say our medallions were the key. Anyone disagree with me putting my medallion on that space?"

"No, go for it." Atu's excitement had overcome his reservations.

Carefully, Jaden lined up the sides and images. Then he placed his medallion over the one carved into the stone. The stone flashed, and Jaden's medallion vanished.

"Uh-oh," Iri said. "That doesn't seem right."

A grinding sound made them all leap back. The wall split into two, forming two doors that swung inward.

"Hmm, I'm a little more hesitant about going in there after the wall swallowed your medallion," Atu conceded.

"I'm not." Jaden bounded inside before anyone could stop him and snatched something off the ground.

"Jaden, what are—" Kayla didn't finish her sentence.

With a broad grin, Jaden held up his medallion. "I think it was a key, just not in the normal sense. It took it in one side and spat it out on the other." Jaden chuckled.

"Cowboy," Han muttered as he waddled past Jaden.

"Worrywart," Jaden parried, but he gave Han's neck a fond rub. Han leaned into his hand, enjoying the contact.

Kayla grinned. She knew the feeling. As if he had sensed her amusement, Jaden turned his incredible blue eyes on her. Kayla smiled sweetly. "Do I get a turn too?"

Jaden laughed, that amazing smile making his face more handsome than anyone's should be. Kayla moved toward him, but Taz stepped in front of her.

"What do we do next?" Taz demanded.

Kayla sighed. Time with Jaden would have to wait. Studying the two riddles, she came up empty. "I don't know. There's nothing more there."

"There must be more," Jaden insisted.

"If it's any help, the ceiling over this area is really high," Iri commented.

Kayla looked up. Although she didn't see the ceiling, she couldn't miss the dark shapes that loomed far above. "Are those what I think they are?"

Jaden directed his attention upward and then groaned. "And here I thought we'd be able to complete this task without dealing with Gaptors."

CHAPTER TWENTY-EIGHT

"Atu, you did jinx us," Kayla accused. To no-one in particular, Kayla said, "Do you think the ceiling's the only thing keeping them out of the Buried Forest?"

"Who knows." Jaden sighed. "But if this ceiling is anything like the barrier that blocked the Gaptors when we were at the tower, it might only be effective for a limited time. Let's get what we came for before they break through."

His grim words forced Kayla to examine her surroundings. Their small group occupied a narrow strip of grass rimming a circular area sprinkled with circular stones, each one large enough to hold a person with their arms tucked at their sides. "What's with all the circles?"

"I don't know, but they smell bad." Iri gagged. "Like something's rotting there."

"Any colors telling you which stones we should avoid?" Jaden asked.

Iri squinted at the stones. "No colors. And the smell is warped by the breeze, so I can't pinpoint the bad stones that way either."

Jaden picked up a pebble and raised an eyebrow. "Here we go again."

He lobbed it, and they all watched as the pebble arced through the air. Kayla held her breath as it landed. Then she wished she hadn't. What happened made her suck in air so sharply that she coughed, but no one else noticed. They were all staring at the gaping narrow pit that had taken the place of the stone.

"Can anyone see how deep it is?" Kayla wheezed.

Jaden clapped her on the back, and Taz took to the air. Kayla gave him a watery smile as the coughing subsided.

"I can't see the bottom," Taz called a moment later.

"That's not encouraging," Han noted dourly.

"I wonder if they're all like that." Atu idly tossed another stone into the circle.

If Jaden hadn't been standing so close, Kayla would've been skewered by the spears that shot out at them. She heard hissing but didn't register the danger. Jaden shoved her to the ground, and she huffed as he landed on top of her, protecting her body with his own. The silence that followed was deafening.

Jaden rolled off Kayla and ran his arms up and down her body, checking for injuries.

"I'm fine," Kayla assured him. "What about you?"

As an afterthought, Jaden looked at his own body. "I seem to be in one piece."

Kayla saw the anger that flooded him as he turned a scarlet face toward Atu. "A little warning next time!"

Atu looked abashed. "Sorry, I didn't know that would happen."

Kayla put a placating hand on Jaden's arm. "Of course you didn't. But I think it's safe to say we don't want to try that again."

Atu nodded, suddenly looking shaken. His legs crumpled, and he plopped down. "How are we going to get out of here?"

"There was a way last time and there'll be a way this time," Jaden grunted.

Kayla knew how much being civil to Atu right then cost him. Taking his hand, she squeezed, hoping he understood she was proud of him. She was rewarded with a tiny smile. *Good enough.*

"Jaden, anything on that star map that might help?" Taz offered.

Kayla had forgotten about the map. Jaden released her hand to drop his backpack and retrieve the cube. He twisted the panels to open it, and the disc fell into his waiting palm. Jaden held the disc up to the light.

"I don't see anything." Then his face changed as he rolled the disc between his fingers.

"What?" Kayla pressed.

"We always thought this was just a chip." Jaden indicated the unobtrusive notch at the edge of the disc.

"Don't I remember it," Kayla said bitterly. The tiny cut it gave her had festered for days, until she asked Atu for healing. "What about it?"

"It looks exactly like that indentation in the grass!" Atu pointed at the lawn next to his feet. It looked like an overzealous weed whacker had chewed too far into it.

"Okay, given there's no such thing as coincidence when it comes to this mission, what does it mean?" Jaden said.

Atu thought a moment. "What if it's meant to show us that we should step on the stones that match the holes in the disc?"

Nobody said anything because there was nothing to say. It was the only thing that made sense.

"May I?" Atu looked at Jaden as he picked up a stone. "By my estimation, working from this chip-slash-grassy marker, the stone that's in this row," Atu stepped up to a row to mark it, "and the second one in should line up with a hole in the disc."

It wasn't only Jaden who checked his positioning. Taz even took to the air to be sure they weren't missing something. When she called confirmation, Atu lifted his arm to throw the stone. After a moment's hesitation, his arm dropped, and he handed the stone to Jaden.

"You know what my aim is like," Atu muttered when Jaden raised an eyebrow.

Nodding understanding, Jaden aimed and then cast the stone. When it landed on the right circle, Kayla tensed, ready for some new danger to present itself. It didn't.

"Alright, I think we're onto something," Jaden said. "Question now is, does the order in which we jump on the stones matter?"

Taz, who was still flying over them, called down, "I think you'll find that if you start with that stone, there's only ever going to be one other viable stone that you can reach."

Jaden compared the disc to the stones in the circle and realized she was right. Her bird's eye (or was that bat's eye?) view was excellent for placing the stones, but he wasn't going to take any chances. Jaden glanced at Han. "Just in case we're wrong, I'll tie that bit of rope around myself before we start. Would you mind holding the other end in case another abyss appears?"

Han gave his toothy grin. "Of course. What are friends for?"

Kayla felt her nerves stretch to their breaking point a few minutes later as Jaden leaped onto the first stone. The fact that Han hovered overhead, the rope in his talons, was small comfort. When Jaden landed without incident, Kayla wilted a little. But every jump after that was just as nerve-wracking.

Trying to keep her mind occupied, she traced the path Jaden took. Although it snaked this way and that, it was generally circular in nature, taking him ever closer to the center. She bit her lip. Would the stones hold if he had to jump back for a return trip? No, she wouldn't think about that. One obstacle at a time.

By the time Jaden prepared to jump to the stone matching the last point on their star disc, Kayla was drenched with sweat. She wiped her hands on her smart suit, trying to dry them. This stone was one removed from the very center of the circular area. She watched Jaden leap. He landed and grinned at her.

Kayla smiled and waved. "You made it!"

"Don't sound so surprised." Jaden chuckled. "It was—"

The pillar that shot up from the very center of the circle scared them all. For a moment, Kayla thought Jaden would fall backward onto one of the unsafe stones, but he wheeled his arms and regained his balance. His smart suit, not to mention the rope, helped keep him in place.

With Jaden safe, they all turned their attention to the pillar. It had risen to about waist height and it sparkled in the sunshine as specks of quartz in the rock caught the sun's eye. They all stared at the pillar, waiting for something else to happen. They weren't disappointed. With a soft whirr, the top split into several sections. Each section peeled back like the petals on a flower, revealing two items nestled in the center: a furled piece of leather and a blindingly white piece of parchment.

Jaden stared at the pillar as if expecting something.

"What are you waiting for?" Kayla called.

"The map." Jaden's attention didn't waver. "I can only see the artifact and that piece of leather. Last time, we got the cube in addition to these two."

They waited, but after five minutes, it was apparent nothing else would materialize.

"Maybe you need to take those two to get the map?" Kayla suggested.

"It's worth a try." Jaden reached forward and gently removed the items.

Abruptly, mist filtered up from the ground. It was thin and wispy at first, but it rapidly grew denser until it swirled around Jaden in thick bands. The bands broadened and floated up, like ribbons being pulled into the air, dissipating as they vanished into the sky above.

"Crackerjack!" Atu whistled. "What happened to the circle?"

Kayla's eyes flew to the ground, and she gasped. Sure enough, the circle, along with its stones and the gaping abyss, had disappeared. Jaden was left standing on another manicured lawn.

"Oh no! The map!" Jaden exclaimed.

"You mean the map's gone now that the circle is?" Atu guessed.

"Yes. It should've been there with these things." Jaden gestured at the parchment and strip of leather in his hands.

"Or perhaps there wasn't one," Kayla offered, thinking again of the strange patterns in the symbols. When Jaden gave her a quizzical glance, she waved an arm in the air. "There was something strange about the symbols on the wall. I feel like I'm missing something, but I just don't know what. I can't figure it out."

"You will," Jaden assured her, walking over and placing his hands on her shoulders. "If anyone can, it's you."

"Thanks." Kayla smiled at him. "I just wish it would click already. It's driving me batty." There was a cough from Taz. "Oh, no offense."

"None taken," Han purred, giving Taz a pointed look.

Taz sniffed and shrugged. "I suppose." She ruffled her wings. "Is it time to leave this heinous place now?"

"After one last thing." Jaden handed the furled leather to Kayla.

Kayla wasn't sure whether to slap her arm or take the leather. Her birthmark was burning, like she had scratched it too much. Gritting her teeth and resisting the urge to touch her arm again, she accepted the piece of leather. But as soon as she unfurled it, her arm felt like it had burst into flame. Dropping the leather, she grabbed at her arm.

Alarmed, Jaden took the hand that held her arm. "What's wrong?"

"Just look at my birthmark. Tell me it's not on fire." Even as she said the words, the flames lost their impetus.

Jaden lifted her arm and inspected it. "Kayla, I don't see anything. Do you want to take your smart suit off so Atu can look at it?"

"No, it's better now." Kayla looked at Jaden because it was easier than looking at the others. "I think it has something to do with that piece of leather. The same thing happened last time."

To her relief, Jaden took her words in earnest. "Are you up for testing your theory?"

Kayla nodded. Jaden retrieved the leather strip, then held it out for her. Just having it close again made Kayla's arm heat up. Squaring her shoulders, she flexed her fingers, then latched onto the strip. Fire flared on her arm. Ignoring the flames, she deliberately dropped the leather. The relief was instantaneous, leaving Kayla with an arm that was hot and uncomfortable, but not unbearably so.

Jaden was studying her. "Yup, it had to do with that leather strip. And no, I don't know why."

Thoughtfully, Jaden nodded and picked up the leather. "Just to be sure, let's have Atu check your arm."

Kayla removed the top half of her smart suit, revealing her t-shirt.

She waited as Atu inspected her arm but wasn't surprised when he said nothing was there except her birthmark.

After sliding back into her smart suit, Kayla beckoned to Jaden. "You'll have to open it for me so I can tell you what it says." Jaden nodded and spread the strip out on the lawn in front of Kayla. Her eyes ran over the glyphs. "Living with hope."

"Super helpful, as always. Can we get more than three words next time?" Jaden yelled at the sky.

Kayla giggled. She knew that had been his intention when he turned and smiled at her. She took his hand. "I agree. Can we leave now?"

Looking back up, Jaden's expression darkened. "Only if we're ready to fight that lot."

What had been a few shadows earlier was now a seething black mass threatening to obscure the sunlight at any moment.

"Just as well we have this." Atu removed the reed Pallaton had given him, put it to his lips, and blew.

"How long should we give them to get here?" Jaden asked Han.

Han studied the ceiling. "When black blood begins flowing over that area, it's time to go."

Jaden nodded, then led Kayla away from the others. When they were out of earshot, he sank onto the lush grass, pulling her down next to him.

"You want some alone time now?" Kayla ventured.

"No, I want you to tell me what your birthmark means," Jaden said.

Kayla frowned. She hadn't told him that the mark had a translation. Maybe if she played dumb, he'd talk himself around in circles. "What do you mean?"

Jaden sighed. "Kayla, I'm not dense. I've seen those symbols on the wall and I've seen your birthmark. Then you told me that the books you learned the language from all had that symbol on the cover. It doesn't take a genius to work out that it must have a meaning."

It was Kayla's turn to sigh. She hadn't planned on telling him the translation until all this was over. Now she had no choice. "It means 'key.'"

Jaden mulled her words. "As in, the books were a key to learning the language?"

"I guess." Kayla shrugged.

"If that's the case, why is that word tattooed, so to speak, on your body?" Jaden didn't allow her gaze to slide away from his.

"That's a question I've asked myself almost every day since we found the tower." Kayla looked down.

Jaden's fingers curled gently around her chin, and he lifted her face so that he was looking into her eyes. "This is no time for games. I need you to tell me what's going on in that head of yours."

Kayla wanted to move, wanted to get away from that intense gaze. His blue eyes bored into her, demanding the truth. When she realized he wouldn't relent, she whispered, "That perhaps I'm a key too." Tears of frustration spilled down her cheeks.

"A key to what?" Jaden's thumbs wiped away the tears.

"I don't know. You think that if I did, I'd still be worried about it?"

Noting the others turning to look at them, Jaden folded her into his arms. "Okay, it's alright. Don't stress. We'll figure this out together. That's what a team's for, isn't it? And look at all the great team members we have." Jaden gestured toward the others who were drifting closer, their concern showing. "Can I share this with them?"

Kayla nodded, giving him permission but not daring to speak. If she did, she wouldn't be able to hold it together. She had agonized over this on her own for so long that allowing anyone else in felt alien. Kayla nestled into Jaden's arms, seeking his warmth as he explained to the others. When Iri's supporting hand went to her shoulder and Taz's warm breath rustled her hair, she almost lost it.

With supreme effort, she restrained the emotions. Finally, she dared peek at the others. "You're not all mad at me for not saying anything sooner?"

"No." Iri smiled. "We've all had our secrets. And I can say from my experience with all of you, this is the best place to share them."

Kayla smiled a little. "Thanks."

The group huddled around her, discussing possible interpretations for her birthmark, until Kayla felt comfortable enough to crawl out of

Jaden's arms and add her own thoughts. An almighty crash overhead interrupted them. A black shape slid down the ceiling. Or domed roof would be a more accurate way to describe the thing that trapped them within the Buried Forest. A moment later, another shape hit the roof and slid down.

"The cavalry's arrived!" Jaden cheered. "Time to get out of here."

CHAPTER TWENTY-NINE

They took to the air before any of them thought to wonder whether they would be able to escape the dome. Only when they were halfway towards the ceiling did Jaden mention this to Han. "Can we get out that way?"

Han shrugged. "As you're so fond of saying, there's only one way to find out."

Jaden grimaced. "Then may I suggest that we take it slow? I would hate for us to hit that thing so hard that we do ourselves permanent damage."

Han nodded. Apparently, they weren't the only ones worried about breaching the ceiling. The other gliders were slowing too and approaching the dome with caution.

"Iri, can you see anything?" Jaden asked.

Iri squinted. "Nope. But we should still be careful."

"Alright, Han and I will go first." Securing his hold on Han's neck, Jaden tensed as the dome neared. Ten seconds. Seven seconds. Five-four-three-two . . .

They broke through. Bedlam reigned. Gaptors fell around them. Gliders streaked past, the shapes on their backs indistinguishable blobs. There was no time to think. Jaden's DD glowed to life, and he laid into the closest Gaptor.

Vaguely, Jaden was aware of the others popping through the dome and joining the fight. The sounds of battle filled his ears: human cries, glider twitters, Gaptor screeches. It was a blur of sound and motion. Jaden's arm flashed up and down and around as Han twisted them through their enemies. The odious blood of slain Gaptors soon coated them.

Markov's voice squawked over the comm, calling plays. Jaden ignored them. Those plays would be for Markov, the Legion, and those who flew with them. Jaden didn't start calling plays of his own for their team. It would only confuse matters. Besides, it was too chaotic for him to find them. Jaden concentrated on what was in front of him. The Gaptors kept coming. And Han and Jaden kept fighting.

It felt like an eternity before the battle ended, but it was only minutes. Jaden surveyed the scene. The dome was littered with countless bodies, friend and foe alike. He scanned the survivors, searching for Taz and Kayla. "Kayla?"

"I'm here. We're safe. Iri? Atu?" Kayla checked.

To Jaden's relief, they got replies from both of them. Jaden glanced to his left as a glider drew up alongside. "Markov! You're a sight for sore eyes."

Markov grinned. "As usual, I have to save your sorry butt."

Jaden laughed. "If you say so." Turning, Jaden saw the rest of his childhood friends drawing closer on their gliders. "I see Sven didn't take long making warriors out of you."

"They were easier to train than you were," Sven boomed from behind Jaden.

"Do you always have to come up behind me?"

"That wouldn't be possible if you were paying attention, no?"

Jaden could only shake his head. "I'm glad you all survived. Anyone injured?"

Bree raised her hand. "Me," she said in a small voice.

Noticing Stovan's glider angling closer to Bree, Jaden said, "Atu, can you work your magic?"

Atu raised an eyebrow at Jaden before speaking to Bree. "Let's find a place we can land, and I'll take care of those injuries."

"Not a bad idea," Jaden noted. "We should probably all head for a more defensible position."

"Lead on," Markov said.

As Han and Jaden turned to comply, Jaden noticed two gliders approaching Kayla. His eyes widened when he recognized her parents. Their exhilarated grins were like people who had just had the most incredible ride at the fairgrounds. Their enthusiastic greetings to their daughter and ensuing animated conversation about the battle just made Jaden shake his head for the second time. *Who would've thought? They're in their element!*

Within the hour, the group descended on a small hill overlooking the surrounding countryside. The vista was peaceful. More than that, it allowed for an unobstructed view in every direction. The group took time to rest, hydrate, and eat. Together, Atu and Kayla made their way through the ranks, taking care of the wounded.

The air began to cool, and Jaden realized twilight wasn't far off. Pulling Kayla aside, Jaden said, "It'll be dark soon. Do you think we should try make it home or camp here?"

"A few of the gliders need time to recover. They took some serious hits. Even though I'd prefer to be home, it'll be better if we spend the night."

"Okay, I'll see what we can do to secure the area." Jaden gave her hand a quick squeeze before crossing to Sven.

Between them, Jaden and Sven worked out a guard rotation and set up a perimeter. When Jaden was satisfied he couldn't make the area any safer, he went searching for Kayla. He was looking forward to some alone time with her. That wasn't on the cards.

He found Kayla with her parents, seated near the middle of the camp around a small fire, their gliders looming directly behind them. From the way the gliders scrutinized every person who approached, they had set up their own monitoring system.

"Evening," Jaden greeted.

"Jaden! How lovely to see you," Sadie gushed. "Come, sit down. Join us."

Smiling, Jaden took her up on the offer. "Thank you. From the way you and your husband were grinning after that battle, I'd say you enjoyed yourselves."

"Wasn't it invigorating?"

Jaden could only chuckle. Settling in, he listened as Kayla's parents told them about their training at Sven's. It wasn't long before Jaden's childhood friends joined them.

Then Sven strolled over. Jaden eyed the bulging shapes outlined against the dark sky behind him. "What are those?"

"A few surprises we brought with us in case we met with trouble." Sven beamed.

"A few surprises, huh?" Jaden quipped, his interest piqued.

Sven chuckled. "You want to see?"

"Without question!"

They rose and traversed the short distance. Without preamble, Sven tossed aside the cover concealing the item beneath. Jaden stared. *Sven came up with this?* Then he shook himself. *What am I thinking? Of course he did!*

"A modified missile launcher?" Jaden guessed.

Sven beamed. "Correct! Except they launch the same current beams your DDs do instead of missiles. I would show you, except they're a little noisy and some people are already asleep."

Jaden recalled the booming sounds during the battle. He had dismissed them as Gaptors being dispatched to wherever they went when they disappeared in all that sound and light. Now that he thought about it, though, some of those booms had been different. "You used them today?"

"We did." Sven chuckled. "And they were more effective than I had hoped. The best part is that they're portable. We can set them up anywhere. I thought perhaps you might like to have some near your compound in the event they're needed?"

No doubt. Sven always came prepared. Jaden clapped him on the back. "Sven, have I told you what a good man you are?" Jaden grinned as Sven's cheeks turned pink with pleasure. "And heck yeah! I'll definitely take you up on that offer. I assume you have more of these stashed away somewhere?"

Sven nodded as he covered the machine again. He gave Jaden a breakdown of how the launchers worked while they strolled back to the group. Joining the others, Jaden listened to the various conversations flowing around the fire. No one seemed particularly tired, despite their battle today. Everyone's adrenaline levels were still way too high. Chatter continued late into the night before everyone finally slipped into their sleeping shells for a few hours' rest.

When Jaden opened his eyes the next morning, they were gritty. He shouldn't have stayed up so late. He groaned as he rose. All around him, the camp bustled with life.

Jaden ambled over to where Kayla slept. She looked so peaceful. If only things could stay this way. He tucked the stray piece of hair that had fallen over her cheek behind her ear. She stirred at the touch. Then her eyes blinked open.

"Morning. Sleep well?" Kayla mumbled.

"Sorry, I didn't mean to wake you."

"No, it's good you did. We should be getting home." Kayla sat up and yawned as she stretched.

It didn't take long to eat breakfast and strike camp. Everyone was anxious to get home. Shortly before nightfall, they reached the outskirts of Daxsos. The familiar landmarks were a welcome sight.

Jaden turned to Pallaton, drifting beside him. "Any suggestions on how we split the Legion? I was thinking that the other voyagers who've joined us can camp out at my friends' homes. But I don't think there will be enough space for their gliders as well."

Pallaton shook his head. "It would be better if the Legion patrolled the area so we have advance warning of any impending attack."

"Excellent." Jaden addressed his childhood friends via the comm system. "Are each of you up to taking some of the new recruits home with you?"

The affirmative replies filtered back, and the group separated themselves accordingly. Kayla, Iri, and Atu stayed close to Jaden and watched the Legion carrying the voyagers to the respective homes they had chosen.

"Honey, your dad and I are going to head home," Sadie informed Kayla. "I desperately need a shower."

"Okay, Mom." Kayla smiled. "Iri and I will join you in a short while."

Sadie nodded, and Kayla's parents sped away. Kayla's eyes were speculative as she watched them leave.

"What are you thinking?" Jaden asked.

"Huh, my mom didn't even complain that I wasn't leaving with them."

"Is that a problem?"

Kayla considered a moment. "Nope. I think they're just tired, although they won't admit to that."

"In that case, shall we all head for my home?" Jaden sensed the others wanted to spend time together, just the four of them.

Eager nods confirmed Jaden's suspicions, and they set off. When they arrived, Han cocked his head to one side as though listening to something.

"What's up?" Jaden asked.

Han only smiled. "I think you'll find a pleasant surprise inside."

"What do you mean?" Jaden demanded.

"If I were you, I wouldn't waste time talking." Han deposited Jaden and left without further explanation. Jaden couldn't ask the other gliders, either, since they followed suit.

Mystified, the teens strode to the rooftop entrance. Before they even opened the door, Jaden heard voices. Shock stopped him in his tracks as he recognized them.

Kayla touched his arm, showing alarm at his response. "What's wrong?"

"I think—" But Jaden's voice failed him. When he saw her reach for her DD, he clamped a hand over her arm. "We won't need that."

Her green eyes were alert, her face still showing concern. Now was not the time for this, but if he was right, he wanted her to know how much she meant to him. Immediately. Before anything else happened.

Unabashed by the presence of the others, he lifted his hands to her face and eased the lines of worry on her forehead. His fingers didn't stop there. They traced twin paths past her lovely eyes and across her soft cheeks, coming to rest at the corners of her mouth. He ran one thumb over her lips, wishing he could kiss her. Really kiss her. But that would be going too far with the others there.

She must've sensed his need because she moved in closer, tucking herself against him. Jaden closed his eyes for a moment, savoring her closeness. Then he moved his hands behind her neck, pulling her forward gently as he planted a chaste kiss on her lips. He would have to make do with that for now.

Jaden drew back, and Kayla tilted her head to smile up at him. "What was that for?"

Mischief and puzzlement sparkled in her eyes. It was an alluring combination. Jaden took a deep breath, steadying himself. "Just a token to remind you that you mean the world to me."

Kayla looked like she had stopped breathing. Then she inhaled her own shaky breath. "Gee, Jameson, yet again you show your capacity for taking a girl's breath away."

Jaden smiled and leaned in close so only she could hear. "Give me some time alone with you, and I'll really take your breath away."

Kayla giggled. "That's quite enough of that. We have an audience."

Grinning, Jaden stepped away and dropped his hands, catching one of hers with one of his. Turning to Iri and Atu, he said, "Shall we?"

Jaden was amused when it was Atu who said, "About time."

Still chuckling, Jaden opened the door. It took all of a second for him to confirm he was correct. Giving Kayla a wide smile, he let go of her hand and bolted downstairs. To his astonishment, Atu was right behind him. The reason became clear as soon as Jaden entered the living room: Atu's resemblance to his father was unmistakable. The short, pretty, dark-haired woman standing next to Atu's father had to be his mother. And next to them were Jaden's own parents.

"Dad! Mom!" Jaden yelled. They ran to each other and embraced fiercely. "When did you get back? How is this possible? Did he hurt you?"

Clara Jameson laughed. "Which question would you like us to answer first?"

"You choose. I'm just so happy to see you!" He pulled them closer again, scarcely able to believe they were actually home.

"Jaden, meet my mom, Taema, and my dad, Sava," Atu said, making Jaden aware that he wasn't the only one with something to celebrate.

Jaden shook Taema's and Sava's hands. "It is so good to meet you. Your son never gave up hope that you were alive. He was determined to find you."

Sava beamed. "Yes, he is a remarkable young man."

Only when Atu introduced his parents to Iri and Kayla did Jaden realize they'd made it into the living room as well. The excited jabber continued as introductions were made and niceties exchanged. Jaden thought his head would explode. He needed answers.

"Can we sit down so you tell us what happened?" Jaden's voice was loud enough to drown out the others.

His mother looked startled, but his father just smiled. "Yes, that's probably best. Why don't we make ourselves comfortable in the kitchen? We can drink some tea while we fill you in."

Jaden itched with impatience as they went through the motions. However, finally, they were all seated around the kitchen table.

Ty glanced at Clara. "Would you like to do the honors?"

Without preamble, Clara began. She told them how she and her husband had decided to wait on the deck for a few minutes to see if Jaden suddenly reappeared. After all, that's what had happened the last time he left. But as they stood there, they heard noises that made them want to put their hands over their ears. Unearthly screeches and inexplicable thumps surrounded them. Before they could run inside, an unseen force struck them, rendering them unconscious.

Jaden nodded. "I think what you heard were Pallaton and his Legion fighting the Gaptors that had just arrived. We didn't leave you defenseless. We left a small force of gliders here to protect you. I didn't want to take any chances."

His mother smiled and covered Jaden's hand with her own.

"Thank you for that. Unfortunately, it seems that didn't work as well as you had hoped."

Jaden grimaced. "Yes, Pallaton and his Legion were overwhelmed by their sheer numbers. We didn't expect the Usurper to send so many. When we returned and found you gone, I decided something had to be done."

"Is that when you gave me this?" Clara took the relic stone off her finger and placed it in Jaden's palm.

Smiling, Jaden took the ring and returned it to his own finger. "Yes, and that resulted in a few unforeseen consequences. But more about our side of the story later. Won't you please continue with yours?"

Clara did. "Well the next part is pretty much what I told you happened in my dream. When I woke up, I was in a dark place, and I could hear and smell your father. The main difference was that I wasn't numb. And I could speak, thanks to you and that marvelous ring. I told your father that your solution was viable and hoped no one was listening in. Fortunately, no one arrived to investigate, and based on that, I assumed I could talk freely. Despite this, your father and I realized we should wait for a more opportune time to escape. Besides, we didn't know where we were or what options were available to us. I will admit that right then I began to wonder if it was possible to change my dream. I wondered whether we might be able to escape and thereby bypass the necessity for you to come and rescue us, keeping you safe and foiling our kidnapper's plans. We must have been there for a few hours before two guards appeared and moved us to a different area."

"Who moved you?" Jaden asked.

"I don't know. Remember, I told you that in my dream the darkness was so thick it was impossible to see. Well, that part remained true. There was no way to determine their identities. That's not the important part, though. What is relevant is that we heard our captors discussing two other prisoners. From their conversation, it was clear these prisoners were related to one of the seekers."

"My parents?" Atu asked, surprising them as usual because he'd actually spoken.

Clara smiled. "Yes. Fortunately, our guards were lazy. They got tired of continually opening two sets of cell doors to deal with us, so they moved us into the same cell as your parents. Since you and your father look so much alike, it was easy to figure out who they were. We told them who we were, that we knew you, and that you were well and doing what you could to bring this abominable situation to an end."

Sava spoke. "After so much time in captivity, we had almost given up on survival. But your parents' words renewed our hope and reignited our desire to fight."

"Oh, I think they were doing just fine before." Clara laughed. "They were resisting enough to make the guards wary when dealing with them."

"They could move?" Jaden asked.

"Occasionally, we all could. Our captors had to let the numbing effects wear off so we could eat, drink, and take bathroom breaks. But as soon as that was done, those monsters applied fresh numbing applications. I must say, I nearly had a heart attack the first time I laid eyes on them. I was convinced they were there to kill us! But they just raised their antennae and sent out another dose of partial paralysis, at least, for your father and Atu's parents. It took a while, but we worked out a system of passing the relic stone around so that we could all talk and move. This allowed us to start making plans."

Ty picked up the tale. "We began gathering information. We noted the names of places we overheard, but we didn't recognize any of them. We were beginning to wonder if we would have to make a blind run for it when something unexpected happened."

"Yes," Clara interjected. "The big man himself came to visit. I don't remember much of what transpired during that meeting because he was so terrifying. But when he opened the breach, that was unforgettable. He was gloating over his achievement so much that whatever trick he used to dull our minds wore off. We were able to remember how he opened the breach."

"I assume he didn't know that you could all move?" Jaden asked.

"No, by then we had learnt how to hide that. I think it was our saving grace," Clara said. "Two days later, we took action. We concluded that the breach was the only way we would get back home. From what the Usurper said, we realized we were no longer in our world. Escaping into his world would have been futile. We waited until our guards came to our cell, and then we overpowered them. We snuck through that fortress until we found the place where the breach been opened. It took longer than planned for us to figure out the control board, but we did, and the breach opened. Your dad and I made it through, but before Taema and Sava could join us, the Usurper appeared. He slammed the breach shut with us on one side and them on the other."

"Where were you?" Jaden breathed.

"That was the strange part. When your dad and I walked through the breach, we thought we were entering a forest. But as soon as the door closed, the landscape vanished, and we found ourselves floating in thin air. There was nothing there. It was a void."

"A void?" Jaden repeated.

Ty had had enough of being quiet. "It was empty. It was quiet. We couldn't communicate because all sound was dampened, and we just drifted there. We weren't going anywhere. That was, until that friend of yours, Zareh, arrived. He waved those cute little arms of his, and before we knew it, your mother and I were home."

"So how where my parents able to escape?" Atu wondered.

"When we got home, Zareh demanded to know everything. We told him all that had happened and gave him the names of the places we remembered. We also told him that your parents were still stuck there. He said he and his minions would raid the place, retrieve them, and bag the bad guy. Regrettably, the Usurper realized his lair was compromised. He was gone by the time Zareh's forces arrived. The best news, though, was that the Usurper's hasty departure meant he abandoned your parents."

"You met Zareh?" Jaden sputtered.

"Yes, he's quite the character." Ty laughed.

"But how did he know where to find you?"

"Apparently, he was able to sense something wrong with the 'alternate reality,' whatever that means," Ty answered.

Jaden nodded. If anyone could ferret out an anomaly, it was Zareh. "So after he retrieved Atu's parents, he brought them here?"

Sava spoke up. "He thought it would be better if the four of us remained together. He put some security in place to ensure we were protected."

"If only he had done that sooner," Jaden commented, "all this could have been avoided. Did he say what security he was putting in place?"

"No, only that we should stay inside the house," Clara answered.

Jaden sighed. "I didn't really expect him to tell you, but I thought I'd ask anyway. I think it's time we celebrated the fact that you're all home. Let's get a victory dinner going!"

CHAPTER THIRTY

The ten of them sat in Jaden's living room. It was early afternoon the day after Jaden and Atu's parents had returned. Kayla studied the group comprising five seekers and Jaden's five childhood friends. They had all made themselves at home. Stovan was seated next to Bree on the couch. Kayla wondered what had prompted Bree to switch her spiky hair tips back to pink again. She had quite liked the purple. Kayla's gaze shifted to Markov. He stood behind Shianna, perched on a dining room chair pulled into the living room to accommodate the large group. Not surprisingly, Tarise sat on her own off to one side, staring right back at Kayla.

Kayla shifted. Tarise's glare always made her feel uncomfortable. Those large gray eyes seemed not to miss a thing. Like Jaden's hand on Kayla's shoulder. Honestly, if Tarise could shoot daggers with her eyes, Kayla would be toast.

Averting her gaze, Kayla focused on Iri and Atu. They sat quietly as usual, listening to the rowdy conversation. Sven took up most of the second couch.

"You made us work like dogs," Markov accused.

"That was nothing. You don't know what real training is," Sven protested.

"It was just as well he did," Shianna remarked. "I don't think we would have been prepared for our first battle if he hadn't."

"Thank you, Shianna. At least one if you appreciates my efforts," Sven grumbled.

That brought a few chuckles. Everyone was in such a positive frame of mind. *Everyone with the exception of Tarise.*

"Speaking of effort, what will it take for you to find a way around those numbing EMP's?" Stovan prodded

Just like that, the mood changed. From what Bree told them, she had been injured because a Gaptor had numbed her. Paralyzed, she fell from her glider, was sliced by the same Gaptor's rotating blades, and then was rescued by her glider. Clearly, Stovan wasn't content with the situation.

"It will take time," Sven admitted. "It is difficult to find a solution when I cannot pinpoint the exact frequency at which the transmissions are made."

"Are you saying we should capture one of those monsters if we want a solution?" Stovan asked.

"That would be excellent, yes." Sven beamed.

"And how do you suggest we do that?" Tarise snapped.

Kayla wasn't the only one to notice her snarky tone. Jaden answered. "We'll have to come up with a plan. Tarise, you're the genius here. What do you propose?"

Anger flashed in Tarise's eyes. "You're supposed to be the leader. Why do I have to come up with the ideas?"

Jaden was taken aback. Kayla grimaced. He either hadn't been paying attention or was totally oblivious to the way Tarise felt about him. Poor man! She would have to enlighten him. And ask him what happened between the two of them. Clearly, *something* had. But what?

Jaden floundered for a second. "Everyone knows a good leader takes the ideas of his group and considers them before making decisions. I just thought I'd give you that opportunity. But if you don't want it . . ."

Well said. Kayla felt guilty pleasure as Tarise squirmed.

"I'll work on some ideas," Tarise conceded, less than gracefully.

"The gliders have fought these aberrations before," Atu noted. "I'm sure they'll have some ideas on how we can capture one."

"Capturing them may not be the problem," Sven said. "The more pressing question is how we will get them to raise those antennae for us, no?"

Jaden frowned. "You're right. Okay, let's set those problems aside for a moment. I want to explore a tangent that my brain keeps going back to. We know the medallions counteract the numbing effect of those EMPs, right?" Everyone nodded. "In the book Awena gave us, the Gaptor was set on stealing Gedrin's medallion. Why was that? I mean, Gedrin was going to die, so why did the Gaptor take the medallion after it killed him? It wasn't like Gedrin needed it to counter the EMP anymore."

"I have an answer for that," Kayla responded. She was amused when Jaden blinked in surprise. It really wasn't his day. In fact, it begged the question: what *was* he focused on? "No, I'm not psychic, it's just been bothering me too. The first time we met Zareh, he told us our medallions were the key. He also said something about the Gaptor —remember, when only the one escaped the battle with Atu's relatives. He mentioned it only reappeared when there was a risk that its enemies would rise against it 'in force.' Then its goal was to take the medallions, not kill the seekers. He only killed the seekers because he took pleasure in it. I think the answer to your question lies in those few snippets."

"Okay, so if the Gaptor was after the medallions when the seekers rose 'in force,' that would imply that there were a lot of medallions around back then," Jaden thought aloud. "Maybe that means we need to get a whole lot of medallions together, and that will somehow help us get rid of the Gaptors?"

"That may be," Sven pointed out, "but how are we going to find 'a whole lot' of medallions?"

Jaden began to pace. None of the others said anything. Kayla watched the group, intrigued that they knew to leave Jaden alone when he was in this frame of mind. *Well, what did I expect? They grew up with him, didn't they? They* should *know him this well.*

Her eyes flicked to Tarise again. For the second time, she found those unsettling gray eyes honed on her. Abruptly, Kayla was angry. Just who did this girl think she was? How could she think she was the only one with any claim to Jaden? In fact, that was totally the wrong way to think about it. Tarise wasn't giving Jaden any freedom to make his own choices. That irked Kayla more than anything else. Defiantly, she glared at Tarise, satisfied when Tarise turned away this time.

"What do you think the Gaptor did with the medallions he took?" Jaden asked, breaking the silence. "From what we know, he couldn't get back to his world, and Slurpy couldn't get here. He must've stashed them somewhere."

"Where, though?" Markov murmured, reading Jaden's mind.

"And are they still there or did he send them back to his master as soon as Slurpy found a way to open the breach again?" Jaden added.

"Unless the Gaptor knew we were going to take him out, he wouldn't have had time for that," Kayla pointed out.

"That doesn't mean they're still here," Sven observed. "It's possible the Usurper sent someone to get the medallions as soon as he could get Gaptors through, no?"

"Possibly," Jaden mused. "But only if Slurpy knew where to find them. What if that first Gaptor didn't tell him where they were stashed?"

Abruptly, Tarise stood. "There are too many unknowns here to draw a valid conclusion. I have some errands to run. Call me when you have a plan."

So saying, she marched out. Jaden stared after her, his face thoughtful. Kayla wasn't going to let Tarise's rude behavior stand. "I'll be right back." Kayla dashed after Tarise and caught up to her on the roof just as Tarise was climbing into her 'pod. "Hold up!"

Tarise glanced back, her annoyance clear. "What do you want?"

"You seem to have a problem with me. Why?" Kayla demanded.

"I thought that would be obvious." Tarise folded her arms.

"Because of my relationship with Jaden?"

"He was mine until you came along. You poked your nose where it didn't belong. You beguiled him with your medallion and your questions. Then you seduced him when you went to Ruby's."

"Hang on a minute," Kayla interrupted. "I did no such thing!"

"Smoke and mirrors." Tarise shrugged. "Say what you want, but you stole him from me."

"Tarise, look, I'm sorry that you feel that way, but Jaden was never yours to begin with."

Apparently, that was the worst thing Kayla could've said. Tarise's face almost turned purple with rage. "He *was* mine. He just hadn't realized it yet. Then you came along and spent all that time with him, time that you stole from this world while you were in that time freeze. You cast your spell over him, and he fell for it. Now you're going to pay."

Tarise slammed the hatch of her 'pod shut as she slid inside and revved the engines. Even if Kayla wanted to say something, Tarise wouldn't hear her over that racket. Kayla watched Tarise speed away, a knot of unease settling in her stomach. Had she done the right thing chasing after Tarise and confronting her?

Troubled, Kayla made her way back down to the living room. The others had moved to the kitchen to sample Bree's delicacies. The sight of the wonderful morsels didn't even make Kayla smile.

A hand slid into hers. "Are you alright?" Jaden murmured.

"No. You do know that Tarise thinks you're hers?" Kayla snarled, unable to stop herself.

Jaden sighed and ran a hand through his unruly blonde hair. "She mentioned that."

"When?"

Noticing the others sending them furtive glances, Jaden pulled Kayla down the hall to the living room where they wouldn't be overheard.

"That day we spent up in the mountains, right after we got back from the tower. Tarise confronted me as we were all leaving. I didn't even know she felt that way," Jaden railed. "I thought I made it clear to her that I never wanted to hurt her. I mean, if I didn't know she felt that way, I could hardly be blamed. *And* I told her neither of us foresaw our relationship."

Kayla guessed there was more he wasn't saying. "And how did she take that?"

Jaden huffed. "Well, she said it was okay, but her body language didn't exactly line up with her words."

"Uh-huh. And you didn't think to follow up on that?"

"I didn't have to. She came to my house the next day with all sorts of recriminations," Jaden remembered.

"It seems you still didn't resolve matters though."

"Tarise didn't give me a chance. She stormed out before I could talk sense into her. What happened when you chased after her today?"

Jaden had switched the focus of the conversation, but Kayla let it pass. Jaden couldn't tell her much more that she hadn't already guessed. "The same thing that happened to you. I confronted her about her attitude, and she yelled and took off before I could say anything to calm her down."

Jaden smiled ruefully. "Sorry about that. I didn't notice she was giving you a hard time today."

Kayla wrapped her arms around Jaden's neck. "You had other things on your mind. Besides, it wasn't what she said. It's what she did. Her actions were hostile from the start. But you can make it up to me."

"I bet I know how." Jaden grinned, bending his head to kiss her.

Kayla never tired of the effect he had on her. The heady sensation, the feel of his strong body under her fingers, the incredible need to be close to him.

"You two really should get a room," Markov commented behind them.

Jaden groaned as he pulled away from her. "Dude, did you really have to interrupt?"

Kayla giggled. It was reassuring to know she wasn't the only one enjoying their kiss.

"Yes, we need to know where you keep the pizza dough. We

figured we'd throw some pizzas in the oven, especially since Bree's here. Aren't the leftovers from her pizzas what we always fight over?"

Jaden grinned. "Yeah, I'll be right there. Give me a minute."

Markov nodded and left them.

Jaden studied Kayla. "Are you sure you're okay? You seem a little subdued."

"I'll be fine. I'm just tired. I'm going to head home for a shower. Maybe I'll feel better after that."

"You want me to get Iri?" Jaden asked, aware Iri had chosen to stay with Kayla while they were back in Daxsos.

"No, let her have fun with the others. She needs to get to know them. I'll be fine on my own. Okay if I take your 'pod and you remote command it home?"

"Yes, but I can come with you if you like," Jaden offered.

"Thanks, that's sweet of you, but did you already forget they need to know where the pizza dough is?"

Jaden chuckled. "Okay, okay, I'll let you go. Let me know when you get home."

"Will do." Kayla gave him a quick kiss on the cheek and made her escape.

Relieved, she sank into the plush interior of the 'pod. She really needed some alone time. Setting the panel to her coordinates, she leaned back and closed her eyes.

* * *

Dank air assailed his nostrils as he entered the black depths. The icy temperature made him boost his body heat a little, but not too much. He couldn't show the fires that burned within. Only the sound of dripping water marred the silence. A perfect place to meet this human. Thoughtfully, Zubiaba ran his finger across the wall, through the green trails of slime marking the water paths. Dried bones crunched underfoot, the remnants of long-dead victims. Rotting leaves, blown into the cave and trapped there, sent their putrid aroma his way, reminiscent of a tasty appetizer. Despite these pleasantries, Zubiaba hated the place. He wanted to be back in his own home.

But that home had been taken when Zareh and his troops had invaded. A fresh wave of fury ramped up his inner flame. He grinned devilishly, savoring the thought that they had neither captured him nor been able to lay their hands on his breaching device. Just as quickly, Zubiaba remembered the loss of the two sets of parents, and his thoughts soured again. He hadn't expected that. It would be interesting, if not entertaining, to see what this girl, Tarise, had to say.

As if his thoughts had conjured her, she appeared at the entrance to the cave. Her nervousness was a balm to his bruised ego, but he couldn't show her he relished her pain, her suffering. She would have to be convinced he was her benevolent benefactor.

"Greetings, Tarise," Zubiaba purred. He stepped forward and took her hand, planting a gallant kiss before releasing it. He hid the smile at her shiver. Excellent! She was afraid.

"Hello," Tarise stammered. "What should I call you?"

At least the girl had some sense. She wasn't going to use the unmentionable name that creature Zareh had given him. "You may call me Zubiaba." The meek way she ducked her head almost made him salivate. What would feasting on her flesh be like? But no, not yet. He had to establish her worth. "The offer you sent via one of my creations—or Gaptors as you call them—sounded intriguing. Why don't you tell me more?"

Tarise straightened, and her eyes lighted with fervor. "I believe we can help each other."

"What makes you think I need your help? Or anyone's help for that matter." Keeping his tone civil took effort. To her credit, the girl didn't back down. If anything, she grew bolder the longer she stood there. Interesting. Her hatred made her resilient. She might be more useful than he'd thought.

Tarise smirked. "I can neutralize those missiles that destroy your Gaptors."

That got Zubiaba's attention. From his spies' reports, the weapons were a problem. "And what makes you think you can do what my best engineers have been unable to?"

"Your best engineers aren't geniuses," Tarise said scornfully. "They also weren't there when Sven designed the weapon. There is something he overlooked, a weakness that can be exploited."

"Why should I give you anything for this information? I could just torture it out of you," Zubiaba sneered.

"You could try."

The girl's total lack of terror made Zubiaba reconsider his options. If she was as intelligent as his reports claimed, she could have put a failsafe in place to prevent that. But what?

To his annoyance, the girl leered at him. "I bet you're trying to figure out what I've done to protect myself. You can just keep guessing because I won't tell you. But you will regret it if you try."

Zubiaba wanted to throttle her right there and then. Watch her eyes bulge as he squeezed the life out of her. He tucked his arms tightly over his chest, struggling to restrain himself. Soon enough, he could linger over killing her. She would suffer for this. The thought comforted Zubiaba. "What is it you want?"

"Nothing that I think would be a burden for you. It might even help your cause."

Would the girl continue to toy with him? She was digging her grave deeper by the second. "Are you going to make me beg?"

Tarise shook her head. "No, I'm not that foolish."

Zubiaba relaxed. He hadn't had to plead with anyone for over a millennia, and he didn't plan on ever doing it again. Her wisdom had spared her an hour of suffering. Or at least half an hour.

"I want Kayla Melmique removed from the equation," Tarise spat. "I want that girl gone. And I don't care how you do it. The sooner the better."

"Anything else?" Zubiaba rasped, his usually mellifluous voice deserting him. Nettled by this slip, he cleared his throat. Had his lapse hinted this was something he already planned? Kayla was an infallible way to draw that wretched boy, Jaden, to Zubiaba now that the boy's parents had slipped from his grasp. And Kayla's parents were beyond his reach, having joined that rabble of Pallaton's. Hopefully, his offer would derail any suspicions on Tarise's part.

"No. But if it will help sweeten the deal, you might want to know that she has a birthmark in that ancient language that means 'key.' How's that for useful?"

Zubiaba had spent years learning to school his expressions, both macro and micro, into a mask of indifference, but this revelation almost ripped the mask clean off. He knew Kayla was somehow needed to complete this diversion Zareh devised—but he hadn't known how or why. His mind ran rampant with possibilities. Zubiaba finally settled on the one that suited him. The girl herself might be the key if the mark was on her body. Either way, he couldn't dispose of her, not until he had the Gatekeeper too.

"I will take Kayla 'out of the equation' as you requested. For your part, you will disable those missiles the Armorer has developed?"

"I'll do my part if you do yours."

Did she know how easily he could reach out and snap that skinny little neck of hers? Her attitude was more than unacceptable. She needed to be punished. Now. His pride would not let him wait. "If we have a deal, then let us shake hands on it."

Tarise stepped forward without hesitation and extended her hand. "We have a deal."

Grinning maliciously, Zubiaba took her hand in his own. He had been waiting for her to say those words. Now he would seal the bargain irrevocably. He was gratified when the pain registered on her face. The smell of her burning flesh where their hands met was heady, and her agony was invigorating.

"Stop, you'll set off the failsafe," Tarise groaned.

Frowning, Zubiaba reluctantly released her. He watched as she studied her hand. Her confusion was comical. "Yes, the bargain brand won't leave any visible mark, yet its effects will remain as a reminder of our deal. If you even think of reneging, the pain will resurface. Now tell me about the failsafe you devised before I change my mind about helping you."

Tarise glared at him as though she knew he wouldn't, but she was smart enough not to say so. Zubiaba smirked.

"I put a sensor in my body that reacts to my pain levels. If they get too high, it will trigger an explosion, killing me and anyone within a moderate radius," Tarise disclosed.

This was another unexpected development. "Why would you do something like that? Most humans are averse to self-destruction."

"If you were prepared to torture me for how to sabotage the missiles, I wasn't going to get what I wanted anyway. So what reason did I have to keep living? And if I was going to die, you should too."

The girl was truly devious. A spark of admiration ignited within Zubiaba. It also told him she couldn't be trusted. He would have to set her straight on that score. Raising a hand, he exerted the force within him. A minuscule clear chip burst from the thin skin covering Tarise's neck, leaving a bloody trail. Zubiaba commanded the tech to himself, then crushed it between his fingers.

Tarise slapped a hand over her neck as she cried out in pain, her eyes wide with shock. "How did you do that?"

"I have more skills than all you pathetic creatures combined. Remember that, if you ever think of double-crossing me." The naked fear that leaped into Tarise's eyes satisfied him. Zubiaba inhaled the sweet fragrance of terror. "Go, before I change my mind about harming you."

The girl ran. Zubiaba guffawed. She looked like a scared rabbit. Excellent! She hadn't missed his implied threat, but he could only hope she didn't choose to betray him. Although Zubiaba would know eventually, he wasn't omniscient like his nemesis. The time delay could be costly. Deciding it was a risk not worth taking, he summoned an underling and gave orders for Tarise to be followed. Reports were to be made to him at least twice a day. When the underling was dispatched, Zubiaba turned to the mission already underway. It was time for an update.

CHAPTER THIRTY-ONE

Jaden watched Kayla zoom away. Should he have gone with her? No, she had been pretty adamant that she wanted to go alone. The whole episode with Tarise had been unpleasant. She would need time to deal with that. Resigned, Jaden turned and went downstairs, his smile returning at the jeers that greeted him from the kitchen.

"Yeah, yeah, simmer down," Jaden tutted. "I'm getting the dough into the prepper. Why haven't you guys grated the cheese yet?"

Bree smiled. "If we do it too far in advance, it gets hard and affects the flavor."

"Of course it does." Jaden grinned. "We can't have that, now can we?"

Bree swatted him with a dish towel. "You probably wouldn't even notice. But I would, so we're going with that."

Chuckling, Jaden disappeared into the pantry. The sudden silence that swamped the room behind him had him reversing direction. Zareh stood in the midst of the group, inspecting them.

"Zareh, I be," he said, waving his furry little arms. "Greet you, I do. Introduce yourselves, will you?"

Shianna bounded toward him, her hands reaching.

"I wouldn't cuddle him if I were you," Jaden warned.

Shianna stopped in her tracks, suddenly wary. "Why, does he have fangs or some other means of hurting me?"

"Yes, you just can't see the fangs," Jaden commented. "Zareh, what are you doing here?"

Zareh stared at him, his beady little eyes boring a hole into Jaden. "Your behavior, improved has not, I see. Kayla, where be she?"

"Not here," Jaden bit out. "Are you going to answer my question?"

Out of the corner of his eye, Jaden noticed his friends gaping. Yes, he wasn't known for being rude. But his atypical behavior had the twofold advantage of keeping his friends away from Zareh and stopping them from conversing with the little fiend.

Zareh ruffled his feathers. "Remember, about the strange clicking sound that you and Kayla heard, told us you did?"

"Yes. What about it?"

"Figured it out, we did." Zareh chortled. "Interpret the Gaptor and Usurper's conversations, we have."

"Well, that's great." Jaden didn't bother hiding his sarcasm. "But you don't usually appear to pass along such inconsequential news. Tell you what, before you do get to that piece of information you have to share, how about you tell me why there wasn't a map with the new artifacts we found?"

Zareh clucked. "Because already in your possession, the map is. Your guide, it has been, since received it you did. Stall me no longer, you must! Wait, the information I must give you, will not. Short, time is. Prepare, you must."

Jaden's anger boiled. Again, Zareh hadn't answered his question directly. Throwing his hands up, Jaden growled, "Here we go again! Why don't you stop with the mumbo jumbo and spit out what we have to prepare for? Oh, and while you're at it, try and explain more clearly how it is that we already have the map, since the first one disappeared in a flame of blue light and the second one isn't offering any additional options."

Zareh cut him off. "War coming, it is! Vast numbers of Gaptors, on their way here now, they are. Yourselves, get ready. Courageous, you be. The words given to you in the Forest, forget not."

Jaden stepped forward, fists clenched, ready to grab Zareh by his cute little ears and shake him. But Zareh was gone. A void filled the space he'd occupied.

"Dude!" Markov breathed. "Does he always appear and disappear like that?"

"Blast! I thought I had him that time," Jaden seethed. "Little runt. He's the most annoying thing in any world. Why, if—" Jaden broke off as Zareh's words sank in. "Did he say we were in for a battle?"

"He did," Sven answered. The others only gaped at Jaden, unable to believe this was the same person they grew up with.

"Bro, are you okay?" Atu placed a hand on Jaden's shoulder.

Jaden took off, taking the stairs two at a time. "Kayla! She's on her own!"

Clattering feet sounded behind him. The group spilled out the maintenance room door onto the roof, confronted by a swarm of anxiously circling gliders.

Jaden didn't stop. He kept right on running, leaping off when he reached the edge. Han swept under him, catching him, and they rose above the other gliders darting in to catch their own voyagers. Only then did Jaden notice Taz. "Why are you still here? Kayla's at her house!"

Taz's reaction sent a chill down his spine. She stared at Jaden as though he was speaking gibberish. Then her face morphed into fear. He'd never seen Taz afraid before. And that scared him more than anything else. Without a word, Taz tucked her wings and streaked away.

"I assume we're following her," Han offered before Jaden could ask.

"Yes—and hurry! Why didn't Taz sense Kayla needed her?"

"Her link with Kayla stopped working, which is why we came. At first we thought that perhaps your proximity to her had obscured the link, as sometimes happens when you two are, uh, close. But the nearer we got to your home without the link reconnecting, the more we were certain something was wrong."

Jaden hunched over Han, trying to think of something else. He shed the clothes he wore over his smart suit. Had Kayla followed

Sven's dictates that they always be prepared and worn her smart suit today? Were the others wearing theirs? From the way some gliders flew with speed and others lagged, not everyone had taken the same precautions. *Well, they'll just have to catch up. I don't have time to wait for them to sort themselves out. I have to get to Kayla.*

Jaden was so engrossed in worrying that he almost fell when Han veered to the right. Jaden's eyes widened when he noticed the Gaptor. And right behind it, another one. No, wait, a whole line of them. He cursed. Why had Zareh taken so long to warn them?

"Jaden, what's the play?" Atu called over the comm.

This was no time to be distracted. Shaking himself, Jaden surveyed his surroundings. The sky seethed with foul, horrid shapes he knew all too well. And there were plenty of them. More than he had ever seen.

Jaden gritted his teeth. "Sven, are those new missiles of yours ready to rock and ruin?" Jaden was unsure whether he would even get a reply.

He breathed again when Sven answered. Evidently the old goat followed his own advice and wore his smart suit at all times too. "Absolutely! I had Markov and some of the others help me set them up on the way in. Time for some fun, no?"

"For sure! Where are we headed?"

"You know those mountains on the western edge of Daxsos?"

"Yes, but be a little more specific. That's a huge area."

"I'm sending coordinates now."

Jaden glanced at his PAL, assessing the location and passing the information on to Han. "Alright, Armorer, we'll buy you some time to get there and get them lined up. Anyone who can hear, the play is eight."

Jaden made the call, although he didn't know whether the plays he, Kayla, Iri, and Atu had learned had been taught to Markov and his group. And despite not knowing how the play would work with so many gliders. Jaden risked a peek behind him. Several gliders were getting into formation. *And so it begins.*

Han dove, and the line of gliders that had formed up behind them followed, catching the attention of the circling Gaptors. They plunged after the line. When the Gaptors were within striking distance, the gliders alternated peeling off to the right and to the left, starting with those at the back.

Jaden grinned. The Gaptors' confusion when this happened was always amusing. They floundered, some of the late arrivals careening into the stationary ones, and the crashing parties spiraled downward in a tangle of limbs. *That at least gets rid of a few.*

Han began the loop to curve them back up on top of their prey. The Gaptors were now even more undecided about what they should do: follow those going left and right, or take after those climbing above them. Their hesitation was their downfall.

When the first of the Legion who had darted the opposite way converged with Jaden and Han, they crossed paths diagonally, making an X. Then each party slanted down over their enemies. The remaining gliders in the converging lines traced the same route, and arcing gliders surrounded the Gaptors. Bolts of light slewed off multiple DDs, obliterating the hovering Gaptors.

Exiting the smoke marking the demolition site, Jaden and Han shot into clear air, crisscrossing with others finishing their own runs. They looped back up to begin the attack sequence all over again.

By the time they had completed three runs, the immediate area was free of Gaptors. Jaden looked down, trying to see through the thick blanket of smoke, but it was impossible to see the ground or figure out what losses their side had taken.

"Everyone okay?" Jaden called over the comm.

Voices filtered back in the affirmative. But the one he was most desperate to hear was absent. Where was Kayla? Had she and Taz been delayed, or were they hurt?

"Han, you can sense Taz, right?" Jaden faltered, remembering something the gliders said when Iri joined them. It was how they had been able to track and find Iri after she took off with Aren. Han's shoulders sagged under Jaden, increasing his panic. "What?"

"I was hoping you wouldn't ask."

"Han, tell me, or so help me," Jaden warned.

"I haven't been able to sense her since just after she left," Han confessed.

Jaden tensed. "What does that mean?"

"Either she's dead or unconscious," Han croaked.

His pain was unmistakable, and his words were so final. Jaden didn't have the heart to ask more questions. What did that mean for Kayla? "Let's head over there."

"We don't have time." Han nodded toward the horizon.

Jaden glanced that way. The sky was no longer blue. From one end to the other, a black stain spread, obliterating the light and moving toward them at speed. "We'll make time. We can detour via Kayla's as we lead that lot to Sven."

Han grunted, but said nothing as he turned them toward Kayla's home.

"Listen up," Jaden said over the comm. "We're headed to the mountains via Kayla's home. We'll have to take the brakes off if we're going to reach that little surprise Sven has prepared before those Gaptors catch up. Keep pace!"

Han rocketed forward, but Jaden wished he could go faster, even though Kayla's home was already visible. Then they were there. Jaden sucked in a horrified breath. Taz lay sprawled on the grass next to Kayla's home, blood pooling around her. Countless cuts covered her body. Her wings were in tatters. One leg was connected to her body by only a thin piece of tissue. Was she even still alive?

Han lurched under him. He wasn't taking this any better than Jaden was.

Aren and Atu shot under them. Atu somersaulted as he dismounted to counteract Aren's speed. He rolled, came up on his feet, and sprinted to Taz. Han was already dropping down, his wings wilted. Jaden leaped as soon as he could, allowing Han to land without having to circle back around. They raced toward Atu. Aren landed beside them, startling them both into attack stances. Recognizing Aren, they lowered their weapons and approached Atu.

"How is she?" Han rasped. Jaden barely recognized Han's voice.

Then again, Jaden didn't think he could get a word past the lump in his own throat.

"She's breathing," Atu muttered, his hands flying over Taz.

This time there was no pretense of ointments and salves. Wherever Atu's hands moved, healing flowed. Jaden watched, awed, as the cuts closed. Atu moved to Taz's near-severed limb, and a golden light glowed over the area, emanating from Atu's palm. When the light faded, the limb knit back so perfectly Jaden couldn't tell that there had ever been an injury.

"You really are the healer," Jaden breathed.

Atu didn't look up. He carried on working, applying the same golden light to Taz's wings. Finished, Atu sat back on his haunches, a frown on his face. Jaden wouldn't believe this was the same glider if he hadn't seen the transformation with his own eyes.

"Well?" Jaden asked, aware Han was too emotional to say anything.

"It's touch and go. She's lost a lot of blood. Only time and rest will correct that. It's a waiting game now," Atu announced.

"Thank you, Healer." Han's voice was gruff as he stepped closer to Taz, putting a wing on hers.

Markov's voice cut in over the comm. "Dude, you need to get back up here. Those beasties are closing in."

"We'll be right up. Lead the others to the coordinates I'm sending you," Jaden ordered.

"Will do," came Markov's terse response. Thank goodness for their long friendship. Markov wouldn't question him.

Jaden put one hand on Han and the other on Taz. He stared at Taz for a moment, still amazed by the healing Atu had wrought. "Han, buddy, we need to help the others. Are you ready to leave?"

"We can't leave her lying here out in the open," Han protested.

"We'll move her to a more secure location," Aren assured him. "Do what you must to avenge the Tazanna."

Jaden blinked. *The* Tazanna? What did that mean? Before he could consider the implications, Han took to the air and whizzed back faster than Jaden could ever recall. Jaden leaped to meet him. Then they were on their way to join the others—only just in time too. The massive group of Gaptors weren't far off.

Would Aren and Atu have enough time to get Taz to safety? Even as Jaden thought it, the Gaptors chasing them altered course, taking a more direct line to where Jaden and Han flew. While it was a relief to not have to worry about Taz, reaching the safety of their friends before that menacing group of Gaptors caught up to them wouldn't be easy.

As if he had reached the same conclusion, Han put on a burst of speed. They wouldn't be able to maintain it for long, but seeing the gap between them and their foes widening was reassuring. As they closed in on their friends, Jaden breathed a sigh of relief. Additionally, the mountain pass where Sven waited was just beyond them. At last, a break!

The group of gliders and riders sped into the valley. As they neared the tapering end, Jaden saw the missile launchers. True to form, Sven had outdone himself. The structures, no bigger than a person, were lined up along a ridge. Heavy bolts held the light frames in place. But where were the stacked missiles?

In answer, bright beams spewed from the slim frames. Of course! These "missiles" had to act like the beams on their DDs. A conventional weapon wouldn't work. Jaden watched, amazed, as the beams struck their targets, drilling lines of death into the approaching Gaptors. At least a hundred were destroyed in that first volley.

Jaden whooped. Several of the other riders joined in. A second volley blasted from the frames. This time, Han turned so he could watch too. The effects were even more devastating.

Their first taste with the beams had given the Gaptors a clue of what they meant. Those that weren't decimated by the blast fled. Squawking, they scattered in several directions. Many of them rammed into one another, going down. But going down wasn't dead.

"Move in and take out those falling Gaptors," Jaden ordered.

The gliders and their riders complied. Sweeping across the sky like dotted lines behind an arrow, they took out the plummeting monsters. Not one made it to earth.

Another round of missiles whooshed out of Sven's frames. Han and Jaden were abruptly surrounded by shrieking Gaptors, some still bent on attacking them, others just on escaping the death rays.

Han and Jaden struck out at any Gaptor within range. They disposed of one Gaptor attacking them only to be confronted by two more. Jaden's nose crinkled as the repugnant odor of the blood of their wounded opponents covered them. Jaden's arm began to burn. Between hacking at Gaptors that were close and flicking currents at those further afield, his muscles were working overtime. Han's muscles quivered under him; he was just as fatigued. But there was no respite. The Gaptors kept coming. Round after round of beams from Sven's launchers cut into their foes.

Jaden was just beginning to wonder how many Gaptors could remain when the unthinkable happened.

CHAPTER THIRTY-TWO

One of the missile launcher frames exploded. The thunderous reverberation echoed up and down the valley, drowning out all other sounds. Before Jaden could blink, the next frame blew up, and the next, until the entire line had been destroyed. Soon, the only thing left were lines of flame marking each launcher.

Jaden shook his head. This couldn't be happening! Had Sven miscalculated? Had the Gaptors deployed some weapon of their own?

A Gaptor sliced past, aiming for Han. Han dodged, and Jaden struck out, sawing off one of the creature's gangly wings. It dropped away, only to be replaced by another Gaptor with its weird antennae aloft.

Movement to his right distracted Jaden. The rider on the closest glider had fallen off. Although his smart suit was compensating to correct his limbs, they weren't responding. The Gaptor must have released its EMP! The rider would be useless for a few hours until the numbing effects wore off. Worse, if this was happening to all the riders, soon only Jaden's team and the Legion would be defending against this attack. And those odds were definitely against them.

Pain lanced his arm. Jaden refocused on the Gaptor attacking him. One of its wing blades had sliced into the meaty part of his forearm, just like his very first experience with a Gaptor attack. He lifted his DD and flicked his wrist. With a thunderclap, the beam struck, and the Gaptor disintegrated.

Jaden quickly sprayed his arm with the glue Kayla had given him. It was a temporary solution, but it would stop the blood loss. Then he swung his attention toward what was fast becoming a rout by the remaining Gaptors. Time to get organized.

"Three!" Jaden shouted over his comm to anyone who could still hear and respond.

Several shapes drifted toward him out the haze of smoke, closely followed by Gaptors.

Jaden didn't wait for them to get closer. "Now!" Han curled into a spiral to take them under their approaching foes. They dropped fast and then rose even faster, coming up underneath their surprised assailants. As Han maneuvered them right under the mutants, Jaden's arm shot up, his DD biting into the bellies of the Gaptors flying over them.

Screeching dissonantly, the remaining Gaptors flew higher to escape the blades of Jaden's group. They smashed right into the other half of the group waiting above. DDs sent off multiple shafts of light, and several Gaptors disintegrated, adding their black ash to the smog already thickening the skies. But the home team hadn't escaped unscathed. Several riders tumbled toward the ground, their gliders frantically chasing after them as they plummeted toward certain death.

There was no time to worry about the fallen. Another stream of Gaptors flowed toward them with their antennae already raised. Jaden grimaced. They had worked out that not all the gliders were impervious to their EMPs.

Jaden and Han watched helplessly as most of the other riders slumped over their gliders, or, more alarmingly, fell into open sky.

The spiky pink tips of a blonde head caught Jaden's attention. Bree! Han must've recognized her, too, because he shot after her.

He wasn't the only one. Bree's glider was hot on her rider's heels when she faltered and dropped like a stone. At first, Jaden thought

Bree's glider was diving to get under her. Then he saw the spurt of blood as her head separated from her body. The insidious form of a Gaptor loomed right behind the gory scene. For a moment the responsible Gaptor glared at them, its ochre eyes on fire. Then it took off after Bree.

Jaden bellowed. Han's muscles strained as he tried to reach Bree first, but the Gaptor had the head start. It caught Bree in its hideous curved claws, viciously stabbing its stinger into her chest, hard enough to come out the other side.

Jaden fought back the urge to vomit. He had to concentrate. The beast was almost in range. It dropped Bree like a limp rag doll when it saw Han and Jaden closing in. *Too late*, Jaden thought, flicking his wrist. The beam annihilated the brute.

Bree was horribly close to the ground now. Han wasted no time. Before Jaden could blink a second time, they were under Bree, and Han was rising. Jaden pulled Bree into the safety of his arms. Blood. So much blood. Her face had already assumed a terrifyingly waxy pallor.

"Bree, stay with me. Bree! Wake up! Can you hear me?" Jaden shouted, patting her cheek.

Her eyes fluttered open. Her mouth worked, but Jaden couldn't hear the words over the roar of the wind as Han hurtled away with them.

"That's right, doll. Keep your eyes open. Stay with me," Jaden cooed.

Bree's eyes were glassy and unfocused, and she had started trembling. Jaden was no medical expert, but he was sure she was in shock. Not to mention whatever the venom in that stinger was doing to her. He remembered how that felt.

Bree was trying to say something again. Jaden leaned down so his ear was close to her mouth. "Tell . . . tell Stovan . . . I'm . . . sor—sorry."

The last word took so much effort Jaden could feel the air puffing against his cheek as Bree forced it out. He lifted his head to look her. When her eyes rolled back and she went limp in his arms, he knew not even Atu could help her. "No!" Jaden's anguished cry cut the air.

He pulled Bree into his chest, the sobs wrenched loose as he held her close. "Why her?" Jaden shouted at the sky. "Why her?"

Han had to have realized what had happened, but he kept going, making for the ground at such a steep angle that Jaden had to use all his skill and the smart suit to stay on. They thumped down hard. Jaden's teeth banged together and took a chunk of cheek in the process. Ignoring the warm blood filling his mouth, Jaden slid off Han with Bree in his arms. He stumbled toward Atu, attending to another wounded rider.

"Atu," Jaden gasped.

His tone made Atu turn toward him. Realizing who Jaden held, Atu bolted over. Jaden sank down, still holding Bree. Atu skidded up beside him. When Atu knelt, felt for a pulse, and gently closed Bree's staring eyes, Jaden knew his worst fears had materialized. His involvement in this ridiculous quest had gotten someone he cared about killed.

Fury such as he'd never known filled him. It wasn't the burning rage he typically experienced; this anger was cold, calculating, and all-consuming. Without a word, he turned and strode back to Han. Jaden's voice was emotionless. "Let's get back to the battle. We have work to do."

Jaden aerial connected with Han, his limbs leaden. They weren't the only frozen part of him. Deliberately, he blocked all thoughts of Kayla. Jaden wouldn't allow himself to think about the fact that she hadn't contacted them yet, that she hadn't used her comms. He couldn't go there. If he couldn't even cope with what happened to Bree . . . Bree, sweet Bree! How could she be gone?

Savagely, he slammed that door shut. He would grieve later. Now he had to make sure her sacrifice hadn't been in vain.

Jaden's brain worked with an icy ferocity, scheming how they could win this battle. The numbers were against them. Realistically, any of the new riders were useless in this fight. They had no protection against the EMPs.

That left him, Atu, Iri, Kayla, and Sven. Sven couldn't fight because Jaden would need him to carry out the plan he had in mind—if Sven could even work that miracle. Kayla . . . no, he wasn't going there. Whatever had happened, it was too late for Jaden to fix it. He focused on what they did have. It was down to him, Iri, Atu and the Legion, or what was left of them. First things first.

"Any riders out there who can hear me, I want you to head to Sven. Don't try and engage any Gaptors. You're defenseless against their EMPs. Just get yourselves to Sven as quickly as you can. Get off your gliders and stay on the ground. There's work you'll need to do." Jaden ended the transmission by giving Sven's coordinates. Then he proceeded to the next item on his mental list. "Sven, can you hear me?"

"Yes," the answer came back, the single syllable tired and defeated.

"I have a job for you, if you can pull it off. Do you have your tools?"

"Of course. Just in case the launchers needed adjustments." Sven sounded more upbeat. "What do you have in mind?"

Jaden outlined his idea. "Think you can make that happen?"

Sven paused. "Theoretically, yes, it's possible. It's an ingenious idea. I only hope I can make it work."

"If anyone can, it's you. We have nothing to lose and the world to gain. You'll have the other riders coming your way soon. Use them to help. Good luck!"

Han glanced over his shoulder at Jaden. "We're to engage the enemy with Iri, Atu, and the Legion until Sven can get the task done?"

"Yeah. I don't know how long we'll last, but we have to give them as much time as possible. You up for the fight?"

Han sent him a grim smile. "What do you think?"

"Yes. Time for a little revenge." He surveyed the Gaptors that still filled the skies around them. None were close, so taking them out one at a time wasn't feasible. The more individual battles they fought, the more likely they would be injured or killed. Jaden had to find a way to get the Gaptors to clump together again.

"Iri? Atu?" Jaden called.

"Here," Iri said over her comm.

"Yeah." Atu sounded distracted.

"Han and I need you guys. We have to keep this horde occupied while Sven cooks up something for them. Can you join us?"

"Tinks and I are on our way," Iri confirmed.

"Be there as soon as I can," Atu answered. "I sent some of the Legion to get my parents. I'm just waiting for them to get here so that they can take over from me."

"Good man," Jaden said as Tinks and Iri pulled in next to them.

"How do you want to do this?" Iri asked.

"Do you know if Pallaton's still—"

Jaden broke off as the stately glider popped up in front of him. "Don't look so surprised," Pallaton said. "Han sent for me."

Jaden stared at Han. "You can do that?"

"Only over short distances," Han admitted.

Pallaton got to the point. "What do you need from us?"

"An organized attack is the only way we're going to thin those ranks. We start by luring the Gaptors to a place which gives us the tactical advantage," Jaden said.

"Where would that be?" Pallaton asked.

"I'm thinking a few valleys over from Sven. There's a thin valley with steep sides that I think will work in our favor. We have to use what we have, and the gliders' agility will serve us well if we can take advantage of it."

"Lead the way." Pallaton emitted a long, low whistle, his call to his Legion.

Minutes later, they were on their way to the valley. If Jaden hadn't spent so many years hiking the mountains with his friends, he might not have known about this place. It was perfect. Admittedly, it was more a canyon than a valley. Thin and narrow, it had tall, unyielding cliffs on either side with plenty of rocky outcroppings.

Jaden glanced behind them. So far, so good. Since all the gliders pulled out of the area at the same time, they had successfully garnered the Gaptors's attention. By the time they neared the canyon, Atu had joined them, and most, if not all, the Gaptors had taken the bait.

When Han saw the valley, he sent Jaden one of his toothy grins. "We're going to do what we did when we faced that first Gaptor in the desert?"

Jaden grinned. "Yeah." He addressed Iri and Atu over the comms. "We need to wait here for the Gaptors to catch up."

"What?" Iri yelled. "Why?"

"They need to literally be on our heels for this to work. Pallaton, while we wait, would you like to take your Legion into the canyon and set up some ambushes?"

Pallaton already understood what Jaden intended because he nodded his massive head. "Yes, this is a solid plan. More effective than fighting our foes out in the open. We will go ahead and set some traps."

The Legion disappeared into the recesses of the canyon. Jaden watched them go before turning to see how close the Gaptors were. It would be a couple of minutes yet.

He waited, anxious, hoping the Gaptors wouldn't recognize the trap. But their bloodlust was heightened, and it seemed all they could see were the voyagers floating in front of them, inviting defeat. They increased their speed accordingly. *All the better for this plan to work,* Jaden thought as the Gaptors came within range.

"Follow our lead," he called to Iri and Atu.

With that, Han darted into the canyon, aligning his flight beside the steep walls. Jaden had forgotten how close Han had to take them. And he had done this without a smart suit before? His grin widened. They'd just be more effective this time.

The first rocky protrusion blocked their way, and Han nimbly darted around it. Jaden heard nothing as Iri and Atu cleared the obstacle. Then the air itself vibrated as the first Gaptor collided with the rock face. Or maybe more than one, from the way the canyon echoed.

The second outcropping loomed into view, and Han zoomed around it. Jaden chanced a backward glance as Iri and Atu skirted it with ease. Then he saw the cartwheeling wings of a Gaptor trying to avoid its fate. The Gaptor veered sideways into two others who thought they had been smart enough to go wide, and all three fell to the canyon floor, shrieking. Gliders peeled from the shadows below to attack the falling Gaptors.

His attention jerked back to where they were going as Han skirted yet another hurdle. This time, Jaden heard no collisions. Well, he knew this approach wouldn't work for very long, but he'd hoped they'd take a few more Gaptors down first. As though Han anticipated this, he suddenly swung to the opposite side of the canyon. The lead Gaptors increased their speed to catch Han out in the open, but by the time they caught up, Han was already tucking them into a crevice. The deafening sounds of more than one collision rang up and down the narrow valley.

Jaden rubbed Han's neck fur. "You're a smart one."

"Seems I'm not the only one with ideas." Han nodded at Aren and Tinks, now striking out on their own. While Tinks and Iri dropped down near the canyon floor, Aren and Atu took the high road, lifting to the top of the canyon and allowing the Gaptors chasing them to catch up.

"I hope some of the Legion are up there," Jaden breathed, watching Aren and Atu shoot over the lip of the canyon into open air.

The Gaptors never stood a chance. As soon as they cleared the edge, waiting gliders picked them off. In seconds, no Gaptors remained. Aren and Atu dived back into the canyon.

Han maintained their flight along the canyon walls. Jaden glanced down, checking on Tinks and Iri. What were the girls planning?

Han suddenly slowed, startling Jaden. "What are you doing?"

"Setting Tinks and Iri up for their run." Han grinned.

Jaden glanced behind him, first at the Gaptors closing in, and then at Tinks and Iri rising up under them. "Oh, now I get it."

Han turned them to face their attackers, and Jaden flexed the wrist holding his DD. The first sizzling shaft separated from the blade and hit the lead Gaptor square in the face, incinerating him. Before the others could react, Jaden sent a second ray, obliterating another foe. The remaining Gaptors flapped their scraggly wings wildly, trying to flee. Loathe to go up because of the gliders there, the Gaptors opted for going down, straight into Iri's waiting blade. Iri and Tinks twisted and turned, rolling through the falling Gaptors, dealing death.

Han swept them toward the Gaptors, now rising reactively, and they began their own attack. They laid waste to the monsters. When they reached the end of the group pursuing them, they burst into empty air.

Taking a moment to assess their injuries, Jaden was grateful that they were mostly superficial. After sealing a cut on Han's forehead to stop blood from running into his eyes, Jaden treated a cut on his own shoulder, deeper than the rest.

Jaden surveyed their progress. Aren and Atu were still leading fresh Gaptors, who hadn't seen their comrades' fates, up to their doom. *Either that or they're really gullible.* Iri and Tinks had switched to hugging the canyon walls again, speeding toward an outcropping noticeably larger than the rest. When they cleared it, a swarm of gliders suddenly appeared from behind the obstruction and assailed the Gaptors who had flown right into their waiting teeth and claws.

Jaden grinned. "As long as we can keep them in this canyon, divided by the natural terrain and apart from each other, we're likely to keep them occupied for a while yet."

Han nodded. "The plan to bring them here was masterful. We have them at a disadvantage."

"Let's keep it that way," Jaden grunted as he and Han threw themselves back into the fray.

Every run they made though the canyon decimated another group. Iri and Atu varied the ploys they used to lure unsuspecting Gaptors into waiting bands of gliders. Somehow they knew where Pallaton had sequestered his troops for maximum effect.

Pallaton was doing his part too. Every so often, a group of gliders swarmed Gaptors that had strayed. The result was a brutal clash of ancient enemies. So far, the gliders were triumphant due to their superior numbers. But the Legion had casualties of their own. They wouldn't be able to keep this up indefinitely.

Han and Jaden varied their own approaches just as the others were. They were holding their own until their next run through the canyon, when disaster struck.

CHAPTER THIRTY-THREE

A slashing beak caught Han's side, making him grunt. From the way they suddenly tilted, Jaden knew this injury was serious. Han struggled to level them, but his movements were slow and lethargic. Time splintered into infinite fragments, each one an eternity, as they drifted into the oncoming Gaptor. Jaden was powerless to stop the whirring blades at the ends of its wings from slashing into his leg, forging four diagonal lines of pain across almost the entire length.

Howling, Jaden clutched at his leg. Between Han lilting one way and Jaden curled protectively over his leg the other, they couldn't defend against the Gaptor. It fell on them, beak gnashing, talons tearing, and stinger stabbing. Jaden's smart suit kept him out of reach of most of the weapons, but Han had no such protection.

With extreme effort, Jaden rolled himself upright and stabbed at the monster. The beast shrieked as Jaden's DD plunged into its chest, then ripped downward. The Gaptor disintegrated in a blinding flash.

Jaden almost whimpered; the next Gaptor was already taking a run at them. But a blurred streak cut through his line of sight—Atu, shooting a beam at the Gaptor as he passed. The Gaptor exploded.

They weren't safe, though. Han was now at more than a forty-five degree angle. They needed to see to his wound, or they would follow the Gaptor's fate.

Atu was way ahead of him. Aren's wings appeared under Han's injured side, lifting them level. Han groaned in pain and wobbled under Jaden, making Jaden wonder whether gliders ever passed out from agony. Such a strange thing to wonder about in the middle of a battle. He would ask Han when all this was over. If they made it.

A soft golden glow seeped from around the underside of Han's wing, illuminating the shadowy crevices in the nearby canyon walls. Han's sigh of relief told Jaden all he needed to know. Han abruptly straightened, and power surged under Jaden as Han flapped his massive wings. Bless Atu!

"Thanks, dude!" Jaden called, as Aren and Atu dropped clear and took up a position beside them.

"Anytime." Atu grinned, but then his face sobered. "Seems that leg of yours needs help too."

Jaden glanced at it. He couldn't feel the pain anymore. Was that a bad sign? In fact, all he felt was cold. That thought made him realize how fatigued he was. He wanted to lean over Han's neck and just rest a little.

He started to slouch forward, but jerked upright when Atu yelled at him. "Don't do that!"

Jaden blinked, watching Atu with bleary eyes as Aren lifted higher. For some reason, Jaden's head weighed a ton. He felt the jolt as Atu dropped onto Han behind him.

"Why are you here?' Getting the words out was an effort. *Why am I so tired?*

"Just stay awake, okay?" Atu murmured.

Dully, Jaden observed the golden light that coated Atu's hands. Was this what dying felt like? The light was so pretty. Then he gasped as icy fingers ran across his leg. His brain kicked back into action. For a moment, the pain was unbearable, but miraculously, it faded, leaving a soothing warmth in its place. Jaden moaned. *Ah, that's so much better.* He blinked as whatever had been supporting him disappeared.

Turning, he caught sight of Atu landing on Aren's broad back.

Under them, Tinks and Iri fended off Gaptors trying to get close. Pallaton swirled overhead with some of the Legion, keeping them free of attack from above. They had been working as a team: the gliders above, Iri watching their six, and Atu supporting Jaden as he healed him.

Jaden glanced at his leg. The shredded smart suit was the only evidence of his grievous wounds. So why did he still feel so weak?

"You lost a lot of blood," Atu told him over the comm, as though reading Jaden's mind. "You're going to feel weak for some time yet. Best you try keep your clashes with the Gaptors to a distance rather than up close and personal."

"Hah, like I have a choice, but I'll try."

Iri cried out, snagging their attention. She was falling clear of Tinks. But why had she screamed? Then Tinks's wing sheared off her body. More than her wing—her shoulder and part of her back too. Three Gaptors had their beaks, talons, and blades embedded in the segment. They had literally ripped Tinks apart.

Jaden retched. As he leaned over Han's side, emptying his stomach, Jaden saw what was left of Tinks drop like a bar of lead. He was so stuck on Tinks that he wasn't mindful of Iri. But Han was. He shot down to where Iri flailed, making Jaden snatch at fur to get a grip.

But Aren and Atu beat them. Atu reeled Iri in when Aren lifted to catch her. She was sobbing incoherently. Atu ran his hands over her as he searched for injuries, then folded her into his arms, comforting her. "She's not injured," he called.

Rushing air behind him made Jaden duck. Han dropped them down a few feet, and Jaden's brain finally broke out of the haze cocooning it. "Han, get back up there. He's going after Aren!"

Han did as commanded. Jaden's DD sliced the stinger off the Gaptor about to attack Aren. Unbalanced, the Gaptor wobbled. Aren moved clear, and Jaden released a sizzling beam. He didn't wait for the usual light and sound show, but swiveled, ready for their next opponent.

While they'd been distracted, the Gaptors had converged into a single group. The Legion were still launching stealth attacks, but they weren't nearly as effective, and Iri was without a glider. Not that she was in a state to fight anyway.

That left him and Atu. They needed a new plan.

"Jaden?"

His comm crackled in his ear, startling him. "Sven?"

"I think we have that solution you were looking for."

"You magnificent man!" Jaden crowed. "We're on our way. Atu, we . . ."

"I heard," Atu interrupted. "Not a moment too soon either. Let's get out of here."

Aren shot ahead of Han, closely followed by Pallaton and the Legion. *Just as well we were on the right side of the canyon when Sven called. I don't think I would've had the strength to fight or trick our way through all those Gaptors. Now we're all lined up. Perfect!*

They took the most direct path out of the canyon, to put a little distance between themselves and the Gaptors crowding behind. They cleared the canyon and angled west, skirting the other valleys that gradually gave way to Daxsos.

Jaden's strength ebbed as they reached the pass that would take them up to Sven. He just had to hold on a few more minutes. Han and Aren shot up the valley, towards the narrow end curving into the mountains proper. The rise was gradual at first, but it was misleading. Sheer cliffs took over after a hundred horizontal feet, making the valley a dead end for anyone without the strength to scale the cliffs. Han sped along the tapering valley, and they were soon fenced in by massive granite slabs on either side. They reminded Jaden of a mortician's slab. He grimaced. Why did he have to think that?

They crossed the imaginary line that offered sanctuary. Or so Jaden hoped. He urged Han onward; they needed to reach the cliff walls and curve back above the approaching Gaptors for their plan to succeed. Han accelerated. Then they were at the wall, and Jaden was second-guessing himself. He should've told Han to slow down, not speed up. They weren't going to make it. They were going to smash into the mountain!

Abruptly, Han arced upward at an insane ninety degrees, taking them parallel to the cliff. Jaden fell flat, grabbing handfuls of fur to stay on. He tightened his knees around Han's chest. If not for his smart suit, he'd be free-falling. Even so, he felt himself slipping before Han mercifully curled sideways and rolled them out of a backward curve. His new path took them back the way they came, now a few hundred feet above the Gaptors. Wheeling them back round to face the cliff, Han slowed as Aren, Pallaton, and the Legion followed his example. Together they waited and watched, anxious to see the results of Sven's work.

The Gaptors were going too fast to change their trajectory. They attempted following the gliders' lead, but they weren't as acrobatic. The front lines crashed into the mountain, sending tremors up and down the valley. As they fell back from the cliff, a second wave crashed into the first, taking out another line. The third wave were just scrabbling out the way when a stream of light shot out from the cliff wall, hitting the remaining Gaptors. Radiance flared, booms reverberated, Gaptors disintegrated, and black ash filled the air.

Before Jaden could take a breath, another beam burst out, then another, and then several more. Sven had done it! Jaden whooped. The remaining Gaptors tried escaping, but Jaden and the others were waiting. This time, they had the numbers. The Legion swarmed the surviving Gaptors, taking them out. Han and Jaden barely got a taste of the action. It couldn't even be called a battle.

Not that Jaden was disappointed. He was so exhausted he didn't even know if he could swing his blade, insignificant as its weight was. When the air cleared, the Gaptors were gone. Jaden searched the skies, sure he would find another squadron, but after ten minutes, he exhaled. They had done it.

But at what cost?

Jaden glanced at Iri, still huddled in Atu's arms. Atu indicated he was going to land, and Jaden nodded, letting Atu know he would follow. As a precaution, Jaden asked Pallaton to post scouts at either end of the valley before allowing Han to glide down. As Jaden dismounted, his limbs protested, tired and stiff. *Ugh, I haven't felt like this since we first started training with the gliders.* He stumbled to Atu, waiting with Iri, and took her in his own arms so Atu could to go to work on the fallen gliders.

Jaden dropped down, still holding Iri but too weary to even talk. It seemed Iri wasn't in a talking mood either, so that was just fine.

"Dude!" Markov landed, dismounting from a glider. Whether that was Markov's original glider, Jaden didn't know.

"Yeah," Jaden acknowledged.

"That was some idea you had! Getting Sven to turn our DDs into more missile launchers. I didn't think he'd be able to do it. The man is amazing!"

Jaden only nodded. Words were beyond him. If Sven hadn't been able to pull that rabbit out of the hat, they would all be dead.

His silence must've told Markov more than Jaden wanted to let slip. "Here, let me hold her," Markov offered, taking Iri from him. Over Iri's head, he mouthed, "What's wrong with her?"

"Tinks didn't make it," Jaden mouthed back.

Markov winced and wrapped his arms around Iri more tightly. She didn't respond, just stayed where Markov held her, her eyes vacant and staring. Hopefully it was only the temporary effect of shock and nothing more serious.

Others landed, and Jaden turned to see who it was. He almost groaned out loud when he saw Kayla's parents. They rushed over, their faces worried. "Jaden, have you seen Kayla?" Mrs. Melmique demanded.

"The last time I saw her was before the battle. She was on her way home to you." Jaden fought to stay calm. Confronted with Kayla's absence, he was almost hyperventilating. He had to stay seated. His legs were no more stable than thin tubes of jelly. "Did you not see her when she got home?"

Kayla's parents glanced at each other, then at him, and then back at each other. Why didn't they answer already? Did he really want them to? Deep down, he already knew what they would say.

"Kayla never made it home," Mr. Melmique said huskily. "When we left the house, the battle was already underway. If she left your house before it started, she should've been back."

Jaden sagged. There. They confirmed it. Something had happened to Kayla. He should've gone with her when she'd left. He had failed at the one thing he wanted most to do—protect her. Crushing weight settled over him, making it hard to breathe.

"Where is she?" Mrs. Melmique wailed.

Mr. Melmique pulled his wife into his arms, dropped his head down to her ear, and said something only she could hear. Then he glanced back at Jaden. "You'll help me find her, right?"

Jaden almost didn't have the strength to reply. "Without question."

Mr. Melmique nodded and went back to consoling his wife.

Jaden gritted his teeth. He knew exactly where they would start their search. That made him wonder how Taz was doing. If he was going to ask her questions, he would have to get back to her. Hopefully her condition had improved.

The sound of running feet made him turn his head a second time: Stovan, closely followed by Shianna and Tarise. Jaden didn't know how much more he could take.

"Have you seen Bree? I can't find her," Stovan moaned.

Jaden's work here wasn't done. Rising on shaky legs, Jaden tottered over to Stovan and put a hand on his shoulder. Stovan's face crumpled before Jaden even spoke. "I'm sorry. She didn't make it."

Stovan's legs gave way, and he fell to his knees, his head in his hands. Shianna dropped down next to him. Her face was white, and her hands trembled as she rubbed Stovan's back, trying to comfort him even though she needed comfort herself.

Tarise stared, her grey eyes opening even wider. "It wasn't supposed to be like this," she whispered.

At first, Jaden thought she was referring to the battle. "What did you think you were signing up for when you went to Sven's for training?"

"Not that." Tarise waved a helpless hand in the air.

"What then?" Jaden challenged.

Tarise blinked. She took a step backwards. "Uh, nothing, it's not important."

Jaden studied her. Tarise looked like she had said something she hadn't meant to. No, she looked guilty. "Tarise, what is it?"

Impossibly, Tarise's eyes grew even rounder. They filled her face, showing terror, and she took another step backward.

Jaden lurched over and gripped her shoulders. "Spit it out. What wasn't supposed to be like this?"

By now, they had an audience. Tarise looked like she wanted the earth to swallow her whole. When she still said nothing, Jaden shook her.

"Easy, dude," Markov cautioned.

But Jaden was beyond caring. In his bones, he knew Tarise was hiding something. Something to do with Kayla.

On cue, Tarise whispered, "He was only supposed to take Kayla."

Jaden's fingers dug into Tarise's flesh, but he was beyond controlling himself, even when tears began trickling down Tarise's face. "Who is 'he?'"

"Jaden, let go. You're hurting me!"

"Who is 'he?'" Jaden shouted, not letting up.

Tarise whimpered. "You know, that scary dude. He said I should call him 'Zubiaba.'"

Jaden released her in shock. "You mean Slurpy? You met with him? When?"

"I don't know who Slurpy is. The person I met is the one sending Gaptors here," Tarise mumbled, rubbing her arms.

"How did you get a meeting with him? No, that's not important now. What deal did you make with him?"

Tarise looked uncomfortable.

"Well?" Jaden took a step towards her, fists clenched and jaw set in a tight line.

Tarise backed up again and hurriedly said, "That he would take Kayla away."

Jaden lunged for her, not sure of his exact intentions, only aware that he wanted to hurt her. "You selfish little—"

Markov stepped in front of Jaden. "Calm down. You don't want to do that. This isn't you."

"You don't know what I want," Jaden snarled, shoving Markov. But Markov transferred his weight to the balls of his feet, ready for any run Jaden might make at him.

"I understand better than you think." Markov's voice was quiet, but it held finality.

Jaden weighed his chances. On any day, Markov was a formidable foe. Today, though, he definitely had the upper hand. Scowling, Jaden stood down. Glaring at Tarise, he spat, "What did you have to do in exchange for betraying Kayla?"

Tarise cowered behind Markov. Her voice was barely above a whisper. "I sabotaged the missile launchers."

"You! It's your fault Bree's dead!" Stovan made his own run at Tarise.

Tarise clutched Markov's back, huddling behind him. "I'm so sorry, Stovan. It wasn't supposed to be like this," Tarise mewled.

"And just how did you think it would go without those defenses?" Stovan demanded, looking for a way around Markov.

Shockingly, Atu stepped up next to Markov. "There's no need for violence. And you're right. Without Sven's missiles, we didn't have a chance. But Jaden came up with a plan and we survived. Let's not defile Bree's memory by attacking someone who was misguided. Let's make sure we win this battle and honor Bree that way." His calm voice had the desired effect. Stovan looked confused for a moment, then stomped away with a disgusted grunt.

Jaden watched him leave, then looked at Tarise. Her face was an odd mixture of defiance and despair, but the despair won through.

"He's going to kill me for this." Without warning, she clutched her hand, and her eyes widened. "He knows!"

Markov gaped at Tarise. "How do *you* know?"

"My hand," Tarise sobbed. "It's on fire where he touched me. It's what he threatened to use to keep me in line. It wouldn't be burning like this if he didn't know." She was howling in agony now, curling in on herself as she cradled her hand.

Jaden eyed her coldly. She had brought this on herself. Truthfully, nothing in him felt anything anymore. How was he going to do this without Kayla? Ignoring Tarise's suffering, Jaden said, "I assume Kayla's still alive?"

"That was the plan—he was keeping her alive, so he could get to you," Tarise sniveled before dissolving into fresh wails.

Jaden turned and stalked away. He wasn't going to give her another second of his time, positive or negative.

"Jaden, don't leave—please," Tarise begged.

Her pleas fell on deaf ears. As though he had known Jaden needed him, Han hovered nearby. Jaden smiled at his glider. There were still some good things in this world.

Jaden's smile didn't erase Han's frown. "You need to forgive her."

"Maybe I will when I get Kayla back. Shall we go see how Taz is doing?"

At the mention of Taz's name, Han's face brightened. "Yes, let's."

Han arced away into a sky streaked with the indigo hues of approaching night. The light was fading, and Jaden had to squint to catch Han as he darted back for the pickup. As Han lifted them away from the depressing scene below, Jaden couldn't help but feel alone. And afraid. And despairing.

How had things gone so wrong? Weren't they the winning team? What was Slurpy doing to Kayla? Where did he have her? A million other questions tumbled out, crushing him, until he felt like there was no air left to breathe. He was drowning.

Exacerbating the sensation, the skies around them dimmed, the high mountains behind him rushing the onslaught of full night. Then the sunlight hit the last angle where its beams could squeeze through the mountain's bulk. A golden light, tinged with pinks, apricots, and creams, shone through for a second.

And Jaden was reminded of the words Zareh had told him to keep close. "Living with hope." He snorted derisively at the sentiment. Then he realized that was all that they had left now. Hope. He had to rely on it to find Kayla. He had to remember it to complete his journey and put an end to all this suffering.

It was night and black as sin now, but the new day would soon dawn. When it did, he would be ready.

BRONWYN LEROUX

* * *

ALSO BY BRONWYN LEROUX

Desperate to know what happens to Kayla? Want to know how it all ends?
Pick up *Duel of Death*, the final book in the *Destiny* series.

Feel like a change of pace? Curious about how this all this began? Pick up
Breach, the *Destiny* companion novella, FOR FREE!

Other books by Bronwyn Leroux:

Breach (A *Destiny* companion novella)

Dawn of Dreams (*Destiny*, Book 1)

Dogs of Doom (*Destiny*, Book 2)

Doors of Destiny (*Destiny*, Book 3 - this book)

Duel of Death (*Destiny*, Book 4)

Forecast of Shadows

IF YOU ENJOYED THIS BOOK . . .

I would love it if you would please share it!

Reviews are the fairy dust that keep my wheels turning, thinking up fresh and exciting books for you - and they help other readers just like you discover new books to enjoy.

You can leave a review at https://bronwynleroux.com/DoorsReview

GET THE FIRST BOOK IN THIS SERIES FOR FREE

Interacting with my readers and building friendships is the most rewarding part of writing. I occasionally send newsletters with details on new releases, special offers and other bits of news you may find noteworthy. If you are interested in writing your own book, you can opt in for the additional bonus of weekly writing tips.

Enjoy these wonderful benefits, including your free book, by signing up at https://bronwynleroux.com/FreeBreach

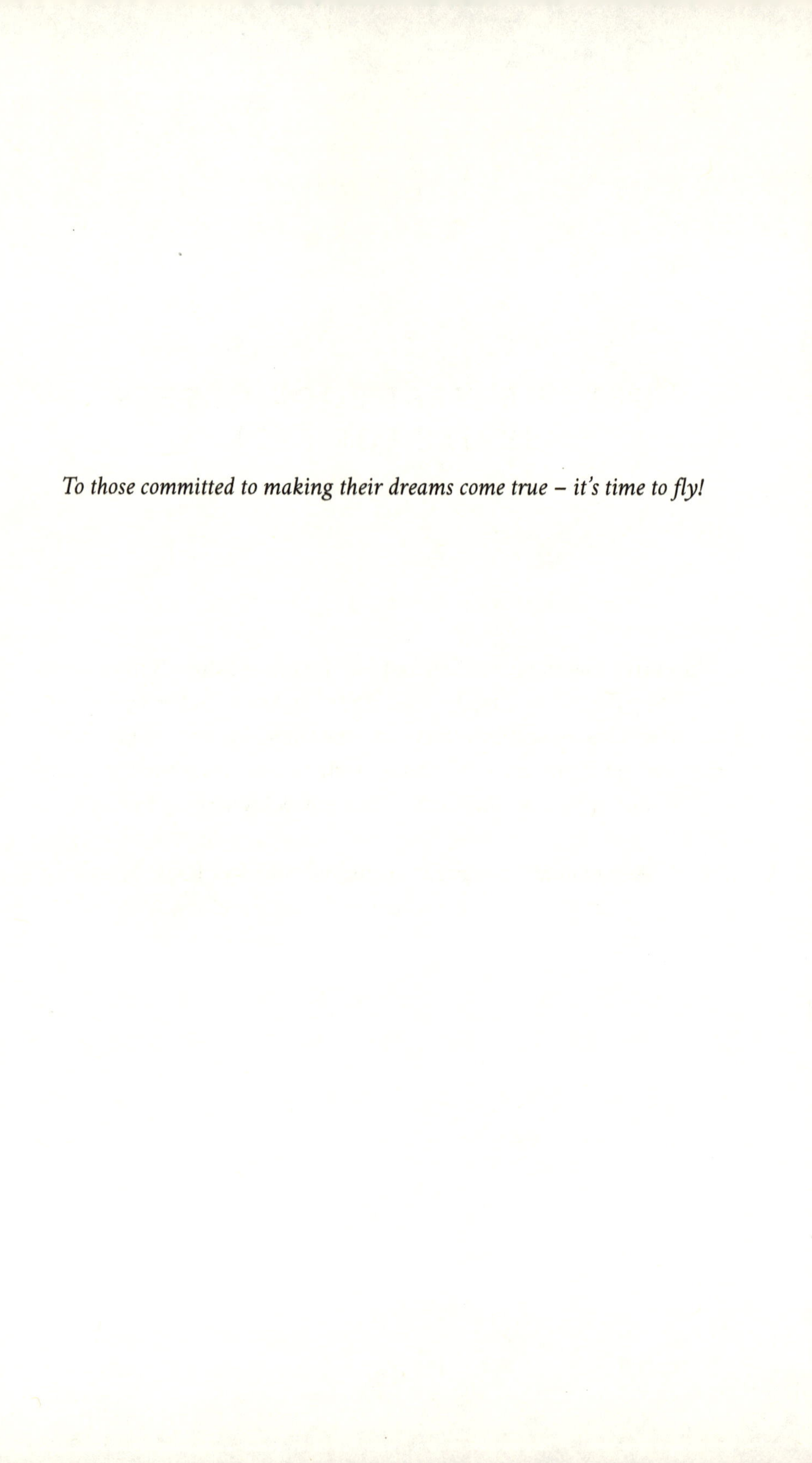

To those committed to making their dreams come true – it's time to fly!

ABOUT THE AUTHOR

Born near the famed gold mines of South Africa (where dwarves are sure to prowl), it was the perfect place for Bronwyn to begin her adventures. They took her to another province, her Prince Charming and finally, half a world away to the dark palace of San Francisco. While the majestic Golden Gate Bridge and its Bay views were spectacular, the magical pull of the Colorado Rockies was irresistible. Bronwyn's family set off to explore yet again. Finding a sanctuary at last, this is Bronwyn's perfect place to create alternative universes. Here, her mind can roam and explore and she can conjure up fantastical books for young adults

facebook.com/AuthorBronwynLeroux
twitter.com/bronwyn_leroux
instagram.com/bronwyn.leroux

www.ingramcontent.com/pod-product-compliance
Lightning Source LLC
Chambersburg PA
CBHW060909190726
48286CB00002B/435